A DEADLY TRADE

A JOSH THANE THRILLER

E. V. SEYMOUR

A division of HarperCollins*Publishers*
www.harpercollins.co.uk

This novel is entirely a work of fiction.
The names, characters and incidents portrayed in it are
the work of the author's imagination. Any resemblance to
actual persons, living or dead, events or localities is
entirely coincidental.

Killer Reads
An imprint of HarperCollins*Publishers*
1 London Bridge Street
London SE1 9GF

www.harpercollins.co.uk

This paperback edition 2017
1

First published in Great Britain by Cutting Edge Press 2013

Copyright © Eve Seymour 2013

Eve Seymour asserts the moral right to
be identified as the author of this work

A catalogue record for this book is
available from the British Library

ISBN: 978-0-00-827153-4

Set in Minion by Palimpsest Book Production Limited,
Falkirk, Stirlingshire

Printed and bound in Great Britain

CHAPTER ONE

Female blowflies can scent the moment of death. I don't understand how this works. But like the blowfly, I had a premonition that the woman I'd come to kill was already dead. I sensed it from the moment I slipped into the darkened room.

Yet I couldn't be certain.

Senses alive, I crossed the floor without sound. Silence is important in this wicked game. And preparation. I'd memorised the precise location of the wardrobe and dressing table and the rocking chair that crouched in the corner. I'd charted the distance from the doorway to the bed: four point eight seven metres. A man my height and build with a smooth gait and a size eight shoe should cover it in less than six seconds. Basic law of motion. I had no fear of interruption. On entry I'd double-locked the front door.

The room was November cold. I could smell booze, brandy at a guess, the fainter scent of expensive perfume almost entirely smothered. When watching her I'd noticed the target appreciated expensive clothes, good quality shoes. She was particularly fond of a charcoal-coloured leather jacket. Personally I never wear leather for a job. It makes too much noise. I'm a clean, crisply ironed open neck dress-shirt with jeans and loafers kind of guy.

When flush I buy my suits from Cad and the Dandy, Canary Wharf.

She lay on her back, one limp arm hanging down. Light from a fading four o'clock moon illuminated her face, neck and the fleshy slope of her shoulders. I leaned over – my eyes are pretty quick at adjusting to night vision – and stretched out a hand towards her, the same hand that would have smothered and suffocated and extinguished life. The cool skin felt inert against the latex of the surgical glove. No breath. No movement. No pulse.

Did I feel cheated? No. Was I angry? No way. I was confused and bunched up with alarm. I had been sent to kill her. Chances were so had someone else. And maybe they'd come for the same reason. Not easily fazed, something coiled slowly in the pit of my stomach.

I crouched down beside her. In death she neither looked serene nor at peace. Her mouth was ajar as if she were mid-snore. Marionette lines ran from each corner to her chin like two deep incisions. The blonde hair splayed across the pillow, dark at the roots, indicated a woman who once cared about her appearance but had lost interest. To establish the rigidity of her flesh, I touched her mouth and jaw. There was some stiffness but not much. There were no visible signs of violence that I could see. No vomit or bruises. No broken nails. No lacerations. I suppressed an involuntary shudder, an earlier memory threatening to erupt. This was now, I reminded myself, not then, not with the blood on the wall and…

Part of me wondered if by strange coincidence she'd died from natural causes. Unusual, not impossible, but as a general rule people in middle age don't succumb with the same unexpected haste as those in the first flush of fickle youth. There was, of course, another possibility.

I took out a pocket torch, slid open the drawer of the bedside table and found a pack of Temazepam. Commonly used to treat those with a history of severe depression, the pills are seldom prescribed for insomnia although many insomniacs take them. Habit-forming and potentially dangerous when mixed in large enough quantities with alcohol and other medications they can kill you. Had she taken her own life? I checked out the blister pack and saw that only three were missing. Not suicide then.

A glance at my watch told me that ninety-five seconds had passed, eighty-five to go. Ideally, I like to be in and out within three minutes.

Moving noiselessly across the floor, I glided out onto the thickly carpeted landing and headed for the study. Ranks of laptops and a high-security computer, massive and squat, glowered accusingly as I sped past. The intelligence stated that the safe, concealed by a rug, was set into the floor at the back of the room. As I approached the combination numbers clattered through my brain like windows in a fruit machine. It would take twenty seconds to open, leaving a little over a minute to steal the portable hard drive and escape. With fingers pumping like a honky-tonk pianist, the door opened and I reached in and connected with empty space. I peered inside, shone the torch around.

Nothing.

Then it hit me; this was no ordinary killing. Anyone can commit murder, but to fake death, to make it look like natural causes, requires skill and subtlety. Whoever had carried it out was a professional assassin, a class act, someone like me.

Footsteps.

Retreating into the shadows behind the now open door, I slowed my breathing, listened hard. This was not part of the plan. But the plan was already fucked. Anything could happen. In readiness I took out the length of cord carried in my jacket pocket for emergencies.

Then I heard the sound of singing, low and haunting, like a chant.

It was so unexpected, so out of key with the situation, my

3

mouth dried as though I'd swallowed coffee grinds. Stranger still, the quiet desperation of the lyrics coupled with the singsong melody awoke sleeping and painful memories of my mother. At that moment it felt as if her ghost were right beside me. But this was not my mother's voice, not even a woman's.

The singing stopped. So did the footsteps. I held my breath. I could almost hear the brain of the person less than a metre away making the calculations: door open, rug askew, safe open, *trouble*.

The light went on. On reflex, my hands flew up, each end of the cord coiled around fists prepared to viper-strike. Raw adrenalin spurted through my veins as the figure shambled into the room. It gave me a couple of seconds to observe the back of my quarry: male, around five nine, a couple of inches shorter than me, wearing a denim jacket, skinny jeans hanging low and exposing the top of the boxers beneath, trainers. I lunged. He turned. *Christ.*

Pale blue eyes stared out of a long-jawed and heavy-lidded face that had only recently made the transition to manhood. His hair was a mess of bleached blonde over brown. In that split-second I recognised that he was his mother's son.

He gaped, managed to eject one word. 'What?'

Instinct told me to kill him. No pointing fingers. No witness. No loose ends. I took a single, silent step forward.

His eyes were wide now, pained, the knuckles on his clenched hands white and shiny. He was probably working out that his mother was either dead or in mortal danger. Suddenly all the dusty years between the boy I was and the man I am now faded away. It was as if the lad had grabbed hold of my sleeve and, against my will, yanked me back to a darker and unholy time. Memories of old grief, misery, rage and helplessness, the seeds for transforming me from an ordinary teenager into a professional killer, swamped me.

'Who sent you?' He hissed.

I blinked, confused, the question odd in the context.

4

'Are you going to kill me?' Sweat beaded his top lip. His wild eyes flicked from me to the open door and back again.

My answer should have been yes.

CHAPTER TWO

I fled. Feet punching the stairs, the floor felt on fire, the air around me sucked dry of oxygen. I exited out of the back door the same way that I'd broken in, and tore alongside the fence at the rear, scaling a wall, landing on the other side, feet square. Not too many people about at that time of the morning. Even if there were I'm not sure I'd have paid them attention. The boy had knocked me way off course.

I was more than baffled by my own incompetence. How could I have missed something so fundamental? I did not make mistakes. I was unaccustomed to failure. I did the homework. As the Americans say, I did the math. Except, on this damn job, I hadn't. Too little time and paid too much money. Greed had made me lazy.

Chill air brought me briefly back to my senses. I needed to get off the streets. I needed cash. Any attempt to access one of my numerous accounts too risky because it would tie me to a location.

I considered my options, which right that moment seemed limited. Truth was, I'd never found myself in this situation before.

It was still dark. Somewhere a dog howled. Shoulders back, I pushed my hands deep into my pockets, affecting a confident stride. No more than five minutes to the underground station, it would allow the wildness to pass and give me time to think. Inexorably, my thoughts returned to the dead woman.

The target, Dr Mary Wilding, a scientist based at Imperial College, London, had crossed up a crime lord. Not so bizarre as it sounds. Fake pharmaceuticals are hot big business, product piracy a prospering market. Without scientists there would be no drugs trade. Rumour had it that Wilding had been paid an exceptional amount of loot and reneged on a deal. My employer clearly wanted what he'd paid for. As for the hard drive, I had no idea what was on it. Not my business. But it *was* my business to know that Wilding had a son who lived in the house with her. I'd truly screwed up on that score and, if word got out, not only would I be finished, I'd be a dead man. The realisation that I'd committed professional suicide punched me hard in the gut. Whatever could be said about my existence, it beat to its own sick and twisted rhythm. I was used to living out of a suitcase, on the run, stakes high, as if each day were my last. What I'd do if I didn't do this I had no idea.

What now?

I strode into the underground at Ealing Broadway. It was two minutes past five in the morning. Conscious of close circuit television cameras, I pulled down my cap to conceal my face, and calmed myself that for CCTV to be effective the cameras need to be positioned at the right angle, most CCTV is recorded over every four days so there is a one in four chance the film will be wiped before it is taken out and studied and, even if an image is captured, it still needs to be identified. A lot of film is grainy, of poor quality and indecipherable. Staring at reels of film hour upon hour will send even the most conscientious viewer into snooze-time. I wasn't really consoled. I'm usually the hunter not the hunted.

Boarding a district line train, I hunkered down in the compartment and glanced around me. My only companions at that hour were solitary, desolate figures wrapped up against the cold and dark, heads down, the kind of people who were scraping by and clinging on by their fingernails, who bust their balls for nothing and knew it was all for nothing.

Like a disorientated homing pigeon, I stumbled out after a couple of stops. Under normal circumstances I'd be covering my tracks and making the all-important call to Wes. I did neither. The boy had seen to that. That I'd let him live when I could so easily have killed him meant that I was unmasked, no longer invisible, that I could no longer hide, not even from myself. From now on it would be like walking down the street stark bollock-naked.

Keen to go to ground, I turned a corner, my eye automatically clocking a café and dossers' establishment, all white and red plastic furnishings. A wall of heat engulfed me as if I'd walked into a bank in Saudi with the air-conditioning bust. Rammed with men who'd slept rough the night before, their clothes stained, gnarled hands clutching mugs of tea, grease and sweat hung tenaciously in the air. Among the vagabond throng a number of unfortunate Eastern Europeans with beaten expressions. I didn't exactly fit in, but it was the best place to go to avoid the attention I had no wish to attract.

I ordered tea, builder's brew, the type you can stand a spade in. When I spoke my voice, so rarely used, felt strangely detached from the rest of me. Low in pitch and without obvious accent, it certainly contained no trace of my middle-class Gloucestershire roots.

'You, alright, mate?'

I turned towards the man serving, the one who asked the question. He had a fleshy face ripe with folds and creases. All I wanted was a mug of tea. I did not welcome chat. I did not want be his mate. I nodded slowly once. His tongue flicked out, touched the side of his mouth, nervous. As he poured the beverage from an urn the size of a household boiler, I glanced at my reflection in the mirrored glass behind the counter expecting a drastic change in my appearance, some giveaway expression in the eyes betraying the disarray in my head, but I looked the same: cropped dark hair, blue eyes, wide nose that had once been broken in a game of rugby and reset, high Slavic cheekbones care of some genetic kink down my father's line.

Counting out the exact change, I paid and took the mug to a corner table with a good visual on the door. Wes would be wondering why I hadn't called. That got me thinking. Wes had insisted that Wilding was unmarried and childless. Had Wes been aware of this crucial piece of information but for darker reasons withheld it from me? Did he presume that any inconveniences would be ruthlessly taken care of? Knowing Wes, he would describe it as 'collateral damage.' This did not alter the simple fact that he had a fucking duty to tell me.

Uninvited, my thoughts cascaded, washing me up next to the wretched boy. No doubt about it, he'd supply a description to the police and thereby identify me. My face grew cold at the thought of a squad of armed coppers lifting me off the street, if I were lucky marching me to a station and Wilding's son picking me out from a line-up. By sparing his life, I'd left myself wide open. I ought to go back, finish what I'd started, except…

Wired, I gulped the tea, scalding the roof of my mouth. By now the lad would have discovered his mother's body. The thought genuinely appalled me, which came as a surprise. Not because Wilding was female – women can be twice as cruel and vicious and calculating as men – but because I wasn't accustomed to this level of introspection concerning the relatives of the targets I'd removed. It was as if some unseen force had taken me over and brainwashed my mind. Truth is, over the years, I'd ripped men from life. Some had been rogues and murderers, some cruel and psychopathic. Some were good men who turned into bad men. Mostly motivated by greed and pride, always vanity, many strayed too far on the wrong side of the tracks and paid the ultimate price. Dr Mary Wilding was one of them. But the boy…

He was like a fly buzzing around my head. I couldn't help but picture his anguish and pain and his devastation at losing his mother. No doubt about it, his life would be changed forever. If he became vengeful one day he'd come after me.

The door swung open and closed. My eyes flicked to the woman who'd entered. Middle-aged, stout, tired around the eyes, something in her manner reminded me of the woman I was sent to kill. Had I not skimped on the job, I'd be able to run through the strap lines of Mary Wilding's life in my head: what she spent her money on, her medical and family history, her career path, her…

The mobile phone I used for the job vibrated. I snatched at it. It was Wes. Coldly furious, I pictured the pretty-boy American with his dark hair, and soft brown down-turned eyes inferring sensitivity that he didn't possess but rendered women helpless. Part of me was looking forward to breaking the news that I'd aborted the job. It would be Wes's stupid fault for screwing with me. The other part was not so keen.

'You didn't call,' he said.

I said nothing.

'What the fuck is going on?'

Good question. I didn't answer. You learn more from staying quiet and letting others do the talking. Frankly, I was too livid to speak.

'You all right?' he began, clearly mystified.

No, I was not all right. 'There's been a problem.'

'What sort of problem?'

'She was already dead.'

'Shit, you sure?' I pulled a face at Wes's loss of volume control. 'What about the merchandise?' he ranted.

Wes had an annoying tendency to imitate lines from the latest action adventure film or crime show. This was not an episode of *The Wire*. 'The safe was empty.'

'Fucking holy hell.'

I dislike excitable reactions, but often they lead to the kind of loose mouth talk that yields vital information. I wasn't to be disappointed.

He lowered his voice in a way that I imagined he might if he were phoning Dial-A-Wank. 'What about the boy?'

I felt a pulse in my jaw tick, Wes's lapse in intelligence unforgivable. 'What boy?'

'The fucking son, you moron.'

I let the insult pass. I'd been called worse. I kept my voice low and controlled to conceal my rage. 'You never mentioned a son,' I growled. 'The deal was for one target only. If there had been two the price would have been considerably more. Your lack of attention to detail could have compromised me. It could cost me my life.' I didn't admit that I, too, had screwed up, that I'd made monumental mistakes.

Faced with the irrefutable logic of my argument, he backed off. I also think he was afraid of me, which was good. 'Look, I knew about the kid, right?'

'You fucking lied to me.'

'I'm sorry, man, but I was ordered not to tell you,' he whined.

'Who by?'

'The guy who's paying.'

What sort of half-brained lunatic was this man? I said something to that effect.

'I know,' Wes said, trying to appease me. 'So there was no boy?' he pressed.

One good lie deserves another. 'No.'

'Holy Christ, that's going to be a problem'. Yours, not mine, I thought. 'The boy is a loose end. He has to be removed.'

This was the equivalent of pouring a can of petrol over my very personal fire. 'Fuck you. I'm out.'

Wes let rip with what could be best described as a full-on curse. I maintained a contrived and dignified silence so that he could calm down, which he did. 'Can't, man. You have no idea who you're dealing with.'

'Who *am* I dealing with exactly?'

'One nasty son-of-a-bitch.'

My laugh was cold. They were all nasty sons-of-bitches. Came with the territory.

'And there's the small matter of the merchandise,' Wes said.

'Which is missing,' I reminded him.

'Says who?'

I neither cared for the tone nor the inference. 'Says I. Don't get smart, Wes. I can track you down any time I like.' And kill you, I inferred. Wes got the drift.

'Hey, I'm not taking a pop at you, I'm only saying how the employer is gonna see it, bud. He's one suspicious dude.'

Most of them were paranoid fuckers. 'So who do you think beat me to it, apart from me, that is?' I added acerbically.

'Search me. You really sure it's missing?' The whine had returned.

'Certain,' I said, clipped.

Wes let out a big sigh. 'You gotta find it.'

I swelled with anger. 'I'm not a private detective.'

'Yeah, I know, but please, you've gotta help me out here. I…'

'What was on the hard drive?' I now realised that the hard drive was more than straight business. The hard drive held the key.

'I don't know.'

Wes was the kind of guy who says no and does yes and vice-versa. I didn't believe him. 'If you want me to find it I need to know.' I had no intention of doing Wes or anyone else a favour. I was done with them. I was only concerned with me.

Silence descended like a safety curtain at a theatre. I imagined Wes feverishly trying to worm his way out of the mess he was in. Finally, he spoke.

'Data.'

'What kind of data?'

'Chemical, drugs, just stuff,' he said unconvincingly, 'Look,

12

I'll see what I can do, talk to the employer, or something. So you're in?'

'It will cost. Stay tuned.' And I hung up.

First rule of the game: don't botch the job. Second rule: don't get caught. I'd broken the first and had no intention of breaking the second, but for what I hoped would be the only time in my life I was going to break the third. Insane, maybe, but I had no choice.

Finishing my tea, I stepped outside. Sun trickled through the cloud. My breath made smoke-rings in the cold morning air. Nice day for a walk. Me, I had other ideas: I was going back.

CHAPTER THREE

Less than four hours after I'd fled, I was holed up on the upper storey of a small boutique hotel, and on the opposite side of the road with a clear view of Dr Wilding's home, a modest but attractive 1930's red brick semi-detached property with a casement window in the front and triple-glazed French windows at the rear. Cutting corners on the job did not mean I'd failed to carry out basic groundwork. Days before, I'd already ascertained that her next-door neighbours were away on holiday and the attached property the subject of a repossession order, the occupants long gone following the collapse of their electrical business.

I'd expected the area to be cordoned off. I'd anticipated rafts of police officers. The view before me was a picture of the mundane, ordinary and commonplace. It spooked me.

As I saw it there were a couple of explanations for the lack of activity. Perhaps the killer had returned, or maybe Wes and his employer had interpreted my response as too negative, swung into action and appointed another assassin to finish off the boy. Doubtful, I thought. Too knee-jerk, too dangerous. Involving more people than you need always fraught with risk. And pointless – the boy's death would not reveal the whereabouts of the hard drive. The gnawing desire to know what was on it made my skin itch, and it occurred to me then that Wilding's murderer had come within a split-second of crossing my path, an awesome thought. If we'd both showed up for the same job at the same time we'd probably have ended up killing each other.

So who was he and who had employed him? If I could trace the guy I'd find his employer and then I could get my hands on the information. Best man to approach for that type of low-down would be Billy Franke. I let out a liquid breath. Easy to say, less easy to do: asking questions would draw attention to my failure, and Billy, one my main employers, didn't like mistakes. I was still chewing this over when almost twenty minutes later the cops arrived. To tell the truth, I was almost relieved.

There were two police patrol units, an unmarked Mondeo with four plain-clothes guys inside, and a police Range Rover. I watched as the occupants piled out and into the house. Within ten minutes or so, a plod appeared doing what plods do: spooling crime scene tape around the front of the building. My stomach clenched. How many bodies?

I leant back then straight back up as a black Land Rover with tinted windows hove into view. It prowled down the street, paused outside the crime scene area for enough time to be significant, and drove on. The number plate bore the prefix 248D, assigned to all Russian diplomatic vehicles. While I swallowed this indigestible piece of information, another less assuming Toyota Land Cruiser with two men inside pulled up on double yellow lines and parked twenty-five metres from the property. Both occupants watched silently, unashamedly, as though they did this every day of the week, as if they operated by a different set of laws to the ordinary citizen. Next, racing down the road, a navy-blue Lexus, one male driver, and one female passenger. I could almost smell the rubber from the tyres as the vehicle cut and swerved into a tight space and parked between two patrol cars. The driver shot out a split-second before the woman. He glanced up the road, jerking his head in the direction of the stationary Land Cruiser.

'What the hell is Mossad doing here?' he said to her.

'Doing what they do best: watching.'

At this, I froze. I have no particularly fluency in languages bar the bare rub-along stuff that buys me a beer and gets me out of tricky situations, but I can lip-read. I've no idea how I do this. Put it down to a predominantly solitary and lonely childhood. Lip-reading aside, I guessed that the woman and her sidekick were British Intelligence. To see so many security services congregated in one place made me more than uneasy. I felt as if I had chipped ice in my blood. Had Wilding been involved in some kind of industrial espionage? Selling trade secrets, maybe? Didn't really compute with what I'd been led to believe.

But then what I'd been told was a pack of lies.

Painfully I tried to force connections, but my mind was swamped with the boy, the dead woman, the damned Israelis whose attendance closely reminded me of someone who taught me everything I knew. Cold sweat nestled in the small of my back. Feelings, alien emotions, played no part in my life. They were a luxury I could not afford.

Think, for Chrissakes. Think clearly.

I'd learnt a long time ago that Mossad had a habit of showing up either at or in the aftermath of all major events. Most recently and to name a few: the death of Princess Diana, the murder of Robert Maxwell, the suicide or murder, depending on your point of view, of Dr David Kelly. Their presence here confirmed that there was more to Wilding than I'd taken the time and trouble to find out. Now I saw why the hit on the scientist had been a rush job: Wilding was a big fish.

I turned my attention back to the woman. Tall, around five eight, full-figured without being overweight, probably a dress size twelve. She had a pale complexion, with a shock of short copper-coloured hair, side parting so that a lock fell over the right side of her face, which was a perfect oval. The lips matched the full figure, voluptuous with a nipped in waist, and she had a neat

16

nose, neat everything. I couldn't yet tell the colour of her eyes but I guessed they were green. She moved with feline stealth, fluid, impressive for a woman of her build and stature. From the way she threw her head back at the Israelis and blew them a kiss, the way she strode ahead of her male colleague, the way he deferred, this was her gig.

I followed her path to the door, half-mesmerised, then she took me by surprise. She turned, looked up, eyes scanning. I chilled. It was as if she were looking not straight at me but *into* me. I stared back, aroused. Then she turned and was gone.

An hour and a half passed. Forensics came. A white van appeared. Two men got out and disappeared inside, re-emerging twenty minutes later with computer boxes. Two trips later they were packed and gone. The patrol cars left. An ambulance showed. The Israelis stayed, mute, unyielding. The driver smoked incessantly. I never saw the Russians again. Then my mobile vibrated for a second time in as many hours.

'Yes, Wes.'

'Where are you?'

'Out and about.'

'Is that smart?'

I didn't respond.

'You still there?' Wes's voice, low and tense, scraped down the line.

'Uh-huh.' My deliberately Neanderthal response suggested that he'd overplayed his card and he knew it.

'That's great,' he said, effusive now. 'Can you meet? Charing Cross Hotel.'

'When?'

'Noon.'

'Make it one. I'm taking an early lunch.' I cut the call and switched off the phone. I don't eat lunch. It makes me sleepy.

At half past ten the house opposite erupted into activity. Two men in plain-clothes came out first, closely followed by the woman's sidekick. Next, the redhead, with the boy bunched up next to her. I let out a breath. He was alive. From this height and distance, armed with a Heckler and Koch military sniping rifle, I could 'remove' the problem at the click of a trigger. Not subtle, but effective. It gave me pause for thought. Would it even do the lad a favour? After the sudden death of his mother what would become his story later on? Would he turn to booze or drugs or sex to relieve his pain? Would he seek meaning in violence, as I had done? I wondered how he'd negotiate a path through a lifetime's maze of hidden obstacles and mantraps and people out to get you. This was not my problem, I reminded myself. What did I care? Except now I realised that I cared more than was good for me, that even if I'd had the necessary kit I lacked the necessary ruthlessness.

Worrying.

A snarling phalanx of hangers-on, grim-faced, came out of the building last. Clear and easy in her movements, the woman directed the boy into the rear of the Lexus, climbed in next to him, but not before turning her back and issuing orders to the others who received their instructions as though ordered to eat dirt. I smiled in spite of everything. The woman running the show came across as direct, in cold control, authoritative and, yes, sexy. If anyone were going to hunt me down it would be her.

The main cavalcade drove away. The boy was out of immediate danger, whisked off by his minders no doubt to a safe house on some godforsaken housing estate where nobody asked questions. I almost envied him.

As for me, there was only one place to go, one man to see, the last person alive familiar with my real name and who could help me. I briefly wondered whether he'd think the time he'd devoted to my education in the Dark Arts wasted.

CHAPTER FOUR

Even in winter and under a sullen sky, Chiswick, moneyed and classy, oozed vibrancy and colour, aspiration and style. Treading an unfamiliar path through a crush of dead leaves, my senses alert to every police siren, every copper on the street, I turned right and left until finally I found myself in a maze of streets and homes that in summer would be hidden from view. It was as quiet as a desert night. Row upon row of classy red brick houses with white railings and balconies lined the wide tree-lined avenue. Suburbia at its finest.

It didn't take long to locate the house right at the end. Screened from the street by a hedge, detached, it was a building of entrances and exits, a metaphor for life and death. It never occurred to me that Reuben might have moved or even died. Reuben, somehow, seemed indestructible.

Murmuring *good morning* to a young pretty mother pushing a baby-buggy, I followed the line of the wall to the rear of the building. A heavy wrought iron gate divided the boundary between the property and the pavement. As I walked back round to the front, the teal-coloured front door with the lion's head brass knocker swung open and a woman stepped out.

In her mid to late thirties, her dark blue coat buttoned up, only the perilously high heels and pointed toes gave the game away. Actually, I lie. She had a satiated, just-fucked expression on her face. And I knew why. Even in middle age, Reuben had projected a strong sense of his own sexuality. A man's man, Reuben adored women. Seemed like this peculiarity of his personality remained unchanged, his enthusiasm undimmed. Before she closed the door I bowled up to her and turned on my most winning smile.

'Private parcel delivery for Mr Greene.' I took out the dummy set of keys I carry with me, rattled them and pointed as if my van was parked around the corner.

She started, a flush of colour spreading across her cheeks. 'Oh right,' she said. 'You want me to take it? Only I'm in a bit of a hurry.' She shifted her weight from one foot to the other.

'It's heavy,' I said. 'No worries, I'll pop inside and get Mr Greene to sign for it first.'

She smiled, grateful. 'Thanks.'

'You're welcome. Sorry to have held you up,' I called after her, closing the door silently behind me.

I stood in the inner porch. I don't know why but I felt as if my lungs were being crushed from the inside. I could hardly draw breath. I hadn't seen the man in more than fifteen years and just because he'd worked for Mossad a long time ago did not mean that he could throw light on current events. Would my unexpected appearance trigger a negative reaction? Would he welcome a voyage into the past? I guessed there was only one way to find out.

The house was long and narrow with pale laminate flooring. Stairs to the right, two doors to the left, ahead a light and airy kitchen with a glass roof and two steps down into a dining area with a view of a pretty walled garden.

I could hear water running. The sound came from upstairs. I crossed to the kitchen, helped myself to a mug of coffee from a pot, still hot, and pulled up a chair near the window. After spending so much time out in the cold Reuben's home felt unnaturally warm.

I saw Reuben before he saw me. The skin under his dark, intelligent eyes was more pouched than before, and his hair, now uniformly grey, thinner on top, yet he was still recognisable. An imposing figure, with a body built to last in spite of being a couple of stone heavier, he wore a dark shirt of needle-cord buttoned to his throat. The sleeves turned back exposed formidable forearms. I'd always believed that he could strangle a man with his bare hands.

I stayed absolutely still and watched as he suddenly registered that I was there. He had total mastery of his physical responses. Only someone who knew him well would be able to divine the thoughts and emotions running through his mind. I read shock in his eyes as if he believed that the day of reckoning had finally arrived and he was to be eliminated by one of his many enemies. Next, recognition, puzzlement, suspicion, and finally pleasure. His full lips drew back into a smile as he crossed the floor and down the steps, arms outstretched. I stood up, opened my arms wide, showing in that one small gesture that I had come in peace. He held me tight, clapping me on the back like a long lost son. His embrace aroused a brief, fleeting need in me to belong. As inconceivable as it was, an infinitesimal part of me flirted with the idea of rejoining the human race even though I knew deep in my heart it was impossible. Reuben was the only person in the world who knew me before and after. He was aware of what I'd become and what I was. He would not judge me. He would not ask awkward questions. He would not ask me to explain. We were never going to have one of those mundane conversations about what I'd done the previous day, week or year. We would not waste time discussing my choice of holiday destination. Relationships were off limits because I had none.

'Joshua Thane, the young man I once described as shimmering with menace,' he let out a loud laugh. 'My God, I thought you were dead. What brings you here? We must eat. We must celebrate. You are hungry, yes? I have pastries and eggs. What would you like? Name it and you shall have it.'

If anyone could give me what I wanted Reuben could, but first he needed to be finessed. As far as brunch was concerned, I settled for eggs, poached, and more coffee. While he hustled around the kitchen he rattled on about the old days. He made no mention of my unorthodox entry. Reuben only ever voiced criticism.

'Remember you asking what it felt like to kill someone?' he said at last with a chuckle. 'I told you that it doesn't feel like anything. It's…'

'Business not personal,' I chipped in.

Reuben cast me a slow sideways look. He knew where I was going with this. My first kill broke the cardinal rule. It was personal and it was supposed to be my last. The fact that I was here sitting in his kitchen meant events had come full circle. I don't believe in karma. If I did I'd be dead a thousand times over, but I definitely felt the pull of something outside my very ordinary human powers. Disturbing.

'Eat,' Reuben said, putting a plate down in front of me. 'Then we will talk.'

We ate in silence. In spite of the unusual and tricky circumstances in which I found myself, I was calm. I trusted nobody, but I trusted Reuben. If I pitched it right, Reuben with his extensive contacts would provide me with the answers I so urgently needed.

At last, when the plates were cleared, I told Reuben what had taken place that morning. I delivered the account without emotion, as he had taught me. I kept my pitch neutral, the information factual, giving as clear a description of events as possible. At this stage, I didn't identify the target. He listened with the acuity I expected from him. He did not express surprise or comment upon my low diversification into theft. He frowned only once, but when I mentioned the surviving witness, he grew angry.

'You did not know about the boy?' Condemnatory, Reuben's dark eyes turned as black as the sharps and flats on a keyboard.

My jaw ground but I said nothing. I'd broken a fundamental rule. 'I…'

'Didn't do your homework,' he barked. 'What have I always taught you: surveillance, knowledge, survival. You check the intelligence then you check it again.'

He was right, of course. It was not Wes's fault. The blame lay with me.

'Have you forgotten the art?' Reuben snarled.

What could I say? Even if I'd elicited screeds of personal details, something told me that I would have missed the one that counted. 'It was a one-off, an unusual job.' More unusual than I could ever imagine, and one I never wished to repeat. Ever.

'How could you be so remiss?' he growled. 'What was it, greed?'

I met his eye. He had a point but I'm not sure it fully explained my incompetence. I've heard it said that there is a particular time in a serial killer's life when he wants to be found and stopped. To facilitate his discovery, he makes a mistake. I was not a serial killer in the sense that the term was generally applied so I didn't believe I fell into this category.

'I slipped up, took my eye off the ball,' I said lamely.

'You got complacent,' Reuben said, contempt in his eyes. After all I've taught you, his expression implied.

'I admit I was reckless,' I said, stubbornly defending my reputation.

'And you let the boy go?' Reuben saw me for the fool I was. This rattled me.

'I did.'

'Why?' In Reuben's book, you took no prisoners.

Stumped for an answer, I said. 'If ordered to kill him I would have done. Nobody gave the order.'

'Then you have taken an unacceptable risk.'

'Yes.' No point in denial.

'The police will be all over it and now they will have a description of you.'

'A description but not an identity.' They couldn't exactly issue a warrant for the arrest of a man without a name. Even so, the boy had dragged me kicking and screaming out of the shadows. Did Reuben of all people recognise this? If so, he didn't enlighten me.

Reuben took out cigarettes and a lighter. I sensed he was playing for time. He offered me the pack. I rarely smoked but this seemed like the right occasion. I took one, lit it. Reuben did the same.

'You need money?'

'Yes.'

'I will see to it.

'Somewhere to hide?'

I hesitated. It would be the smart move yet I could see now that it would be too easy for Reuben to slip back into his old role as mentor and me as pupil. I no longer responded well to criticism. 'No, just give me the cash, I'll be fine.'

'As you please.' Dark-eyed, he took a drag of his cigarette, drawing the tobacco deep into his lungs.

'The reason I'm here,' I confessed, 'is that I went back.'

'Back?' he spat, 'Are you out of your mind?'

'To finish the job,' I lied.

Reuben met my gaze with watchful eyes. He nodded briefly.

'After I arrived,' I continued, 'the place teemed with British, Russian and Israeli security services.'

Most people would have reacted. Reuben was not most people. He barely flinched. 'The woman,' he began. 'You said she worked at Imperial College.'

'That's right.' I inhaled deeply. 'Dr Mary Wilding.' I floated her name as if it were a smoke ring. A pulse fluttered in Reuben's thick neck. I checked any natural response of my own.

'The microbiologist,' he said slowly, as though his brain had suddenly filled with sludge.

I blinked. 'She was a research scientist.'

His eyes narrowed. 'You didn't bother to look into this aspect of her background?'

Unforgivably, I had not. I glared at him. He said nothing, his expression one of sheer disbelief. He took another drag of his cigarette, flicked a flake of tobacco from his tongue. 'So who did she upset? What was her crime exactly?' A shrewd glint entered his eyes.

I told him what I'd been told, then I said, 'As the security services are all over it, I assume she committed industrial espionage.'

'*Assume*?' Reuben's damning expression ripped right through me.

'It's a fair…'

'Clearly you were not familiar with her sphere of work.'

I said nothing. My brain was in overdrive, misfiring and failing to make connections.

'She worked at the Department of Virology at Imperial College,' Reuben said.

'Virology,' I repeated, sounding leaden.

'The department she allegedly worked in was a front,' he added, darkness in his tone.

'For what?'

Reuben did not answer my question directly. 'The college has *many* departments,' he continued, cool-eyed. 'Some more secret than you can ever imagine.' His voice assumed a forbidding note. It felt as if a chill easterly wind gusted across the room. I felt faintly nauseous and it was unconnected with brunch.

'Meaning?' I said.

'Bio-weapons,' he snapped. 'Chemicals that kill,' he added as though I didn't get it the first time. 'As deadly as nuclear but more vile in its application.'

'And illegal,' I flung back at him. This was Britain, for God's sake, not some far flung Russian outpost.

Reuben threw me a contemptuous look. 'Yes, which is precisely why any sane government ensures that it has counter-measures in the event of a biological attack. Wilding was working in strategic defence.'

I contained a groan. This had catastrophe written all over it. No wonder the security services were all over it like typhoid in an Indian slum. Christ Almighty, what was on the hard drive? Reuben read my expression and asked the same question. I shook my head.

'*Why* don't you know, and when the hell did you become a common thief?'

I opened my mouth to protest. Reuben waved away any attempt at excuses with a flick of his wrist. 'And your American friend, how does he fit?'

I gave no names. I explained that Wes was the fixer, the guy who acted as a middleman. 'Crime lords have their own contract killers on the payroll, but sometimes they need a specialist job that puts enough distance between them and the intended victim.' Safe to say, I usually got involved in the dirtier end of the business although I drew a line at abduction and torture.

Reuben stared at me with distaste. 'And this character, you have operated with him before? He is reliable?'

'As much as anyone.' Except, of course, he'd lied royally to me.

Reuben nodded slowly. I realised he was trying to work out a way to save my reputation, my skin. Thank God for that.

'You want out?'

I did my best to conceal my shock. How could I? Was it really possible for me to rub out the past, get a nine to five job, settle down and start over? Straight answer: no. My silence lurked like a restless ghost in the room.

Reuben gave voice to what I was thinking. 'We all want out at some time in our lives but it isn't always possible. Few have the necessary requirements for this type of activity,' he added with false delicacy. 'What I am trying to tell you, Joshua, is that you cannot change who you are. You can change your name, your address, your friends and you can run away from problems, but not from yourself.'

This I already knew. I didn't want a lecture. 'Then I'd appreciate your help. You could find out what the Israelis are after. It would give me a lead to find those responsible for the theft.'

'And then what?"

Take them out. I shrugged, a *go figure* expression on my face.

He shook his head. 'I no longer have those type of contacts. Your only option is to finish what you started.'

'What the hell do you mean?'

Reuben hiked both shoulders, raised both hands, palms up in supplication. 'It will be difficult but...'

'I will not kill the boy.' This took both of us by surprise. I cleared my throat, drew heavily on the cigarette. 'It would be too tricky,' I added. 'He's probably in a safe house.' Seconds thudded past. Silence washed into the room like sea invading a stricken vessel.

At last, seemingly forgetting the boy, Reuben asked, 'Who took out the contract?'

I shook my head. 'His anonymity was part of the deal.'

'You were paid well?' Reuben's voice thronged with cynicism.

'Handsomely.'

He thought for a moment. Easy to guess what he was turning over in his mind: that no paymaster would rest easy with such a poor return on his investment. I was, in effect, a dead man walking.

'What was on the hard drive, Reuben?'

He didn't answer straight away. He seemed to be weighing something up in his mind. The stillness in the room was so tangible you could have heard a feather fall.

'Have you heard of Project Coast?' he said tentatively.

I shook my head, perplexed by the sudden change of subject. Once more he stared at me for a moment with what seemed genuine indecision, then when he finally spoke he had a certainty about him that I normally found reassuring. That morning I wasn't reassured.

'Project Coast was a programme that originated in South Africa. It involved the creation of an ethnic specific biological weapon. The weapon only attacked blacks.'

I wanted to interject, to lean forward. I didn't flicker so much as an eyebrow. Reuben had taught me well.

'The project was run by the Pretoria government. Deeply secret, it ran during the 1980's. The then Defence Minister oversaw it. The work was still at the embryonic stage when the apartheid regime collapsed. Certain individuals assisted in the government's twisted endeavours. One was an American, Dr Larry Ford, a gynaecologist who allegedly worked for the CIA, his role to create and develop biological weapons. Years later, he was found dead with a gunshot wound to his head. The official version was suicide, his involvement with the CIA, as one would expect, denied. When the police opened the refrigerator in his home they found enough toxins to poison the entire state of California.'

I wondered why Reuben was telling me this. His information seemed rehearsed and readily given, a little too pat. Irrationally, I had the sudden sick sensation of being played. Resisting the temptation to speak for a second time and with a deep, growing sense of unease, I nodded patiently for Reuben to continue.

'You knew nothing of this?' he said, a sharp edge to his voice.

I shrugged my ignorance. It was Reuben's turn to go silent. I realised what he was driving at. 'You think I had a hand in Ford's murder?' Suddenly I saw the connection to Wilding.

He did not answer straightaway. He studied my face with the same penetrating gaze as a man shining a spotlight into my eyes. I hoped that he was satisfied with what he saw. I am a gifted liar, but I wasn't lying this time. 'It was a particularly inept piece of work,' he admitted. 'I would have been disappointed in you.'

'When was this, exactly?'

'Spring 2000.'

My mind reeled back. I was twenty-four. Russia. My first gig for Mikhail Yakovlevich, a Russian thug. 'Nowhere near. I can prove it.'

Reuben sipped his drink, nodded in agreement, accepting my explanation at face value. Glad we'd cleared it up, I was less happy that I'd fallen under suspicion. 'You think there's a pattern, someone bumping off scientists?'

'Perhaps.'

Shit, and now the security services were on my tail. 'You were saying,' I said, trying to lose the thought and get him back on track.

'Certain groups of people have individual genetic character-istics. As you probably know, there is an entire industry devoted to the creation of drugs to target specific genes responsible for certain genetic disorders.'

I nodded.

'An entirely commendable endeavour, of course, it involves the precise sequencing of DNA. But there is a less benign application. By a rigorous process of selection, there are those who hope to develop pathogens to attack targeted individuals based on either their racial orientation or their sex.'

'Hope? You mean it's been developed?' I said.

Reuben's accompanying smile was claustrophobic. What was once a sick dream had assumed a reality of nightmarish propor-tions and, well out of my normal sphere of operation, I confess it shook me. 'Think how such a thing could be turned into a military weapon,' he continued, without missing a beat. 'So obsessed with the threat of nuclear destruction, most politicians retain a blind spot for other more diabolical possibilities.'

I had no tremendous interest in politics, but I was certain this wasn't true. Governments knew, all right. Only the general populace remained ignorant. And thank God for that. Reuben picked up on my dismay. With cool, he disregarded it.

'Which is why there are secret departments to counter the possibility of such an odious attack.'

'You think Wilding was involved in this type of research?'

Reuben shrugged his massive shoulders. 'Never a good idea to jump to conclusions, but it is credible.'

I blinked and cursed my stupidity. Even for a man like me there's a big moral distinction between slotting bad people one at a time and annihilating innocent individuals en masse. What if such a weapon fell into the hands of a rogue state or terrorists? Aside from what they could do with it, it would provide the perfect means for blackmail. Christ, you could hold entire countries to ransom with that kind of leverage.

'You think this was why she had to die?' Already I was thinking her death politically motivated and unconnected to organised crime. For sure, the security services would be after my hide.

Reuben did not answer, just looked. I scratched my ear. 'The U.K. is a melting pot of races. Which target group are we talking about?'

'That I can't tell you.'

'Can't?'

'Because I genuinely don't know,' he spread his hands.

'But, surely, there are treaties and agreements…'

'Which can be broken.' He leant towards me once more. 'Government exists to protect its people. One has to fight any threat, however vile, accordingly.'

I didn't speak. Not for a moment did it occur to me that Reuben was mistaken. Whatever Reuben said about being out of the game, my old mentor had always been the kind of man who kept his ear close to the ground. There was no reason for me to suspect that this had changed. What scared me more, instead of coming to Reuben to pick his brains and borrow money, I'd discovered a conspiracy of unimaginable proportions. And I was at the centre of it.

'Let me show you something,' he said, climbing to his feet. He gestured for me to follow and retraced his steps through the kitchen and back out into the long hall. On his left, a wooden door, which I'd assumed led to a cupboard under the stairs. Taking a key from his pocket, he unlocked the door, opened it, flicked on a light, and descended a short flight of wooden steps to a basement room where, against the farthest wall, there was a sofa. Facing the sofa, and fixed to the wall nearest the stairs, a fifty-inch plasma screen sitting astride an antique desk, the remaining walls lined with books.

Reuben invited me to take a seat. I obeyed and watched as he touched a catch underneath the drawer in the desk revealing a false compartment from which he removed a brown sealed envelope that he placed to one side. Sliding the back panel of the dummy drawer to the left, he revealed a secondary hiding place. From this, he picked out a DVD with skull and crossbones drawn crudely in black marker pen along the spine. Reuben slipped off the cover and fed the disk into the DVD player. Nothing much happened. A lot of flicker. No sound. Lots of grainy moving images like the flaky footage you find on a pirate video. Then Reuben switched off the lights and it felt as if I was being swallowed whole. I blinked, fused in concentration.

Picture the image: a cavern, sides made of solid rock, wide metal ducting as if to pump fresh air into the bowels of the earth. At ground level, men dressed like astronauts walking slow-limbed. Some, who wore thick gloves and held clipboards, had their attention fixed on a chamber with transparent walls around twelve metres wide by twelve metres high, although difficult to tell. A metal tube fed into the domed glass roof. Inside, a group of people: an emaciated-looking white guy and a young teenage couple holding hands alongside two other men and women who stood separately. If I had to take a guess I'd say the non-whites were Chinese, Korean maybe. Their tattered clothes hung on them like shrouds, their expressions one of mute rank terror, the like I had never seen and I've seen a lot of fear in my time.

31

A cursory nod from one of the 'astronauts' or rather scientists, as I now believed them to be, signalled that something was about to happen, but I didn't understand what. I pitched forwards, straining to comprehend, rapt by the figures in the glass dungeon. Within seconds all seven cupped hands over their faces and fled to the outer extremities of the see-through prison. The young couple herded desperately together, eyes agape with fear. Within a minute, two of the women were vomiting. One man, with blood issuing from his nose and mouth, crashed to the ground. Another turned purple, leaking through every orifice, body in spasm. The white guy, unaffected by the spreading contagion, collapsed to the ground and, with hands over his head, knees to his chest, rocked in despair. Blood and bile, faeces and vomit spattered the floor and glass. They were shouting, screaming, but I heard no sound, only a chorus of unheard voices. I am rarely moved, but my fists curled and found their way to my mouth. I longed to look away, to escape, and to empty my mind but I remained transfixed.

At last, buckling under the vicious assault on her nervous system, the last surviving girl, bloodied and broken, leant towards the dying boy and kissed his mouth. I thought my hardened heart would seize up.

Reuben's voice shattered the silence. 'The killing process took three minutes,' he said matter-of-fact, switching off the film and switching on the lights. Same length of time I'd allowed myself to steal in and out of Wilding's home, I registered.

'What about the white guy?'

'He was taken out and shot. Experiment over.'

'So he was immune?'

Reuben nodded, held my gaze in a vice-like grip. 'In simple engineering terms, it's a tremendous feat to divide one human genome from another, but…'

'Excuse me,' I said, stumbling past Reuben and upstairs.

'The cloakroom is on the right by the front door,' he called after me.

I found it and threw up in the sink. Adrenalin dump, I convinced myself, totally unconnected, to what I'd just watched. Splashing water over my face, I gaped at my reflection in the mirror. Apart from my obvious pallor, I thought I'd be unrecognisable. I thought the man I believed myself to be was hiding but he wasn't.

'You are shocked,' Reuben said as I emerged and rejoined him in the kitchen.

'We're talking about biological genocide,' I snapped. 'I take it the clip is genuine?'

'It has been authenticated although we are not entirely certain where this took place. The footage emerged over a decade ago.'

'Bearing in mind you didn't show me this shit as a form of entertainment, what's the *exact* connection to Wilding?'

'I am simply making you aware of possibilities,' Reuben said, pulling his punches, 'I'm giving you the context within which I believe she worked.'

'Why?'

An unnerving gleam entered his eye. 'To save your soul.'

Too late for that. Redemption was beyond me: I'd committed too many acts of violence. I shook my head.

'You are indifferent to death?' he said, his turn to be shocked.

'I'm indifferent to life.'

Reuben frowned. I think he found my response glib and irritating. 'Joshua,' he said, with a stern and penetrating expression. 'What about the lives of others?'

I took a deep breath. I'd spent my entire professional life singularly unconcerned by the lives of others. I didn't do noble and I didn't do self-sacrifice. And yet…

Reuben was still talking. 'I do not know how far such weapons have progressed because I no longer have the kind of connections I once had, but it's a safe bet that you are mixed up in something of apocalyptic proportions.'

In spite of the outward show, the content of the video-clip

and the spectre of mass murder taunted me. I thought about Wes, about the so-called data on the hard drive. Assuming Wilding had been engaged in defending the nation, someone had stolen it with the intention of neutralising our defence capability. It might also have been stolen to trade with individuals intent on carrying out an atrocity. Like it or not, I had to face the possibility that certain unscrupulous people, individuals I dealt with on a daily basis, wanted this type of material to sell on. I didn't give a damn about my own survival but, as Reuben had already pointed out, the lives of others were now at stake. Locating the hard drive suddenly assumed increased urgency. What I was going to do with the material when I got my hands on it I hadn't a clue.

CHAPTER FIVE

Hiding me in the rear footwell of his Volvo Estate, Reuben drove me into town, dropped me off and I returned as quickly as I dared to my lock-up near King's Cross. My only official claim to property it housed the tools of my trade and, aside from weapons, included bikes, wigs, uniforms, props like walking sticks, and hair dyes; anything that could aid a metamorphosis in my appearance. There, I had a quick shave, changed into a smart cashmere coat over tailored trousers and brogues, and popped contact lenses into my eyes, transforming them from blue to brown. It was a detail. It would only count if someone got up close and personal but as detail had tripped me up I wasn't keen to repeat the error. To complete the disguise, I chose a pair of glasses with plain lenses in black rectangular frames. I took a briefcase containing a pair of high-spec binoculars and a Cannon PowerShot digital camera, a false passport and false credit cards linked to the passport. It's commonly assumed that these are difficult to acquire. They are, but fifteen or so years ago, when I was starting out, and the Identity and Passport Service was lax, they were a doddle.

Confident that I could not be recognised, I felt more at ease and made my way to the hotel to hook up with Wes. Despite his outward show, I'd always had the impression that he was a nearly

35

man; nearly made it into the higher echelons of organised crime; nearly made it into accountancy. Never had enough bottle for the former and lacked application for the latter. Now I had my doubts. Now I believed he was more involved in the Wilding job than I'd given him credit. Why else would Wes lie about the boy and the reason for the scientist's murder?

Stepping into the large foyer with its L-shaped reception area, I veered to the right into a wide corridor with booths down one side, lifts on the other. It was cathedral quiet. At that time the place was virtually empty. Wes was sitting three slots down. His eyes flickered with lust as a handsome-looking forty-some-thing woman wearing a power suit and heels clicked by. He never could resist the call of the wild. As I approached he glanced up, no recognition in his eyes. I strode past as though making for the grand staircase. Like a guy who has forgotten something, I checked my pace, turned, strode back and slipped into a seat opposite. Wes blinked wide, sharply retreated into the leather, his olive skin two shades lighter. I met his startled gaze with a level expression.

'Fuck, and holy fuck.' His body braced. His dark eyebrows assumed two angry points in his forehead. For a moment I thought he was going to lean forward and punch me hard in the face. Fortunately his survival instinct kicked in.

'Hello, Wes.'

Wes jerked towards me. 'Have you seen the news? It's on every television channel, every radio station. And the boy was there. He saw you, man. Your identikit picture is gonna be in every mother-fucking newspaper. You fucked up, Hex. You screwed me over.'

I glanced away, let out a long slow breath, a technique to control my urgent desire to smash his jaw into five pieces. '*I* screwed *you* over?' My voice sounded ugly.

Wes looked me straight in the eye and leant in close. Fat beads of sweat dotted his brow. I realised then that he feared his employer more than he feared me. 'The British security service is all over this one,' he hissed.

'And the Russians and Israelis. Now why would that be?'

'Russians?' He had the desperate look of a man crashing through a rain forest trying to evade a Cassowary.

'You didn't know what Wilding was up to her pretty white neck in?' I said, a *do me a favour* expression on my face. 'And you've got the fucking cheek to get me here to deliver a lecture.'

His shoulders dropped and he glanced away. 'The employer is getting mighty jumpy.'

'Then he needs to get a grip.'

Wes ran his fingers through his dark hair, his expression flashed from anger to anxiety to beseeching. 'You have to find the material.'

'I don't *have to* do anything.'

He held my gaze for a moment then looked down. 'You have three days,' he mumbled.

Wes wasn't making a lot of sense to me. What he said, his body language, everything about him was off. 'Three days until what?'

He hiked one shoulder then he seemed to collapse into himself. He did not look up.

I let out a laugh to cover my nerves. I was thinking about the snuff movie with the biological twist. 'Is this a threat?'

'They hire you for slotting,' he said, looking me in the eye again, this time urgent. 'They have their own for torture.'

Oh do they? I thought. 'Who is this bastard?' I said.

His face was a stone. 'We had a deal.'

'We did, but the deal is off and the rules just changed. You can have the money back.' Which was a fair offer and, in any case, I didn't want it any more.

'No way, man. I'm risking my skin already.'

I am an infinitely patient individual, but Wes was pissing me off and I was getting nowhere. I struck hard and fast, grabbed his throat with one hand and dragged him half way across the table.

'I'm going to run through possible candidates and you're going to agree or disagree.'

This was bluff on my part. I wasn't going to disclose my personal list of clients to some creep like Wes.

'Break my neck, if you like,' he managed to croak.

I increased the pressure. Wes's spaniel eyes popped. His lips clamped shut. 'I suspect our dead scientist was engaged in a little more than finding the cure for the common cold. Right?' I didn't get a nod. I got a double-blink. Good enough. 'She was working in strategic defence against bio-weapons.' I didn't know this, but it would do. I said nothing about my source, nothing about secret departments. Wes tried to swallow, difficult under the circumstances. 'In an enterprise like this I'm guessing we're talking dirty bombs, chemical warfare, terrorism. Nod if I'm on the right trail.' He didn't nod. I released my grasp. Wes coughed, cleared his throat, and shook himself like a wet dog after a walk in the rain.

'I have to go to the men's room,' he rasped, standing up.

I stood up opposite him. 'I'm coming with you.' It would be easier to work him over in the tiled confines of a public lavatory.

He gazed up at me with defeated eyes, saw I wasn't screwing with him and, with the same raised hands that had undressed dozens of women, showed me his palms in surrender. 'Okay, okay,' he said, slumping into the leather, 'but you didn't hear it from me.'

I sat back down. Right, now we were getting somewhere.

'Wilding was working on a blueprint.'

'A blueprint for what?'

Wes looked round, furtive. 'Some new kind of drug, works in a different way. I don't know. I'm not a chemist.'

I stared at him and read deceit in his eyes. Again I cursed my own stupidity, lack of professionalism and downright criminality for embroiling me in something unspeakable. Without doubt, I was treading on unhallowed ground.

'Honest, that's all I know,' he burbled, distracted. He ran a hand through his hair again. It stuck up in dark tufts. Pale, his face a mass of lines and edges, he looked genuinely stricken. I hadn't just opened a can of worms. I'd eaten them.

'I don't believe you.'

He squirmed in his seat, desperate to escape. There was no escape. He seemed to come to the same conclusion because the fight went out of his body and he leant in close and dropped his voice to a whisper. 'Drugs that kill certain types of people.'

My face stiffened. 'This is a bit of a departure from your usual line of business, isn't it? I thought the object was to get addicts hooked, not kill them. Who exactly?'

Wes shook his head, his expression contorted. 'I don't know,' he said shooting me another beseeching look. 'On my mother's life.'

I looked him hard in the eye. 'Fuck's sake, Wes, don't you care?'

He shook his head sadly. 'Man, it's business. It's money. Just money.'

I swallowed hard. No point in getting into a fight with Wes, snake that he was, about moral distinctions. I had no stomach for it and it would have been supremely hypocritical. 'So the data for the blueprint was what I was ordered to steal, right?'

'Yeah.'

'Who wants it?' I'd tried before and got nowhere, but I was all for catching Wes unawares.

He recoiled as if I'd thrown boiling oil in his face. 'I can't, man. He'll kill me.'

'*I'll* kill you if you don't tell me.'

'You have no idea what this guy does. His victims suffer agonies.'

'Then tell me and I'll kill him before he gets the chance.'

A flame of indecision flickered in his eyes, guttered and blew out. There weren't many men who could inspire that level of fear. Impressive, I thought.

'Okay,' I said, resigned. Something I've learned in life: don't expend energy on people or things you can't control.

Wes's relief was plain to see. 'Can you do it?' he said. 'Can you find it?' His eyes glistened with hope and fear.

'I don't know.' I wasn't telling the truth. I *had* to find it but when I did I wasn't going to hand it over to Wes, or anyone else. 'Let me get this straight, Wilding wanted to trade but welshed on the deal?'

Wes swallowed. 'Yeah, I think.'

'Think?' I snarled. 'How much was she paid?'

'I don't ask questions, man. I follow orders.' He swallowed again, looked at me pleading.

'There's something not…'

'Three days,' Wes said, scrabbling to his feet. 'Meet me in the usual place, usual time.'

'Are you insane?' Our usual hook-up was the Placa de Catalunya, a square in Barcelona.

'Thursday morning. Be there. Make sure you have the hard drive with you.'

CHAPTER SIX

Even if I found the goods, no way was I travelling on a scheduled flight. My description would already be circulated to every customs officer in Europe. I still intended to show up at the appointed hour on the appointed day because my gut told me that if I were smart I'd find the man who'd employed me for the job. If I could pump him for information, it could give me the vital lead I needed to find who was also in the market for the stolen hard drive. It was a risk. Wes might turn up in Barcelona with backup in place.

I decided to call in a favour. A fan of the two birds with one stone scenario, I also wanted to chase down the Russian lead.

One of my main clients, Mikhail Yakovlevich, was currently in London. He had houses in Russia, France and Britain. His British home, in Kensington, was worth a cool ten million. Having made his fortune in the steel trade, he'd specialised in supplying raw materials to factories in short supply. This was the shorthand version. In reality he had clawed his way to the top of his particular grubby pile through the cultivation and maintenance of friendships within the FSB (formerly KGB) and the relentless elimination of his enemies. I knew this because I'd carried out most of the eliminating. His FSB connection was what interested me.

I arrived outside the white stucco porch, gazed up at the four-storey dwelling, and hoped he was in. Eight marble steps to the lacquered front door, and before my foot touched the first, one of the most sophisticated security systems in the world clicked into action. Yakovlevich took his own safety seriously; evidenced by the entourage of former convicts he hired to protect him. Most of them looked as though they'd been conceived in Frankenstein's laboratory.

I rang the bell, one of those old-fashioned hand-pull affairs. The door swung open. There is a saying that behind each powerful man is a good woman. In this case, behind each discerning butler is a heavy-duty thug. Once the butler established that I was not there to arrange the flowers, Yuri, Yakovlevich's lieutenant, stepped out of the shadows towards me. I found it difficult to meet Yuri's eyes. Not because I was afraid of him, but because the tattoos on his face obliterated his features.

I slipped off the spectacles, popped out the contacts. 'Hex to see Mr Yakovlevich,' I said.

'You have an appointment?' Yuri knew full well I didn't.

'No.'

'Wait.' His eyes never leaving mine, he took out a mobile phone, pressed a few digits. A quick burst of Russian and I was allowed over the threshold. As usual I removed my shoes and was subjected to a full body search. Unpleasant and humiliating but essential if I was to gain an audience with Yakovlevich.

I followed Yuri upstairs to a first floor drawing room of immense proportions with fabulous views of a walled garden. The room should have been stunning. It was if one's taste was one of decadence meets burlesque. Thick-pile rugs on oak flooring, gaudy ornaments atop highly decorated French furniture, and a series of floor to ceiling paintings of Yakovlevich's young mistress in various states of undress, the last verging on pornographic.

Yakovlevich lay half-sprawled on a cream leather sofa. He was wearing one of his signature outfits: dark Italian suit, now crumpled, white shirt and silk tie. Red-faced, he held a glass of Chivas Regal in his hand, the half empty bottle sitting on the marble-topped coffee table in front of him. Chugging on a Cuban cigar, no doubt from Davidoff on St James's, he welcomed me with a cheery wave.

'Hex, my friend, come in, take a seat. I hope Yuri did not treat you roughly,' he boomed, deep-voiced. I smiled as if being treated in such a degrading fashion happened to me every day, and sat down opposite him. He stared at me blearily. 'Drink?'

'Thank you.' Refusal would only invite censure.

Mikhail summoned his butler. More whisky poured, I settled back, glass in hand. I was used to the drunken fool routine. A frustrated actor at heart, Yakovlevich was no more inebriated than his butler. He knew I knew but we all played along.

'So what brings you here?' His Russian deep-set eyes fixed on mine like barnacles clinging to the rusted hull of a wreck.

There was no point in using an obtuse approach with Yakovlevich. Well-connected, it was only a matter of time before he worked out my angle. In any case I really wanted to see if I could smoke him out. Making no distinction between commodities, the Russian was the kind of man who would do a mean trade in 'babushkas' if there were a ready market. It was rumoured that Yakovlevich had personally paved the way for the transportation of nuclear material from an old and decrepit nuclear facility. I never did discover who the buyer was and where it ended up. A man without scruples, Yakovlevich would not hesitate to deal in other forms of trade, including bio-weapons, as long as there was good money to be made.

'Nerve agents,' I said, suitably obtuse.

'I know nothing of such things.' Yakovlevich smiled broadly. 'Only what I hear on the grapevine, as you say.'

I nodded, smiled encouragingly and took a long swallow of whisky. I had the feeling I was going to need it.

'I remember some years ago,' Yakovlevich began, a sage expression on his fleshy features, 'Something about a stolen smallpox virus from a bio-containment laboratory in Siberia. A terrifying prospect.'

'There are still bio-labs in Russia?'

'All old. All crippled,' Yakovlevich said morosely. 'Before the break-up of the Motherland, there were many scientists working in the field. Many worked for Secret Department Twelve.'

I made an educated guess. 'Part of the former KGB?'

'The KGB's First Directorate responsible for biological espionage,' he explained.

'What sort of research?'

'The study and creation of toxins and substances specifically designed to poison reservoirs, pharmaceutical drugs and contaminate air conditioning systems.'

I stifled my interest by taking another snatch of whisky. 'Where are these scientists now?'

'Scattered to the four corners of the earth.' He snorted a gust of thick aromatic smoke into the atmosphere.

'To work for the highest bidder?'

'Something a man of your obvious talent can surely appreciate.' The chill in Yakovlevich's eyes tempered the smile on his face. I returned the expression. A snake in a suit, Yakovlevich dreamt, slept and ate in terms of profit margins, marketing potential. 'I understand there is a market for such commodities,' I said softly.

He sat up, knifed me with a sharp smile. 'You think I, Mikhail Yakovlevich, would trade in such things?'

'Not at all,' I said.

'Good,' he said bluntly.

'But who would, Mr Yakovlevich?'

His face assumed a dolorous expression. 'Look at the world around you, my friend. Think of the turmoil. Think of the threat from Islam. See what they have done in Chechnya. Now that Bin

Laden is dead there are any number of young radicals keen to avenge him and spill the blood of ordinary Russians.' He leant towards me, a hawkish look in his eye, 'What if such a commodity fell into the hands of fundamentalists?'

I snatched at my drink. Faced by such an appalling prospect it was hard to think, let alone think in clear straight lines. I attempted to factor this possibility into the context of my work. People for whom I worked, gangsters and felons, pimps and pornographers, could fill a criminal version of 'Who's Who.' Many based abroad, all fell under the wide umbrella of international organised crime, yet I could no more envisage them doing deals with al-Qaeda than Santa Claus. Yakovlevich remained an exception and I knew for a fact, aside from the grandstanding, that he wasn't choosy about his trading partners.

Temporarily forgetting his drunkard impression, he said, 'I am guessing you did not come here for philosophical debate.'

My turn to smile, I leant back, took a verbal detour, eager to bring down the conversational temperature. 'I need to be in Barcelona in three days.' Which meant I had less than forty-eight hours to trace the hard drive. 'You once offered me the personal use of your helicopter, remember?' Originally Yakovlevich had suggested it in the particular context of a job he wished me to carry out. I'd declined. I'm not keen on flying coffins. He later proposed it in the form of a bonus. Now seemed like the perfect opportunity to make good on his offer.

'I haven't forgotten, Hex.' He puffed out his massive chest. 'I am a man of my word, a man of honour.'

He was neither of those things but I didn't argue.

'That's most generous of you.'

'Not at all, I am sure you will return the favour,' he said, with a wily smile. 'I will speak to my pilot and put him on standby.'

We discussed the finer details of pick-up and time. Yakovlevich took a big gulp of whisky and leant back, making the leather creak. 'These scientists to whom you allude,' he said slow-eyed, picking up from where we left off. 'How is this of interest to a man like you?'

I evaded giving a direct answer. 'In the light of the brain drain, Russia's bio-weapons systems must be set back a couple of decades, at least.'

Yakovlevich closed his eyes. He looked half-cut. The more inebriated he seemed the more interested he was. 'Officially, Russia has no interest in such things. Unofficially, who knows?'

'Is this why the FSB are interested in the death of a British scientist?'

'The Kelly affair,' Yakovlevich ventured with another slow blink. He leant forward and deposited the remains of his cigar into an antique marble ashtray.

'More recent, the Wilding affair.'

'Ah, I heard something about it on the lunchtime news. Most unfortunate. They are saying that she died in suspicious circumstances.'

'Unconfirmed, I believe.'

Yakovlevich held the glass to his thick lips, fixed me with a dragnet stare. 'And you say this is of interest to the FSB? Since when did you work for the organisation?'

I let out a laugh. 'I don't.'

'So?' he pressed, his lips drawn back into a lazy smile.

'I keep my ear to the ground. As do you.'

Yakovlevich let out a snort of laughter. 'I like this game you play, Hex.' He took another drag of his cigar. 'Tell me what you have heard.'

'A Russian diplomatic vehicle was seen outside Wilding's home this morning.'

'I know nothing of this.'

'A pity.'

I played my next card softly. 'I heard something was taken.'

His dead eyes briefly sparked with life. 'Robbery? Fascinating. What exactly?'

'Information,' I said, obtuse.

'Making the possibility of murder more likely,' he said with a complicit smile. 'In my experience, people are removed either because they threaten one's interests, they know too much, or are offered the opportunity of collaboration but foolishly decline.'

I am not a rude man. I believe in go along to get along. Charm gets you further than aggression – to a point. I did not tell Yakovlevich that he was taking the linguistic equivalent of the scenic route and failing to answer my question. The fact he was prevaricating told me quite a lot. The wily old bastard was buying himself thinking time. Yakovlevich issued a sly smile. 'My memory is not so good but didn't Wilding inspect old bio-labs in Russia?'

'I've no idea. When?'

'Early 90s, I believe. Part of a UK/US delegation.'

'She must have been a junior member.'

'Who knows?' Yakovlevich said, dismissive. 'Many laboratories were closed down. Many good men were put out of work. Russians have long memories. Perhaps she was killed out of revenge.'

A fair point, a new angle, and one I wanted to explore. 'Could she have been working on something that was of particular interest to your people?'

His smile was caged.

'I have no firm evidence,' I continued, 'but there's a possibility that Wilding was working on bio-weapons. In a defensive capacity, of course,' I added swiftly.

'Of course.' He smiled without exposing his teeth. 'And how did you come by this information?'

'On the grapevine, as we say.'

He threw his head back, laughed, full-throated, then returned to his woozy eyes half-closed act. One glance at his watch was my cue for leaving. I duly obliged and drained my glass.

'Forgive me, Mikhail, I've taken too much of your time already.'

'Think nothing of it. A pleasure, always.' He lumbered to his feet. 'We must do business again soon.'

I cleared my throat. I wasn't sure what to say, the concept of taking on another assignment strangely unsettling, then Mikhail handed me over to Yuri who, resembling a creature trapped between night and day, escorted me from the building.

I did not go far. I crossed over, walked to the end of the street and loitered in the descending mist. The air, dank and chill, nipped at my clothes.

Yakovlevich emerged fifteen minutes later wearing a dark cashmere coat slung rakishly over his shoulders. For him to venture out alone without a minder in tow a rare sight.

I followed at a respectable distance, the thickening fog concealing my pursuit. As I trailed from street to street, out into the glare of Knightsbridge with all its sleek and not so subtle charm, then dropped onto the Brompton Road and eventually to a residential maze of leafy squares and railings, I wondered where the big Russian was heading with such abandon. In his enthusiasm, he seemed to have forgotten the basic rules of tradecraft.

Yakovlevich was now quite a way in front, the grey and gloomy streets deserted apart from the odd cyclist. A glance at my watch informed me that it was not yet four in the afternoon. Then he was gone.

I paused, bent down as if to tie a shoelace, and listened. Muffled voices drifted from a garden square ahead. Screened from the road by railings and dense foliage, it provided an ideal location for a meet. I didn't know who was on the other side of the conversation.

No gambler, I was more inclined to study a quarry and calculate his actions accordingly. All men had a price and Yakovlevich was no exception. Superficially, he seemed like any other gangster, the acquisition of huge wealth and riches his reason to get up in the morning. In reality, he was a power junkie, which explained why he rubbed shoulders with those who could really shake things up and make them happen: his cronies in the FSB. Straining my ears, I heard Yakovlevich's deep bass voice speaking in his native tongue. I had no clue what was spoken, but I calculated that Yakovlevich's garden guest was a Russian intelligence officer. Had Yakovlevich personally ordered the hit, he would have kept his distance. The fact he was here, reporting back to base, indicated that Wilding's blood was not on Yakovlevich's hands. The same could not be said of the Russians.

Straightening up, I squinted through the murk at the empty street. Frustratingly, there were few places in which to hide. Acutely aware that if I got close enough to see Yakovlevich and his friend, they could also see me, I backtracked and sloped across the road and stole down a flight of stone steps leading to a base-ment flat. Hopefully, the occupants were out. Concealed behind a boundary wall, I slipped the camera from my briefcase and waited.

Yakovlevich emerged first, followed by his friend. They crossed the road together, passing dangerously close to where I crouched, breathless. Taking a snap, I got a good look at the other man: middle-aged with short grey hair and a distinctive scar on the left side of his chin. Seconds later, they shook hands; Yakovlevich walking one way, 'Scar-face' the other.

Mission accomplished, I slipped the camera back into the briefcase. I probably had another hour, if lucky, before the light entirely faded, smothered by the thickening murk. Within an easy stroll of Imperial College in Exhibition Road, I decided to head that way. The Israelis' London Station, embedded in the Israeli Embassy on Palace Green, was also within striking distance. Reuben once told me a small team operated there from several floors below.

Cutting back into a crush of shoppers, I allowed myself to be buffeted along on a human tide. A fragment of me wondered what it would be like to run alongside and join them. The thought lasted seconds.

It started to spit with rain as I turned a corner and walked up

Exhibition Road past the Natural History Museum, the V&A on the opposite side, and glanced up at the main entrance to Imperial College with its geometric glass and steel winking in the gathered gloom. By now the woman from the British Security Service would already have paid a visit, interviewed Wilding's line manager and asked all the usual questions: were all security restrictions in place; was anything missing; was Wilding behaving oddly; had she trouble sleeping; was she depressed? I wished I could have been a fly on the wall when that conversation took place. But I had other ideas.

I'm a big believer in timing. Wrong place, wrong time exists, but it's rare. It underlines the theory of calculating the odds. Match a certain set of events with a number of different players and chances are those players will end up bumping into each other, the fact my path almost crossed with Wilding's assassin a fine example. Given the circumstances, it was actually surprising that we didn't meet. I hoped my theory held up now.

Taking a left into Kensington Gore, I sauntered parallel to Queens Gate with its classy hotels and wide residential streets of Victorian buildings and white stucco grand six-storey edifices, similar to those found in central Moscow. I felt peculiarly settled in the shadows and I walked slowly, softly, in the direction of Kensington Palace Gardens, more specifically Palace Green, the most secure and exclusive road in Kensington and beating heart of Embassy land. Within its half mile stretch of prime real estate lay the red brick former home of the novelist and essayist, William Thackeray, its current occupier the Israeli Embassy. As one would expect, security around the embassy remained extremely tight. Fine by me. I had no intention of straying too close.

My field of vision restricted, my hearing constrained by the hostile elements, call it intuition, but I sensed the redhead at Wilding's house that morning would be chasing down the same leads, perhaps within the same time frame. All I had to do was pick a spot and wait.

I set down the briefcase beside me and took up a position leaning against a plane tree. Surrounded by a collection of moving shapes, silhouettes, the gauzy light of cars and lorries, I took out a pack of cigarettes I'd bought earlier in a backstreet newsagents. Fog stretched over my face in a damp embrace. There were many approaching footsteps, some fast and staccato, others flat and heavy. Still I waited.

Two cigarettes later, the last crushed against the heel of my shoe, I heard a purposeful yet even tread. Having devoted years to identifying the idiosyncrasies of others, I knew, without the smallest doubt, the gait and pace belonged to the woman with the flame-coloured hair.

I struck hard and fast. Action is faster than reaction. There are exceptions. The woman, highly trained, was one. As my hands clamped around her throat, she flicked her head up, the crown striking my jaw. Next, she raised her right leg. For this I was ready. Before her knee could make the connection with my groin, I flexed, and substantially increased the pressure on her neck. I had to be careful. A man can be rendered unconscious in three seconds, dead in fifteen. I needed her alive, articulate and co-operative.

I am a strong guy. My shoulders are broad. I used all my body weight to push her against the base of the tree. She didn't scream. She couldn't. Even so, you'd think someone would come to her aid. Nobody did.

I released the pressure on her neck. I did not clamp a hand over her mouth. I removed her earpiece, stuck my hand in her jacket and lifted her phone, scrolled through, switched it off and shoved it back. I let her recover, but I stayed up close and very personal. I could smell her perfume: floral, contemporary, notes of citron, cedar and musk. Anyone walking by would assume we were lovers about to get it on. I put my mouth close to her ear and whispered, 'If you're smart, you'll understand I haven't set out to kill you.'

51

'What do you want?' Nice voice, low and melodic, well spoken. Her eyes, an iridescent green, shone like a cat's in the night. She hadn't asked me who I was and that told me the boy had talked and she had paid attention. I smiled. She was smart. We were going to get along fine. I loomed over her, using my body to put a barrier between her and anyone else in the street.

'Wilding was working on something big. What was it?' No way was I prepared to suggest a blueprint for a biological military weapon let alone any possible ethnic aspect. Way too hot.

'I don't know what you're talking about.' Not smart, reckless. I flew at her throat once again. 'Do you enjoy killing women?' she spat, her voice low and accusing. I let my hands drop as if I'd touched molten steel.

'I didn't kill Wilding.'

'You were there.'

'I don't deny it.'

'If you didn't kill her, who did?'

'We wouldn't be standing here having this conversation if I knew.'

'This isn't a conversation. It's an assault.'

'How did he kill her?' Call it professional interest.

'Fuck you.'

I admired her spirit. Faced with a force field of barely suppressed aggression, most keel over. Not this woman. 'My guess is that he injected her with something.'

'You should know.' Her cold smile reminded me of light on icy water.

'I already told you. I didn't do it.'

'So what *were* you doing?' The green eyes narrowed to two feline slits.

Tricky one. 'Searching for information.'

'What exactly?'

I shrugged. 'Data on a hard drive.'

She blinked slowly once, a cover for the interest she undoubtedly felt. She now recognised that we were dancing on the same stage. 'Where is it?'

'I don't have it.'

'You insult my intelligence.'

'I wouldn't dream of it. I don't have it. Someone wants it. May even have it. And now I want it.'

'Who's the someone?'

'That's what I'm trying to find out.'

Her brow wrinkled in concentration. 'You don't know who contracted you for the job?'

I didn't care to be reminded of my failure. 'You understand how the game is played. The man who instigates mayhem is five times removed from the action. You don't think your average suicide bomber meets the mullah who commissioned him, do you?'

'Rich,' she sneered, 'me taking lectures from you.'

'I'm just saying that...'

'You don't have a clue who you work for.' She glared at me in disbelief.

'I don't. Not on this particular occasion.' I'd cocked up.

She gave me a long hard, venomous stare. When she spoke her voice scorched with contempt. 'You might think you're a somebody, but you have no idea what you're involved in.'

'I do.' I didn't. I was like a pilot making a crash landing. God knew where I'd fetch up.

'No, you don't,' she repeated flatly.

'Then enlighten me.'

Her laugh was dry as tinder.

'I'll take that as proof I'm on the right track. Wilding was involved in something most sane people would prefer not to think about.'

'It's proof of nothing,' she said, tight-lipped. I looked into her eyes. I thought I detected weakness. She looked torn between keeping her mouth shut and wanting to trade. Getting down to the nitty-gritty, the gathering of intelligence is all about give and take, and I was the best lead she'd had all day. I decided to try and tempt her.

'I'm thinking Wilding would hardly store A-grade information in her home, but then it would depend on what it was and what she planned to do with it.'

Two spots of colour flashed across her cheeks.

'I accept I'm running ahead of the evidence,' I riffed. 'Must be virtually impossible to steal anything from Wilding's place of work. The security arrangements would be strictly monitored, bombproof even. Then again, she didn't need to steal anything. She already had it in her head. What should I call you, incidentally?'

'Whatever you like, this isn't a social engagement.'

'We could help each other.'

At this she laughed again. Low, from her belly, this time. It was a good laugh. 'I don't think so.'

'Secrecy's my middle name. Your superiors wouldn't have to know.'

She issued another cold, cynical look. 'Unlike you, I have rules to obey.'

'But surely they could be bent a little?'

She smiled without warmth. 'What are you trying to do, end my career? Sorry, I'm not open to corruption.'

'Not even if it helps save the day?' I let that sink in.

She looked at me, sullen, eyes revealing nothing at all.

'Toxins, nerve agents?' I goaded, desperate to get a rise.

Her full red lips pressed together. I noticed she wore brick-red lipstick, very Forties starlet. I continued to barrage her with questions. 'Who would be in the market for it?'

'You've been reading too much spy fiction,' she glowered.

'What about your friends at the Israeli Secret Service? Do they have an opinion?'

Her face betrayed no emotion.

'Funny, they showed quite an interest this morning.'

She let out a surprised breath and her body tensed beneath me. I smiled. 'Your sidekick has quite a crush on you, did you know? The other guys hanging around were regular police officers. Judging by their sour expressions, they don't care for the security services pulling rank.' As soon as the words exited my mouth, I realised I'd said too much. For reasons unknown I'd wanted to impress her, to let her see that I was worthy. Vanity, Reuben had often reminded me, was a capital offence. 'How is the boy?' I said, changing tack.

She fixed me with hard eyes. 'Safe from you.'

In spite of every effort to curb a reaction, a pulse above my left eyelid quivered. Like a shark scenting blood in the water, she spotted my weakness.

'Why didn't you kill him?'

I had no answer. If I wasn't careful she would lead me to a place I'd no desire to visit. It was her turn to smile.

'Your failure reveals worrying inconsistency. It's as if you give a damn.'

I swallowed hard. She wasn't finished. 'I wonder what the hell that's all about,' she said, her turn to goad. 'Care to share?' I did my best to retain a blank expression. Her lips curved into a superior smile. She was onto me. I stepped back. 'You're free to go,' I said. She didn't move an inch. I had the impression of her staring right into my soul. I wanted to break her hold on me. Her gaze dropped, eyes fixed on a point beyond my shoulder. I turned minutely. Next, her hand thudded into my chest and she was gone.

I bent down to see if she'd taken the briefcase. It wasn't there. She'd performed a classic disappearing trick. Like I said, she was smart.

CHAPTER SEVEN

Conscious she'd call for reinforcements, I took a fast, circuitous route. Whether she believed me or not was incidental. We both knew what we were dealing with. We both knew what we wanted. Whether or not she would play on my team, I'd no idea.

A creature of shadows, I liked the dark: my milieu. But that night I wasn't paying enough attention. The memory of the MI5 girl's laugh, her penetrating stare, a blizzard of green, had side-tracked me. Quite suddenly, I found myself in a shabby lane, a cut-through between two rows of houses within spitting distance of Earls Court, reminding me of the many *hutong* you find in the Forbidden City in China – without the bikes and rickshaws. Lights from neighbouring streets cast a sickly glare through the gloom. I could hardly see but I could imagine the shattered walls that flanked the alley, the corrugated iron and outbuildings in varying states of disrepair. Weeds grew in knots between the cobbled stones beneath my feet. I didn't hear another, no telltale breath, no loud footfall, but I recognised that I had company. Too late, I turned.

The guy exploded into action, raining blows, several cracking my jaw and head. I darted, lunged, parried. Bone connected. Blood spattered. Mostly mine. My adversary was bigger than me in every respect, a wall of muscle, a human Pit Bull. Grabbing me by one ear, he yanked me close with one hand, by the throat with the other. He had a bad case of halitosis; his breath reeked of garlic and Guinness.

'Where is it, you fucker?'

'Where's what?'

'The fucking hard drive.'

We were eyeball to eyeball. Blood streamed from my head. Shot through with pain, I wasn't so far gone that I didn't notice his strong Belfast accent.

'You've got the wrong guy,' I moaned through bloodied teeth.

Predictably he released his hold on my throat so he could mess me up some more. I arched, thrust my body back, felt my ear tear, but I was free. Enraged, he came in again at close range, fists, head and feet. Whoever he was, this clown meant business.

Under this level of fire thought vanished like the mist swirling around us. Fortunately I had good instincts and my instinct was to draw him back through a terrain of empty cans, litter and used needles towards a derelict building. He sensed my game and changed tempo. The pressure increased. I mostly absorbed the pain, landing the odd blow without doing him any serious damage. Acting the vanquished, I drew him close. Close enough to…

The length of wire flashed quicksilver against the dark and twisted round his neck with the speed of a cobra strike. In two steps I was behind him, hauling back, putting my full weight into hanging on, the struggling man twisting and turning and grunting, shoes sliding in the dirt. His fingers scrabbled to loosen the wire before it became embedded. I hauled some more. A fine spray of blood released and cascaded into the night. He fell back heavily, knocking the air out of my lungs as I collapsed beneath him. '*Think like him and never stop thinking like him until he is dead*' Reuben had taught me. Men can do extraordinary things even when dying. I didn't doubt that if I let go my assailant would

57

produce a knife and make one last attempt to kill me. I clung on with grim determination until the spray became a pumping torrent of plasma and his heels drummed on the rough surface. My arms and shoulders juddering with strain, I gave one final wrench and it was over. A noise, like water gurgling down a plughole, rasped, rattled and hissed into the night.

I slid out from beneath him and dragged him by his feet into the remains of an empty building partially boarded up and smelling of piss. Rifling through his clothing revealed a wallet with five hundred pounds in sterling, no credit cards, no identification. He also carried a gun. Difficult to tell what it was in the stuttering light, but it felt like a Colt. I briefly wondered why he hadn't used it, and pocketed both.

To conceal the bloodstains on my coat, I took it off, turned it inside out and put it back on. Retrieving the wire, I wiped it on the dead man's trousers, returned it to my pocket, and made my way back to Reuben's.

This time I used a conventional form of entry: I rang Reuben's doorbell. He let me in, invited me through to the sitting room.

'You look like hell.'

I shrugged off my coat. 'This needs to be disappeared.'

He took it from me without a word and told me to take a seat. 'I will get something for the cuts and bruises.'

A fire blazed in the grate, throwing shadows on the walls. I realised how cold I was and stood and warmed myself. Reuben was halfway down a bottle of red wine. There were three glasses, one empty, one his, one used.

Reuben returned with a medical kit and expertly cleaned me up. It stung.

'Who did this?' he said.

Had it not been for my assailant's mean and precise line of questioning, I might have thought I was the victim of a stranger attack. If you walk in those sorts of places you're likely to meet trouble. As it was, had to be someone with more than a passing interest in Wilding although I didn't believe it was anyone in an official capacity. Not their style. As for the accent, well, who knew? Plenty of out of work thugs from that part of the world. I wondered whom he worked for.

'A guy with no name built like a banned breed of canine.' I was spent and dejected. My head and ear throbbed. I flinched as Reuben traced my face with his thick fingers for fractures.

'You're fine,' he said.

I grunted thanks. I felt anything but fine and gladly accepted his offer of a drink, a Grand Vin and premier cru of a fine vintage from Bordeaux. He asked nothing more of me. He knew that I'd speak when ready. We sat in awkward silence for some minutes until I chose to deliver edited highlights. I did not tell him about my audience with a Russian crime lord and his theory that the motive for Wilding's murder was revenge. I did not tell him about my personal run-in with the British intelligence officer. I wanted to keep her to myself. Instead, I told Reuben that Wes wanted the hard drive returned in three days. Seemed like Wes was not the only person who wanted to get his hands on it, any number of parties after the same thing. Made my job a hundred times more difficult.

'To give it to whom?'

'I don't know but I intend to find out.'

Reuben did not react.

'Who in hell wants to inflict biological ethnic genocide?' I snapped.

'You lack the evidence to support your claim,' Reuben softly reminded me.

'You're now saying I'm wrong?' After all you told me? My mind reeled back to my conversation with Wes. *Drugs that kill certain types of people.* What else if it wasn't this? And McCallen hadn't exactly blown out my allegations about nerve agents. I wildly wondered whether the Israelis harboured a desire to annihilate their Arab neighbours by twisting the genetic key, and vice-versa. I asked Reuben.

He smiled broadly and shook his head. 'Israelis and Arabs share similar genetic characteristics. They are both of Semitic origin. In simple engineering terms, it would be a tremendous feat to divide one human genome from another. Any pathogen developed in a test-tube would result in mutually-assured destruction.'

I gaped at him. He leant forward, rested a paw of a hand on my knee. 'Do not worry, Joshua, you come from a mongrel race. It would be extremely difficult to wipe out you and yours.'

Then whom in God's name were we talking about? Orientals? I looked him in the eye. For reasons I could not describe I found Reuben's fervour neither convincing nor reassuring. Difficult was not the same as impossible. The white man in the Korean showcase had been chosen for a reason. My mind unravelled. I'd narrowly escaped moving from the steal-to-order market into something more deadly and dangerous, maybe even state sponsored terrorism. And what of the Russian connection? By now, MI5 would have disseminated the contents of my briefcase, trawled through my false identification papers and studied the photographs on the camera. I wondered whether they'd yet identified Yakovlevich's mystery contact.

Reuben broke into my thoughts. 'I have not been idle in your absence. It's all right I was discreet,' he added in response to my obvious consternation. 'I have an old contact who passed on some timely information.' I retained a mask of inscrutability. That very morning Reuben had tried to persuade me that he no longer had connections. 'The London station chief received a visit this afternoon from MI5's Inger McCallen.'

Inger McCallen. I silently drank in her name, rolling it round my mouth like a fine wine. Suggestive of a Scottish origin, it explained the pale colouring, the copper-coloured hair, and flinty manner. It intrigued me. I mused whether Scandinavia played a part in her background. In my reverie, I clean forgot that her name was in all probability fictional. Reuben was still talking.

'Apparently, Dr Wilding was killed by a bubble of air injected into the jugular vein.' The suspected method used to kill Robert Maxwell before he was chucked overboard from his yacht, I remembered. I also remembered that in my foolish enthusiasm to impress McCallen I'd offered this as a possibility. In Wilding's case, the combination of pills and alcohol would have masked the prick of the needle entering her skin. She would have put up no defence. As a method, it was brilliantly conceived, her assassin clearly taking advantage of available conditions on the ground – a masterstroke.

'According to my source, the British are unusually upset by Wilding's death.'

I gave a snort of frustration. 'I'm not surprised.'

'To be expected, indeed,' Reuben said. 'With the lingering stink over the Kelly affair, the security services are bound to be at the centre of a swirl of new allegations. They will not welcome renewed attention.'

I didn't react. With every appearance of calm, as if Wilding were nothing more than a humble computer programmer setting up a new project, I said, 'What if Wilding had her own agenda? What if she was working in an offensive capacity?' Why else would the information be at her home?

He spread his hands and gave a wide shrug. I frowned. Reuben was doing the equivalent of feeding me titbits and then running away. 'Whatever it was, this is well outside my experience,' I said. 'More than likely a foreign security service is responsible for her death.'

'Then why were you employed?'

He had me there. Wes dealt exclusively with international organised crime. Silence invaded the room like a conquering army. I stayed still, tuned out. Finally Reuben broke the deadlock.

'The British have an asset within a newly emergent fundamentalist Muslim splinter group based in the Midlands.'

'Terrorists?' I said, with a snatch of alarm.

'Yes.'

I remembered Yakovlevich's take on young Muslim radicals. I eyed Reuben with suspicion. 'How do you know and how is this relevant?'

He let out a tired sigh as though I was particularly stupid. 'Muslim groups are always relevant. The uneducated masses still declare death to Israel and death to the West.'

I suddenly didn't buy Reuben's alleged ignorance. 'Reuben,' I added sternly. 'You are forcing connections and speaking in riddles,' I said, exasperated. 'Frankly, this is political dynamite and I don't do politics.' Nor religion nor fundamentalism, I could have said.

Reuben flashed a smile and hunched his shoulders. 'I may be out of the game, Joshua, but there are certain things that a man like me can divine.' I looked deeply into his eyes. He met my gaze with a considered expression. 'McCallen is meeting the asset tomorrow here in London.' He gave me the details.

'Divination is one thing,' I said deliberately. 'If you're so out of the game, how come you know about the meeting?'

Reuben slow-blinked, issued a wily smile. 'Remember that everyone is there to be used.'

Dissatisfied, I stood to leave. Reuben got up, too, and followed me out into the hall and to the front door. Before he opened it he rested a hand on my arm. Despite the lightness of touch, I could feel the power of the man radiating through his fingertips. He quoted a motto of which he was particularly fond: *By way of deception, thou shalt do war.*

CHAPTER EIGHT

I bought some electric hair clippers from an open all hours' chemist and booked into one of many cheap budget hotels near Paddington. Not the most comfortable establishments but they had their advantages. Within close proximity of train stations they offered the best chance of escape, and they employed the type of temporary staff inclined to be less discriminating. The night porter barely lifted his eyes let alone paid attention to my battered appearance as I asked for a room for the night.

Reuben's intelligence was non-specific in certain aspects, precise and detailed in others. Caught in a slimy net of events beyond my understanding, it made me suspicious. With this firmly planted in my head I fell asleep quickly and came to a couple of hours later, restless, awake and wired.

Logically, Wilding's murder looked politically motivated, a foreign security service responsible for her death. And yet, as Reuben had pointed out, someone had been willing to employ a guy like me. In the same vein, my unknown assailant didn't strike me as an 'in-house' professional. Whoever he was, I intended to find out – maybe Wes could offer an opinion – but first I'd keep my date with McCallen, the thought of crossing paths with her again strangely exhilarating.

In the past, my rare encounters with mostly foreign women had been restricted to the one-off, passionate and no holds barred variety, commonly termed the one-night stand. In the heat of the moment, terrific; hollow in the aftermath. I didn't believe a woman like McCallen would ever look twice at a man like me and yet I briefly wondered what it would be like to sleep with her, how she would feel and taste. Wasn't a simple case of sexual attraction, it was more elemental. Before the Wilding job I would have said that we were flip sides of the same coin. We both moved in murky worlds. We both had secret lives. We both hewed the rich seam of frail and foolish humanity. Long-term relationships were out. Neither of us could make promises, nor offer commitment. Alike in so many aspects and yet, I had to admit, light-years away in others. With this swilling around inside my head, I lay back down, resting in the shadows, then finally turned over and fell into a fractured sleep.

Low in spirit, smudged by fatigue, I rose at six in the morning. An hour later and, thanks to my new electric hair clippers, I had a brand new image. Along with the bruises and swelling around my left eye and torn ear, my freshly shaved head added several years to my appearance. Tag on a pair of outdated spectacles and scruffy jacket and I could pass for a recently released guest of Her Majesty.

Before leaving the hotel room, I wiped away fingerprints, paying particular attention to door handles, lavatory seats, anything that bore my personal insignia, then headed back to the streets and found a newsagents, part of a large chain, and rifled through the day's newspapers. The identikit picture of me was particularly poor. Had McCallen protected me? I quickly dismissed the idea as wishful thinking.

Her meeting was scheduled for nine forty-five in a precise corner of Kensington Palace Gardens. (Reuben had all but given me the co-ordinates.) Arriving half an hour early, I walked up the road and entered the park through a wide set of gates that always reminded me of the elegant entrance to Pittville park in the Cotswold capital of Cheltenham, my home town.

Out of nowhere two black-clad police officers, carrying Heckler and Koch MP5's, walked along the street towards me. Heart thudding in my chest, I curbed my natural instinct, which was to turn and leg it. Still they came, their gaze seemingly unfocused, the weapons held close to their barrel chests. At any moment I knew these guys could spring into action and empty a couple of magazines into me. The closer they walked, the more I sweated. My hearing went, my tongue stuck like bubblegum to the roof of my mouth. All I could see were the men and the guns, nothing else. Forcing my legs to move, I nodded *good morning*. They both nodded back, strolled past, oblivious of my real identity. I turned into the park and let out a painfully contained breath.

In spite of the Arctic weather, joggers ran, halting to perform the occasional squat thrust. Tourists milled about, snapping photographs. Footpaths were slippery and coated in frost. I meandered left, eyes raking my surroundings, and eventually walked past a bench that offered privacy without secrecy. If McCallen's asset was as high-grade as Reuben led me to believe she would want him secure and in a place where nobody could slot him and get away with it.

Falling in with a bunch of Australians admiring the late Princess Diana's old home, I waited when, eventually, a slightly built man in his mid-twenties rocked up. Hands thrust deep into a padded jacket, woollen Beanie hat close over his ears; he wore a desert scarf in a black and white chequered design, rebel republic style. A soft dark beard offset his pinch-faced features. Watchful and wary, he had standout eyes that made him look as if he wore eyeliner. He could easily pass for an Afghan, I thought.

He sat down with a bump, hunkered down into the seat in an effort to reduce his visibility, and clapped his hands together against the cold. His boots stamped the frosted ground. Swarthy complexion, tinged with blue, he looked frozen. With my freshly shaven head, I totally got where he was coming from. Slipping out the mobile phone for the Wilding job, I hastily took his picture and jammed the phone back into my pocket.

McCallen arrived a few minutes later. The latecomer's way of asserting authority, of stating who's in charge and calls the shots, McCallen was very much displaying her credentials. Giving her time to settle, to re-establish a rapport with her contact, I turned my back and wandered over towards a water fountain. Bending down, I helped myself to a drink. The bitter cold set my teeth on edge. At this level McCallen was directly in my eye line. I fixed my gaze on her full-lipped mouth.

Looking straight ahead, she engaged the youth with the standard openers of conversations recited all over the world. She called him Saj. Saj replied that he was well and that his family were just fine. Next she asked after a guy called Mustafa.

'Zealous as ever.' A faint smile played on the young man's thin features.

'And the group's more recent activities?'

'Lying low after the attack plan attracted too much heat and was aborted.'

'And they had no idea you were responsible for the tip-off?'

'None.' Saj seemed like a polite and quiet individual. With McCallen at his side, he had lost some of the nervousness he displayed earlier.

Then she moved on to the heavy stuff.

'You've heard of Dr Mary Wilding?'

Perplexed, he said, 'The dead scientist.'

'We believe she was the victim of blackmail.'

At this we both frowned. Me, because it was something Wes should have told me; Saj, because he was unable to fathom any possible connection to himself. He said as much to McCallen. 'What sort of blackmail?'

'She had access to pathogens with a variety of uses.' My interest spiked. I wondered what form of blackmail would persuade

Wilding to risk her job, her reputation, her life and indeed, as it now turned out, the lives of others. Against every instinct, I was reminded of the dying Koreans, the blood and ordure. Saj nodded, gravely assimilating the information. 'Are you aware of anyone making overtures to Mustafa?' McCallen pressed him.

'Something like this would not be brought to my attention. Above my pay grade.'

'With this particular type of material on the market we fear Mustafa will be approached.'

'Who by?'

'Our only lead is a British assassin. Around six feet, maybe a shade under, strong, with a slim to medium build. He's dark haired, blue-eyed, striking with flat high cheekbones. We think he may attempt to trade.'

I tuned out after *assassin*. She was wrong. She didn't believe me. And she wasn't going to get anywhere if she concentrated her attention in a wasted direction. The idiocy of it made me flare with anger.

'Anyone like that cross your radar?' she concluded.

'Never.'

McCallen flexed her shoulders, dissatisfied. She wasn't alone. The tip of her nose glowed red from the cold. Her eyes scanned the human landscape. I turned away so that I missed her contact's follow-up question. When I turned back McCallen was speaking once more.

'The hit was professional and accomplished. The killer escaped with vital information concerning a certain bio-weapon.' Too true, I thought, wondering about the exact nature of *this type of material*. 'Do you think you could persuade Mustafa to test the market, to put out the word?' she said.

'Use him as bait to draw the killer out of the shadows?'

'And lead us to those who have the information. Would Mustafa deal with a white guy?'

'You mean would he bargain with an infidel?' Saj flashed a

rare grin, the question rhetorical. 'The world has changed. For Mustafa, this is all the more reason to ramp up the violence. We do business with whoever will aid our cause.'

'If you could persuade...' She changed position so that I could no longer read her lips. Fuck.

Her contact blew out a breath, sending a plume of warm air into the chill atmosphere. 'Can you be more specific about what exactly we're touting for?'

She bent towards him then drew away. Irritatingly, she still had her back to me. Suddenly, her contact twisted round, facing her, his eyes bright like polished mahogany. I couldn't hear but his bearing shrieked outrage. 'The British government sanctioned *this*?'

She leant towards him for a second time. Frustrated beyond belief, my eyes locked onto the young man's thin lips.

'It should have been destroyed.'

She reached out, rested a hand lightly on his shoulder, squeezed it, said something else then got up and strode away.

I followed at a distance. She walked quickly, soft shoes pumping, frequently changing direction. I felt out of sorts, possibly because I hadn't eaten for hours, probably because I was a marked man and I could be arrested at any moment, mostly because McCallen had shone a fiery light on a dirty corner. I thought about Reuben and how McCallen's revelation chimed with what I'd witnessed in his basement. I thought about Wes and the pack of lies he'd told me. I thought about my own presumption of Wilding's greed and guilt.

In no time we were in the heart of trendy affluence and bowling along Notting Hill, finally looping round towards Holland Park tube station. As we neared the underground her pace changed and she cast a long slow look behind her. Thinking she was on to me, I had no option but to take my chances and keep moving. If I darted out of view she'd definitely make me.

The closer I came the more her eyes seemed unfocused. She

was looking but not seeing then two things happened in fast succession. McCallen drew out her phone and answered it, her voice drowned out by an ambulance followed by a fire engine, both with sirens blaring, racing down the avenue. Meanwhile her eyes did all the talking. She was clearly in receipt of important news. I just didn't know what it was.

CHAPTER NINE

Riveted, I followed her into the underground and stood well back as she waited to board a tube train on the Piccadilly line. Her profile was neat and symmetrical. I liked the way her black roll-top sweater contrasted with and maximised the copper in her hair. I liked the way she stood: relaxed, confident, striking. I admired everything about her.

Two minutes later, the thunderous noise of a train's approach. People surged forward, including McCallen. I stayed rooted, immobile, like a relic frozen in time.

Gasp of hot air, blinding lights, driver's eyes, heat running through my veins, hammering in my chest, giddy sensation. Get close but not too close. Anxious I might be sucked off the platform onto the live rails and crushed and chewed into oblivion. Then the man next to me toppling, falling, plunging…

I blinked. McCallen had boarded. My abrupt lapse in concentration cost me and I took a hurried step forward. The doors squeezed closed, shutting me out, then suddenly snapped apart, ejecting McCallen. For the second time I thought she'd catch me in her visual crosshairs. Maybe she did, but she didn't react.

I retreated into a crowd of students, recent shambling additions to the platform. My eyes followed as McCallen walked a short distance away, waited for and stepped onto the next tube. This time she stayed on board. I knew because I was in the next-door compartment. Together we rode as far as Oxford Circus where she changed onto the Northern line and got off at Embankment.

Outside the Thames looked choppy, white spume cresting khaki, the sky overhead milk-white as though it might snow. There were too many people. Hot-dog vendors and roast chestnut sellers plied their wares. Jugglers tossed flaming batons. A black guy break-danced to an admiring crowd of onlookers and a steel band thumped out reggae. The carnival atmosphere was intoxicating but I was too shaken by Saj's violent reaction to whatever McCallen had said to get high.

She mooched towards an underpass where a number of skateboarders showcased their skills. One guy, older than the rest, gathered speed and careered off the edge of a ramp, taking a death-defying leap, soaring through the air and coming down with a tremendous clatter. Others zoomed in and out of pillars, pirouetting and contorting, agile and speedy. McCallen stopped, ostensibly to watch. I could tell it was a blind from the way she inclined her head. She wasn't there to take in the show. She was there because she was waiting for someone. I slipped behind a pillar and waited with her.

Fifteen minutes elapsed.

A woman approached. She had shoulder-length raven hair, eyes the colour of double espresso. Her black wool coat fell from her shoulders in two vertical lines, the dress beneath a vivid blue, the neckline plunging. Not to put too fine a point on it, she was stacked. It was easy to imagine her naked. To my surprise, she walked straight over to McCallen and greeted her. Then my heart sank. I know enough Russian to translate *privyet*, which means hi. After that I was lost although, frankly, fascinated by McCallen's obvious linguistic talent. I glibly wondered why she worked for MI5 when her skills would find a more appropriate home with the Secret Intelligence Service.

The rapid-fire discussion between the two women lasted roughly ten minutes. This time, my lip-reading skills wasted, I could only rely on body language.

McCallen started by flaring the fingers of one hand, as if about to reach out, reinforcing her desire to project her ideas and thinking. In return, the Russian sliced the icy air with the flat of her hand, eager to cut to the chase, the gesture eventually reciprocated by McCallen cupping her palms, begging for agreement. At one point the Russian tapped her nose in a classic conspiratorial gesture. McCallen nodded grimly and, finally, clenched her fist, a symbol of her determination. The display gave the impression that they were nothing other than two people on opposite sides of a fence, exchanging and pooling information, each having something that would benefit the other. There was no overt animosity. No power play. To the casual observer, they seemed like equals. *Seemed.*

Practiced in the art of deception, they could not quite contain their facial expressions. The way the Russian inclined her head, pressed her lips together into a smile, touched her mouth lightly to conceal a lie, revealed she was less than an honest broker in the negotiations. By contrast, McCallen, outwardly calm, touched the tip of her nose and subtly shifted her weight from one foot to the other, almost rocking. Yeah, she was definitely anxious. Was it possible that Yakovlevich's mystery contact was the subject of the discussion?

They parted without a backward glance. I watched, waited, and moved away. There were people I needed to talk to and I had a ride to catch.

CHAPTER TEN

I headed back to the lock-up, exchanged my scruffy jacket and jeans for a navy Italian single-breasted suit and camel-coloured overcoat and, to hide my battered features, wrapped a fine Morino woollen scarf around my neck and chin, and topped it off with a trilby. I resembled a character from a romantic wartime novel, fine for the environment I was about to inhabit. Next, I selected a worn leather briefcase, one of my favourites, containing another set of I.D. plus a change of underwear and enough euros to bribe the most reluctant customs officer. I wanted to take the Colt accessory and spoil of war. Out of the question. Yakovlevich would never sanction it. I'd have to travel clean and pick up a weapon, as usual, at the other end.

My thoughts centred on blackmail, close country cousin to bribery and extortion, and blood relatives within the great family of organised crime. How and who had blackmailed Wilding? These were questions I wanted to pose to Wes, preferably with my hands around his neck. Flakier by the hour, Wes was starting to look less like a loosely involved link man and more like an integral player. Time I found out what Wes was really up to.

There's a gentlemen's club in Pall Mall populated by arms dealers, spooks, criminals and oddballs. Eclectic best describes it, and exceptionally discreet. It opened its doors at lunchtime and, in spite of my wanted status, I paid it a visit.

I was hoping an American called Ron Tilelli would be at the club. Tilelli had taken British citizenship a decade or more before. A driver for various watering holes, ironically one with a drink and gambling habit, he was a happy combination for me because it made him highly corruptible. Word on the wire said that several intelligence agencies had him in their pockets – another reason for having a chat. I wasn't sure how true this was. Filled with enough sour-mash whisky, Tilelli could make some fairly extraordinary claims. I'd learnt over the years, however, that even the most unlikely stories contain grains of truth.

The club was decked out like an old country hotel with wood-panelled walls, tartan-patterned upholstery, and distressed-looking leather sofas the colour of old cognac. An overweight golden Labrador snoozed by the fake, but no less convincing, gas log fire. An assiduous Polish waiter took my coat and drink order.

Tilelli had a regular spot in one corner, the equivalent of the foreigner erecting his windbreak on a particular stretch of sand and marking out his territory. A bear of a man, with a mop of sandy-coloured hair, his face a mesh of thread veins in which small light-brown eyes sat like pebbles. He had a raucous laugh and Tilelli laughed a lot. It was one of the things I liked about him. The opposite of me, he was a glass half full merchant.

Tilelli held court with his usual flair, this time and to my relief he imbibed coffee. Around him, a coterie of hangers-on, or liggers as I sometimes described them. It included one man with whom I'd regularly done business. I called him Guy. Small, dapper, shiny-shoed, he looked more financial advisor than small arms dealer. He met my eye, winked and moved away. The others, whom I didn't recognise, took one look at me and fled as though they had the Grim Reaper stalking towards them. In a sense, I suppose that's exactly what I was. Tilelli stayed put, met my gaze with a smile. We got on as well as I get on well with anyone.

'Hex,' he said, clapping me on the back. People called me Hex because it had connotations of witchcraft. Considered first-rate at what I did, I was clearly no magician. 'Good to see you,' Tilelli enthused. 'Say, what happened to you?'

'A minor collision with a door.'

Tilelli was shrewd enough to accept my poor excuse. 'Drink?'

'Got one, thanks.' I tipped my head in the direction of the approaching waiter who put a tray on the highly polished table in front of me. Bombay gin, plenty of ice, tonic, and a slice of lime. Tilelli leant forward, swooped up the bill in his big, fleshy fingers, handed it to the waiter.

'Put it on my tab,' he said.

'Certainly, sir. Are you eating with us, gentlemen?'

'Not me, thanks,' Tilelli said, patting his stomach, the buttons under considerable strain.

'No,' I told the waiter who disappeared with the speed of a greyhound. Perhaps he, too, was scared of me.

I thanked Tilelli for his generosity. 'My pleasure,' he said graciously. Nothing in his bearing suggested he associated me with the man wanted by MI5. I wasn't surprised. It was a rubbish picture. 'How's tricks?' he said.

I smiled, 'Average.' Tilelli didn't expect a rundown of my latest business ventures no more than I expected him to tell me whose payroll he was on. I had, however, revealed in one single word that all was not quite as it should be. Tilelli picked up on it.

'There's a lot of frightened folk out there and when folk get frightened they make mistakes and then those mistakes need taking care of.'

I nodded sagely. 'Any folk in particular I should know about?'

'Just making a general observation.'

He was right. Tough times usually meant an increase in my line of work.

I said, 'Seen Wes lately?'

Tilelli frowned. 'Not for a while.' He didn't ask me why I asked.

Wouldn't have been sensible or clever. *Why?* Was not a question to which I responded with warmth. 'I heard he was banging some older broad,' he added.

'Wes would bang his own sister if he had one,' I said, to which Tilelli hooted with laughter. 'Any idea which outfit he's operating for right now?'

Tilelli shook his head disappointed he couldn't help. 'Like I said, I haven't seen him in a while.'

'Nothing about him on the wire?'

Another shake of his head followed by another gulp of booze.

I followed his lead, took a pull. Terrific. The coniferous tang of gin drowned my nausea. Nothing, however, obliterated a sudden vision of mass casualties, the morbid results of a vicious dirty bomb.

'You all right, Hex? You look a little haunted, if you don't mind my saying.'

I flashed an easy smile. 'I'm good. Tired, that's all.'

'Doing nothing sure is tiring,' he snorted, taking out a silver hip flask. He unscrewed the top and poured a slug of booze, presumably brandy, into his coffee cup. 'Damn cold out there,' he said as if by explanation.

I leant forward, dropped my voice several notches, baritone to bass. 'I'm looking for a guy. He carried out a hit two nights ago.' As soon as the words left my mouth I wondered why the man in the alley hadn't presented himself to me as a potential candidate. Just because he'd questioned me about the hard drive didn't exclude him. Maybe he'd killed Wilding but some other party had stolen the information. Then I contrasted the crass, brutish attempt of my attacker to the neatly conceived and slick execution carried out by the assassin: no comparison.

'This guy,' Tilelli eyeballed me, 'Is he pissing on your patch?'

My answering smile was without mirth. I flicked an imaginary mark from my trousers, deliberately suggesting that I wanted to flick the guy who'd rained on my parade out of existence.

'Got anything else on him?' Tilelli's eyes were alight with interest.

'His working method tells me that he has a high level of skill and nerve.' Whether or not he bore the scars of his trade with relish, I'd no idea. I didn't need to spell out to Tilelli that the nature of the work meant that we were loners, anonymous, secretive and deadly.

Tilelli clicked his tongue. 'Not that many on the circuit with your particular skills, especially for the more exotic gigs.'

I knew. I'd come across a few, foreigners mostly. I guessed Wilding definitely fell under the heading of *exotic gig.*

'With regard to the legitimate market,' Tilelli continued, 'Governments all over the world, including democracies, employ security services who employ specialists to carry out wet operations.'

I knew this too. The Israelis had kidon. *Grey Ghosts* carried out assassinations on behalf of the Pentagon, or so Reuben, feeding my boyish imagination, once told me.

'Reckon there's a lot of hypocrisy on the subject,' Tilelli chuckled, clearly on his own pet subject and loving every second of it. 'There's not a dime's worth of difference between their dirty work and your dirty work.'

'I just happen to work in the private sector,' I flicked a cool smile, making Tilelli laugh out loud. The politically motivated murder once again took precedence over the criminally motivated, to my mind. Tilelli was still rattling on.

'Any clue to this guy's mojo?'

I shook my head. Most were driven by money, some by cruelty. There were a few who, once they had the taste of blood in their mouths, were unstoppable. Neither money nor cruelty made me tick.

Tilelli lifted the coffee cup to his lips. 'And the victim?'

'A scientist.'

The cup loitered mid-air. Actually, it shook a little. Tilelli's eyes widened. Deep furrows appeared on his brow. 'The scientist, Mary Wilding?'

'Uh-huh.'

The rim of the cup pressed hard to his lips, Tilelli drained the contents, and returned it with a clatter to the saucer. He paled. For a man in the know it seemed inconceivable that Wilding's death was suddenly headline news to him. I'd pressed some kind of button, but I didn't know what.

'You okay?' I said.

'Sure,' Tilelli forced a smile. He didn't look it.

'The man who killed her has something that doesn't belong to him,' I said.

Tilelli took a big gulp of air as though about to dive into the deep.

'You know anything about it?'

Tilelli shook his head, jowls wobbling. 'What was taken?'

'Information. It's been confirmed she was the victim of black-mail. Might be connected, might not. There's all kinds of people with their snouts in the trough.'

Tilelli grimaced. 'What kinds of people?'

'Your kind,' I said elliptically. 'Think you can help?'

'Sure would like to but I'm kinda busy right now.'

'Thought things were a little slow.' My voice cut like a razor.

Tilelli glanced at his feet for a moment then looked up. I narrowed my gaze to one of cold steel. Sweat broke out on Tilelli's brow. The tip of his tongue grazed the corner of his mouth. His eyes shot wide. 'I'll triple your fee,' I promised.

It took a matter of seconds for the power of my words to penetrate Tilelli's booze-sozzled brain. When it did his large frame relaxed. The muscles in his face went slack. I recognised that expression, one of sheer, unadulterated greed tempered by fear. I stayed absolutely still and observed him making the mental deductions. He was working out how many crates of Bourbon he could buy with that kind of loot, how many games of roulette he could fund. Finally, he grinned broadly, slapped one hand against his thigh and ejected a nervous laugh. He stuck out a hand. 'Always a pleasure doing business with you.'

I took and shook out of courtesy. I had no need to remind him that the consequences of breathing one word of our conversation would result in instant and final retribution.

'How will I get in touch?' Tilelli's eyes gleamed like two shiny pebbles at the bottom of a stagnant pond.

'I'll find you.' I stood up and left.

The sun had given up trying to punch a hole in the sky and had sensibly retired. There was a whisper of sleet in the air. I had the strong sensation of events out of control and swirling around. I hoped McCallen was having better luck because then the hard drive would be in safekeeping and maybe McCallen would realise that she'd got me wrong. Somehow that was important to me.

I caught a tube to Richmond, walked into a supermarket, head down, basket in hand, checking for tails, then, ditching the basket, walked out and caught a bus to Kingston where I picked up take-away coffee, and changed to the 459 to Woking Station.

Every step risked exposure and I spent the journey coldly checking faces, watching those with mobile phones and I-pods, trying to distinguish who was who, whether any posed a threat. The constant and universal blare of music in shops, cafes, garages, and on the street had mostly worked to my advantage in the past. Now I was the hunted it spooked me.

From the station I hailed a cab that took me to Chobham, a charming historic village that had fallen prey to the tourist trade according to Billy 'Squeeze', the man I was going to visit. Billy's real name was William Franke, but nobody I knew called him that.

To the outside world, Billy was another wealthy landowner who'd made his millions in the City when times were hot. Only a select few knew the truth. I doubted his family had a clue that the upstanding, generous husband and father who dominated their lives possessed a hidden dark side, a side where men were dispatched with the same ease with which Billy shot and bagged a pheasant. They didn't know about his legendary cruelty, that he had once squeezed a man's brains from his head, or that their world was built on the proceeds of drugs and the spilt blood of others.

'You a friend of Mr Franke?' the cabbie said.

'Yes,' I replied.

'A real gentleman, grand fella. We do a lot of business with him. Generous as they come.'

I couldn't disagree. Spotting what he called 'raw talent', Billy had given me my first early jobs in the trade and provided me with an influential contact in the States. For this I remained indebted. His impressive list of contacts was what drew me here now. Whether or not, he'd play ball was a different matter. Billy always drove a hard bargain. He thought he was being fly. I thought he was a mean old bastard. Unlike others with whom I'd had dealings, Billy had no airs and graces. I was as likely to find him with his sleeves rolled up fixing the crankshaft of one of his vintage motors as sitting in his study working out the logistics for his next shipment of cocaine. I smiled, catching the driver's eye, and as quickly wiped the humour from my face. The way in which he watched me in the rear-view mirror made me uneasy. My description, although poor, was out there, in circulation. Concerned that I looked familiar to him in a way that he couldn't yet fathom, I arranged my features into one of stark uncompromising hostility. It worked. Unnerved by my stony expression, he wittered on about Billy's wife and kids. I grunted another reply and, not keen to engage, turned my head aside. I didn't need an association with the great man to protect me. I could do that on my own. Thankfully for the cab driver the distance to Billy's place was less than five miles. Wouldn't have been good for him to push my buttons.

Eventually we swung into the grounds via a set of large electronic wrought-iron gates and drove uphill along a sinuous gravelled drive with fields on either side. Symbols of Billy's success stood like monuments at every twist and turn: the man-made lake on which sat a rowing boat anchored to a post and chain; an old Victorian dovecote beautifully preserved; a folly glimpsed from within the manicured gardens. With a shudder, I realised then that the trappings of great wealth counted for nothing against a weapon of grotesque proportions.

At last we drew close to the entrance of a substantial black and white timbered farmhouse. I paid the fare and, as I handed it over, it occurred to me that I was no different from Billy. My rewards had also been earned from the deaths of others. The driver took my blood money and, pretending affability, nervously asked me to pass on his best wishes.

Brief conversation with a housekeeper informed me that Billy was last seen in the stable block. She suggested that I head that way. Other men would employ more stringent security measures. I could have been anyone. It was a measure of the man's ruthlessness that Billy saw no need for extra protection. I knew that if he wanted to kill me he could, and probably smile in a moment of sober reflection afterwards.

By now the air was raw. A low-lying sun streaked the sky a bloody red. My footsteps sounded clipped and loud, reflecting my racing pulse. I was taking a risk, but I reckoned most disasters in life occurred because of chronic complacency or apathy rather than sudden and decisive action.

Following a stone path that sparkled with ice, I passed a horsebox and trailer, and inhaled the heady odour of dung and wet straw, then the wonderful warm smell of leather and saddle soap, as I stepped quietly inside the loosebox. With his back to me, bent over, Billy gave no indication that he was aware he had company.

Quietly spoken, he said, 'Hello, Hex.'

'Hi, Billy.'

A short man, lithe and wiry, he groomed a massively muscled

animal, black as night. I knew nothing about horses yet I sensed that beneath the gleam and shine lurked a brute of neurotic and spiteful unpredictability. Sure enough, at my approach, the horse jerked its head, ears flattening, nostrils flaring, and lashed out. Billy leapt back, the beast missing him by a millimetre.

'Pack it in,' Billy snarled, slapping its rear hard with the flat of his hand, then turned and grinned. Clean-shaven and permanently tanned, he had deep-set eyes, the colour of currants, sharp cheekbones. He'd had the same hairstyle for the past fifteen years: ultra-short at the sides, shaped flat on top so that it looked as if it grew vertically. Still dark, no grey, Billy's hair was quite obviously dyed. I'd always thought it a strange affectation for a man comfortable in his own skin and whose steely determination was a cover for the sheer viciousness of the personality beneath. 'Sorry about that,' he said. 'Milo sometimes forgets his manners, don't you, lad?' He patted the brute with obvious affection. The horse tossed its head, snorted hot air through is red shiny nostrils, yet it was smart enough to recognise Billy was boss.

'Personally I can't see the attraction,' I said.

Billy grinned some more. ''Ah well,' he said. 'Me and Milo share a lot in common. Sired a fair few offspring and he's an evil old git. Killed a man up north. I had to jump through all sorts of hoops to save him from the knacker's yard.' He cast me a long slow look. 'Don't suppose you came here to discuss the price of horseflesh.'

'I came for a chat.'

'Not sure I can help but I'll try. Give me a minute.'

I watched Billy as he cleaned out the stallion's hooves with an implement that resembled a bottle-opener, painted them with oil and, finally, rugged the animal up. Finally, he took a sugar lump from his pocket, laying it on the flat of his hand, offering to Milo who scooped it up with rare delicacy.

'So,' Billy said. 'Looks like you've landed in the shit.'

News travelled fast. 'I didn't do it.'

Billy inclined his head. Seemed like an angle he hadn't considered. 'It's your signature.'

'Forged by someone else.' Christ, I thought. Had I been set up? Billy read my thoughts.

'Maybe you need to look behind the curtain. Think someone's out to get you?'

Tilelli implied the same. Wasn't rocket science, any number of hard men would like me dead. 'Perhaps,' I said.

'Could be the finish of you, son.'

I knew this only too well. Nobody was indispensable. In a flash I saw that it wasn't about me any more – easy to imagine the quicksand of time closing over my bones after I was gone – it was about averting catastrophe. 'Ideas on a postcard?'

Billy pinched the bridge of his nose with his fingers. 'Plenty of young guns will knock someone off for a couple of grand. But you're different. You're high-end. Class. People like me employ a man like you because you don't leave a mess. To you, killing is an art form.'

'Thanks for the glowing reference…'

'But not much help.'

'Not really.' I let out a sigh. 'Billy, I don't expect you to name names, but what kind of players would order…'

Billy put the flat of his hand up, gave me the look. I shut my mouth, choked off the words before they could breathe. There were not many men I feared. Billy was one, perhaps the only one. 'Can't answer that.'

I nodded. I probably shouldn't have asked. Gloomily I realised that my visit was a dangerous waste of time.

'Judging by that slapped-arse look on your face, you know why she was killed.'

I nodded again.

'Dodgy stuff?'

Dodgy didn't really cover it. Wait a minute, I thought, feeling as though I was skating on black ice. 'How did…'

'Listened to the lunchtime news on the radio. 'Course it wasn't spelt out,' Billy said, 'but seemed to me like she wasn't your average bear. Did you know she'd worked at Porton Down?'

I shook my head.

'Not good. Not good at all. Hell, Hex, how did you get mixed up in all this?'

'It's something I've been struggling with.'

'Well, that's a fucking relief,' he flashed a grin, 'Because seems to me as though you're the only one who can sort it. Word of advice, to find the player you look at the commodity. If we're talking drugs and guns, slappers, even, I can point you in the right direction, but we ain't talking drugs and guns.'

'No,' I said.

'See, men in my line of work, they're proper blokes, got wives and kids. They ain't the type to go messing in stuff they can't control. Enough said.'

I thanked him. He touched my sleeve. Billy was not the tactile type. I appreciated the gesture. 'Anything else I can help with?' he said.

'Got jumped the other night by a big Irish guy. Ring any bells?'

Billy went very still, thought for a moment and shook his head. 'Want me to make some enquiries, on the quiet?'

'That would be good, thanks.' I turned and started to walk away.

'What happened to him, your Irish mate?' Billy called after me.

I turned back, met Billy's eye and gave him my best weapons-grade smile.

CHAPTER ELEVEN

I took a cab to Fairoaks, an airfield surrounded by hotels and Spanish restaurants. There, I booked in for the night and, using a payphone, made a cryptic call to someone I used for background checks on employers, the anonymous employer for the Wilding hit a regrettable exception.

A computer analyst by day, Jat, was a hacker by night. Our lives had crossed many years before when I was starting out when as a student Jat had fallen foul of the Asian Mafia. Certain organised crime syndicates targeted poor and gullible Asians by offering to pay for their degree courses – the most popular: law, accountancy and I.T. – in return for 'help' later with such activities as illegal immigration, smuggling and cyber crime. Unwittingly involved, Jat had tried to extricate himself. This was where I stepped in, the rest history. Unable to pay me, we came to a sensible working relationship. Through Jat, and via the Internet, I was given unrivalled access to a parallel universe and mine of information.

An hour later, Jat showed. Taller than me, he walked with a low lope, shoulders rounded. He had a shock of dark hair, dark sideburns. His toffee-coloured eyes were slightly too close together to make him conventionally good-looking, but no way did he fit the nerdy, bespectacled stereotype most associated with I.T. geeks.

'Beer?' I said as he sat down.

'London Pride, if they've got it.'

I went to the bar, paid for two pints, returned to our table. We never indulged in pleasantries. I wasn't interested in his life no more than he was interested in mine. We got straight to business. I passed him my phone, showed him Saj's mugshot.

'I need you to check out this guy,' I said, keeping my voice low.

Jat nodded, took out his phone and transferred the picture from mine to his. I took a sip of my pint. 'His name is Saj.'

'Saj what?'

'I don't know.'

Jat smiled. 'Have you any idea how many men go by that name?'

I didn't answer. As far as I was concerned this was a problem for Jat to solve. Jat swallowed some beer. 'All right,' he said. 'I'll work on the photo. What else have you got for me?'

'Our man is based in the Midlands, your home patch.'

Another smile. 'Birmingham, West Bromwich, Tipton, Wolverhampton, where exactly?'

I shrugged a *don't know.* 'He's part of a terrorist splinter group.'

Jat's eyes widened. He let out a low grunt. I knew what he was thinking before he said it. 'He is not a potential employer,' I added with emphasis.

'Target?'

I knifed him with a cold stare. I never used him for targets. 'Not the way I work.' Perhaps if I had, I wouldn't be in the mess I found myself in.

Jat took another long swallow of beer. I'd like to say he looked relieved. He didn't. 'Which group am I looking at?' he said.

'No idea.'

He let out a deep sigh. I continued, relentless. 'Find out what he's up to, who he hangs out with, any detail however irrelevant it may seem. His boss is a guy called Mustafa. You'll have to be careful because this Saj character is an informer for MI5.'

Jat hunched over, closed his eyes tight then looked up at me, imploring. 'You can't seriously expect me to get involved in something like this.' His voice was a whisper.

I smiled and winked. I could. And he knew it.

'OK, OK,' he said, taking a deep breath, 'but already I can see a big practical problem. Groups of this nature,' he said delicately, 'communicate with hand-written notes and word of mouth. They don't talk to each other through phones or computers. I'd basically be mining a barren seam. I take it you're not expecting me to run around the Midlands raiding bins,' he said, acerbic.

I am a reasonable man. I didn't want Jat getting himself into all kinds of trouble. 'All I'm asking is that you give it your best shot.' I took out my wallet. Jat shook his head. 'Come on,' I said. 'This isn't an ordinary job.'

'Afterwards, maybe.' Then he drained his pint, stood up and left.

I spent the remainder of the evening drinking beer and thinking over what Billy said. Had I been set up? It was worth consideration. While the security services were chasing my tail, the real assassin was delivering the hard drive to the elusive Mr X. Maybe Mr X and the guy who contracted me to kill Wilding were one and the same. It was something I wanted to put to Wes, preferably with a gun pointed at his head. In fact, I was positively looking forward to our meeting, not something I could say about my impending flight.

I don't scare easily. I am unafraid of instant death. I am fatalistic. If your number is up, that's it. Flying has always played a big part in my life. I don't enjoy it but I am cool with it. I prefer big planes to flimsy 'Buddy Holly' numbers. It's simply a matter of preference. Helicopters, however, file under a different category.

I appreciate that 'Big Birds' are nifty in tight situations; brilliant for air sea rescue, dispensing supplies in famine and earthquake stricken zones where roads have disappeared and rivers have burst their banks; vital in the arena of battle. I admire the mad and 'devil-may-care' guys who fly them. But, aerodynamically, they don't work for me. Helicopters are like cats that moo. As a consequence, I slept badly, got up early, met Sergei, my pilot and his co-pilot, Valery, around eight. I speak few words of Russian and the Russians spoke few words of English. We were going to get along fine.

From the sheer size of the waiting vehicle, I guessed it was an Agusta 109, but I could have been mistaken. I was no expert. Blue and white exterior, the nose of the machine pointed, it closely resembled a shark. Apposite, I thought grimly. Inside, plush tanned leather seats and thick-pile carpet. I climbed in and sat in the back behind the pilot like a visiting dignitary, headset clamped to my ears. Had I been a praying man I would have offered one up.

There seemed to be a lot of hanging around but eventually we got going. First stop, Le Touquet, where we were set to clear customs. It bothered me. If pushed I'd offer a bribe. If really pushed, I'd disappear. I needn't have worried. Sergei, or rather Yakovlevich and his extensive network of contacts smoothed the way: nothing but greetings, smiles and cursory glances at passports and papers. Same old: if you have the right amount of currency you don't need to speak the language. From there we flew to Tours, stretched legs, grabbed something to eat, then taking to the air for a short hop, refuelled then headed south towards Biarritz and up and over the Pyrenees, a bleak and forbidding range of mountains that divided France from Spain and stretched coast to coast. Transfixed, I gazed in awe of the sheer scale and drama of the peaks below, sparkling and seductive and deadly. If we came down we stood zero-chance of survival. I knew it. The Russians knew it. I could tell from the silence.

A fiery sun finally slipped from the sky, leaving a trail of gold and pink like spun candyfloss, its dying light catching and tumbling into the snows beneath. Enthralled, I watched until with nothing else to do I slept.

We arrived at Sabadell around nine, Barcelona time. I had less than three hours to clear Customs, find a base, hook up with my armourer, and meet Wes at mid-day. Again, Yakovlevich's word worked like a magic charm. I thanked the Russians and caught the first bus heading towards the city.

I got off near the University, walked down Ronda Sant Antoni, and checked into the kind of small anonymous establishment that suited my purposes: no dining room, no room service, a simple place to sleep and bathe.

The safe was housed behind a panel in the wardrobe. Creating a code, I opened it and put one of many false passports and euros inside. Couldn't be too careful. La Rambla was notorious for pickpockets. All I took was my 'dummy' wallet containing cash and the litter of someone else's life in the form of false receipts and bills, in other words a paper trail of lies.

By half past ten I was back on the street, walking briskly along magnificent, wide tree-lined avenues with wrought-iron balconies on every apartment building, each a subtle reminder of my past. My mother had lived in a classic Regency apartment in an exclusive area of Cheltenham, known as the Suffolks. Living primarily with my grandparents, I'd sometimes drop by unannounced on a summer's evening and find her, gin and tonic in hand, sitting out on the balcony and listening to music. A child of her time, she adored Led Zeppelin though, when I thought of her now, I associated her more clearly with Jim Croce or the Moody Blues or early Roxy.

I blinked, snuffed out the memory.

Past the first floor offices of a private investigator, I crossed the main square and hub of the city where I fell in with a sea of sightseers. Together, we surged forwards down the main tourist drag, the thoroughfare flanked by market traders selling birds, hamsters and ferrets; and jugglers, fire-eaters and mime artists, including a couple of formidable-looking Visigoths painted gold. They drew quite a crowd and I stopped, too, because by now I was certain I was being watched. I'd sussed out the first tail as I rounded the corner near one of the more expensive hotels off the square. Male, my height, Mr Average, he showed out simply by virtue of the fact he was trying too hard. His signature pony-tail, although alive and well in Spain's second city, looked like it had been stuck on. The rest of his routine was pretty good. He didn't touch his earpiece. He didn't talk into his collar. He walked with a nice even gait. Well-trained, I'd say, but I could sniff out guys like this at a hundred paces. Part of a team, he had a female in tow, ordinary looking, no distinctive features, a good sound covert operator. Again something about her, possibly the slightly circuitous way she walked down the street, put my foe-detector on high alert.

I came to a pedestrian crossing with the lights on green and the driver with right of way. Fortunately a community officer stepped out and held up the traffic. I surged over the road to the other side, joining a crush of people heading for the indoor market. Glancing idly over my shoulder, I almost did a double take at the sight of McCallen. How the hell had she found me? Meant someone had tipped her off. My mind pitched back to the tube station, to McCallen taking the call, the important news she'd received. It was about me, I realised. *I* was the news. Only one person knew about my trip: Yakovlevich.

Automatically I rounded my shoulders, dropped my head so that my chin tucked into my chest, and barrelled into the food hall, disappearing into a blast of chatter and colour. Indoors, one great deli of raw and cooked meat, cheese, fish, fruit, nuts, breads, chocolate and vegetables. Rammed with shoppers, it was almost impossible to move. Not good for me. Not good for the people tailing me. With even odds on both sides, I tried to second-guess my watchers, put myself in their shoes. They'd expect me to walk out the other end. It's what professionals were taught to do, either that or exit on a different level. I did neither. I killed time, bought and ate a pastry filled with apples and cream, bartered my overcoat for a trader's donkey jacket, then sneaked out the way I'd entered. Crossing back to La Rambla, I stole down a side street signed the 'Potters Gateway,' which opened up onto the medieval part of the city known as Barri Gotic, a tangle of alleys and ancient dwellings. At its beating heart lay the Cathedral. I glanced over my shoulder once more. No McCallen. Looked like I'd shaken her off.

The air was raw and still. I moved with speed. Among the cloistered streets, gargoyles stared down from every corner. An eerie, sinister atmosphere prevailed. Open a door here and you'd likely encounter an open yard with lemon and olive trees and steps up to a silent home. Or maybe not.

I paused outside a door covered in graffiti. Challenging, in your face, on a different level to other more predictable art, this was hostile, threatening, a collage of monstrous faces, the equivalent of telling the unwary to fuck off.

I knocked long and loud and waited.

Footsteps. A grille slid open. A set of wary eyes peered out. The grille slid back. Next cursing then the sound of bolts being shot and keys scraped into a lock.

'Hola,' I said as the door finally opened and Isabell emerged with a timid yet enchanted smile.

'Benvinguts,' she said, speaking Catalan. *Welcome.*

I leant forward, put my hands on her shoulders and kissed both cheeks then her lips. She shivered in delight. This had no connection to what I'd love to believe was my magnetic personality and every connection to the fact that Isabell did not receive a lot of kisses. A boyfriend once took a blowtorch to her face. At her request I killed him. At my request I refused payment. We had a mutual understanding.

She looped her arm through mine and ushered me inside to a cobbled courtyard filled with weeping figs and vines. A straight flight of stone steps led to her home. Beneath, an armoury contained every conceivable weapon for the modern assassin.

'Aren't you going to lock the door?' I said.

Isabell reverted to English. 'Hex is in town. I don't need to lock the door.'

I gave her a wry look and she laughed. 'Here,' I said. 'I'll do it.' Once I believed I was invincible. Not any more.

'It's so good you're here,' she beamed with happiness. 'I have much to show you.' When she wasn't supplying arms, Isabell painted great abstract pictures that I couldn't get my head around. She tugged at my sleeve expectantly in a way that made my hardened heart crease.

'Can't stop. Business not social.'

She took a step back, dismay in her expression.

'Hey,' I said, touching her chin with the crook of my finger. 'You're looking great.' And she was. In spite of her ruined looks, Isabell dressed with panache. Slightly built, she favoured soft, layered clothing, silks and linen, brightly coloured scarves and shoes. She reminded me of an exotic tropical bird.

She rested her hands on her hips, kinked her head to one side and smiled. 'What do you want, Hex?'

'A pistol, something small, light, easily concealed.'

She rolled her eyes. 'This is what you say *every* time.'

I looked towards the steps and the hidden door beneath. Before the Wilding job my excitement, almost sexual, would hardly have been contained. I visited roughly three times a year and each time I got a buzz. For reasons I hadn't processed it felt as if the thrill had gone. I turned to her and forced a smile, keen not to reveal my change of mood. 'Shall we?'

She flashed a grin and slipped out a set of keys. I followed her across the cobbles and watched as she unlocked the steel-clad door, leant inside and switched on the lights. Two steps down and I was assailed by the smell of weaponry and gun oil.

The cellar extended across the width and length of the house. Near the door, a desk on which sat a laptop and mobile phone. To the left of the desk, a collection of carrying containers for musical instruments, violins, mostly. Not every busker in Barcelona carried a clarinet or oboe in his music case. They were as likely to be used for the transportation of weaponry.

Rifles, bolt action and automatic, hung on freestanding racks. Pistols and revolvers housed in separate display cabinets lined two of the four walls. Submachine guns had their own department in an L-shaped section that ran underneath the kitchen. And there was a new addition: a glass cabinet containing an array of hunting knives and Samurai swords. I arched an eyebrow at the sight of a fine looking Kukri.

Isabell flashed me a triumphant smile. 'Very on trend,' she said, making me laugh. She spoke good English, full of colloquialisms and modern twists.

Parking her small rear on an easy chair, she tucked her legs up underneath and from nowhere, like a conjuror, produced an apple into which she sank her small white teeth. 'Want a bite?' she said, offering it to me. I shook my head, distracted. Once I would have stayed for days. I didn't have days not even hours. I advanced towards a nearby cabinet, my attention grabbed by an M40 Firestar. Made in Spain, one of the Star series of pistols, it was a nice slim and compact piece of kit, especially for the calibre. Dead easy to conceal, accurate and powerful with a magazine capacity of six rounds, I thought it perfect for my purposes. I asked Isabell if I could take a closer look.

Isabell nodded, skipped over to the desk, unlocked a drawer and withdrew a bunch of keys. She opened up the display cabinet, took out and handed me the gun, which I held with gloved hands. Nicely weighted, I thought. I went through the usual routine of clearing it, checking the chamber, squeezing off the trigger. All satisfactory.

'Magazine?' I said.

'Sure, and a spare?'

'Please, and a holster.'

'On your tab?'

'Gracias, I'll settle up next time.'

'No worries,' she said, scooting round the corner, returning minutes later. I checked the action of the gun several times then loaded the weapon, shrugged off my coat, snapped on the holster and slipped the gun securely inside. It felt familiar. It felt good.

I glanced at my watch. Time to go. I slipped my arm around her, drew her close, and gave her a hug. 'Take care, Isabell.'

'You, too, Hex. Fins despr'es.' *See you later.*

I emerged into the courtyard and finally back out into the alley where the sun was shining, and took a less scenic route well off the tourist trail.

Shoes padding across the cobbled stones, I passed cafes with dark, brooding interiors, down-and-outs clustered outside a theatre that had fallen into disrepair, inebriated peddlers, and middle-aged hookers with laddered tights and laddered faces. When I finally emerged into Placa de Catalunya, the hub of the city, I thought I'd taken a fast ticket from hell to Paradise.

Two minutes to mid-day. Wes would emerge at any moment and take a seat at the usual bench in the usual spot. Checking to see if he had backup, men who would take a pop at me in the mistaken belief that I had what they wanted, I scanned the scene: statues, fountains, the iconic Café Zurich, diehards outside smoking cigarettes and drinking coffee, a Romanian beggar with one hand cupped, the other with fingers pressed to lips in a 'feed me' gesture, dogs, buses, taxis, scooters. From here all things radiated, the bus and rail systems, the Metro, the good, the bad and the…

McCallen was sitting on a low wall close to a newsstand. Her eyes met mine. She held my gaze, victorious. I stared back, fascinated and furious. I'd seriously underestimated her. I did a three hundred and sixty degree turn to find out where the rest of the crew loitered. Couldn't see them. McCallen's generous top lip curled into an almost smile as my gaze fell back in her direction. Around me the rest of the city seemed to come to a standstill, as if everyone, apart from McCallen and me, were frozen in time. I blinked in some vain hope that the picture before me would change. It did. And not to my liking. As I opened my eyes I saw Wes emerge from Rambla de Catalunya, about to cross the square. If I went to him now, McCallen would make the connection. If I hung back, did nothing, Wes would return to his employer empty-handed and I would be none the wiser. I couldn't follow him without McCallen following me. My only hope was to make a brush contact with Wes, alerting him to trouble, and hook up with him later. Timing was crucial. I'd have only seconds to warn him and pass on by. I couldn't waste words. Everything relied on my expression. Balanced against this, the place was crowded with lunchtime shoppers and office-workers, in theory providing enough cover for us to escape in different directions. We had done this once before. It would work only if Wes were sharp enough to catch on and play the game. I wasn't sure he was that sharp.

I stepped forward intent on heading Wes off and preventing him from coming too far in so that I could make a fast getaway into the traffic and shops and seething streets. As I made my move, McCallen stood up, hands in pockets. Wes kept on coming. He looked grim. There were shadows underneath his hangdog eyes. He had a fresh and open cut on his mouth. A livid bruise paraded on one cheek. I didn't like it. I didn't like it at all. It felt wrong.

So far he hadn't seen me. I dreaded his first moment of recognition, maybe raising his hand, shouting across the square, increasing pace. Whether it was imagined or not, Wes looked petrified.

On I walked. A glimmer of recognition flashed across his eyes. Expressionless, I pounded ahead at a brisk pace, no eye contact, acutely aware of McCallen behind me. Traffic was dense, slow moving. In contrast to London and other capitals, Barcelona was in motion all the time. Off the multi-lane highway, a light blue

Seat swerved and cut in close to a bike stand. A series of images flashed before me: driver at the wheel; engine running; two passengers out; slammed doors; headed my way. Shit, this was a trap.

Alternatively, these weren't killers. These were kidnappers. A cut above, they looked professional and capable, and the type of men who work to a formula. The code being *out, grab, back,* the abduction taking no more than twelve seconds. A variation on that same theme: *rabbit punch, garrotte, get the hell out.* I know.

Killers or kidnappers, I didn't change pace. There was no tension. Now I understood what was going down I felt calm. Breathing steadily, I slipped my hand into my jacket pocket, reached for the gun. Wes frowned and half-turned. Part of me registered Wes being grabbed around the neck, dragged back to the waiting car, each step choreographed with speed and skill; the other sentient part of me concentrated on the bigger of the two abductors: thick-necked, square-jawed, cold-eyed, the one sent for me.

But I wasn't going anywhere. I had a job to do, a last job, and this two-bit piece of shit wasn't going to stand in my way.

I could do things the easy or the hard way. I'd had enough of fists flying, broken teeth, split lips and spilt blood, and the crowd reaction that kind of attention drew. I did the easiest thing in the book. I took out the pistol and shot him.

Chaos erupted behind me. People screamed. People ran. Without breaking stride, I continued, coldly detaching myself from the scene, my eyes fixed on the waiting car, the registration. Some kind of dispute was going on inside. Wes's frightened eyes stared back at me out of the rear window, locking onto mine like my face was the last he'd ever see, then the driver gunned the engine, reversed back into the traffic and fishtailed down a one-way street followed by McCallen astride a motorbike.

This stopped me in my tracks. I looked around, noticed a young Spaniard with a biker's helmet cursing the empty space once occupied by his bike. A victim of hijack, he threw hand signals into the damp air, his gaze trained on the retreating vehicles. Isabell taught me a little Catalan, enough for me to advise and strongly encourage the biker to contact the *Policia* on 092.

'Si, si,' he said, pulling out a mobile phone.

Cops in the city were among the most courteous in the world. They were also speedy. I reckoned they'd respond in minutes. Tracing the bike might take a little longer. Fine by me. It would give me more than enough time to walk to the main police station in the Old Town.

CHAPTER TWELVE

As cop shops went the station in Nou de la Rambla ticked all the boxes. An arrangement of grey breezeblocks, it resembled throwback British architecture of the 1960's. Outside, a strange smell of drains and drunks pervaded an unprepossessing street of downtrodden shops with metal grilles at the windows. I inserted myself on the opposite side of the street, skulking in a doorway, hoping I wouldn't be noticed. Tough to imagine, only a stone's throw away, one of Barcelona's finest landmarks, the Palau Guell, an extraordinarily flamboyant mansion built by Gaudi.

Either unknown others had got a taste of the action, which was scary, or maybe the 'jumpy' employer had finally gone into meltdown. The guy I'd shot dead provided a lead only if his real identity could be established. I wasn't about to stroll back to the square and make enquiries.

Fifteen or so minutes later, a police car sped past and halted outside the main entrance of the station. A blue clad anti-crime officer stepped out. Handcuffed to him, a grim-faced McCallen. It was tempting to rush across the road, point the handgun at the driver's head and demand McCallen's immediate release. I did no such thing because I don't issue threats on which I'm reluctant to deliver. I had only ever killed one police officer in my life. His name was Michael Berry and he had murdered my mother.

I watched as the arresting officer kept McCallen close, tapped the roof of the car and signalled the all clear to the driver, and took her inside.

It would probably take the Spanish no more than an hour of phone calls to corroborate McCallen's story, to prove that she was telling the truth and for them to realise their massive cock-up. I didn't have an hour. If I were to find Wes I needed McCallen. With no time to waste, I crossed the road and entered the police station. I knew exactly where I was going. McCallen's voice, loud with protest, led the way.

At a glance, I saw chairs, a clock, people milling around, two screened compartments, one for dealing with theft and muggings, and the other for booking in and processing clients. This was all I saw. I wasn't looking to write an inventory. McCallen was spitting junk out of her pockets and remonstrating with a burly desk sergeant. I expected she carried the same amount of bogus material as me. Not that it helped. The cops looked out of their depth. People out of their depth behave irrationally. McCallen was minutes away from a chilly police cell. If I didn't pull off the biggest stunt of my life I'd be joining her and all would be lost. To spring her I had to change the dynamics, keep things tight and sharp. I had to assume total control. I also needed to lie and I needed to lie well.

'British Intelligence,' I swaggered, marching straight up to the arresting officer. The colour of vintage Marmite, his eyes widened. He evidently realised that this was not going to be an average day of pickpockets, pimps and muggers. 'You speak English?' I demanded arrogantly.

'Yes.'

'Good. You've just arrested a British intelligence officer. Release her.'

He stared, slack-jawed, gawping from me to McCallen and back again. McCallen, keen to escape, played along.

'I said you'd made a mistake,' she said, with cool.

Unfortunately this was not a view shared by the desk officer who reached for the phone.

'I will check…'

'You don't believe me?' I spat, imperiously drawing myself up to my full height. Something in my deadly expression hit the mark. The officer moved his hand away from the receiver as though it might bite. The arresting officer gabbled something to him in Spanish. We all glared at each other. An awkward silence descended. Everyone in the police station stared our way. You could describe it as a high noon moment.

I leant in close to Marmite eyes, dropped my voice, for his ears only. 'The man shot in the square was an asset. My colleague here was attempting to hunt down his murderer. Are you going to release her, or do I have to contact your superiors? Perhaps the Director General of Centro Nacional de Inteligencia would welcome a call?'

He blinked, nodded vigorously. 'Si, I…'

'For God's sake, hurry up, man,' I said, fronting it out. My jaw ground and I caught McCallen's eye. She stared right back, combative.

Five minutes later, and amidst a welter of confusion, we headed down the concrete clad stairs. As we hit the street, I grabbed McCallen's elbow, propelling her in the direction of the waterfront and the Metro. McCallen had other ideas. Far enough away from the police station, she shook me off and turned on me, green eyes flashing with cold anger.

'What the hell are you doing?'

'Coming to your rescue.'

'*My* rescue?' she tilted her chin.

'Be grateful I didn't simply put a gun to his head.'

A sarcastic smile glanced across her mouth.

'You'd have got out eventually,' I admitted, 'probably with a lot of red faces and apologies all round, but you're in a time sensitive business.'

'Don't tell me what business I'm in, Mr…' She faltered, arched an eyebrow, no doubt expecting me to fill in the gap. Looked like she didn't buy the false identification papers I'd left in the brief-case.

'You should be pleased,' I said.

'I *should* be arresting you.'

'Try, if you like.' I stabbed her with a cold look of my own. I was armed. She wasn't. That gave me a major advantage in the arrest stakes.

'Wanted by Interpol, your description issued to every police force in the United Kingdom, you've got some nerve, I'll give you that.'

What did she expect? Assassin was on my C.V. The reality: I was fighting for my sorry soul. I wanted to tell her this. I didn't. McCallen was still spitting poison.

'You've just killed a man.'

'Regrettable, I admit, but necessary. The question you should ask yourself is *why* I killed him.' She said nothing. She'd seen what happened at the square. She understood that it was a case of kill or be killed.

She narrowed her eyes. 'Who is he?'

'I don't know.'

'But you knew the other guy, the one they took.'

'Yes.' No point in lying.

'And?'

'He's a fixer, a middle-man.'

'The one who lined you up for the Wilding hit?'

'Yes.' No point lying about that either.

She skewered me with her intelligent eyes. Her accompanying smile was nasty. 'So you don't deny it?'

I clamped down on my jaw to mask my growing frustration. 'I don't deny being asked. I do deny killing her. You've wasted a lot of time looking the wrong way. I thought you people were trained to peer round corners, not walk to the end of the road and stay there.' A man of few words, I'd delivered the equivalent of an essay. It was a measure of my anger and dissatisfaction. I had no problem with taking responsibility for my actions. I was damned if I was going to be blamed for something I hadn't done, or stopped from something I needed to do: namely, find the missing hard drive and destroy those who had it.

'Okay,' she backed off.

Glad we got that straight. 'Now what?'

'I'm going to find your man.'

Couldn't have put it better myself. 'What happened to the car?'

'I lost it near La Sagrada Familia.'

'Then we'd better get back there.'

'We?' When McCallen frowned the tip of her nose creased. It creased now.

'You don't want to lose me again, do you?' I locked eyes with hers.

'What? Me trust you?'

The question should have been mine. I had more to lose. Did I trust McCallen? I couldn't afford to. Not yet. Perhaps never. Distrust was as ingrained in me as the DNA in my body.

I answered McCallen's question for her, 'Yes.' Her eyes flickered, revealing hesitation. I bet she wanted nothing more than to hand me over to her masters, but then she'd lose the only lead she had. In effect I was of more value to her than she to me. Then again, I didn't know what I needed any more. I drifted in uncharted waters.

She didn't like it, but she agreed to take me with her. 'Are you still armed?' she said. I nodded. Normally I'd have ditched the gun. In a strange city, with too many people chasing me, I was hanging on to it. 'Good,' she said.

With the square swarming with cops, the area in lock-down, traffic brought to a standstill, people were heading for the Metro in droves. Only way to go: on foot.

We cut down towards the port, passing vast historic buildings, including the Columbus monument. On the other side of the road, the wooden walkway and footbridge that leads to the mouth of Port Vell. Continuing along the busy palm tree-lined waterfront, shoals of sailors in white uniforms and white shoes posed for photographs with pretty foreign tourists. Heads down, faces turned away, we criss-crossed through a maze of back alleys peppered with sex shops and peep shows, tattooists and taxidermists. Everyone chugged on cigarettes. Dark-eyed, people looked suspicious, even the kids.

McCallen moved with a fast sure stride and with the same easy grace I'd observed the first time I clapped eyes on her. We were a good fit. Neither had to adjust pace for the other. We didn't talk. She kept it professional. It would have been nice to believe that we were on the same side, but I recognised that working together was no more than an illusion. Each of us was exploiting the other. That being said, I'd started to draw conclusions about the woman who could denounce me. Mistress of the slow-blink, McCallen exuded cool without the arrogance of some that stumbled across my path. Her fast thinking in hijacking the bike and going after Wes had earned her brownie points in my eyes. She had nerve. I wished I'd done the same. The best bit for me was that she was good at working alone. Then again, she was a spook. What else should I expect?

At last, within spitting distance of la Sagrada Familia and Barcelona's answer to the Eiffel Tower, we came to a wide street, derelict office buildings on one side, decrepit residential the other. A play area for kids consisted of two swings, one ripped out, and a broken seesaw. Dog shit littered the only scrub of grass. Beyond, squalid dwellings with rows of washing lines and grubby clothing hung out to dry in dirty traffic-laden air.

McCallen broke stride at the apex of two roads near a row of fast food joints and cheap bars where salmonella came free with the paella. She looked down a corridor of slung-together dwellings. I followed her green laser gaze and pinpointed a pale blue

Seat with a dented rear and same registration as the vehicle in the square. Neither of us spoke. Changing direction, we moved as one.

The way ahead lacked charm. Twentieth century mouldering edifices with lumps eaten out of them, either by the elements or someone having a laugh with a bulldozer, bore down on us like mixed-up teenagers angry to be born and furious with the world. Machinery lay dormant. Cars rusted. Dogs barked. Babies screamed. Adults screamed louder. You didn't have to speak the language to recognise violence in your midst. It was the kind of place where even the sun dared not shine.

As we entered the street four lads hanging round a stairwell, drinking and smoking, turned their slow eyes towards us. A couple clicked their tongues at McCallen who ignored them. Their avaricious stare burnt into the side of my head. I slowed, listened, waiting for the inevitable scuffle of footsteps. Noise behind me, I swivelled round, locked eyes with the leader, his swagger distinguishing him from the rest of the pack. Opening my jacket, I gave him an exclusive opportunity to view the holstered weapon, the message clear and deliberate: *don't mess with me.* He backed off, signalling to the others to do the same.

When I caught up with McCallen she was viewing the Seat thrown up on the kerb, empty apart from a fresh bloodstain on the rear seat and the only sign of recent occupancy. I looked up: grim towering constructions with walkways and parapets and plenty of get-away routes. Door-to-door enquiries with *please can you help* questions and *I'd be glad to* answers were not going to win the day. I bet the cops only visited in groups of ten.

'There.' McCallen pointed out a boarded-up window on the third floor. To be fair, it was not the only one. However I could see her point. If you measured a line from the car to the window, the trajectory made sense.

I nodded. 'What about exits?'

'Windows are too high unless you happen to be Spiderman. You cover from the left. I'll approach from the right.'

'You're not armed.'

'I don't need to be.' She gave me a cold stare. I had no idea how good she'd be in a scrap. At that moment I thought she could kill with a look.

'Here,' I slipped the gun from its holster. She flashed me another of her cool stares and took it without hesitation. The way she handled the weapon I could tell she'd used one before. I suppose I was taking a risk, a calculated risk. I didn't think McCallen would waste time on me. Yet.

'What about you?' she said.

I grinned a wolfish smile. 'I'll be fine.'

We split up. McCallen disappeared inside. I crossed to the other end, venturing through a barren patch of what loosely could be described as a front garden and was now home to a burnt-out car and several months' worth of rubbish, and stole inside a dark and urine-encrusted entrance. From somewhere above my head, I could hear the raucous din of gangsta-rap.

McCallen was fine but lightweight and a tad too gullible. She should never have put so much trust in me and I should have insisted on making the running. In fact I should have…

I whipped round, lashed out, shoved whoever it was against the wall, smothered them with my own body. That's when I heard the double click of the safety catch slipped off.

'Touch me and I'll blow a hole in you the size of your own head,' McCallen hissed, the barrel of the gun pressed against my gut.

Most guys would have moved away, raised their hands, and done the expected. I stayed still. Rapidly reassessing my 'lightweight' prediction, I realised that, should she decide to take the shot, this would be a most painful way to die. I turned my head a little and murmured, 'Did you find anything?' She was breathing so hard I swear I could feel her heart banging against my chest. Maybe it was my own.

She nodded slowly, colour in her cheeks. I altered my stance, eased off. She almost looked disappointed. At that precise moment I had a huge visceral urge to kiss her, better still to fuck her. I stepped back. She put my gun back in her jacket pocket. 'You won't be needing it,' she said, a grim light in her eyes.

I didn't argue and followed her in silence back the way she'd come. Nobody batted an eyelash at the door off its hinges. Nobody commented on the smell of opened bowels emanating from the room with no view. I doubted anyone noticed anything around here. McCallen pointed for me to go first, which I did.

A body hung from a rope attached to a hook in the ceiling. Straightaway I knew it was Wes. I walked over, looked up at his battered face, the skinned knuckles, broken nails, evidence that he'd put up a desperate fight. I wasn't surprised. The desire to live is the most powerful drive in all of us. It's programmed into our DNA. Wes was no exception. He loved life and sex and colour too much to go quietly.

'Your friend,' McCallen said.

I pictured Wes's frightened eyes, the way he'd looked at me that last time. He must have known then that he was finished. *His victims suffer agonies,* he once said. And he was right. There was nothing clean about his death. The psychological trauma would have been intense. Stringing someone up like that smacked of sadism and cruelty. It appalled me on every level. Whatever could be said about me, I'd always prided myself on a clean kill. In birth we don't expect to be dragged into life. No more should we be yanked into death.

'You realise what this means?' McCallen's tone was defeated.

I turned towards her and, without a trace of irony, I said, 'Dead end.'

CHAPTER THIRTEEN

I'd outlived my usefulness, a state of affairs with which I was familiar. Five out of ten jobs emanated from someone living beyond their sell-by-date. Either they became a dangerous liability or were in danger of revealing information they shouldn't. McCallen was all for shipping me back to Blighty and offering me up as a human sacrifice. The gun in her pocket imbued her with a sense of importance that failed to impress me. For a start, it was my gun.

'Is this the moment you call in the rest of the team and parade me in front of them?'

'What team?' The accompanying frown looked genuine.

'The man and woman tailing me this morning.'

McCallen shook her head. 'There is no team. I'm here alone.'

This took me by surprise. Looking deeply into her eyes for signs of deception, I could read nothing. I would not go so far as to say that I believed her – she was trained to lie – but giving her the benefit of the doubt left me with a problem. Who was after me: legion forces of law and order, or unknown others? Without the time to properly reflect, I cut my losses, moved on. 'So how did you know where I was?'

'Intelligence. It's what spooks do.' This time there was a trace of a genuine smile. Good, the woman had a sense of humour. 'Something you seem to know a lot about,' she said, serious again.

I said nothing.

'Don't play me,' she said sharply.

I made light of it. 'I'm not. Any knowledge I might have is based on sheer bravado.' I waited a beat. 'You had a Russian tip-off, right?' Sometimes things fall into place with me unexpectedly and all at once. I didn't think Yakovlevich was responsible. He'd hardly fly me all the way to Spain to sell me out to the British security service. Scar-face, the man he met in the garden square, was different. I'd no idea what was spoken, what knowledge had changed hands, but I reckoned Yakovlevich would be untroubled by revealing information on a source to a man like him.

'You don't seriously expect me to comment.' McCallen's smile failed to conceal the hard expression in her eyes.

No, I didn't. 'Are you hungry?' I said.

She slow-blinked, made a tsking sound with her lips. I didn't believe she was squeamish or the type of self-obsessed woman who counted calories, although one could never be sure. More likely, she was thinking me mad to suggest we share a common-place activity in the middle of such persistent chaos. 'I need to eat,' I said plainly. And delay whatever she planned to do with me. I also wanted to talk, to find out what made her tick, what she knew, and whether I could turn it to my advantage. Hopefully she was thinking the same. To serve in the intelligence services you had to be *intelligent*. The clue lay in the title. I reckoned McCallen was as sharp as they came. 'Come on, your chance for a debrief, or whatever you call it,' I said encouragingly.

She relented. 'Where?'

I smiled. 'I know the perfect place.'

We were a few minutes walk from an area known as the Diagonal, an upmarket shopping district. A few paces from there, the quiet sophistication of Hotel Astoria on Carrer de Paris. Frequented by many it hardly shrieked secrecy and that was the point. Dirty deals weren't cut in backstreet dives that could be watched, in some cases bugged, and draw attention.

In common with many Spanish hotels, the Astoria served a standard three-course lunch until three-thirty in the afternoon. I ordered a table and informed McCallen that I was going to the men's room. She didn't look happy and obviously thought this my cue for heading for the hills.

'What are you suggesting, that you come with me?' I said, faintly amused.

'It has been known.'

'Wait outside, if you like.'

She liked. So off I went, did what I had to do, and joined McCallen a couple of minutes later. 'Do I get to wait outside the 'Ladies' when you want to pee?'

'Already been.'

'So you *do* trust me?'

'Rather pushing the envelope,' she said, unsmiling.

The vibe in the restaurant was cool and modern. With its white painted walls and minimalist décor, it reminded me a little of an art installation at Tate Modern. McCallen ordered mineral water. I ordered the same. I hardly looked at the menu. Neither did she. I scoped the room. She scoped the room. Anyone entering drew our attention. When the waitress came to take our food request McCallen asked for soup and fish. I chose and ordered soup and meat.

There were several others diners, couples mostly. The restaurant burbled with a low undercurrent of convivial conversation and the chinking of glass and white china. McCallen leant across. She smiled although the tough expression in her eyes didn't meet the twist of her lips.

'So here I am face to face with the Widow-maker.'

'People call me Hex.'

She didn't react. Not a flicker. Perhaps she already knew. 'The man with no friends, no career, no life, no moral code.'

I wouldn't have put it quite like that, but I could see where she was going with it. Not a woman to pull punches, McCallen was trying to draw me out. Perhaps she thought by insulting me I'd defend myself and reveal a tasty nugget of information.

McCallen was talking again, nice and low, nothing nuanced in the question. 'The guy hanging from the ceiling, what's his name?'

'Wes.'

'That it?'

'Yes.'

'And to recap, he's the facilitator between you and the client?'

'Correct.'

'You've had dealings with him before?'

I grunted a yes. I wanted to give McCallen every impression that I was prepared to co-operate.

'When?'

'A couple of years back.'

'Where?'

'England.'

'How did you meet?'

'He approached me in a club in London.'

'Which club?'

'I don't remember.' I did, but I wasn't telling McCallen.

'Is this how you routinely pick up business?'

'I don't do routine, or normal, or nine to five, or Sunday lunch.'

McCallen waited a beat, her eyes locked onto mine like a cruise missile. 'How did you intend to kill her?'

'Kill who?' That was the other thing about people like McCallen. They asked the same questions again and again either in the vain hope of getting a different answer, or tricking you into saying something you shouldn't. In her heart she still believed that I had a major connection to the bigger picture. In one small respect, she was right. Mostly she was wrong.

'Wilding. How would you have killed her?' She repeated it as if I had the I.Q. of a cockroach.

'*Would?* At last you admit I'm innocent. Progress.'

Tsk, tsk, again. 'You had every intention of murdering an innocent woman. That makes you guilty.'

What could I say? 'If you had every intention of seducing that man over there, the one with the wedding ring,' I said, jerking my chin in the direction of a neighbouring table. 'Does that make you guilty?'

'Hardly the same, is it?'

'Depends on your point of view. Not sure his wife would see it with the same level of detachment.'

She slow-blinked. For a moment she was silent, or at least quiet enough for me to get a word in. 'Look, I know what I am. I know what I've done. But…'

'Next you'll be telling me you don't kill decent, law-abiding citizens, that you're really doing me a favour, removing scum for other scum.' The blood in McCallen's face drained to roughly a millimetre below the surface of her creamy-white skin. Her features assumed a constrained expression. She was angry. Days ago I might have agreed with her analysis. Self-awareness had never been my strongest suit. I wasn't finished. 'I don't want to do it any more.'

Her bloodless lips didn't scowl in disdain. They were more a firm, straight, unyielding line. 'You expect me to believe you?'

'I expect nothing.'

'What are you going to do, join Amnesty?' In the absence of a reply, she said, 'Humour me, why would someone like you pack in killing for a living?'

'Because the stakes are too high.' I wasn't going to bear what passed for a soul to a stranger. By saving the boy, I'd set off a train of events that, admittedly had made me vulnerable, but all that really mattered to me was averting another vision of hell: the sight of bodies bleeding and nervous systems collapsing. For

111

the first time in my life my fate was intertwined with the lives of others.

She elevated an eyebrow. 'What about the guy in the square?'

'That was different.'

'Always is,' she said, contemptuous.

'Look, I need to find Wilding's murderer as much as you.'

'That I very much doubt.'

'No, you're wrong.'

'Spare me,' she said, flexing the fingers on her right hand in a supremely dismissive gesture. 'Men like you can't trip a switch and become someone else. You're nothing more than a cold-blooded contract killer. You chose to be that person and that's all you'll ever be.'

I leant across the table so sharply she jumped. 'Talk to me as though I'm dirt if you want to. I'm not looking for respect. But maybe it takes a killer to catch a killer.' And perhaps you should play nice, I was tempted to say but didn't.

Fortunately the soup arrived. We ate. She was so vexed, some of it splattered on the tablecloth. I'd rattled her and now she viewed me with open loathing. It wasn't the start I'd hoped for. As far as I was concerned questions remained that required answers. I might have been out of options but I wasn't out of ideas.

'Do you believe Wilding was innocent?' I floated this as though the thought inconceivable.

She lifted her eyes to mine. 'Is this a pathetic attempt to justify your actions? Next you'll be assuring me all the people you've slotted, clipped, rubbed out, murdered, however best describes it, had blood on their hands.'

This too I would have agreed with once upon a time. Now I realised that I'd clung to that belief because it made what I did for money easier to live with. Truth was Dr Wilding's death had made me more contained, less certain, confused. I shook my head. 'I'm trying to get to the truth.'

'The truth is that she was an innocent woman doing her job and I don't need to defend her to a bastard like you.'

'Look, Inger,' I said, trying to put our relationship, for want of a better description, on a more personal footing. Whether it was her real name or not was debatable, the fact she answered to it all that counted. 'I hear what you say, but you have to face the possibility that Wilding was trying to trade. She wouldn't be the first scientist or the last.'

She looked at me as if I were the most despicable individual on the planet. I changed tack.

'Do you think it's possible that she was the victim of a revenge attack?'

'I don't follow.'

'Could her death be connected to her work in Russia?'

She frowned surprise. She sneered 'no way'. 'Is your knowledge based on *sheer bravado*?' she said, 'or did you make this discovery tripping through Google?'

I gave her the type of look that would reduce most to a snivelling wreck. McCallen remained impervious. 'It was on the news,' I said, although I thought this unlikely.

'Wilding worked in an extremely junior capacity as part of a weapons inspection team on one occasion, and it was decades ago.'

'No link then,' I said, calmly stating the obvious.

She didn't comment. Had she been a school examiner, I'd have received an 'ungraded.' I tried again. 'The briefcase you stole.'

'I wondered when you'd get round to that.' The accompanying smile was nasty and triumphant.

'The picture you found on my camera, who was the guy?' I said.

'Vasily Felshtinsky.'

I was surprised by her candour. 'And?'

'Works for the Russian defence ministry's research and testing institute.'

'And unofficially?'

She shrugged, looked right through me. Play hardball then, I thought. 'FSB? They're not exactly shy at dropping the odd toxic cocktail when the need arises. Perhaps you should talk to him.' I now understood her reason for meeting up with the cute Russian in the party dress.

'How did your paths cross?' she said, failing to answer my question. The flinty glint was back in her eye. I saw how this was supposed to work. McCallen gave me a useless thread of information. In return, I spilt my guts. I looked at her straight. I wasn't about to drop Yakovlevich in the dirt yet, not until I had a better handle on how he fitted into the great scheme of things. Yuri, on the other hand, I didn't give a shit about. I said, 'There's this guy, Yuri, an enforcer. Works freelance. Brains not required. It's rumoured he played a minor role in the theft of fissionable materials, leaning on officials, usual stuff. Hangs out with all sorts of guys,' I said, getting creative.

At this she sharpened, 'Felshtinsky?'

'I guess,' I lied. 'Perhaps Yuri thought he might be shopping for more profitable commodities.'

'Why would he do that?"

I gave another shrug.

'What sort of commodities?'

I looked her straight in the eye. 'Biological weapons.'

Something unreadable flitted behind her eyes. 'What's this got to do with Wilding?'

Grain in my tone, I said, 'The portable hard drive stolen from Wilding contained high-grade information.'

She leant toward me, her voice low. 'Who said the information was high-grade?'

'You did.' I didn't spell it out. I didn't refer to her conversation in the park and her reference to Wilding having access to pathogens with a variety of uses.

'No, I didn't.'

'All right, not in so many words, but you inferred it.'

'How?' she frowned.

'*Where*? would be a more appropriate question.'

She frowned some more, the bridge of her nose creasing. The distant look in her eyes told me that she was running events through her head, working out who said what and when and where, and considering how I was the recipient of such information and wondering about my contacts.

Unprepared to reveal my lip-reading skills, I said, 'The fact is I *know* that Wilding was involved in research on biological weapons, admittedly in a defensive capacity, so let's stop pretending otherwise.' I did not mention the ethnic-specific angle. It would have revealed too much.

McCallen rested her spoon on the plate beneath the bowl. 'You can't know,' she said, dismissive.

I put on my warmest, most winsome smile for her. She met my eye, unsmiling.

'Where do we find Yuri?'

I gave a huge *don't know* shrug. 'He's probably back in Moscow, his normal place of operation.' I continued breezily, 'Now we're all clear on that, why would Wilding, a good woman according to you, become a very bad woman?'

McCallen retrieved the spoon and finished up the dregs. She didn't offer a protest. She didn't utter one single word. This was turning into a monologue.

'Perhaps she was being blackmailed,' I said wide-eyed.

'Right up your street, I'd have thought.' She clearly believed that I was hazarding a lucky guess because the slow-blink returned followed by silence. The soup bowls were removed. Waiting for the main course to arrive, which with typical Spanish speed and efficiency they did within moments, I poured more water and tried again.

'Cards on table,' I began, 'Whatever was stolen has fallen into the hands of organised crime.'

'You can't know that.' This was the first time I got a straight-forward, co-operative response.

'Stop telling me I can't know things. You know very well I can, which is why we're sitting here having this conversation.' Why else, for goodness' sake?

She fixed me with a sullen and begrudging look, hating me on sight yet recognising I couldn't be ignored. 'All right, how do you know?'

'Every security service in Christendom, and beyond, is looking for it. You guys talk. I know you do,' I said with more fervour than intended. 'It's in everybody's interests to exchange informa-tion, and you are exchanging like crazy, but you're all coming up empty. Someone, somewhere would have talked, probably along the lines of some flaky scientist prepared to sell his expertise to a rogue state, and now one of its agents has the contents of the safe. I don't know. You can write the strap lines better than me. Apparently my poxy theory that Wilding was knocked off by the Russians isn't credible.' I waited a beat to see if she'd interject. She didn't.

'My guess is that you are meeting a wall of silence, that there's an information black hole. It explains why you're all over me like a rash. I, piece of trash that I am, apparently hold the key to the kingdom.'

She continued to hold my gaze, her lips very slightly parted, which I didn't think was intentional. Forget the essay, I was building up to writing a thesis. 'Like I said, the most pressing question for spooks is why? You know that people like me work principally for organised crime.'

'Really? I thought you worked for anyone prepared to pay.' She glanced away.

I was obviously not getting her attention. 'I have an IPad list of clients.' I'd like to say she was intrigued. Instead, she looked vexed. 'All right,' I forced a laugh, aiming to re-engage with her. 'I don't really have a list. It's all inside my head.' She looked me in the eye again, scowling in irritation. The way she saw it, she was being forced to deal with Mephistopheles. I soldiered on, 'Inger,' I said, because I needed to impress upon her one last point. 'The people I deal with, believe it or not, have standards. Everything has a value. Drugs, trafficking women, arms, oil, blood diamonds, these are their stock in trade. As you know, it's a different world out there. Gangs will now lift nuclear material from crumbling nuclear facilities in Russia. You know more about this than me. If there's a market for bio-weapons, you can bet someone with an eye to the main chance will be willing to deal, but I don't personally know anyone from my circle of feral rich who would. Added to this, I've heard nothing on the grapevine. It's as if there's been a news blackout.' In itself extremely odd, I had to admit.

She treated me to a frozen smile. 'You told me you didn't know the name of the client for the Wilding job.'

'True.'

'In which case you can't be sure whether or not anyone *from your circle of feral rich*,' she said with heavy irony, 'has the kind of barbaric intentions we're discussing now.'

And she was right. Ethics never my strong point, I didn't remind her that barbarism was a two-way street. Whoever wanted to get their hands on the material was indisputably nuts, yet it could also be argued that the British government had sanctioned an abominable form of research. Knowing what I know of human nature, I couldn't rule out the possibility that there were darker motives in play.

'Which is why I'm keen to locate whoever it is,' I said, ice in my voice. If only to make sure the bastard never issued another contract again.

'How does it feel?' she said, tight-faced.

'How does what feel?'

'To know you were paid to kill for such a purpose?' She'd got me. And she was right. It didn't feel good. It felt as if I were damned. Strange, only days ago I'd have felt indifference. 'Ignorance is no defence,' she added, her top lip curling. She was definitely correct on that score, but not for the reasons she believed. Ignorance had got me into this mess.

She sat back, studied me in that all-seeing, all-knowing style of hers. I noticed her breasts swell a little beneath her sweater. Then her phone went off. She withdrew it from her jacket and pressed the 'receive' key. I thought she'd at least walk away to take the call. She didn't. Her eyes remained on mine. I had the feeling that this was for my benefit, as though permissions were to be granted. Either that, or I was being set up. No doubt in my mind, I was deemed expendable.

'Yes…I have him here…I don't believe that's necessary…Dead end, I'm afraid…Yes, I understand… Do we know who he is? … I see… Yes, I'm sure that would work.' She looked at her watch. 'Can do, thanks.' She closed the phone and pushed her plate away untouched. I did the same. I'd lost my appetite. Then she did that weird thing that women do when they're struggling with saying the unsayable: she traced her index finger over the pattern of the tablecloth. I sipped some mineral water and waited.

'Right,' she said, letting her hand fall. Her eyes locked onto mine like a magnet to cold steel. 'I'm going to take you at your word. Where are you staying?' There had to be a catch, but I was curious. I told her. 'Get the bill,' she said, 'You're coming with me.'

CHAPTER FOURTEEN

We returned to the hotel without delay. Once inside the room McCallen checked for electronic listening devices. She was methodical, starting over by the balcony and working her way back to the door and bathroom. She paid special attention to the telephone on the bedside table, the lamp near the window and the cushions on the chair. Had there been carpets, she would have lifted them. While she carried out the sweep I retrieved the contents from the safe.

Finally satisfied, she told me to sit down so I sat. A bit of my brain registered that I was being manipulated. Takes one to know one.

'When were you last in the States?'

'Why?'

She flickered one of her most deadly smiles. 'You don't seem to understand. I ask. You answer. Ever been to Connecticut?'

'Never.'

'Massachusetts?'

'Once, but it was a long time ago.'

'How long?'

'Nine years.'

'Virginia?'

'What is this, a geographical version of *I Spy*?'

'Answer the damned question.'

'Passed through twice, 2003 and 2007, both times en route to Washington D.C.'

Judging by the look on her face, I wasn't coming up with the right answers. I remembered Reuben's remark. Seemed distinctly possible that McCallen also had me down for carrying out murders that had nothing to do with me. 'What were you doing in these places?' she said.

'Sightseeing.'

She stared through me like I was clear glass.

'I'm guessing this is relevant,' I said speculatively. I wanted to quiz her about ethnic-specific toxins. I wanted to pick her brains on the subject of Dr Ford, but it would display unhealthy interest.

'At the risk of repeating myself,' she said sternly, 'when were you last in the States?'

'Sixteen months ago.'

'Where?'

'New York.' This was a lie. I was actually in Boston.

'Another job?'

'Yes.'

'Who was the target?'

'For me to know and for you to find out.'

She ground her jaw and spoke through gritted teeth. 'Who employed you? Or don't you know,' she added, her voice scathing.

'In common with journalists, I never reveal a source.'

Cornering the market in cold smiles, she issued another spectacularly icy variety. 'You aren't really helping your cause.'

'Neither are you.' Just wasting time, mine mostly. Locked in conversation about my past prevented me from finding the data. The thought of what might happen if I failed stabbed me in the chest. 'Instead of dancing around the edges, why don't you give me dates and names of victims? You never know I might be able to help.' I was ruthlessly fishing and she knew it.

She glanced away, tapped her nimble fingers on the table, buying herself thinking time. I expect she was gauging how much to divulge. Depended upon what the powers that be had sanctioned. She looked back, dropped her voice several decibels even though it was just the two of us in the room. 'In the past three years a number of individuals from the scientific community have died in suspicious circumstances. Not all were scientists; some were software analysts working in the biochemical industry and allied fields.'

Nicely put. In reality, code for something nasty. I remembered the toxins in the fridge. I remembered the dying Koreans. 'In the States?'

She nodded.

It chimed with her opening gambit and the list of locations. Harvard in Massachusetts, Yale in Connecticut, the Smithsonian in Virginia; all had prestigious scientific communities, though the Smithsonian's Biological Institute veered more towards conservation and research into the survival and recovery of endangered species. Seemed apt in the circumstances.

'You still reckon there's no connection between Wilding's murder and foreign security services?' I was pushing a point, but I needed to be sure.

'No evidence,' she said smartly. 'Deaths ranged from accidental falls from suspension bridges,' she continued, 'messy suicides with no prior history of mental disorder or any of the typical stressors commonly found in those who want to take their own lives, and muggings involving extreme violence.'

'Muggings?' I said with distaste.

'A loose description,' she conceded. 'Consequences for victims in every case were fatal.'

'Any record of wallets or briefcases being stolen?'

'None,' she said.

'Amateur and clumsy,' I said conclusively. 'What you're describing is an abject lesson in how *not* to remove people. No class. No subtlety. No anonymity.'

'Not your thing?' She said, impaling me with a cold look.

'And interesting for that reason alone.' I'd always preferred the staged suicide, my speciality the sex game that went tragically wrong. I tried to put it out of my mind. I'd have plenty of time for reflection later – if there were a later. 'The victims,' I said, 'Were they linked in any other way?'

'No,' she said, her eyes stony. 'Biotechnology the only connection.'

'Get rid of the scientists, you get rid of the science.'

'Not that simple.'

'No, but it serves as a hell of a warning for anyone thinking of specialising in that particular arena.'

'You think that's the purpose?'

This was going better than I could have hoped. She was actually displaying an interest in my opinion. Or rather pretending an interest. No point in getting too carried away. 'Could be,' I said. 'If people can get radical about nuclear power, and vivisection, think how exercised they'd get about this stuff?' Her arch look made me realise that I'd given too much away. If I were McCallen I'd be wondering how come this low-level button-man seems so on the ball. Does he have a degree in clairvoyance? I went for a verbal diversion. 'On the other hand, it could as easily be a method for removing the competition. Crime bosses use it all the time. Get rid of the rivals to getter a bigger and better share of the market.'

She studied my face as though trying to fathom me out. I smiled. She didn't return the gesture. 'What exactly do you know about biological weapons?' she said, pointedly.

'They're illegal and they kill.'

She gave me another arch look. 'Heard of ethnic-specific weapons?'

I gave a slow nod. Might as well own up. 'The logical next step,' I said.

'To what?' Her expression assumed the cutting efficiency of a freshly sharpened Samurai sword.

'To wiping out enemy armies.' I said this with a big shrug as if everyone were familiar with the concept. 'Not nice, but a future reality.'

'We aren't necessarily talking for military purposes,' she said, eyes cool and betraying zero emotion.

I lifted an eyebrow. I hoped she couldn't hear the pounding in my brain. Against the military bad enough, but the consequences for a civilian population were cataclysmic. 'Anybody heard of the Geneva Protocol?'

'Prohibits use of biological weapons but not production.'

'Jesus Christ, if they exist they can be used. Ethnic-specific bio-weapons elevates them to a deadly sub-category all their own. For Chrissakes, when...' I stopped. I'd said too much. Welcome to the murky world of espionage.

She met my eye. I'd like to describe it as a moment of trust between us. In reality, she'd smoked me out and she knew it. What she said next blew me away. 'There's a Research Institute in North Korea, south of Pyongyang, called Institute 398. We believe scientists have developed a weapon to eradicate the white population.'

I recalled the monstrous film footage and my conversation with Reuben. I remembered the white guy crouched in the corner. I guess I'd always hoped that my mongrel race status conferred some kind of protection. I was wrong. 'Developed? Surely, impossible to pull off in engineering terms.'

She inclined her head, looked at me in a way I've seen women look at me before, as if she couldn't quite believe that the brain inside the thickened skull was fully functioning. 'No longer impossible, I'm afraid.'

I wondered if I'd misheard. I opened my mouth to ask her to

repeat what she'd said, but she carried on talking. 'The key is to isolate the critical differences in the human genetic code. The differences may be infinitesimal. We're talking less than one per cent. Once identified, pathogens can be developed to target individuals based on racial characteristics. Even eye colour can prove the distinguishing feature.'

'And the Korean weapon is aimed at white Caucasians?' I needed to get this absolutely clear in my head.

She nodded twice. It didn't take me long to work out the political implications. North Korea had a rare ally: China. China was a rising super-power. If China had military ambitions against the West, it possessed the capability to wheel out the big daddy of weapons.

'Wilding was working on an anti sera,' McCallen said.

Relief, warm and clear, washed over me. Wilding had been a force for good. I'd seriously misjudged her, my cross to bear. More crucial, the existence of anti sera meant there was hope. 'Government sanctioned?'

'Of course,' she said, a little too sharply.

'Was this all she was working on?' Old habits died hard. In my dystopian world you had bad guys and worse bad guys and rules were broken all the time.

'You have to remember,' McCallen continued, robustly evading my question. 'Wilding was working on strategic defensive measures.'

By whatever means necessary, according to Reuben. I didn't say this. McCallen looked pretty fired up, usually a sign of someone on the run. Or perhaps she was just plain passionate, which I admit excited me.

'To produce an anti sera, she first needed to create the toxin,' McCallen said with a dark look that drew me up short.

'Created? You mean she succeeded?'

'She did.'

I tried not to swallow. If this was what I was ordered to steal then I was in deep shit. I hadn't yet stopped to think why McCallen was confiding in me. I was too involved in the moment. I scratched my head. 'I was only ever told to remove a hard drive. I don't even know what a toxin would look like.' I presumed it would resemble something out of a chemistry set.

McCallen gave a wintry laugh. 'The world has taken a few turns. We're not talking about theft of the actual toxin.'

Thank Christ for that. 'Then what are we talking about exactly?'

'A hard drive containing data for a genetic blueprint.'

'Is this supposed to reassure me?'

She shook her head firmly. 'Afraid not. Whoever has the blueprint has acquired the capability to…'

'Create a toxin and inflict unspeakable evil.'

'Yes,' she said, giving me a level stare.

I realised that somewhere round the globe a scientist was on standby waiting for the blueprint so that he could translate the formula and rush it into production. The only loose comparison I could make was with the drugs trade. Most of my contacts in the sphere of banned recreational substances were doctors who'd been struck off and students who'd either failed their chemistry degrees or had taken too keen an interest in the compounds they studied. What McCallen was talking about scared me senseless. It was one thing to have suspicions, quite another to have those suspicions confirmed.

'You've talked to Wilding's colleagues?' I said.

'Extensively.'

'And?'

'Nothing. Wilding, by all accounts, kept an extremely low profile. A dedicated professional, she lived for her work.'

'What about her dark side?'

McCallen looked vacant.

'Everyone has a dark side.' I wondered about McCallen's. I had her down for a deeply competitive individual. Amazing what people will do to further their ambitions. 'Even you,' I murmured.

'Let's leave me out of it,' she snapped. 'Wilding might not have had any obvious weaknesses per se but there were other issues.'

Sounded like bureaucratic-speak to me. I raised an eyebrow.

'She had one vulnerability, her son.'

I flinched. The weakness I'd missed. Strange to say, he was my weakness, too. Or maybe he was my saviour. I spoke in a vain effort to keep the shadows at bay. 'She was being pressured?'

'Yes.'

At last, she was admitting it. 'By whom?'

'Your close friend.'

'I don't have close friends.'

'Associate then.'

'I'll go with that.'

'The man bundled into the back of the car, the man hanging from the ceiling. The man you call Wes.'

'He threatened Wilding's son?' I said taken aback.

'Yes.'

This wasn't Wes's style at all. 'No,' I shook my head. 'Wes wasn't that type of guy.'

McCallen was insistent. 'There were a couple of nasty incidents, both verified by Jake Wilding himself.'

Jake, so that was his name. 'What sort of incidents?'

'Unknown assailants shoving the lad into the boot of a car with a bag over his head and driving him around for a couple of hours.'

'And Wes actually made threats?'

McCallen nodded.

I thought this unaccountably careless of him. Why the hell would he have taken such risks? Come to think of it, why would he have made my job more dangerous? I thought about the impact on Wilding and the boy. No wonder she was on anti-depressants. She'd allowed herself to be compromised. 'Are you saying that, in return for the safety of her son, Wilding was being forced to give up the blueprint?'

'Why look so surprised?' McCallen scoffed.

'Because this is all news to me,' I snapped, mainly because it shouldn't have been. Had I carried out a more forensic background check, I would have discovered this.

The cool expression in McCallen's eye told me I wasn't believed. There was too much circumstantial evidence implicating me. 'Are you sure she wasn't paid?' I said, grasping at thin material and watching it tear.

'Nothing in her finances confirms that's the case. Tell me about Wes.'

'You've already asked and I've already told you. Way outside his comfort zone.'

'Where's he from?'

'Hell, I don't know. I think he hailed from the East Coast.' I soon as the words left my mouth I realised their possible impact. McCallen had asked whether I'd ever been to Connecticut or Massachusetts, both on the East Coast – as was Boston. She didn't respond. Either she was super smart or she didn't make the connection. My money was on super smart.

'Your gang had no intention of honouring their side of the bargain,' she said, giving me a level look. 'Once they got Wilding to do what they wanted they wheeled in a killer: *you*.'

This time I held her gaze in a vice-like grip. In return, hers was so penetrating I felt swept away. 'I was never part of a gang. It wasn't how I operated. I was never ordered to kill the lad. I didn't even know of his existence.' I thought again about Wilding's son, the boy I'd spared. If he were a cat he'd be two lives down and seven to go. I scratched my head, miserably trying to find something to cling on to. 'How's Jake doing?'

She flexed her shoulders. The stern look returned. 'Bored, emotional, snarling at everyone.'

I struggled to prevent a sleeping memory from waking up.

'Setting aside the horrible situation he now finds himself in,' McCallen continued grimly, 'he's not doing too badly.'

I cleared my throat to hide my growing sense of déjà vu. To this day, I could still picture the vivid scene of carnage that had greeted my adolescent eyes when I found my mother. Bewilderment and devastation didn't really cover it.

'I get the feeling that underneath his understandable grief, he's quite a spirited young man. It might actually save him.' She crossed her arms, the boy dismissed with the same ease with which she dismissed my opinions. Not a woman with a natural maternal instinct.

Watching my face like a raptor views road-kill, she said, 'You honestly knew nothing about the threats?'

'Why would I? Outside my area of expertise.' Not keen to dwell on it, I fired a question of my own. 'What do you know about Wilding's history with the opposite sex?'

'Why?' she said, suspicious.

'Because it's a good question.'

She shrugged. 'No suggestion of any serious relationships, or any relationships at all.'

Which was exactly my take. 'So she lived like a nun?'

McCallen flashed a cool smile. 'She got her kicks out of her work.'

'What about the father of her child?'

'No mention of him on Jake's birth certificate. No record of his existence. It's not that unusual,' she said as if to ward off any disparaging comment I might make.

I conceded the point. 'I realise her son was being threatened and if, as you say, Wilding was dedicated to her work, would she so easily have risked the blueprint falling into the wrong hands? Why didn't she go to the cops? I mean how could she possibly have lived with herself?'

A shadow appeared to pass behind McCallen's eyes. 'Are you going all moral on me? The fact is she didn't go to the police. What has to be established is where it is now.' She leant towards me as though sharing a confidence. 'We fear the data will fall into the hands of terrorists or possibly a rogue state.'

As Reuben had predicted. 'I've never dealt with terrorists.'

'How do you know?'

'Because I do my homework.' As soon as the words left my mouth she had the drop on me.

'Doesn't look like you bothered too much this time.'

I recoiled from her. She flicked a smile like a chess-player taking an opponent's queen. 'The data on its own is useless, but traded with the right people and converted would prove devastating. Bio-weapons with an ethnic variant remain attractive because they give the terrorist the ability to make a huge racial point and inflict massive casualties over a large area.'

I knew this only too well. The memory of the film was like a shard of glass lodged in my brain. Against every effort to resist, I felt myself mentally transported back to the basement room, to the glass dome, to the scientists with their damned clipboards, to the men and the women and the kids and the gore. 'The psychological trauma on an unsuspecting population would also be enormous,' I murmured.

'So you know something about it,' she said with another icy, penetrating stare.

'Something,' I said, with a return stare of my own. 'I follow the news, that's all,' I added lamely.

'What we're discussing doesn't feature in the news.'

She kept her eyes on me for longer than felt comfortable. I tried to break the link in her thought process. 'How do you know it will work?'

She met my eye. 'Both toxin and anti-sera are effective in laboratory conditions.'

Jesus. I'd always imagined my own demise as being fairly instant. You live by the sword, you die by it. I did not relish the thought of a slow, lingering biologically induced death. 'Once this bloody stuff is created what's the method of delivery?'

'Drop it into the water supply, or any air conditioning system should do it.'

'So its specific in delivery, specific by nature.' Unlike a virus, which would be random. Thank Christ for small mercies. 'Aren't you scared?' I was amazed by her sang-froid.

'I'm paid not to be.'

'There are some fairly crazy people out there.'

'Present company excepted,' she said without a flicker of humour.

I thought for a moment, tried to digest the information. 'Surely there's a time lapse between the theft of the formulae and going into full-scale production?'

'In a perfect world, yes.'

No such thing as perfect, black and white, right and wrong. 'Is this time sensitive?'

'Do you want to take the risk? Clock's on countdown.'

'What's the official line?'

'On you?'

'I can guess on me,' I said with cool. 'I meant with regard to the current position of the British government. I presume cabinet ministers are in the know.'

'Two, and the P.M.'

'And the British population stay in the dark. I guess experimentation with this kind of stuff wouldn't reflect well,' I said with cynicism.

'This isn't about public relations and damage limitation,' she said sharply. 'Fuck the politics, think of the mass panic it would create if this leaked out.'

Civil unrest, racist attacks, World War Three. I rubbed my jaw, awed by the prospect. One question remained. It was like the elephant in the room. Why was she telling me this? 'Aren't you in breach of Official Secrets?'

She flicked a slow, seductive smile. That's what the call was about, I realised. She'd got permission to deal: my co-operation in return for freedom. Except the freedom ended as soon as the respective genies were put back into their bottles. Frankly, after everything I'd done, I'd never be free. The prison was of my own creation.

'You want to recruit me?'

'Hardly,' her lip curled.

'What then?'

'You will help us unconditionally,' she said, emphatic.

'Do I get protection from other interested parties?'

'No.'

I waited a beat. There was a low noise, like the sound of distant thunder, probably a train rumbling through a nearby station. I wished I were on it. 'So I have access to people you don't, and you're party to information I don't have?' Plus massive technical resources, I should have said.

'This isn't a deal,' she flashed with irritation.

'Then what is it?'

'A lifeline.'

I expressed my contempt. 'What if I don't want one?'

'You have two choices...'

'Two? That's generous.'

'Either we have you removed, or we let one of your employers think you sold them out...'

'And let them do the removing.'

'You're getting the idea,' she smiled without warmth.

'Seems like a fairly temporary arrangement to me.'

She didn't disabuse me of the notion. To reinforce how things stood she offered a 'take it or leave it' shrug. I glanced away, tapped my index finger on the table. 'What exactly do you want me to do?'

'Use your contacts.'

Something I'd been doing for the past couple of days and got nowhere. She and her bosses clearly thought I was better connected than I actually was. Fine by me. I'd give them what they thought they wanted and in return I'd find out what they knew. A little like inviting the target to look the other way in

131

order to kill them. I believed the French executioner responsible for detaching Anne Boleyn's head from her shoulders had employed a similar method.

I smiled. 'When do we start?'

CHAPTER FIFTEEN

What a man says and does are often two different things. McCallen thought she'd painted me into a corner. She believed she could use me. I intended to give her every reason to think she'd made the right call.

My pact with the she-devil made, I had a couple more questions of my own. I asked whether or not the identity of the man I'd shot had yet been established.

'No, but the Spanish will co-operate with us on it.'

'What did you do, threaten to shut down their tourist industry?'

She flashed a smile. Believing she was holding the puppet strings, she was starting to warm to me. I pushed my luck. 'I'd be more use to you if you let me go.'

She ignored me, looked at her watch and asked to see my passport. I handed it over. She glanced at the name, regarded my face, hitched a disbelieving eyebrow and said we were returning to London. This very much suited my purposes. No matter what McCallen said, I hadn't yet fully ruled out the Russians and their dodgy link to Yakovlevich. It came back to motive. Curious to know what she had in mind, I said, 'To do what?'

'To talk and establish the facts in a more appropriate environment.'

Code for taking me to a soundproofed basement and beating the crap out of me. 'Who to?'

'Others.'

'Do these 'others' have a name?' I imagined burly men with sadistic tastes. Her responding smile was more smug than enigmatic.

I left it at that. I didn't ask how, as Europe's most wanted, I was supposed to be smuggled through Customs and put on a flight to the U.K. I supposed it fell under the umbrella of Spanish co-operation.

McCallen wiped my gun clean of prints and ditched it in the safe, ordered a cab and we set off for the airport ten minutes later. I'd like to say that she trusted me. She wasn't even acquiescent. I was on the back foot and she knew it. I was already plotting my escape.

Check-in went smoothly, not even a raised eyebrow, and we finally boarded an Easyjet Flight WW1992 at twenty-five minutes past nine that evening. I sat in 07E near the window, McCallen next to me. I wasn't in the mood for conversation. As I glanced around the packed cabin, I considered how many empty seats there'd be if eighty per cent of the occupants were simply not there any more, McCallen and me included. I thought about deserted cities, decimated towns, rural wastelands. Depressed, I slept. After years in the killing game, I no longer had a body clock. I was like the old Martini ad: any time, any place, anywhere. We arrived two hours and five minutes later, half past ten British time.

We passed through Border Control after a clipped, businesslike exchange, McCallen using her considerable authority in a way that no amount of money could buy. I was impressed. I knew the price of every border guard, but Brits at this elevated level were impossible to bribe. I'm not sure what accounted for this streak of honesty. I suspected it was connected to some weird atavistic *Rule Britannia* gene.

A black Lexus was waiting. McCallen pushed me inside and sat beside me and behind the driver who flicked the light on and turned round. He studied me without expression for a second or two, then as if he'd lost interest flicked McCallen a warm smile. I recognised him as the man I'd seen her with at Wilding's house. Oddly, in the reduced light, I thought he looked a little like me. He had the same basic bone-structure. I wondered if the admiring gleam in his eye was mine too.

'Everything all right?' Mr Doppelganger said.

'Fine,' McCallen replied. 'Let's go.'

We turned out of the airport and followed the main route for Central London along the Great South West Road and finally left onto Great West Road. Nobody spoke. I had no idea where they were taking me. I didn't think it was Thames House, MI5 Headquarters. The men and women in grey wouldn't want to sully their carpets with someone like me. Doppelganger indicated to pull over into the right hand lane as we crossed the Hammersmith flyover and onto Talgarth Road. Up until this moment traffic had been fluid, moving reasonably quickly, but there seemed to be a snarl-up ahead so that we slowed to snail's pace. McCallen leant forward in her seat, frustrated by the lack of motion.

'What's up, Blake?'

'Don't know. Could be an accident. There's a car up ahead with its hazards flashing.'

McCallen sat back with a thump, dejected. I got the impression that she was not the most patient individual. She and I were poles apart in this respect.

I gazed out of the window, watching the flare of lights from vehicles, lampposts and neighbouring houses. I'd noticed the steep drop in temperature as soon as we'd left the airport. Already, a thin sheet of frost coated roofs and pavements. Now would be the perfect time to slip into the night and disappear into the urban sprawl.

'Don't even think about it,' McCallen said, reading my thoughts, warning in her voice.

'Hadn't crossed my mind,' I lied, my attention caught by the sight of a couple of figures wearing hoodies, hands plunged deep into pockets. I had them down for street robbers, teenagers most probably. With so much stationary prey on offer, pickings were rich. It took only a little nerve to wrench open a car door and lift out the latest phone, camera, purse or laptop.

I turned back to McCallen, wondered if she'd seen them, but she looked straight ahead, in shutdown mode. I changed position, caught a whiff of chewing gum coming from the front. A deep bass beat thudded out from the vehicle behind in striking contrast to the silence ticking inside the Lexus. I stared back out of the window to escape the rising temperature of tension. Without warning, my mouth dried, my ears closed to sound. Figures in silhouette approaching, not teenagers, older…

I was wrong. They weren't street robbers. They'd come to kill me.

A blam-blam sound battered my ears as the tyres were taken out. Next the rear window shattered. The door-locks burst open and I threw myself out and onto the road, dragging McCallen with me. Shots from a semi-automatic whistled over our heads and I hauled her round to the front of the vehicle. Metal offered zilch protection against gunfire and at any moment I expected shots to pierce the metal casing and kill the pair of us.

Screams and shouts catapulted into the night sky, dark and cold, the only illumination the mottled glare of street and car lights.

Hunkered down, I squinted, making out two shadowy figures grappling in the gutter, Blake locked in combat with one of the gunmen. Pushing up from my feet and propelling my body forwards, I rushed them, crashing both men to the ground, the pistol spinning out of the attacker's hand. At the same time McCallen threw herself at his friend, clinging to him to deflect his line of fire. Scooping up the gun, I twisted, squeezed the trigger, firing two shots into his head, missing McCallen by millimetres then turned back to the man still down and drilled a hole in his face. Other drivers were on their mobiles, screaming for emergency services. Around me chaos: horns blaring, people shouting, women shrieking then the staccato clatter of more gunfire as two men hurled themselves out of a Peugeot four vehicles behind. For a split second, I thought that they were backup for Blake and McCallen. Their demeanour and body language persuaded me otherwise. These were part of the same attack team whose primary members were exsanguinating in the road.

Blake was now back on his feet and made a grab at my gun. I chopped him hard, the side of my left hand connecting with his throat. He collapsed like a building under demolition. Simultaneously, I fired at the secondary team, dropping them both. As I turned to disappear a hand clamped on my arm. It belonged to McCallen. I raised my weapon and pressed the muzzle against her temple.

'Don't make me,' I growled, meeting her steely gaze.

She hesitated, breathless, tried to swallow then let her hand drop. The sound of sirens brought me out of the zone and back to my senses and without looking back I raced down the road, my own demons in pursuit, and into the cold black night.

CHAPTER SIXTEEN

Far enough away from the core of mayhem, I slipped the pistol beneath my jacket, into the rear of my waistband and against the small of my back, and forced myself to slow my pace to a moderate walk. Immediately I had a flashback of the night's events, the shocked expression on McCallen's face, the fear that was hers, and the loathing that was mine. Would I have pulled the trigger? Would I have watched as her life-blood flowed into the gutter? Conflicted, I persuaded myself that I would never have done such a thing, not even with her standing in the way of my freedom and my quest to find the data. But how could I be sure?

There are many locations in which to hide in a city. When a place is in lockdown it's assumed that it's impossible for an assassin to evade detection. Not the case, not even in broad daylight. Add dozens of distressed witnesses, darkness and dead men, and the odds were stacked in my favour.

An affinity with graveyards and burial grounds, I quickly lost myself in the maze of streets that connect the deathly triangle of Hammersmith, Fulham and Brompton Cemeteries, my goal to weave a way towards one of the no star hotels near Earls' Court. Near the scene of crime, area packed with heat and crawling with police, I calculated that it was the best place to go to ground.

My room for the night was a dirty box with a bed inside and bathroom facilities down the corridor. I took out the gun, a Jericho 941, Israeli-manufactured and commonly known as a Baby Desert Eagle. I flicked the catch to remove the magazine then, with brute force, pulled back the slide and ejected the round in the chamber. The ammunition was 9mm black talon, not in regular use. A version of the hollow-point, the tip had a distinctive black coating and sharp barb-like tip. These bullets made big holes in human tissue, expanded on impact and killed instantly. Western police departments had banned them because, aside from scything through the human body with the same force as a miniature chainsaw, they penetrated Kevlar. To be more specific, only certain individuals would be up for using this type of ruthless accessory. Shaken by the implications, I reloaded the weapon and took out temporary membership of their club.

The television worked, which was a pleasant surprise. Even more of a surprise, the picture was in colour, the TV digital. For the price, I thought it might be black and white, analogue and useless. I turned the sound down low and switched to 'News 24'. Amateur footage, possibly from a mobile phone, captured the moment when the secondary backup team joined the party and unleashed a volley of bullets. The next frame jerked back to me, my face in shadow, striking the MI5 man then opening fire and dropping both attackers. It was both graphic and damning. Next up, a bright-eyed reporter, microphone in hand, talking to camera. I watched hard, listened harder.

'Three dead, one gunman critically injured, the police aren't yet sure whether this was a targeted attack or whether the off-duty police officers were victims of random robbery. What remains incontrovertible, this was a vicious and violent assault carried out by a gang who displayed a callous disregard for the lives of innocent bystanders.

'The police are eager to trace the have-a-go hero who came

to the aid of the officers. Without the man's quick thinking, the two would most certainly be dead. If anyone...'

I sat down on the grubby bedspread and scratched my ear. *Have a go hero, off-duty police officers.* I particularly loved the street thugs scenario. I wondered how those who'd issued the directive would feel about that. I also wondered how the news media squared the circle vilifying me one minute and lionising me the next. Did they even realise that I was the same man?

I switched off the television, lay down, tucked my hands beneath my head and tried to pin down what had actually taken place and, more importantly, why.

I remained in no doubt that I was the target. The assassins were at pains to avoid my MI5 minders, McCallen and her driver, which struck me as odd. In a hit bodyguards are first to be eliminated, even if unarmed, in order to expose a clear line of fire to the intended victim. The deliberate spray and pray approach that I'd witnessed contradicted standard operating procedure. Thinking back, it seemed as if the team were trying to wrong-foot and scatter the MI5 officers to get them out of the way. Bottom line: they were not to be harmed. And it had cost them.

Other aspects of the operation were exactly what I'd expect. The first team had moved with speed, stealth and surprise, key elements for a successful assassination. Typically, as soon as they'd run into trouble, backup moved in but by then the tide had already turned against them. Crowds of frightened people made for unpredictable and volatile situations. Fail to get your man in the first minute, the sand starts to run through the timer. If you don't take control and dominate events within the next two, the sand runs out and you're basically fucked. And they had been. Even the best could make a mistake. And they were the best.

I flexed a foot to ward off a spasm of cramp in my calf.

The most effective killers in the business were not people like me. They were those from whom I'd learnt my craft, their skills passed down the generations and, for me, conveyed through one man. It's why, from the moment the secondary team arrived, I'd identified my unknown assailants as 'kidon' – the killing elite of the Israeli Secret Service. Contrary to how they were often portrayed, the Israelis cared greatly about collateral damage, hence the decision to spare Blake and McCallen at all costs. Why they wanted me dead at this particular juncture I wasn't certain. This was not their fight, as far as I could tell. Had they been involved in Wilding's death, I'd no doubt that her murder would have been a low-key affair: a car accident on a dark night with no potential witnesses. Again, it put me in mind of the assassin. He too had slipped up. Like me, he'd missed the boy.

I flexed my shoulders, trying to work the tension out of my muscles. I guessed the Israelis' desire to slot me could be for no other reason than they took the view that I was a dangerous loose cannon that should be eliminated. I scratched an ear. Try as I might to believe this, it didn't stack up. The attack was too daring, too fraught with risk. Hell, they could have killed passers-by. No, the arrival of Mossad on the scene revealed a line of enquiry I refused to countenance. Not because I was squeamish. Not because the stench of betrayal was more than I could stomach, but because I needed more evidence. Right now, I had other priorities. Israel's security service was not my immediate problem. In spite of the cover-up, they wouldn't risk another public relations disaster and ensuing embarrassment, let alone the serious political fallout. This didn't mean that I was off the hook. Mossad always got their man. They might wait years or decades. The moment of exit might be a car bomb, a sniper bullet, or an aerosol in my face containing a poisonous and lethal substance. I'd killed their own on a London street, admittedly in self-defence, and one day they'd come calling – but not tomorrow.

I slept fitfully in my killing clothes, woke early and, in the absence of hot water, stripped and took a tepid shower. Getting dressed again, I slipped out of the hotel as night became day and caught an early morning bus to Pentonville Road, Kings Cross. Uncomfortably aware of my 'wanted' status, I tried to behave as normally as possible. I didn't want some sharp-eyed member of the public identifying and shopping me.

The capital that morning seemed to stretch, shake off the excesses of the night and wake up bleary-eyed. I arrived at the lock up at twenty minutes past seven. At that time the alley was empty. No stray dogs, no foxes, no people.

Around my neck, I wore a gold chain on which hung a single key. I slipped off the chain, took the key and slid it into the padlock, letting myself in. Shutting the heavy door behind me, I breathed in the dark aroma of gun oil in the same way a lover inhales the skin of his beloved. For me, this was home. It contained landmarks that proved to me that my life was not a worthless waste ground.

I possessed no photographs of my former life, nothing that could unmask me. My only mementoes were a few sparse belongings. I had a Jim Croce album in vinyl that belonged to my mother, a scarf she often wore that still bore her perfume after all these years, a couple of paintings and books. On her birthday I buy flowers, freesias, her favourite. Anyone could be forgiven for thinking I had some weird Oedipal deal with her, that her death and the nature in which it came calling had kinked my mind. This wasn't so. It was about memory. It was about keeping someone alive in your mind when others wished or chose to forget.

I started up the generator, powered up the heat and light, and checked my most current phone and the one I used for Billy Squeeze. On it, one missed call, timed for eighteen minutes past four on the previous day. Most of my clients were hardworking individuals. Billy was no exception. I called him straight away.

'You called.' I never used names. Billy never used pleasantries.

'Meet me.' He cut the call.

I glanced at my watch, threw on a hoodie, took a tube to Belsize Park where Billy used a café there for 'briefings'. When I arrived he was tucking into a bacon and egg sandwich, a stack of newspapers in front of him. I sat down opposite and he pushed a selection towards me. They were full of the previous night's events, front page in the late editions. I picked the one with the most lurid headlines, the stuff written about me a pack of lies. I bore no resemblance, whatsoever, to the heroic individual portrayed in the newsprint, unlike the picture of me taken by someone with a mobile.

'You like living dangerously,' he said, wiping a trickle of grease from his chin. Not the type to inhabit a room with the power of his personality, he gave an impression of benign insignificance.

I shrugged. 'Wasn't me.'

'Looks like you.'

'Coincidence.'

Billy stared at me with dead eyes. 'Let's hope so, shall we?'

My eyes locked with his. Something in his tone had me nailed to the floor. 'So what have you got?' I silently prayed it wasn't a job.

'I checked out the Irishman,' Billy said. 'Goes by the name of Black, real name Dermot McMahon. Rumoured he had dealings with the Provisional IRA as a lad, running arms and general gophering.'

'Did he serve time?'

'No.' When Billy said no you could take it as Gospel.

'Thoughts on who he currently works for?'

Billy shook his head. I grunted thanks. I wasn't too fussed about the political label. Black sounded as though his stint with the Provisionals had been at street entry level. A lot of men like him who dabbled in groups with political aspirations would be as happy joining a band of armed robbers. Since the introduction of the peace agreement many low-level thugs refused entry to new radical splinter groups were forced to find other means to feed their addiction to violence and easy money. I expected Black was one of them.

'Any further forward, son?'

My thoughts skewered, I shrugged. 'Got a few leads, nothing ground-breaking.'

'Word of advice,' Billy said, taking another mouthful and chewing vigorously. 'Go to ground. I'll put a word in for you, smooth things over with the big guys. Doesn't have to be the end.'

I swallowed. I didn't doubt that Billy was capable. I'd seen him in action once before, showboating to save the life of someone he deemed worth saving. A generous offer, it wasn't one I could take. I had to find the hard drive before it got traded. If it got traded, I had to prevent production of the toxin. In spite of what I'd told McCallen, I didn't care how many criminals I killed along the way, just as long as I averted a catastrophe of sickening dimensions. 'I want to sort this out first.'

'Stubborn bastard, aren't you?' Billy flashed a smile.

'I'm grateful, Billy, but…'

'You want to play it your way, I understand. Always been your own man, Hex. I'll say that about you. Admire you for it.'

I burnt inside. Days ago I'd have received this as a compliment. And now? I pushed back the chair, thanked Billy for his support.

'Take it easy,' he said.

'Yeah, Billy, you, too.'

I returned to the lock-up and stayed there until mid-day. How McMahon fitted into the mix I didn't yet understand. Could be a hired hand. Could be deeply enmeshed in a plot that assumed alarming proportions with every passing minute. If I stopped to think too hard about what was at stake, that someone somewhere held the potential to destroy thousands if not millions of lives, I'd cease to function. I could only engage and concentrate on the next step in front of me, not the one ahead. The next step boiled down to the name, real or assumed, of the man I'd killed in the alley.

Back at the lock-up, I packed a new briefcase with a new

identity, popped green contact lenses into my eyes, donned a pair of wide-framed spectacles, and changed into a black overcoat over a navy-coloured suit. Lastly, I slipped on a pair of dark grey leather gloves. I always wear gloves – even in summer. I chose a Glock 17 with ammunition as backup. Forty per cent of the weapon made from polymer, it was extremely light and portable. This one had a moderator, or silencer. It didn't remove noise when fired, but dampened it sufficiently.

I took the only piece of jewellery I owned apart from the chain I wore around my neck, a plain gold band that was a close and lethal fit for my middle finger. Secreted in the underside, a .22 bullet triggered by a tilt mechanism, the same kind of device found in certain types of mine. I rarely used it for a job, but it had saved my life on more than one occasion. My life was worth jackshit, but I wanted to stay alive long enough to thwart those who had the data. My other luxury and burglar's friend: a custom-ised gadget for decoding domestic security systems. It worked in the same way as global positioning systems are designed to show the exact location of aircraft and maritime vessels. Simply put, these small hand-held units, no bigger than a mobile phone, read the indentations on an alarm box and transmit the data back, enabling the would be burglar to disable the alarm.

Suited and armed, I returned to Pall Mall. I needed to run down Tilelli, my American gambling, all-seeing and all-knowing friend to see if he'd turned anything up on Wilding's assassin. He wasn't there. This didn't faze me. Drunks are like wildebeest. They have the same number of watering holes. I tried every one of Tilelli's favourite hostelries. No joy. Either he was blowing his ill-gotten gains or, as I suspected, he was laying belly-low.

Aware of his sexual predilections for young foreign men, I decided to try a gay haunt tucked away in a basement bar on the Cromwell Road. There I found Tilelli giving a performance worthy of the best stand-up routine, an adoring bevy of good-looking sycophants fawning over him as though he were the last Emperor

145

of Rome. As I walked in the thread veins on Tilelli's cheeks turned white and retreated below the surface of his skin.

I ordered a straight malt whisky and took my drink over. At my approach Tilelli whispered into the ear of a dark-skinned, fine-featured guy from Somalia called, Gaal. Gaal had the reputation for being a hard man. Anyone can be hard fizzed up on drugs. Foolish in the extreme, Gaal gave me the look. I gave him the look back and he melted away, his mates in tow. I slipped into the booth next to Tilelli who now resembled a comedian dying a death on stage.

'Drink?' I said.

'No,' he said, 'thanks,' he added with a forced smile.

'We had some business, remember?' I took a gulp, rolled the whisky round my tongue and swallowed.

'Yeah, sure,' Tilelli said, his pebbly eyes darting from me to the door to the floor.

'The information I asked for.'

'You didn't say you needed it in a hurry.'

I have an A class personality, demanding of myself and very demanding of others. One thing I can't stand is excuses. I said nothing. The lead-weight of silence crushed Tilelli into a response.

'I haven't had a lot of time,' he burbled. 'Hell, it's only been a couple of days.' Tilelli shuffled his large rear.

'Did you find time to spend the money I wired you?'

Tilelli cleared his throat. Sweat broke out on his brow. Every sinew in his wobbly frame strained with fear. I could feel him inching away from me. He looked like a guy who, right that moment, wanted to borrow someone else's life. 'I had debts to clear.'

I clicked my tongue, a cover for slipping the Glock from the holster. 'That's very disappointing.'

'If you give me a little more time, I'm sure I…'

'So you turned up nothing?' I pushed the muzzle of the gun into his paunch, well below the level of the table. Tilelli's wet lips opened into a perfect 'O'. His eyes receded into his face. It wasn't a pleasurable experience, but in the circumstances it was exactly the kind of treatment he could expect. Simply put, Tilelli was lying his head off. 'No idea who stole my gig?'

'As a matter of fact, I might have something for you.' Tilelli's thick pink tongue flopped out and licked the corner of his fat lips.

'*Might?*'

'I wasn't sure whether it would be relevant, if you get my meaning.'

'Yes, I think I get your meaning,' I said deadpan.

Tilelli dropped his voice. He was practically crying. 'Do you think you could remove that thing,' he said. 'It might go off, accidentally, or something.'

'If it goes off it will be no accident, I assure you.' I let it sink in. 'You were saying?'

'I'm sorry but I can't reveal the source,' Tilelli gulped.

'I don't expect you to.' I did, but I thought I'd humour him first.

'Sorry, Hex, I've no idea who killed the scientist, but,' he rushed on, 'I heard a couple of names on the wire, the type of men who might be after you.' I eased off the pressure on Tilelli's gut. I wasn't keen on him having a heart attack before he'd finished telling me his news. 'A guy who calls himself Black.' Tilelli waited. He looked like an abused child, unsure whether he was going to receive a hug or a slap. I covered my disappointment with a smile.

'This is good, Ron.' I didn't tell him that Black was currently rotting away in a back alley and that I already knew his name, care of Billy.

Encouraged, he said. 'Also known as Dermot McMahon. He hires himself out to anyone who will have him.'

'To do what exactly?'

'Enforcing mainly. Heard he also offers his services in the removals business.' Tilelli licked the corner of his mouth again.

I frowned. No way had McMahon killed Wilding. I'd discounted it before and I was discounting it now. What struck me as odd was that Billy had failed to find this out. Maybe he had but, for reasons of his own, didn't want to share. 'Who to?'

'All over.'

'Don't dick me around, Ron. I said who, not where.'

'I don't know.'

I glowered some more. 'And the other name?'

Tilelli opened his mouth. No words came out. For a moment I thought he was going to croak. I nodded at him, forced a smile of encouragement.

'Lygo,' he whispered, eyes darting like popcorn in a hot oven, 'Frank Lygo.'

I'd never heard the name before. 'Who is he?'

Tilelli vigorously shook his head. 'It's just a name. I don't know him. Never come across him in my life before.'

I threw him a dead-eyed look, increased the pressure once more. 'Are you sure?'

Tilelli looked from me to his stomach and back again. I think he was weighing up whether to be blown away now by me or at a later date by Mr Lygo. In ninety-nine per cent of cases, deferred death is generally more acceptable than imminent departure.

'Certain. I heard he's new on the scene, usual racket,' Tilelli stuttered, eyes darting.

'Nationality?'

'American,' he stammered.

I felt a shadow pass over me. I wondered if Lygo had a connection to the dead scientists across the pond.

'Or maybe Canadian,' Tilelli swallowed hard. I gave him a sharp look. I don't like it when people get creative with the facts. For the time being I was prepared to stick with North American.

'How long has he been operating here?'

'I don't know.'

'This is getting repetitive, Ron.' Tilelli looked genuinely

terrified, as well he might. 'Does he have any connection to Mikhail Yakovlevich?'

'Who?' he gulped

'Don't give me that moronic look, Tilelli,' I said, prodding him hard.

'I don't know. I mean I have no idea,' he burbled, 'Honest, Hex, I'm telling the truth.'

'Anything else?'

'Black worked for Lygo.'

It was as if someone had made a grab at my throat. Black knew about the missing information, or as he'd referred to it, the hard drive. If he took his orders from Lygo, stood to reason that Lygo had taken out the contract on Wilding. Lygo was Wes's employer and, by default, mine.

'Where do I find Lygo?'

Tilelli opened and closed his mouth. He looked as dispirited as a car factory that's gone into receivership. 'And don't tell me you don't know,' I added with menace.

Tilelli's voice came out several octaves higher than usual. 'I could maybe find out.'

I prodded the muzzle of the gun through several layers of fat. 'You do that, Ron,' I said and left.

CHAPTER SEVENTEEN

In the space of less than an hour the weather had turned. Pavements feathered with snow. A chill, bitter wind blew from the east and squeezed tears from my eyes. It was cold enough to shatter teeth. Hardy I might be, but I needed somewhere warm and quiet in which to think, essential I planned how to nail Frank Lygo.

A stone's throw from Knightsbridge, and taking a calculated risk, I shopped for jeans, sweaters, underwear and a pair of tan-coloured Rockport boots. I bought basic toiletries. I also bought a baseball cap.

The streets were rammed with early Christmas shoppers and bankers with bonuses to spend. Blending into the glossy environ-ment, I booked into a small, well-appointed hotel off Sloane Square. At over two hundred pounds a night, it fell outside my usual choice of residence though well within my budget.

Taking the lift to the third floor, I let myself into my new home without hassle for the night, a room at the rear of the hotel well away from the street, and felt something akin to pleasure. I hadn't always been rootless and nomadic. Fine linen, thick carpets and state of the art sanitary ware could still delight me. After taking a long hot bath, I shaved, dressed in my new clothes, picked up the phone and asked for a line out. I called Billy.

'Yeah?'

'I chased down the lead you gave me.'

No comment.

'Black was linked to a guy called Lygo, Frank Lygo.'

There was a moment's silence, a silence in which I could feel my own pulse racing.

'Don't ever call me again,' Billy snarled and cut the call.

I stared at the phone. Did this explain why Billy had been less than forthcoming with information? For Billy Squeeze to be given the creeps Lygo must be formidable. As for Billy's sudden change of attitude towards me, I refused to think too much about the consequences. Short term was all that counted. I'd found my man. Lygo didn't hold the equivalent of the smoking gun in his hand, but he knew more about the state of play than either MI5 or me had been able to fathom.

With regard to the stolen information, I assumed it was either traded or about to be traded, the final recipient having one hell of a lot of leverage at his disposal. The thought made me want to throw up. No wonder Lygo was sore at losing such a prize. It certainly explained his decision to send McMahon after me.

I stretched out on the bed. So what of Frank Lygo? Part of me wanted to climb inside his head and crawl around to see what he was like. Another recoiled. Something of a novelty that Lygo had not registered on my personal radar before, it inclined me to think he was a man of the moment and someone who shouldn't be underestimated. How and when he'd crashed onto the scene and where he'd served his apprenticeship, I hadn't a clue. It was difficult to appear from nowhere, especially in the States, somewhere I had good contacts. I felt the tug of common ground. My father still lived there, as far as I knew. He'd walked out of my life when I was three. It struck me that I knew as little about my own father as I did Lygo.

Sweeping the thought aside, I had no idea where Lygo hung out. I didn't know the scope of his empire, and I wasn't holding out any hope that Tilelli would come up with anything extra. He was too scared.

But I knew something about Dermot McMahon, his prior links to the Provisional IRA, his crass and brutish attack on me. Was it pure accident that I happened to be on a job in Boston, a place known for its fair share of Irish-Americans, during the period of the assassinations? Tilelli maintained that McMahon hired himself out to anyone who would have him, an employer who wanted to off a string of scientists, perhaps?

Inspired, I picked up the phone once more, dialled a number I rarely used to a woman called Ellen Greco. Greco was a woman who put the 'ruth' in ruthless. As the line re-routed and finally connected I imagined the unassuming street in Boston where she lived in a four-storey red brick house squeezed between a garage and a diner and from where she ran a syndicate for the Italian Mafia. The Mafia, a shadow of its former self in that part of the world, was down but not out.

'Ellen, it's Hex,' I said.

'Hex, how are you?' Her voice husky from a twenty-a-day small cigar habit, she sounded genuinely pleased to hear from me.

'Good. And you?'

'Good, too.'

'Still burning rubber?' She had a weakness for riding motor-bikes at high speed.

'Of course, how else am I supposed to get my kicks?' I smiled. Gutsy on every level, Ellen played a dangerous game in a predominantly male environment. I might no longer admire her for what she did, but I admired her for surviving so long. 'So what can I do for you, honey?'

'What's the current state of play with Ireland?' Anyone eavesdropping would assume a reference to the country. Only Ellen knew what I really meant. Organised crime split two ways in the city: the Mafia in the north, Irish gangsters in the south. Sometimes they formed alliances; sometimes turf wars broke out.

Ellen had taken up the reins of her husband's empire after Irish mobsters killed him a few years before, Stefano Greco a casualty when relations were less than cordial.

'Favourable,' she said.

Ellen was nothing if not pragmatic. 'Heard of a guy called McMahon, Dermot McMahon, sometimes goes by the name of Black?'

'Yeah, low-level employee in the O'Grady's removals business.'

'Has he done any house clearances recently?'

'Not that I know of.'

'He sometimes works for a guy called Frank Lygo. Does that name ring any bells?'

'It's familiar in the sense I've heard the name before. These Irish guys sound all the same,' she gave a dry laugh. 'In the same business, you say?'

'That's right. I'd like to contact him.'

The line went quiet. I heard her inhale and exhale. At last, she spoke. 'Sorry, Hex, not sure I can help.'

'It's okay, probably a long shot.'

'If I get a lead I'll let you know in the usual way.'

'Thanks, Ellen, appreciate it.'

To jack up my thinking, I made myself coffee from the welcome tray, took the cup over to the window, glanced out onto the yard below. I didn't see anything or anyone suspicious. McCallen was most likely caught up explaining to her superiors how she'd come to lose me, an uncomfortable situation, I imagined. Again, I reflected on what she'd said and, more revealingly, how she'd said it, sifting through the debris of our conversation, hoping to find gold. As guarded as someone of her calibre should have been, there were a couple of giveaways. When questioning me on how my path had crossed with one, Vasily Felshtinsky, I'd assumed she was feeding me a useless thread of information. Her breezy dismissal of any Russian connection made me think that she'd showed her hand. I'd failed to put the pieces together, but pieces there were.

Night was made for concealment and killing so I put on my gloves, wiped the room clean of prints, shrugged on my coat and left the hotel. Stepping out into the street, the darkness pressed against me. I avoided the main routes and returned to Yakovlevich's lair in Kensington where I hid in the shadows and waited and watched. Drapes open, every facing room glittered with light from dozens of chandeliers. Cabs came and went. People like me didn't appear on guest lists, but some faces I recognised and some I didn't. Most of Yakovlevich's visitors were young, excitable women, their raucous screams of laughter due to the fact that they'd dressed for the beach instead of the current Arctic-like conditions.

Two hours passed without incident. I'd stay all night if I had to. Like vampires, men like Yakovlevich only operated when the sun went down.

As my watch ticked into the next hour I believed I'd lucked out. I was wrong. A black Volvo suddenly hove into view and cruised down the road, turned around and, with lights facing, parked close to the party house. I shrank back into the shadows. The lights went out in the vehicle. I made out the silhouette of the single male occupant and smiled. I'd have preferred McCallen to be at the wheel instead of her sidekick, my Doppelganger, the man called Blake, but it confirmed my thinking.

The front door to the big house opened, except it wasn't Yakovlevich piling down the steps and onto the street at one in the morning, but his lieutenant, the ornately tattooed Yuri. I glanced across, expecting the Volvo to take up the chase. It stayed exactly where it was.

Blowing a smoke ring into the chill night air, I stepped out into the road, took a long taunting look back then, using myself as bait, turned as if to follow Yuri on foot. Behind me the door of the Volvo flew open, followed by the sound of pounding footsteps. I didn't flee. I walked. Timing the intelligence officer's arrival, I whipped round and punched him hard in the stomach, chopping him once across the back of his neck as he doubled up. My blow, precision-aimed to disable rather than kill, he hit the deck, unconscious. I dragged him up, hauled one of his arms over my shoulder, supporting him like he was my drunken mate, and carted him back to the waiting car. In raw haste, he'd left the keys in the ignition. Easy enough to open the boot, and pile him inside, which I did. As a precaution, I flicked out his earpiece and removed his mobile phone. Satisfied he wouldn't choke or run out of air, I climbed into the driver's side and started the engine. The episode had taken less than two minutes, but two minutes was all Yuri needed to disappear.

I drove into Old Brompton Road and from there into Gloucester Road where fortune smiled on me. Up ahead, I caught sight of Yuri, his off-centre gait suggesting he was very drunk. Cutting my speed, I dawdled, pulled over, waited and pulled back out in time to see Yuri pitch up at a bus stop in High Street Kensington and board an all-nighter. Keeping a car's distance behind, I followed.

The trail led to Earls Court Road, through Chelsea, via St Johns Hill, Clapham Junction and on towards Wandsworth Town Station where Yuri got out. The journey at that time in the morning had taken a little under twenty minutes. I parked the Volvo at the side of the road, climbed out and followed Yuri's retreat into a maze of ugly, badly lit streets and empty buildings in terrain that smacked of social breakdown and anarchy. I could smell it on the air, just like I sensed the eyes peering out from every squat and dwelling.

Two hundred metres ahead, on the opposite side of the road, a collection of storage sheds, disused offices and old factory units. A light glowed from a second floor window of what looked like a warehouse. Yuri crossed over and beat a path to a side entrance, and disappeared inside.

I counted to ten then crossed the yard and looked up at the vast three storey brick-built building. Over a wide entrance of huge closed mahogany double doors a sign read: 'Black's Brewery.' Whether this referred to the dead Black or was banal coincidence, I couldn't say. Whatever the truth, I didn't believe Yuri was there for the beer.

I hovered until past three-thirty in the morning at which point Yuri emerged and retraced his steps back to what passed for civilisation, and I returned to the car. Drumming my gloved fingers against the steering wheel, I wondered on what errand Yuri was running. Another possibility: he was moonlighting. A financially savvy crew, blood, honour, loyalty amongst Russian Mafia was non-existent. It was all about defending the rouble, the dollar, and your patch, and you got a lot of nasty people fighting over turf.

Turning this over in my mind, I drove back to Kensington and parked in exactly the same spot outside Yakovlevich's house. Judging from the blare and lights, the party was still in full swing. It wasn't the only noise. The clamour from the boot assured me that my lift for the night had regained consciousness.

I stepped out of the car and headed off down the street. Taking out Blake's mobile from my jacket, I called the emergency services alerting them to the possibility that someone was stuck in the boot of a car, gave the registration and location, then cut the call and dropped the phone in the nearest rubbish bin and walked away. In less than an hour's time the capital would be stirring. I didn't want to stick around for the wake-up call.

CHAPTER EIGHTEEN

Every lone wolf needs to eat. I was no exception. I stopped off at an all-night café in Fulham. Half the clientele were finishing off the night, the other starting the day. I was somewhere in the twilight zone.

I ordered and ate a full English with tea, strong and sweet, and returned to my hotel to grab a couple of hours sleep. By mid-day I was showered and keen to follow up the brewery connection. First, I found a callbox from which to phone McCallen, her number memorised on our first encounter like a tattoo on my frontal lobe.

She answered on the second ring. 'Yes?'

I went straight for the kill. 'The FSB guy, Felshtinsky. What was he doing at the research institute?'

'Hello, Hex. Where are you? Perhaps we could meet.' She didn't miss a single beat. She didn't curse. She didn't ask how I'd got her number. I liked that about her. Always in control and didn't scare easily.

I laughed. 'I don't think so. Your Israeli pals might want a slice of the action. Oh, and sorry about this morning. Has your colleague fully recovered?'

'I suppose I should thank you for not murdering him.' Her voice was like cold rolled steel.

'You should pay more attention to what I say. I told you I don't clip police or security officers. I don't kill people.' Not any more. Not unless I have to. Not for money, at any rate.

'Unless they happen to be Mossad,' she said dryly. I smiled. Nice of her to give the game away. Proved we were both grown-ups.

'A clear case of self-defence. What was that all about exactly?'

'You,' she said with menace. 'Aside from the absence of protocol, I completely understand where they're coming from. You threatened to kill me, remember?'

My blood curdled. I hated being reminded. 'So where were we? I've got plenty of time. I know you aren't tracing the call.'

'*How* do you know?' I detected slight anxiety in her voice.

'Because after the foul-up I expect you've been demoted to babysitting duties. How's Jake doing, incidentally?' I imagined her twitching the nearest curtain, peering outside, scoping the street to see where I was.

'You'd better not try anything,' she growled.

'Trust me, we wouldn't be having this conversation if I wanted to *try* anything.' I didn't tell her that Jake's welfare mattered to me. There was a sort of irony that a boy I'd failed to kill caused me so much difficulty.

'Really?' she said, withering.

'Really.'

She went quiet. I could almost hear her thinking. Then there was a sound like rushing wind, deafening. Aircraft, I realised. She coughed loudly then started talking. What she said took me by surprise. 'Thanks to you, my career's screwed.'

'I'm sorry.' I genuinely was. For a darkly ambitious woman this would be destroying.

'I didn't think apology was part of your repertoire.'

'Proves how little you know me.' I didn't have a clue what was running through her head. I wanted to believe that she hoped to know me better. I wanted to hope that, somehow, I was worthy of making a connection with her.

'What were you doing last night?' she said.

'Following a lead.'

'Like to be more specific?'

'Quid pro quo?'

She let out a dry laugh. 'Depends.'

I took a punt and told her.

'Yuri, as in the elusive enforcer who allegedly has contacts with Felshtinsky but actually works for Mikhail Yakovlevich and returned to Moscow?'

I didn't deny the pack of lies I'd given her. No point. The presence of MI5 at Mikhail's pad meant the intelligence services had already checked out the connection.

'Where did he go?' she said.

'He didn't. I lost him in Bayswater.'

She went quiet again. I don't think she believed me this time. 'Do you think his boss is in the market for the missing material?'

'Yakovlevich is an opportunist,' I said. 'I don't believe he had a direct involvement in Wilding's death, but I think he'd like to profit from it.' I fell silent. Right now she was probably getting more educated answers from me than her masters. If McCallen believed her career was on the skids, perhaps she saw me as a vehicle to reinstatement.

'So Yakovlevich could lead us to the missing information?'

'Us?' I said.

'MI5,' she said, waspish.

'Perhaps.' Not if I get there first. I had a clear advantage. I had a name: Frank Lygo. I tried a different angle.

'That guy I shot in Spain.'

'What about him?'

'Who is he?'

'Antonio,' she began then broke off. 'What is it?' I heard her

say. 'No, give me a moment…I *said* I'll be with you in a moment.'
I waited during a muffled exchange. Eventually she came back
on the line. 'Antonio Blanco,' she continued, 'a Spanish national
and former police officer.'

'Former?'

'Left five years ago pending an enquiry into a drugs bust that
took down three of his colleagues.'

I got the picture. Lygo was a traditionalist who surrounded
himself with an international bunch of felons with varying degrees
of form. First, a former IRA guy, and now a dodgy Spanish cop.
Maybe I had more in common with him than I first thought.
'Do you think the Spanish connection significant?'

'Hard to say. Al-Qaeda controls a lot of criminal networks in
Spain. It's also rumoured they have links to a number of radical
groups but the intelligence on that is sketchy, to say the least.'

I scratched my nose. I couldn't determine one way or the other
whether Spain had any bearing on the big picture. Bearing in
mind McCallen supplied the information freely and without me
doing the verbal equivalent of twisting her arm up behind her
back, it looked unlikely. McCallen only told me things that suited
her purposes. With regard to the alleged links between terrorists
and criminals, I needed to see how my friendly hacker Jat was
getting on and whether he'd been able to unearth information
on McCallen's asset, Saj. 'Seems like you'd better go,' I said, about
to wrap up the call. McCallen wasn't finished.

'You can't run forever. You know that, don't you?'

'Doesn't sound to me as if you're in much a of position to
make threats.'

'You'd better believe me, your days are numbered.'

'From where I'm standing, looks like all our days are numbered.'

I grimly cut the call and made another. Jat answered after three
rings.

'Yes?' One word, one question, the tone steeped in anxiety, and
I didn't think it was because I was on the other end of the line.

'Find out anything?'

Jat let out a deep breath. I got the impression he was expecting a call from somebody else and was relieved to hear from me, a novelty in my experience.

'Not yet,' he said. 'I'll keep trying.'

'Are you okay?' It's not something I usually ask but I sensed all wasn't as it should be.

He let out another big sigh. 'Family problems. I thought you were my mother. My little brother's acting up and she's bending my ear every five minutes.'

I didn't know what to say. Families weren't really my thing.

'I might have to go back to Brum for a bit,' he said, sounding dejected.

I brightened at the prospect. 'Might be useful but don't do anything stupid,' I warned. Hanging up, I stepped outside the call box. Big heavy flakes of snow tumbled from the sky like torn up bits of paper. A crucifying easterly wind slashed the street, the temperature plummeting to sub-zero. I rolled up the collar of my jacket, kept my head down and made my way to the nearest underground station where I took the northern line to Clapham.

Emerging from the underground, it took me fifteen minutes to walk to my destination. The nice thing about Yuri's choice of after-hours venue was that, like him, it was as ugly by day as by night. A bit of snow didn't change things. With plenty of disused buildings in which to insert myself, it took only a little ingenuity to find a spot on the upper floor of an old factory building with a view of the three-storey brewery and yard. From here, I could see lights on inside, two vehicles parked outside: an Audi Q-5, confident if a bit bland, and a classy black Mercedes with tinted windows, low on its wheels. I blinked with recognition. I'd travelled in the Merc on several occasions. A variation of the walk and talk, Yakovlevich preferred his car for business meetings, his feeling that it provided a more secure location in which to deliver his next set of orders. That Yuri had driven it here without his boss was inconceivable. I craned my head, expecting Yakovlevich to pop out of the crumbling brickwork, but there was no evidence of the big Russian, no sign of human activity. In fact precious little activity of any description; no indication of brewing in action; no personnel coming and going; no delivery lorries travelling in or out. At every level, the place shrieked front.

I turned my attention back to the Mercedes, more especially the low-slung suspension. Armour plating provided one explanation, the presence of a body in the boot another. Bearing in mind the Mercedes belonged to Yakovlevich, the latter a strong contender.

Shifting my weight from one foot to the other, trying to work blood into my frozen limbs, I attempted to work out the reason for Yakovlevich's visit. I didn't generally work on hunches. I was a believer in strong evidence, and the Mercedes was the strongest indication I had yet that Yakovlevich was chasing down a deal. McCallen also sensed the mighty Russian was on the trail. For this, I had to take responsibility. It was me who first visited and alerted Yakovlevich to Wilding's murder, me who inferred that something valuable had been stolen. Sometimes you had to put out to get anything back. McCallen worked in the same way. Why else did she engage with a creature like me? I wondered again whether I could tempt her to go off-message, whether I could exploit her ambitions and turn her dark desire for success to my advantage. If I were honest, I wondered if we could work this thing out together, and whether I could then attract her and become her guilty pleasure.

A side-door opened and Yuri stepped into the yard followed by an older thickset man with a top-heavy boxer's build. Swept back from his face, an impressive head of silver-grey hair that I guessed once upon a time was a dark match for the eyebrows. With his colouring, he could pass for Italian or Greek. Strong featured, with a forehead like a shelf, the craggy lines around his eyes suggested he'd spent time underneath a desert sun. He had wide nostrils, full mobile lips. Deep-set lines around his mouth gave his jaw the appearance of belonging to a ventriloquist's dummy. I estimated his age as fifty-something, maybe a little younger. Those crevasses on his face made it difficult to tell. I distrusted him on sight and my instincts are pretty good.

Watching him engage with Yuri provided a master class in human behaviour. Yuri, a difficult man to dominate, was subservient to the point of deference. He stood, hands crossed lightly over his genital area, head bowed while the other guy, his features fused with concentration, chopped the air with the side of his hand like he was cleaving stone. I leant forwards, watched his mouth with the same tenacity a blind man reads Braille.

'I want them gone by tonight,' he said, jerking his head towards the Mercedes.

'I can do this,' Yuri said. 'You want that I dispose of them also?'

'You have some place in mind?'

Yuri smiled. 'A perfect place, full of tradition.'

'Fuck tradition,' the man scowled.

'All I meant,' Yuri said, taking a step forwards, remonstrating, 'Yakovlevich, he has many enemies buried there.'

The man's lips pulled back into a smile. He had great teeth. Obviously took his dental care seriously. 'Cool, I appreciate the sense of irony.'

The muscles around Yuri's tattooed mouth twitched. 'Will you be needing me again, Mr Lygo?'

I smiled in awe as my man, Lygo, looked at his watch and shook his head. 'You've got a busy night ahead of you. Take a couple of hours. Back here for six with the girls.'

Both men went their separate ways. Lygo retreated into the brewery. Yuri left on foot. I stared at the Mercedes as if it were an unexploded bomb. Yakovlevich would never sanction the use of his vehicle for such an enterprise. And it was beyond Yuri's wit to carry out such an act and conceal it from his boss. The obvious conclusion: the body in the boot was Yakovlevich.

I rested back, tried to come up with credible answers. I suspected a simple case of double-cross. A scenario with which I was familiar, typically they were inter-family affairs. Yakovlevich probably went to do business unaware that his own right-hand man had signed up to serve another master. I expected Lygo lured Yuri away, perhaps to replace McMahon, or perhaps Yuri jumped ship for reasons of his own. In the final analysis it didn't much matter. Lygo ran the show. Any executing taking place he sanctioned. This a routine set of events: new guy on the block takes out old guy. Who better to carry this out than the old guy's own right-hand man?

According to Lygo, there was more than one stiff. I wondered how many. No doubt he'd be able to provide the answer. Now that he was alone, I thought a formal introduction long overdue.

CHAPTER NINETEEN

Withdrawing the Glock from its holster, I padded down the steps to the ground floor and, using the vehicles as cover, crossed the yard to the main building. Finding the side-door unlocked, I slipped inside.

I had never been into a brewery before. A cross between factory and warehouse, although smaller and more basic in scale, it had high ceilings with iron girders, mezzanine floors and staircases with metal treads. To my right, two doors marked 'toilets'. To my left, steps leading to a platform and presumably another storey. Ahead, a bar with several pumps for dispensing ale. Behind the bar, and marked 'No Admittance Beyond This Point', an open door led off to another room or, because it was hard to tell, several. At the far end, on a raised area to the left of the counter, two enormous stainless steel vats, a 'masher' and a 'copper.' Beyond these another set of steps.

I'd expected the heady aroma of crushed hops and yeast to hang in the atmosphere like fog. In fact there was little odour. Everything, from the slate floor to the equipment, shone, scrupulously clean, which was how I spotted the unexpected: blood. In two separate locations. Not fresh. Not old. The first this side of the bar as if the victim had been caught unawares while enjoying a pint, and blood in a quantity great enough to suggest that it had been pumped out of a body; the second, no more than a metre inside the entrance, less devastating in volume, a spatter of tiny droplets and, therefore, easier to read.

Working on the basic rule that the smaller the droplet the higher the velocity and that velocity indicated a weapon, I reckoned it was certainly from a firearm. The lake of plasma over by the chute however, suggested a blade attack involving close contact with a major artery.

I crossed the floor silently on the balls of my feet, shimmied up the steps to the next level where a large clock told me that it was a quarter to four in the afternoon. Straight ahead: a glass-fronted door. Locked, it didn't appear to reveal very much other than the office area behind it. Eyes scanning the upper storey for signs of Lygo, every door was closed. Every corridor held the potential for danger. I felt an odd familiar fluttering deep in my chest, an ache in my groin. I didn't sense Lygo was close. I *knew* it. Watching and waiting, his breathing shallow, finger in all probability dancing on the trigger of an automatic.

'Hi,' a voice carried from above. 'Come on up.'

I swivelled my gaze, saw another shorter flight of steps that led to another mezzanine floor and room with a double set of doors flung open. Whoever held the higher ground had the advantage. Only a fool would allow himself to be lured into a killing zone.

'You come down,' I called back.

I waited, heard the steady thud of footsteps. Lygo appeared with an easy smile and walked down to meet me. Close-up he looked taller, more bulky. Some would find his physique challenging, intimidating. For me, it was his eyes. His forehead imposed to such an extent on the rest of his face you could barely see them and when you did they looked as though something had crawled in behind and given up the ghost there a long time ago. I needed no reminder that I was face to face with a man

166

who wanted to inflict the most unspeakable suffering on innocent people.

'Hey, put that thing away,' he launched another smile. 'You and me are on the same side.'

'Are we?' I held onto the Glock.

'Sure we are.'

No expert on dialects, I reckoned time and travel had smoothed Lygo's voice to the cultured, softly spoken American commonly adopted by diplomats, giving no clue as to his state of origin.

'Frank Lygo,' he said, extending a hand, flashing a heavy-duty signet ring made of white metal, platinum at a guess, rather than the more traditional gold. Whatever it was, he wore it on the little finger of his right hand, suggesting to me that he was left-handed.

I didn't take it. I said, 'Did you send McMahon to kill me?'

'A misunderstanding, in the heat of the moment.'

'What about Antonio Blanco?'

Lygo smiled some more, let his hand drop to his side. 'He made an unfortunate mistake and paid the ultimate price.'

'Seems like your employees make a lot of mistakes.' I did not include myself in my summary.

Lygo smiled again, conceding the point. 'Blanco misinterpreted the brief. I simply wished to talk to you. Nothing more.'

'What about Wes?'

'Extremely unfortunate, I admit. Things got out of hand. It happens.'

Lygo was talking bullshit, and he knew I knew, but we continued the charade, the game.

'What did you want to talk to me about exactly?' I said.

'About how we can get this back on track.'

I had never done 'we' but I didn't trouble to point this out. I needed to reserve my energy for bigger issues. 'You're satisfied I don't have the hard drive?' As this was what I was tasked to steal, I thought I should refer to it in this way. No point Lygo thinking me too knowledgeable. If he discovered that I knew about his wicked game, I'd be finished.

'I am.'

'Then who does?'

'That's what I need to find out.' He inclined his head, an enigmatic expression on his face. I wasn't taken in, but thought more could be gained by offering trust. I put the Glock away. He extended his hand once more. I shook it anticipating an attempt to pull me in, smash the back of my neck, for Lygo to reveal his true colours. Nothing happened. Looked like we were on the same wavelength for now, probably because we both wanted things from the other.

'Good,' he said, eyes glittering like icicles in the sun. 'Let's go some place warmer.'

He turned, retreated back up the steps to what he called his office. I followed. Quick observation told me that this was Lygo's lair in every sense. Aside from the usual clerical paraphernalia, the room was kitted out with a fridge, a two-ring hot plate and a fold-up campaign bed. A one room fits all purposes. Like me, this was a man accustomed to living on the hoof. It didn't look as if he planned on sticking around longer than strictly necessary.

He poured coffee for both of us, offered cream and sugar, which I declined. I took a couple of gulps of the dark steaming liquid. It was the best coffee I'd tasted this side of the Atlantic.

He surveyed me for a few moments, a faint smile playing on his lips. The man had expended considerable energy trying to bring me to heel and here I was of my own volition. He genuinely appeared pleased to see me. I wasn't taken in by his sudden show of friendship. I had Lygo down for the type of man who, in a classic Mafia don move, drew you close, got your trust, then struck and crushed. He sat down in a leather chair, leant back, feet apart, nice and easy.

'So what happened, Hex? What went wrong?'

'The intelligence was poor.' I didn't point out that I'd been lied to wholesale. I didn't admit that the botched job was my cock-up, my fault. To my surprise, Lygo didn't waste time berating me. He played Mr Reasonable. Encouraged, I delivered a factual account of events on the night of Wilding's demise. I said nothing about her son. He listened without interruption, the dead light in his eyes giving nothing away.

'So someone else got to her. Who?'

'I don't know. Plenty of others in the game.'

Lygo nodded, thoughtful. 'Any idea about the man behind the contract?'

I frowned. 'Beyond my remit.'

'You're not interested?'

'Should I be?' I wanted Lygo to believe that I was nothing more than a hired gun.

'As a professional, yes, you should.' His eyes locked onto mine. He was gauging how much I really knew. I looked blank. I hoped he would elaborate. Either he didn't know or wasn't saying. 'Do you have any idea what's on the hard drive?'

I shook my head.

'I'm surprised and a mite disappointed,' he said. I was obviously failing in every respect. Good, I thought. 'Curiosity is key to survival,' he intoned. 'You should know that.' He leant towards me, worrying intensity in his seemingly sightless eyes. I said nothing, worked out the moves, estimating how long it would take me to snatch the Glock from the holster and drill a bullet through his forehead should the need arise. If I did this, my one thin lead to the hard drive vanished.

'Does it ever occur to you that governments lie to people, even their own intelligence services?'

I was becoming a specialist in frowns. I expressed my best: three straight lines along the forehead.

Undeterred, Lygo continued his pitch. 'I'm a scientist by training, genetics my speciality. Haven't worked in the field for a long time but it has relevance to what I'm about to tell you.'

Genetics sparked my interest. I masked this with a barely stifled yawn.

'What if I told you that the British government sanctioned the development of ethnic-specific weapons?'

I shuffled in my seat, expressed shocked surprise. Without warning I had a vivid memory of Kensington Gardens and McCallen's conversation with Saj, most specifically his reaction to it. *The British government sanctioned this?* I recalled how McCallen had explained things to me, but had she told me the truth, or was there another agenda? The thought that I had become a pawn in a game between the powers that be and someone who could threaten vested national interests and security made me feel dizzy.

Lygo bore down on me. 'Let me explain,' he said with a dark smile.

Crime lords and the type of individuals who employed people of my ilk were not in the habit of giving explanations for their actions. Generally they were not that highly educated. Occasionally they'd go off on a psychopathic rant, usually when things weren't going their way. But Lygo wasn't some newbie boss fresh on the scene. Lygo was unique. His provenance was different. Charismatic, he spoke with authority.

'Sanctioned by the British government, Wilding was working on ethnic specific toxins that have the potential to kill certain groups of people who are troublesome. Out of greed, she decided to peddle her knowledge and sell the genetic code for a toxin that would wipe out Arabs and, by default, Jews.' He paused as if I might be eager to dive in with a host of questions.

Apart from the fact I was stunned, experience told me to stay silent. I was, after all, playing dumb. 'I couldn't let that happen,' he said tonelessly. 'Blowing the whistle wouldn't work – too many vested interests.' He gave a rueful smile, 'And actually nobody would believe me.'

Me not *it*, I thought. Somewhere along the line, it appeared that Lygo had fallen foul of the system and been discredited.

'I tried to talk to her,' he said airily. 'As one scientist to another.'

I broke cover. 'You approached her in person?'

'Appealed to her better nature, but she refused to listen.'

'You mean you wanted her to destroy the research?'

'Of course,' he snapped, visibly offended.

I did not ask the question that was gnawing at my mind. Why, in God's name, would the British government sanction such a programme? Instead, I said, 'Surely there are others working in the field?' I didn't understand how removing Wilding eliminated the threat.

'Not at such an advanced level.'

'So you sent in Wes to soften her up?'

He nodded. 'If she wouldn't do as I asked, I had to force her to hand over the genetic codes for the weapons. And the rest you already know.'

Except I didn't believe I did. I hadn't forgotten Billy Squeeze's fear of the man. I hadn't forgotten Yakovlevich and Yuri. 'You've involved a number of people, Mr Lygo…'

'Call me Frank.'

I forced a smile, 'Frank,' I repeated. 'It's possible one of them talked.' No such things as total security. Human beings were primed to open their mouths from the moment of birth.

'You think we have a leak?' His voice sounded as if it had emerged from somewhere cold and shadowy and faraway.

'It's the obvious conclusion, surely?'

Lygo considered this for a moment. He looked as if it had never occurred to him. I was surprised and a little alarmed. It wasn't exactly brain surgery.

'What were you going to do with the information?' I said.

'I already told you, destroy it.' His brow lifted to better reveal the expression of affront in his eyes.

Was Lygo a superannuated whistleblower with a grudge, or an out and out liar? Clearly he wanted me to believe that he was a force for good. A big part of me wanted to be convinced, that there was another interpretation, some higher motive at play. Strangely, in my heart of hearts, and even at this late stage, I wanted to believe that I was on the side of the angels. The flipside: I was the one being exploited. I was the patsy. I was the fool.

'Mr Lygo,' I began, studiously hesitant.

'Frank,' he reminded me, smiling smoothly.

'It's taken some time to find you, Frank.'

'I appreciate your trouble.'

'I had to ask questions.'

The smile froze on his face.

'Discreetly, of course,' I added.

'I understand.'

'I found out that that a number of American scientists…'

'Have died in suspicious circumstances,' he said, another smile emerging and fluttering on his lips. 'You think Wilding was killed by the same outfit, is that what you're saying?'

'I'm not saying anything,' I said evenly. 'I'm surprised you didn't think it a line worth checking.'

'How do you know I didn't?' Lygo sat back in the chair, making the leather creak, a self-satisfied smile on his face. Confidence oozed out of his pores. It struck me then that this was not a man I'd like to sit down with over a hand of cards. He was impossible to read.

'Did you find a connection?' I asked.

'To Wilding? None.'

He poured out more coffee, gave his words time to sink into my brain. Then he fixed me with a vulpine stare. 'The boy,' he said. I flinched. I'd never mentioned the boy. 'You must find him.'

The abrupt change of direction took me by surprise. I was only just getting my head around Lygo's wild and monstrous allegations against the British government.

'Find him? That's not what I do.'

Lygo's dark deathly eyes retreated into his head. It felt like I was staring at a blind man. 'You found me,' he said softly.

He had a point. In the same obsessive way I'd hunted down and found Michael Berry, my mother's murderer, I'd tracked down Frank Lygo, but I genuinely couldn't fathom Lygo's motivation. Did he hope the boy would shed light on the real assassin? Or did Lygo fear that he'd identify me and, if I got picked up, I'd talk? Surely, Lygo was aware of the hit man's code of silence? Serve time if you have to, but never breathe a word about a target or a client, assassination or the man who paid for it.

'You're still under contract. You owe me.' His voice rang low and threatening.

I've never questioned those who paid me. With Lygo, I was prepared to make an exception. Changing times. 'Mr Lygo, Frank, I'm a professional assassin not a private investigator.' I didn't remind him that I was already on the run and a wanted man, and that any move risked exposure to the intelligence services.

'Neither are you a thief but you were prepared to steal.'

And how I regretted that decision. 'Stealing doesn't require thought,' I said, wondering why the boy, and not the location of the hard drive, consumed Lygo.

He flashed a chill smile. 'False modesty, Hex. We both know you're one very smart guy.'

'Not smart enough to find and break into an MI5 safe-house.' I wasn't lying. Apart from the fact I wouldn't do it, even if I gave it my best shot I held out little hope of success. 'You've read the news. Jake Wilding is under the protection of MI5.'

'I'll pay you double the original fee.'

'This isn't about money.'

'It's always about money.' He smiled broadly, though the warmth on his lips failed to connect with the expression in his eyes.

'My answer's the same.'

He glanced away, his face tightening into an expression of deep irritation. 'What if I gave you a list of MI5 safe houses?'

I blinked to hide my amazement. 'You have addresses?'

'I do.'

Only someone with contacts within the intelligence services could access that type of information. I had a sudden hunch about Lygo. Then again, if he were that powerful, I wondered why on earth he'd bothered to employ me. 'A list could take days to check,' I told him.

'Your point?' he said, no shine in his eyes.

'Even if I found out where he was it would be impossible to spring him.'

'I don't want him sprung. I want him killed.'

My veins felt packed with ice. 'I don't kill children.' I spoke softly, without passion. It was vital that Lygo believed I was still onside. Now that I'd found the bastard, I was determined never to let go. In spite of every effort to cover my reaction, my cheeks burned.

Lygo threw back his head and laughed. His deeply tanned throat, exposed, looked like bark. At that precise moment I thought him more than capable of carrying out the job himself. 'A child?' he sneered without a trace of humour.

I was definitely missing something, Lygo's sudden fixation on the boy strange. Then again, I was accustomed to the sometimes frankly weird and often sadistic obsessions of paymasters. 'I don't understand why you didn't take him out when you had the chance,' he probed, incredulous. There was no accusation in the tone. He seemed genuinely fascinated, as if it were a perplexing matter of academic interest.

I repeated what I'd already told him, admittedly with more heat.

'He is *not* a child,' Lygo said, grain in his voice. 'He can sink both of us. Think of it this way, I'm giving you a chance to make amends, to restore your professional reputation.'

So he was trying to protect himself, which made a warped kind of sense, Lygo's fixation classed as falling within the normal range of Mr Big obsessions. A loose end, potentially dangerous,

Jake could screw the pair of us. In this, Lygo was absolutely on the money. But I reckoned there was more to it. The urgency with which Lygo wanted the boy dead made me suspicious. I didn't know why or how it fitted, but Jake Wilding held the key.

I waited several beats, as if openly giving myself a chance to reconsider. 'Okay,' I said with a chill smile. 'I'll do it.'

CHAPTER TWENTY

Lygo wanted me gone. I was happy to comply. Running into Yuri would only complicate matters. Neither did I have any desire for a close encounter with Lygo's women. I'd studied enough of the breed to notice that most gangland bosses had heavy tastes when it came to sexual predilections, whether for young women or young men.

As for Lygo's presentation, or *schtick,* as Reuben would say, I thought he gave a bravura performance. Whether I believed the detail of his story, whether he was a geneticist, whether or not he'd uncovered a plot by Wilding to sell her wares, was almost incidental. What spun me out was Lygo's damned claim about the originator and true nature of the research in which Wilding was engaged. In the absence of evidence I stuck with facts I could verify. Fact: Lygo had given the order for Wilding's murder. Fact: he wanted Jake Wilding killed. My main priority now was to find him.

The list comprised several pages of U.K. addresses. Of the London locations, most were on the outskirts. I'd need wheels to check them out. One, however, leapt out of the print and it was geographically doable on foot.

When I'd made the call to McCallen I'd identified the distinct drone of aircraft overhead. Many homes in the capital sat directly below a flight path so nothing unusual about that. Not all, however, happened to be on a list of MI5 safe houses. I decided to give it my best shot, no pun intended.

I walked to Battersea, bought a train ticket from Clapham Junction and took the 17.55 from platform six, arriving in Hounslow thirty-three minutes later. My first port of call was an unprepossessing boozer with Sky TV, jukebox, pool table and fruit machines. A sign proclaimed karaoke on Saturday nights and live music on Sundays. 'Unchained Melody' oozed out of the speakers. The roast of the day was pork. At that time the bar was filled with men popping in for a swifty on their way home from work and those who looked as though they'd been camped there since the morning. Clustered around the bar, the regulars emitted a strong fuck off vibe: our territory and you're in it. I could take a hint. I wasn't one to look for trouble. I ordered a pint of Directors from a pleasant-looking girl called Sally. Dyed dark hair, mid-brown eyes, heavy build, naked flesh, pendulous breasts, big childbearing hips. Not my type. Probably held more appeal for someone like Wes. Except Wes was dead.

'Wonder if you can help me?' I said.

She looked hesitant. I smiled. She smiled back. 'I'll try,' she said, relaxing a little. I told her I wanted to look up a long-lost cousin who I believed was living in the area. I gave her the name of the road in which I thought he lived. It wasn't a ploy I used often. Would never have dreamt of adopting it on a kill mission.

'About a mile away, off the London Road,' she smiled helpfully. 'I can order a cab, if you like.'

'It's fine, a walk will do me good.'

I finished my beer, bought a pack of cigarettes, and shuffled out of the pub and into the night. My demons followed me. Something about the air, the familiarity of the chase, the fact that I'd been here a hundred times before had a dangerous effect. I felt like a hunting dog on the prowl. I felt as if I were operating at a different speed. Everything seemed more vivid and intense, my thrill for secrecy and the edge of the seat excitement that went with it stoked. Rarely reflective, and more often than not practicing self-deception, I recognised that I loved this aspect of the game: the thrill of the chase. Couldn't help myself. For me, killing had always been secondary. What turned me on was the next call. Who this time? What line had they crossed? Not normally given a reason, it didn't stop me from attempting to calculate the why of it. Nine times out of ten the contract to kill was for entirely plausible and consistent motives within the strange context of the villains who employed me. Appalling really. Suddenly what had seemed hazy in the warm confines of my hotel room, in the chill of night began to take form and shape: I would be for ever haunted by the desperate years and the many lives I'd destroyed, both the dead and the living. For a man without conscience I walked in alien territory.

The safe house was a Thirties-style bay-windowed detached dwelling in a quiet, well-lit cul-de-sac. The location was good, only one main entry point visible from the road, the house itself presumably blessed with more than the usual number of entrances and exits. Normally, I'd walk past, clock as much as and, as if I'd wandered into the wrong street, turn and get another eyeful on the return journey. No such precautions needed tonight. Curtains open, in darkness, the place was empty.

Thwarted, a tad spent, I leant my back against a plane tree well away from any lamplight, took out cigarettes, slipped off the cellophane, shook one out and lit it. The house stared back at me, taunting and mocking my failure. I blew out a thin plume of smoke and considered whether McCallen and the boy had ever been there.

Settling into the dark, I remembered the earthiness of her laugh, the intense expression in her luminous green eyes, the way her nose creased in concentration, her cold anger, the sound of her voice, the way she triggered whispers of imaginary conversations in my mind. '*Bored, emotional, snarling at everyone.*' McCallen's observation of Jake Wilding and her reaction to him had taken me by surprise. It lacked sensitivity, to say the least. What else did she expect?

Uninvited, a flood of memories washed over me. Skipping school. Going to my mother's flat. Finding her. Bed linen covered in fresh cranberries, or so I thought in my confusion. Blood, the amount so terrifying I didn't think it possible that a human being could contain so much. Sprayed onto the ceiling, the walls, soaked into the carpet, the floorboards. I later learnt that a cut artery is like a burst water main, spurting in frenzy, each jet of fresh plasma reflecting the dying beat of my mother's heart. I'd stood there mute, numb. It was as if someone had taken a scalpel to my chest, sliced through flesh and sinew, carved out my heart, chopped it up, and awkwardly shoved the mismatched pieces back on the wrong side and in the wrong place.

I had a hazy memory of collapsing against a doorframe, my face buried in my hands, body wracked with sobs. My grandparents on whom I relied, withdrew, as if I were tainted by her death, their silence proof of my contagion. Days and weeks passed in a blur and so did the growing sense of helplessness and abandonment. No, stronger than that, as if I'd be forsaken.

My only certainty was the macabre knowledge that she was stabbed over forty times. Someone had blood on their hands, on their clothes, someone close.

The failure of the police to identify her killer fuelled my madness. My intense rage ate me up from the inside out. The only way back to sanity was to hunt her killer down myself. And so, half-mad, I'd burst into Reuben's house, begged him to help. At first he refused. He sympathised with my desperate longing for revenge, of course, but he said that my rage would pass, that things would get better, that I had a life to live, that to choose any other way would set me on a path from which there was no turning back. But it didn't pass. It didn't get better. It crystallised.

In his role as a long-standing friend of the family, I told him that he had a moral duty to help. He was the only person who could.

In the end, he did and, unlike in the Wilding job, I did my homework. I was meticulous. What I discovered was mundane, unoriginal and tawdry.

Michael Berry, a serving police officer with the MET, was a married man who lived in London. Using work as a cover for his affair, he'd stay with my mother whenever he could. But Berry was a man who was on his way up. Tipped for the top, he had a sparkling future ahead of him. When my mother put pressure on him to leave his wife by threatening to reveal their relationship, he got violent and lost it. Forty stab wounds is a lot by anyone's standards. I never actually met him when he was with my mother. I only discovered the facts surrounding his existence later. My mother could be clandestine. Most alcoholics are.

I blew a perfect smoke-ring into the air. I hadn't given it a thought in the intervening years. The agony of loss, the sickening sensation of hopelessness and absence of any certainty was no longer raw and bleeding. It had scabbed over, dropped off and left a small, ridged scar. Reminded of it now felt as if I were viewing the teenage me from another planet, a little like coming face to face with Jake Wilding on the night I was supposed to kill his mother. Now I saw that to have been at ease with killing a woman, a mother like my own, proved how far I'd travelled to the dark side, how desensitised I'd become. Dr Mary Wilding was innocent, a woman caught up in someone else's wicked game. I'd always known it. Even then. I just couldn't admit it. No more than I could admit that what I did for a living was wrong on every level and from every perspective, that morally and spiritually I was bankrupt.

I recognised it now and sorry would never cover it.

And that's why I'd come to find Jake Wilding. To make some gesture of peace, to tell a stranger that he didn't need to become a man like me to survive.

I took another drag, tiptoeing up to the past for one last look. Reuben had driven me hard. My abiding memory was one of days and nights of training defined by high tension and brutality, interspersed with boredom, frustration and despair.

And when my teenage impetuosity got the better of me, when I wanted to go out and simply kill without thought or elegance, Reuben would clap a hand of restraint on my shoulder, calm me down and remind me that we are all alone in life, that my pain was no more, no less than others'.

I didn't thank him for it at the time, no more than Jake Wilding would thank me now, but he was right. Too late I'd learnt that if you hold onto grief beyond a reasonable time, you have no room in your life for anything or anyone else. In every sense living is messier than dying. I'd been a fool and a coward not to realise it before.

Dropping the cigarette on the pavement, I wondered precisely at what point Reuben regretted the expenditure of so much energy, when exactly he took the decision to betray me. With that weary thought, I made my way back to the hotel in preparation for my early start the following day. I hadn't yet found Jake, but I knew where to find Lygo's bodies.

Daybreak but still dark, I needed wheels and knew how to get them.

My bag packed, I left the hotel, my destination a sports suite of a private members club in Kensington. With nobody manning Reception, I crossed the foyer to the changing rooms and checked inside. Nobody in the showers. Nobody using the lavatories. Next, I scanned the lockers where everyone stored belongings. Fortunately, not everyone took advantage of the keys provided.

Three rows down, left-hand side, locker number twenty-four, the metal door was ajar. I opened it, reached inside and hooked out a set of car keys and slipped them into my pocket with a satisfying chink. Back outside in the private member's car park,

I pointed the keys and pressed the transponder on the key fob and the lights on a Jaguar XKR four cars along flashed as the vehicle unlocked. By the time the owner missed it, I'd be miles away.

The journey through the capital was tortuous. I passed the time by rifling through the glove compartment where I found a pair of sunglasses, which I put on, partly as a disguise, partly to shield my eyes against a low, if feeble, winter sun. Released onto open road, I made one unscheduled stop at a set of road works. Waiting at the temporary traffic lights, I noticed that the work crew had sloped off for a tea break, their tools propped up by the side of the road. Before the lights changed, I slid out of the Jag, picked up the nearest shovel and threw it into the boot, and offered my warmest smile to the bewildered female driver of an Audi TT in the queue behind.

I drove for twelve miles and, by eleven that morning, arrived on the periphery of Epping Forest. Yakovlevich's enemies lay in burial grounds within its six thousand acres. On the big Russian's orders, three men had been disposed of at separate times in the vicinity. Only someone who'd been there before would recognise the exact spot. I was that someone.

The cold weather had turned, sun in retreat and replaced by pewter-coloured skies and fog. Everything dripped. Climbing out of the car was like stepping into a winter swamp. I ditched the shades, and swinging the shovel over my shoulder, stuck to the road for roughly a mile on foot then, mindful of nature enthusiasts and the Conservation centre, turned towards the heart of the forest. Fortunately the appalling weather played in my favour. Visibility was poor. Nobody in his right mind would walk in this murk for pleasure however ancient the oak and beech trees.

Steering away from the trail paths, I came to a clearing that disappeared into a maze of bridleways and grassy plains. Another quarter of a mile revealed an incline and more densely wooded area containing the remains of an Iron-Age hill fort. Beyond a ditch and the daddy of all Hornbeam trees. This was the marker. I stopped, looked around, and keened my ears for the sound of another. All I heard was the patter of rain escaping from over-hanging cloud, the steady trickle of moisture. With a careful tread and using the shovel as an improvised walking stick, I picked my way down a steep-sided hill into a shallow ravine to where the earth had been most recently disturbed. On previous occasions I'd taken a less circuitous route. Dead bodies weigh heavy. The farther you carry them the greater the risk of discovery. I have only ever disposed of one body at a time. It set me thinking that Yuri must have had an accomplice. I wondered who that might be.

I started digging. Yuri was a strong man. I feared my job would be arduous. I hadn't bargained on the Russian's indolent streak. Not only hadn't he bothered to dig much beyond a couple of feet, or cover them in quicklime to mask the odour, he'd slung both corpses into the makeshift grave together, one atop the other.

The smell of death is like no other. At the sharp end, my job was always over before it reached gagging proportions. This time there was no escape. This time I was faced with the consequences of actions. Sweet, rotting, faecal, the odour forced a rush of bile into my mouth as I uncovered first Yakovlevich and then a middle-aged man whose throat had been cut. I was no pathologist but, judging from the reasonable condition of the bodies, I estimated they were both killed within a thirty-six hour timeframe. Close inspection revealed an in-and-out wound, the rim burn behind Yakovlevich's right ear suggesting that the shot had been at close range, probably with a .38 calibre. I felt an eruption of fear unconnected to my close proximity to a couple of stiffs in a public place because I now had the clear sense that events were closing in and Lygo was on a clearing-up mission. Once I'd done what he expected me to do, I too would be 'taken care of.' Should I fail him, same outcome, what you might call a lose-lose situation. And if I were to die the trail would grow cold and any hope of preventing catastrophe extinguished.

Roughly re-interring the dead, I ditched the shovel and retraced my steps to the Jaguar. The owner had considerately left an old dog blanket in the boot on which I was able to clean the mud from my boots before losing it in thick undergrowth.

I drove back in the direction of London on the lookout for a pub with the greatest number of vehicles in the car park, somewhere popular, flooded with people, where I could blend in unnoticed. I thought it would be easy. It wasn't. Recession hit Britain had made its mark in the suburbs. I ended up ditching the Jag on a side street in Barking and taking the underground to Tower Hill. After a short walk I fetched up in a wine bar throbbing with testosterone and well heeled booted and suited young bloods necking Dom Perignon by the bottle as if the world was about to end. For a majority, it might.

I hacked my way through the crush to the bar where mobile phones littered the counter like weapons at an arms fair. One guy in a dark trench coat had three. Every so often he'd pick one up, flick a few digits and put it back down. I ordered a drink, paid for it, stuck around, my attention seemingly concentrated on a chalkboard of food. When the nervous guy with the trio of phones disappeared to the gents, I swooped. I was certain he wouldn't miss one.

Back out on the street, and with a fast, brisk gait, I cut left then right until far enough away I felt secure to make a call on the stolen phone. McCallen answered slowly. Her voice sounded flat. I deduced she was having a rough time.

'Where are you?' I said.

She gave a dry laugh. 'My line, surely?'

'EC3. Are you still babysitting?'

'Why?'

'You sound bored.'

'I'm not.'

'Good.' Boredom is a gift to a killer. 'Want to come out to play?'

'What are you after, a date?' She didn't sound flattered.

'Can't you get someone to stand in for you? What about your mate, Blake?'

'He's not my mate,' she said tartly.

'Someone else then.'

'Why?'

'I've got something to show you.'

She didn't wisecrack. She didn't blow me out. I guessed she was probably weighing up my offer against her current duties and considering whether it would improve her situation.

'It's not a trap,' I assured her. 'But nobody else must know.'

'What makes you think I'd want to tell anyone?' She sounded cynical as hell.

'Look, I've discovered two dead bodies. One of them is Yakovlevich.'

'The other?'

'That's where you come in.'

'What makes you think I can help?'

'Fine, if you're not...'

'Give me one sane reason why I should oblige?'

'Because I'm your only ticket back to success.'

She went very quiet. I didn't push it. I had no need. She was weighing up my offer. Politics wasn't just for governments. Right now, she was working out the politics of her situation. I didn't doubt that there were officers more senior to her, superiors who called the shots. As pecking orders went, I reckoned she'd been downgraded, the flat tone of her voice told me so. But I rated her an independent thinker prepared to take risks. She had *winner* stamped all over her. Finally, she said, 'You have to give me more than this.'

'Does the name Frank Lygo mean anything to you?'

'No, who is he?'

I took another big decision, broke my own code again. Desperate measures. 'My elusive employer. He's the guy who ordered the contract on Wilding. That's just a taster.'

'Give me ten minutes.'

She cut the call and I bought a sandwich and coffee from a takeaway shop. Technology is a wonderful tool but I didn't think McCallen would be able to trace Lygo's history in a matter of minutes. When she phoned back she made no mention of him.

'This better be good. I've had to call in a favour.'

'You won't be disappointed.'

'Where do we meet?'

I gave her the name of a disused factory in West Ham. At the end of a street that had turned into wasteland it had the advantage of not being overlooked. Conversely, anyone wanting to scout me out would stick out like a trade union leader at a Conservative party conference. 'Meet me outside. You'll need wheels, preferably a four-wheel drive.'

'I'm not a bloody car salesman.'

She made me smile, quite a feat in the circumstances. 'And bring a torch.'

'Anything else?' she said, testy.

'Is Jake okay?' In the absence of a response, I said, 'Be there soon as you can.' I hoped my smile would translate down the line, then I hung up and lost the phone down the nearest drain.

Two hours later she showed up in a VW Touareg. I climbed into the passenger seat. She thought she was going to make a quick getaway. I had other ideas. I leant over, switched off the engine, flicked on the light and, against a flurry of protest, cupped her chin in my hands and squeezed.

'What the…'

'Tell me again about the toxin Wilding was working on.'

She started as if I'd thrown boiling water in her face. 'Were you too stupid to take it in the first time?'

'She worked in a defensive capacity rather than offensive? You're sticking to the script?'

'It's not a bloody script.' She flashed with fury. Formidable. I let my hand drop. 'Do you realise the risk I'm running by even mentioning it?' So her bosses hadn't sanctioned that part of the exchange of information. Looked like we were both up for chucking out the rulebook.

I stared at her hard. There were red marks on her face. Shaking with ire, she stared back, undaunted.

'All right, I accept what you say.' Until I had proof otherwise was what I meant.

'Fuck you, Hex, tell me about Frank Lygo.'

And with that I told her how I'd tracked Lygo down.

She broke in, accusing. 'You followed Yakovlevich's second-in-command to Wandsworth?'

'Yes.'

'You said you lost him. You lied to me.'

'I did.'

'So how do I know you're not lying now?'

'Because you have my word.'

'*Your* word?'

'Look, Lygo asked me to kill Jake Wilding.'

'I don't see the connection. When did he ask?'

'Six o'clock, or thereabouts, yesterday evening.'

'On the phone, or what?'

'No, I met him.'

'Christ,' she let out. 'Where?'

'I'll tell you later. The thing is…'

'What did you say to him?' she cut in again.

'I said I'd do it.'

She gave me a long slow stare. Her top lip curled. Stony.

'You *know* I wouldn't.'

Her eyes stayed fixed on mine. Against the dark they shone.

'No, I *don't* know.'

'I didn't kill him when I had a perfect opportunity so why now?'

She didn't pursue it, but from the tight expression on her face

I knew she was saving that one until later. 'Does Lygo have any idea who has the data?'

I shook my head.

'Think he's lying?'

'No.'

'What was he planning to do with it?'

'Destroy it.' I kept his wild allegations to myself.

She flinched. 'At the risk of repeating myself, think he's lying?'

'Yes.'

She sighed, smacked the steering wheel with both hands. 'I'm missing something.'

On this we were simpatico. Unlike McCallen, it wasn't in my nature to openly get screwed up about it. Easier for me; I didn't have one eye on a possible promotion. I had nothing more to lose. 'Anything else show up?' I said.

'No chatter. No intelligence. Nothing at all.'

This was quite some admission. In a flash it seemed that the obvious was staring me in the face. I'd been too caught up to notice. 'Perhaps, that's it: nothing.'

She thrust me a sharp look that would silence most. I'm not most. 'There's no hard evidence that anything has been taken,' I argued.

'How about an empty safe?'

'Precisely: empty.'

'You're saying there was nothing in it?' She looked at me as though I'd lost my mind.

'Why not?'

'You believe we're all wasting our time?' The derision in her voice should have been bottled and used to disperse oil spills.

'Wouldn't put it quite like that.'

McCallen shook her head. 'I'd love to believe it's true, but we can't afford to take a punt.'

'All right, maybe the data's been taken so that it can be destroyed.'

Colour drained from her face. I thought it an odd reaction. 'Then why the dead bodies?' she agitated.

'Fear. Simply put, they knew too much.'

'Or served their purpose.'

'More worrying,' I admitted.

'Brings us straight back to Lygo.'

'Who alleges he's in the dark about the hard drive.'

She shook her head. I couldn't tell whether she disagreed with me or not. 'You'd better take me to him.'

'To do what?'

'Bring him in.'

I didn't voice what I really thought about her lousy suggestion. Nobody was going after Lygo unless it was me. Alone. 'He's not going anywhere. We check out the bodies first.'

'Who the hell is in charge here?'

Squabbles about status never impressed me. I reached for the door. She snatched hold of my sleeve. I turned slowly, looked at her hand, looked back up into her eyes. Apart from breathing, she didn't move a muscle. Static filled the air, the atmosphere in the car electric. I think we were both sweating. I don't know how long we stayed fused together like that. The urge to kiss her intense, I leant towards her. She moved minutely forward then drew back with a faltering smile. Her hand dropped as if she'd touched fire. 'You win. Where exactly are we going?'

Women confound me. 'Epping Forest,' I said, thinking how clichéd.

She gave a shaky laugh and turned the key in the ignition. We travelled in silence for the first few miles. There was no sign of anyone tailing us, intelligence services or otherwise, nothing suspicious at all. McCallen had stayed true to her word. I realised then that she wanted to make her mark more badly than she wanted to kow-tow to her superiors. Give me a woman with a fine maverick streak any day. It put me in mind of Ellen Greco. I wondered if she'd managed to dig up any dirt on Lygo Stateside.

'Can I ask you something?' I said.

'You can ask.'

But it didn't mean I'd get an answer. Fair enough. 'When the Mossad team tried to kill me MI5 put out a cover story.'

'What about it?'

'Why protect them?'

She glanced across at me. 'The Israelis are our friends.'

'Friends don't shake down their mates for money.'

She laughed lightly. I pressed the point. 'You're happy to let them run amok on London streets?'

'Of course not, but for a whole host of political and diplomatic reasons it's deemed expedient. Don't get me wrong,' she said, glancing across again. 'We weren't thrilled. It caused an almighty stink, actually, but Mossad provide expert assistance in monitoring groups from the Middle East based in the Capital. With our overstretched resources the help is greatly appreciated, believe me. We couldn't afford to jeopardise the relationship.'

Which made Lygo's scandalous allegations against the British government even more unlikely. 'So you became the scapegoat.'

She shrugged. 'I messed up.'

It struck me that her life would have been easier if I'd been killed. 'Did they say why I was important to them?'

'Not in so many words.'

'Like to explain?'

'They maintained you had terrorist links.' Sounded like the equivalent of a get out of jail free card to me. When in doubt, whisper one word: terrorism.

'Is that what you think?'

'I don't know,' she said.

I stared out of the window, watched the world spin by, wondered which crime had put me on a collision course with arguably the most professional and effective security service in the world. Thinking back over more than a decade of 'removals' it would be difficult to fathom out. Was it as a result of a lethal injection administered in a crowded street? An overdose? Or was it a fall from a ten-storey hotel room, or the crash of a light aircraft with contaminated Av-Gas in the fuel line? Embedded agents were superb at concealment, which meant it was entirely possible I'd eliminated one of them unwittingly. A more likely scenario, I'd removed one of their informers. However I viewed it I came up empty. I doubted I'd ever discover the truth. I probably wouldn't live long enough to find out.

Under the cover of darkness, I got her to drive close to the dumpsite. We both clambered out. A full moon illuminated the earth. McCallen took out a torch and flicked it on.

'This way,' I said. She followed as I retraced my steps and picked out the route. When it came to the final descent I offered my hand. McCallen grasped it, her fingers strong against the leather, and together we slipped and slid down the steep-sided hill to the gully below. At the bottom I asked her to flash the torch around so that I could retrieve the shovel. I started to dig while McCallen stood and watched wordless. She didn't shiver in the cold. She didn't talk. She didn't recoil.

I pulled out Yakovlevich first. McCallen crouched down, took a good look, nodded, satisfied.

'Next,' she said. I obliged and closely watched as she studied the dead man's face. Her expression remained impassive, only the small outtake of breath as it mingled with the night and formed a smoke ring in the chill air told me that something had dropped into place for her.

'Who is he?' I said.

'Sergei Petrov.' I was surprised she could be that specific. Dead men looked much the same to me.

Pesky Russians again, I thought. 'Is he someone I should know?'

She looked up into my eyes. 'Petrov's a Russian scientist who once worked at the Russian Defence Ministry's research and testing institute.'

'For Vasily Felshtinsky?' The FSB officer with whom Yakovlevich did business, and the reason McCallen had engaged in such a heated conversation with her attractive Russian contact.

'Originally, but Petrov skipped the Motherland and was last sighted working in a bio-plant in Iran.'

'When was this?'

'Three years back. He disappeared from Tehran around six months ago.'

'Disappeared?'

'Skipped the country. No easy task. Scientists are routinely interrogated and subject to strict travel restrictions. If they do manage to attend the odd scientific conference, they always have at least a couple of minders in tow. Not even money can buy you a 'holiday' out.'

'Do you think he was exfiltrated by the Russians?'

She shook her head. 'Wasn't them.'

'Strikes me he had heavy duty connections.'

She shone the torch full beam into my face. 'You'd better start talking about your boss,' she said, an ugly twist in her voice. 'And don't pretend you know nothing about him.'

Fickle, I smarted. One moment you fancy me the next you want to quiz me with menaces. Leaving out Lygo's claim about the ethnic element of the toxin, I told her what he told me. She could pick the truth from the lies.

'So Lygo's a scientist.'

'Genetics, that's what he said.'

'Was he convincing?'

'Convincing and telling the truth are two different things.'

'I realise that,' she said, acerbic.

Now I came to think of it, Lygo hadn't exactly chosen an occupation impossible to check out. 'Easy enough to confirm his credentials and find out if he's lying. Maybe he was using a snap cover.' Or maybe he didn't give a damn.

'But he said his path had crossed with Wilding.' A troubled

expression flashed across her eyes so fleeting I almost missed it. 'How did that come about exactly?'

'Didn't spell it out.'

She considered this for a moment then I told her about the list of MI5 safe houses.

'You have it with you?' she sharpened.

I reached into my jacket, handed her the pages. She snatched them out of my hand and studied them in disbelief. 'They're out of date but some of the locations are still operational. Christ,' she glared, pocketing them. 'I knew we should have gone after Lygo first. Where do we find him?'

'Black's Brewery.'

Her lips very slightly parted. If we weren't up so close and personal I would never have spotted her reaction. It struck me as odd because McCallen was pretty good at concealing her physical responses.

'Is there a particular problem?' I said

'A brewery is all you need,' she said, chill in her voice.

'For what?'

'Production. To brew beer you use living organisms. Biological warfare works on the same principles. It's time-consuming but possible, and brewery conditions provide a perfect environment. By adopting new genetic engineering technology, toxins can be produced in significant quantities.'

'I thought this was supposed to be technically complex,' I said shaken. 'You make it sound as though, given a couple of demijohns, anyone can knock this stuff up.'

'No,' she said flatly. 'First, the appropriate strain of disease pathogen has to be acquired, then you have all the risks of handling it, scaling up production and finally dispersal.'

I registered how Petrov fitted into the picture. 'You think Lygo wants to get his hands on the data, not to sell it, but so that he can go into production?'

'Either that or so he can test its veracity.'

I glanced at the dead scientist and spiked with fear. Petrov had outlived his usefulness. Lygo was lying through his teeth. He'd sent me on a wild goose-chase to keep me occupied 'Maybe he already has it.'

'If he does we're screwed.'

I rocked back on my heels and remembered my conversation with Billy Squeeze, about me being set up and used as an elaborate smokescreen. 'Come on,' I said, straightening up. 'I'll take you there.'

CHAPTER TWENTY-ONE

We were ten minutes into the journey when McCallen received a call. She listened hard, eyes fixed on the road ahead. I couldn't see her reaction. Her voice remained neutral. Then she suddenly pulled over.

'Does anyone else know?' she said. I couldn't hear the reply. 'Keep it to yourself for now… Yep, what else do you have?' She didn't say anything for several minutes. It seemed to me that she was getting some heavy low-down. Occasionally I'd been a bystander to telephone altercations like these. They usually kicked off when a drugs bust had gone wrong and someone was being held to account and threats made. I got the impression that McCallen was in a similar position. Finally, she chewed on her lip and said in a clipped voice, 'No, I'm fine. Trust me… No, I don't know how much longer…Yes, I'm sorry…Just cover me for another hour or so.' She finished the call and, pensive, turned her gaze back into the night, started the car, stepped hard on the gas and pulled back onto the road.

'Who was that?' I said. She didn't answer. I tried again.

'Did you give errand boy the task of checking out Lygo?'

She glanced across at me. 'Blake found out that Frank Lygo is former CIA.'

It fitted. Deep down, I'd suspected a security service connection. It explained his knowledge of safe houses and the reason he was not an established 'face' in organised crime circles. It explained why he wanted to get his hands on the data. More worrying, it suggested knowledge that was way above my intellect and possibly McCallen's clearance and pay grade. It did not explain his desire to kill Dr Mary Wilding, still less his obsession with her son.

'He left under a cloud three years ago.'

'The sort of cloud that leads to vengeful retaliation?'

She shook her head as if my guess was as good as anybody's. 'Lygo's patch was the Middle East, Iran,' she continued slowly, no energy in her voice, as though someone had removed her batteries. 'He had an intelligence officer high up in the Iranian regime as an asset,' McCallen continued.

'Sounds like a genius idea.' For Lygo to enjoy any degree of success testified to the talented and flamboyant style of the man. Pitching to an asset was a delicate business, nothing like the crude methods I employed to force someone to get me the information I wanted. Any sortie into the Middle East was like treading on fine porcelain in the fond hope it wouldn't break.

'It was, initially, but the officer was peddling drugs…'

'Get found out and you wind up hanging from the nearest crane,' I cut in. 'Iran has one of the toughest set of laws on drugs.'

'Officially, yes. In reality it depends who's doing the dealing. Certain elements in power collaborate with the drugs trade.'

My political knowledge was sketchy, but my geography wasn't bad. Iran bordered the Caspian Sea. One of the biggest exporters of caviar, it was no big stretch to imagine smuggling out other commodities. A nice little earner, I didn't doubt.

'All right, so our Iranian engages in a bit of moonlighting.' Not so terrible where I came from. Business was business. 'How does Lygo figure?'

'He did more than turn a blind eye to his asset's activities. He acted as an accomplice. When his Iranian pal got arrested, interrogated and hung from said crane, Lygo fled and disappeared.'

Understandable. 'How the hell did he manage to vamoose from the mighty CIA?'

'Not as difficult as you might think,' she said, a disparaging note in her voice.

'Does Blake have anything else on him? Presumably Lygo's fluent in Arabic.'

'Farsi and Pashtu.'

'What about family history?' Personal details revealed a man's strengths and weaknesses. They disclosed what made him tick.

She glanced across at me longer than was safe for either of us. 'Are you always this persistent?'

I think part of her was fascinated, the other deeply suspicious. I didn't blame her. I flashed an apologetic smile. 'Habit.'

She nodded thoughtfully. 'Born in Missouri. Father: Irish American. Mother: Algerian. Frank used his mother's maiden name, Assad, during his stint with the CIA, smart move given his sphere of operation.'

…Out of greed, she decided to peddle her knowledge and sell the genetic code for a toxin that would wipe out Arabs…

I did my best not to swallow, not to react, but I was genuinely worried. What if I was wrong about the British government's intentions? 'This changes things substantially,' I said unable to muzzle the dull realisation in my voice. I also realised that Lygo was well outside Ellen Greco's international circle of movers and shakers. I hoped she hadn't gone to too much trouble on my account.

'I guess we now know exactly who and what we're dealing with,' she said.

Except, as far as I was concerned, *we* didn't. It depended on the specific purpose of the data. It came down to whether McCallen was speaking the truth or Lygo. If the stolen information related to the production of a toxin that targeted the white population, as McCallen maintained, Lygo with his half Algerian, half Arab heritage, was immune. On the other hand, if Lygo truly believed the blueprint was created to target Muslims, the ramifications of such an act too obscene to think about, he might have been speaking the truth about wanting to destroy it. Who would trade in something that, if unleashed, would kill them and the people they loved?

My mind meandered, something that happens to me when I'm tired and overloaded with adrenalin. I thought again about Billy and his connection to Lygo. Had Lygo trampled all over one of Billy's cocaine deals and threatened him with God knew what? *People like me employ a man like you because you don't leave a mess*, Billy told me. Maybe Billy had passed my name to Lygo with a personal recommendation. I'd often receive jobs this way. Or maybe Billy had made a few too many enquiries about McMahon, Lygo found out and consequently put the frighteners on him. Whether or not Billy was coerced, whether he gave my name and regretted it, it was unlikely I'd ever know. I never envisaged doing business with him again, or anyone else, for that matter.

McCallen cut into my thoughts.

'Nearly there,' she said. 'When we arrive, walk in under the pretext of wanting to talk. I'll be behind you and then we take Lygo down.'

'We?'

She turned and looked at me swift-eyed. 'This time I came prepared.'

'Thought you weren't supposed to be armed.'

'Only on babysitting duties.'

'Let's hope Blake doesn't cop for it then.'

'Not funny,' she said, jabbing me with a stony look.

We pulled into the yard. The place was deserted and consumed by silence. I climbed out. Neither of us closed the car doors. Too much noise. I slipped out the Glock. McCallen followed suit. Together, we approached the building. Tense. I expected to break the lock, but the door was already open and I slid inside the sterile interior, my gun hand outstretched, my other hand flicking on the lights. As far as Lygo was concerned I'd come in peace. As far as I was concerned I needed to have a good visual if I was going to immobilise him with a bullet.

I crossed the floor and scaled the metal staircase to the first level and then snaked up the short flight of steps to Lygo's lair, McCallen a breath away behind. The double-doors closed, I reckoned he was coiled and ready for me on the other side. I silently signalled for McCallen to spread out and wait. She nodded, veered off to the right. Sweat leaked out between my shoulder blades, across my forehead, along my top lip. Americans had guns hardwired into their psyche. Trained in firearms to the highest level, Lygo was my idea of the adversary from hell. I kicked out, my heel connecting with the weakest part of the doors, forcing them apart. The expected volley of bullets failed to materialise. Puzzled, I sneaked inside and found the office empty. More than empty, cleared. It was as if Lygo had never been there. Stunned, I turned to McCallen who stared at me with undisguised scorn.

'Is this part of the plan?'

Biting down hard to prevent a torrent of expletives from pouring out of my mouth, I skirted back down the steps. She yelled after me along the lines of *where the hell do you think you're going?* My reply was to barrel along the corridor and throw open every door to every room in a doomed attempt to unearth evidence that didn't exist. No computers. No lab equipment. Next, I covered the ground floor. No sign of girls. No sign of anyone or anything. Even the bloodstains had been removed. Seemed to me Lygo had been on the point of wrapping up and clearing out the moment I hurtled onto the scene. Those orders to Yuri to get rid of the bodies the first stage, his order to me to eliminate Jake Wilding the second. Recalling the malice and passion in Lygo's unseeing eyes, there was no doubt in my mind that he wanted the boy dead, no loose ends.

Feeling spectacularly unsuccessful, I headed for a door marked 'toilets.' There, I could sluice my face with cold water. It might bring me to my senses.

I went into the men's, checked the stalls out of habit, and going to the nearest wash-hand basin, ran the tap and splashed water over my face and into my mouth. I should have paid more attention to the ceiling, to the girder above where Yuri lay hidden like a funnel web spider waiting to strike. The force of him landing on me was the same as if I'd been crushed by a Grand Piano hurled from a tall building. My head smacked against the sink. My lungs emptied of air. He ripped the gun out of my jacket and, with his thick fingers, dragged me up and smashed my face into the mirror, cracking the glass. Blood streamed into my eyes as he drew me close against his immense physique and prepared to impale me on the taps. I arched and thrust my body back, whip-lashing my head into his face, temporarily forcing him to let go. Severely outclassed, I twisted round, punched Yuri on the jaw, skinning my knuckles, making no impression. He didn't even rock. As I was about to deliver a follow-up, he punched me hard in the stomach and let out a great gale of laughter. This was sport to him. Must have been saving this up for quite a while, I registered, breathless, my mouth full of blood and bile. As I doubled over he launched himself at my neck, grabbing hold of me, and hooked his right leg inside my left, kicking backwards and throwing me onto the tiled floor. Dazed, I tried to roll away, my body crunching on the mirrored shards. I wondered fleetingly where McCallen was when I needed her.

Yuri threw himself on top, pinning me down, his powerful thighs astride me. With one hand, he powerfully punched me repeatedly in the chest, the other around my throat, gripping my larynx so hard my breath rattled painfully in the fast decreasing space. Stars shot in opposite directions before my eyes, hands flailed like skate caught on a line. Seconds away from losing consciousness, I let my body sag, my head go limp and my arms drop. Yuri eased off, leant over. Big mistake. Shooting out my right hand, I hooked it round and clamped it to the back of his neck. Grimly staring into his eyes, I depressed the trigger on the ring-gun, turning away at the last second as the bullet made its entry, destroying the brain stem.

One hundred and seven kilos of human flesh collapsed on top of me.

Choking and spluttering, I disentangled myself, staggered to my feet and rinsed the blood from my face. I thought I was going to throw up. Pain held me in a vice-like grip. Not just my head, my whole body throbbed in uproar. In haste, I retrieved my gun and headed back to McCallen. It took less than five seconds to find her. In front of the bar, she was sitting down, still as statuary, palms resting on top of her thighs, her face ashen. Behind her a woman who could pass for a man held a blade to her throat. Suddenly, the *girls* that Lygo had referred to assumed a very different meaning, this specimen of femininity a clear candidate for assisting Yuri with body disposal.

'Hey,' I said, issuing my best winning smile.

The woman eyed me with dark suspicion. 'Where is Yuri?' She was tall, big-boned with forearms that rippled with muscle and sinew. Her flat, heavy features reflected her Russian accented English, thick as cement.

'Taking a leak. Yuri told me to get rid of her.' I drew my pistol, pointed it at McCallen who turned white then, raising the muzzle, shot the big Russian in the face. As the blade clattered to the floor, McCallen exploded from the chair and came at me. I opened my arms in the fond belief that she wanted to express her grati-tude. She wrenched the gun from my hand.

'Don't move.' She took a step back, breathless, the Glock trained on my chest.

'Sorry,' she said, clipped.

'Thank you would be more polite.'

'Don't get clever,' she glowered. 'Down there,' she said, jerking her head towards the rear of the bar and a closed door marked 'No Admittance Beyond This Point'. For some reason, when I'd clocked it before I'd paid it little attention, which was odd, although no hanging offence.

I crossed the floor, twisted the handle, and entered a room that linked to another, the door dividing the two hanging from its hinges.

'I had to bust the lock,' McCallen said. 'Take a good look inside.'

It looked like a shower block housed in stainless steel. Beyond this, another steel compartment with two Hazmat suits hanging from the back of the door. Thick white protective garments, they each had breathing apparatus in the form of masks linked to oxygen cylinders worn on the back, like diving suits. I stared back at McCallen. 'This is where it all happens,' she said. 'I'd broken open the locks, disabled the systems when our Russian shot-putter showed up. Understandably, she wasn't thrilled.'

'Is it safe to go inside?'

She nodded. 'It's empty,' she said by way of explanation.

Another door to another chamber followed by yet another airlock. 'Ultra-violet,' McCallen stated. 'They're separate staging-posts to ensure the destruction of all traces of bio-hazard.' She waved the gun for me to continue. Next stop the lab itself. I'd never been inside a high-tech laboratory before – ecstasy labs didn't count. It was basically a vision of white and stainless steel with identifiable bits of kit that I recognised from a passing interest in chemistry: Petri dishes, centrifuge tubes and centrifuge machinery, microscopes, cloning cylinders, general scientific glassware, pipettes, an autoclave for sterilisation, an incubator, and what looked like a fridge but had *test chamber* written on the side. It resembled a combination of pathology suite and a top of the range minimalist kitchen from 'Masterchef'. Looked like Lygo had moved things along to a critical stage.

I turned on my heel, faced McCallen. 'You've made your point. Why the gun?'

'I have no choice. You're turning yourself in. It's expected. It's how the game's played.'

'I can't help any more than I already have.' The words came out staccato, like bullets from a machine-gun.

'Not the opinion of my boss.'

'Your boss?' I flared in frustration. 'I don't like being played.'

She hiked one shoulder. Take it or leave it.

I narrowed my eyes. 'Does your boss know you're here with me?'

'Irrelevant,' she said.

'Have you any fucking idea what we're dealing with?' I blinked to rid my mind of the prospect of biological Armageddon. 'This isn't about what's at stake,' I snarled. 'This is about your damn career. You screwed up and now you want to offer me up like a cat presents a dead mouse to its owner.'

'As we're using animal analogies,' she continued, chisel-faced. 'I'd say you fall into the rat category.' She threw the car keys at my head. I caught them one-handed, took vicious aim, sent them flying straight back. As they connected with her face, with what I hoped was acute pain, she swung and fired, missing my left foot by a millimetre. Splinters of ceramic tile flew from the floor like sparks from a fire. A difficult shot. Had she wanted to put a bullet in my chest, I didn't doubt she could have done. I was impressed. I didn't think she was that good. I didn't think she had the balls. Cardinal error on my part: never ever underestimate the opposition.

'Don't make me,' she said, eyes narrowed, payback, undoubt-edly, for my previous threat to kill her. Blood seeping from where the skin was nicked, an ugly bruise blossomed on her cheek. Then her phone rang. Keeping the Glock steady, she slid it out of her jacket and pressed the phone to her ear.

'Yes,' she said. Her green glistening eyes drilled into mine. Even from several metres away, I could detect Blake's voice. Although I couldn't make out the words, the pitch suggested he'd made a significant discovery.

'Slow down,' McCallen said. 'What have you got exactly?'

Next a distant crackle, like a firework going off, a fair possibility given the time of year, followed by several more cracks. McCallen's eyes widened then narrowed. Her face drained of colour for a second time. 'Blake,' she said, looking at the floor. 'Are you still there? Blake, talk to me. Are you...?' She closed the phone, switched her ferocious gaze back to me. Full of strain, skin the colour of wood ash, she tightened her grip on the gun. 'You double-crossing bastard.'

I didn't ask what happened. I already knew. The sound was gunfire. The safe house was blown. 'This has nothing to do with me.'

'You expect me to believe you?'

'Screw what *you* believe, what about Jake?' I spat. 'What about the slow and agonising death of thousands of people? Unlike you, I give a damn.' As admissions went, this was a big one. It took even me by surprise.

She lowered her weapon. Progress. I was relentless. '*I* contacted *you. I* took *you* to the bodies. But if you care more about your precious career than defence of the realm and the innocent lives you're protecting, fine by me. Either way, your sidekick and Jake are in deep shit. We have to get to the safe house.'

She swallowed hard and started for the exit, and I followed.

CHAPTER TWENTY-TWO

McCallen drove at warp speed. Focused, she stayed silent. I daresay she blamed herself for exchanging places with what we both assumed now was a dead man. As for Jake, I held out little hope. It pained me. Lygo had got to him, either in person or by proxy, which made me think that he'd employed two assassins: one to carry out the deed, and another, me, as fall guy. That was my working theory for now. As for the discovery of the lab, the implications were too confused and scary to contemplate with any degree of clarity.

The safe house turned out to be a two-storey Victorian end of terrace near Shoreditch in an up and coming though not particularly trendy part of the capital. In the early hours, everything was quiet. I liked it that way, my kind of time, my kind of place. You'd never know the house provided sanctuary, a hideout. You'd never guess anything untoward could happen there.

McCallen wrestled a bunch of keys from her jacket and leapt out of the VW, gun in hand. I moved slowly after her. No point in getting exercised. The killer was long gone, either by road or rail, the train station minutes away providing a perfect exit.

Her immediate goal to check the status of those inside, McCallen plunged on ahead. I hung back unwilling to confront the reality of the dead boy. There was a time when the professional in me would want to compare the killer's skills to mine, to find out whether he was as good an operator, and why Lygo had chosen him over me. No more.

The front door, on the side elevation, displayed no sign of forced entry. From the entrance, a staircase and two doors. One led to a front room around five metres square. It looked barren and not much in use. From a security perspective, it was too exposed to the street outside. The second led to an inner room, the equivalent of a citadel. It had a traditional layout; sofa against the longest wall; two chairs and television; magazines on the floor; empty ashtray on the coffee table. No signs of struggle, no overturned furniture, no chaos.

From here a door to a galley-style kitchen with an exit into a narrow corridor that led to a downstairs bathroom. Here, the more mundane odour of absence was masked by a more visceral smell of blood. Immediately I noticed the mirror and the clean glass fracture from where a bullet had impacted at high velocity. McCallen, ahead of me, crouched next to the body of the man I only knew as Blake. She checked for vital signs. A pointless exercise: dead is dead. Nevertheless I stood respectful, my attention drawn to the number of shell casings littering the floor. Not good, not good at all. For a job of this nature I would have favoured a snub-nosed .38 revolver, the big plus, apart from speed and accuracy, no telltale cartridges, no debris for ballistics experts to collect and analyse. Quick observation told me that seven shots had been fired, two finding its target. Amateur.

McCallen glanced up, caught my eye, and shook her head. I shrugged an apology. 'Don't touch anything,' she warned, straightening up and heading back to the main body of the house and the stairs to a half-landing and upper floor. Like an apprentice, I trailed along behind, silently noting the security cameras, every one of the screens shot out.

'Jake's not here,' McCallen called down to me.

I frowned and paused, got my bearings: single door off to the left, four stairs to the right and two more doors to two double bedrooms. The heavy odour of adolescence denoted the room occupied by Jake Wilding. I walked inside the cramped confines, checked under the bed, stood on top and pushed open the loft space. No boy. No nothing.

'Looks like he's gone.'

'Taken,' McCallen frowned. 'I don't get it. Why not kill him?'

Good question. 'Leverage?'

'For what?'

I genuinely didn't know and said so.

'Is this Lygo's work?' she said.

Before we arrived I'd believed this a possibility. Now I wasn't certain. I didn't know what to make of it so I said nothing.

'You said Lygo wanted him dead,' McCallen pressed.

Yes and if not Lygo, who? I shrugged and walked back out onto the landing. Looking up, I noticed that the cameras on the upper storey were intact. Problem. I'd been caught on film and I bet the images were a lot sharper than the average CCTV.

McCallen followed my gaze. 'I'll take care of it.' I'd no doubt she would. My presence here would incriminate both of us.

'The killer disabled the cameras downstairs,' I pointed out to her.

'Then why leave these?'

'Because Jake was downstairs when the gunman struck.' At around three in the morning, I estimated.

'A bit late for him to be up, don't you think?'

I flicked a smile. 'You obviously know little about the activities of teenage boys. There's a simple explanation.'

'Yeah?'

'The ground floor bathroom. He probably needed to take a leak. Run the film and I'll bet you'll see him walking past and padding downstairs.' We trooped back down to the scene of crime. 'Blake was armed, right?'

McCallen maintained he was.

'Where's his gun?'

'On him, I presume.'

Presume nothing. 'You didn't find it?'

'I didn't look.'

Careless, I thought. 'Check him.'

She did. 'No, not here. Glock's gone.'

As someone regularly armed, I factor in the possibility that I can as easily be disarmed and my own weapon used against me. Given this scenario, however, I thought it unlikely. Whoever got in would be tooled up to the teeth. They wouldn't need extras. She read my thoughts.

'Hardly likely to be shot with his own weapon.'

'I agree.' Then why and who would take Blake's gun?

McCallen moved into the kitchen and checked the back door. 'Locked from the inside,' she said. She examined the window. This, too, was undisturbed.

'What's out there?' I said.

'A jungle garden surrounded by a high wall.'

Anyone hacking a way through would leave a flattened trail. I flicked on an outside security light, peered across a vista of grass and brambles at waist-level. 'Could the attacker have entered through the front door?'

'You mean Blake knew him?'

'That's my guess.'

McCallen vigorously shook her head then checked herself. 'Christ,' she let out, glancing at her watch. 'I should phone in.'

'Not yet.' Not until I was several miles away, at least.

'What else do you suggest?' she said, her manner terse. 'Whichever way you look at it, I'm fucked.' Royally, I thought. 'Suspension, enquiry, career over,' she added as if I didn't get the point the first time around.

A bright girl like McCallen would find other openings, I was sure. I didn't say this. It would be like telling her that there were plenty more fish in the sea when she'd set her heart on lobster.

She chewed her bottom lip. 'I should never have left.'

'You did and it happened. Self-recrimination is a waste of time.'

'But Blake is dead, the kid's missing, and it's my fault.' She looked stricken.

'The only person responsible is the person who killed him.'

'But I'm…'

'What's the drill?' I cut in. 'Does H.Q. send round a clean-up team?'

She gaped at me as though I'd asked her to take her clothes off. 'This isn't *Three Days of the Condor*.' Pity, a film I'd watched several times over, at least then I'd know what the hell was going on and, more to the point, how it was going to end. 'Within minutes of my call the place will crawl with intelligence personnel, police and forensics,' she continued. 'I'll be hauled in for a debrief and asked to explain my absence.'

Good, she was starting to think instead of emote. 'What are you going to tell them?' Not the truth, I hoped.

'That I got a lead.'

'They'll want detail.'

'Yes,' she said with a heavy sigh. I didn't doubt that she'd come up with something plausible. Her survival depended upon it. If McCallen were a plant she'd be bamboo, her ability under pressure to bend in the wind formidable.

'What happens if you don't make the call?'

'They come looking for me.'

'Seems like you don't have a choice.'

Subdued, she agreed.

'Did you tell anyone that you were with me?'

'Of course not.'

'Not even Blake?'

She inclined her head and smiled. 'You still don't really trust me, do you?'

'Had it drilled into me from an early age never to trust a soul.'

'Who told you that?'

That could keep for another day. I smiled back, elusive. I thought we were going to have one of those 'shall we, shan't we' get it together moments, but her face suddenly darkened. She didn't need to say what she was thinking. Whichever way you viewed it, this was a terrific mess and she was responsible for it. 'All right,' she said, as if she'd come to a huge decision. 'I make the call, sound the alarm and reveal everything I know about Lygo.'

'Without mentioning me.'

She arched an eyebrow. 'Without mentioning you,' she conceded. 'I take the flak. I get suspended.'

'Forgive me, but your suspension isn't going to figure much if Lygo has his hands on the data or worse still, God help us, a viable toxin.'

'Point taken,' she said with a pale smile. 'Think he's in it for revenge?'

'Revenge for what?'

'Coming unstuck with the CIA?'

I shook my head. 'Look at Lygo's background in economics,' I said glibly, 'he's simply doing what he's always done. This is about trade, loot, filthy lucre, making money.' No different to all the bad men I'd ever dealt with.

'Something you share in common then.'

Cheap shot, pointless and unexpected, but she was right. And McCallen was entitled to feel tetchy. In a few minutes she was going to be facing the music – an entire symphony's worth. I let my silence do the talking.

'What next?' she said, catching me unawares. I didn't presume there was going to be a 'next'. I was pretty clear on what I wanted to do.

'We meet,' I said without giving it a second thought. Aside from what was going on around us, I had to see her again. If I were honest she didn't look as keen.

'Not that easy. I'll be watched. They might put A4 onto me.'

Where I came from A4 was a paper size. I looked suitably baffled.

'Specialist surveillance,' she insisted. 'Crème de la crème of watchers. I wouldn't recognise them from ordinary Five officers.'

'Then we come up with a plan and screw them.' Where was the problem? I quickly offered possibilities. One got her vote. 'When can we hook up?' I said.

She looked at her watch. 'Give me twenty-four hours.' I wasn't sure whether she expected me to synchronise like they do in movies. I didn't. I named the perfect place. From the cunning smile on her lips, I could tell this met with her approval.

'What are you going to do?' she said.

What I should have done all along. 'Find Jake Wilding.'

CHAPTER TWENTY-THREE

I crossed streets that were risky by day and even more dangerous by night, and boarded the first train out of the station. Like butterflies, ideas fluttered into my head and fluttered out again. I wanted to net them but they proved too elusive.

The motive for Jake's abduction bothered me. Kidnap was a uniquely time-consuming and costly business, fraught with unpredictability and the constant threat of exposure. Why would Lygo, or indeed anyone, take the risk when a more important game plan was in motion? Maybe that was the point, another distraction from what was really going down. I had a horror that, as I floundered, a shadowy meeting was in play, deals done, bargains struck, money changing hands. Then again, if nothing had been taken, this opened up a whole new dimension and, comforting though this appeared superficially, it meant I was really missing something.

I looked out of the window at the grey, defeated landscape, the sky heavy and pendulous with snow. So busy searching for the devious I wondered if I'd neglected the obvious. Wilding's son had no value that I could divine so maybe abduction was only an assumption. According to McCallen, Jake was a spirited individual, code for petulant and difficult. He was also a teenager.

Aside from his grief, he'd feel frustration. Undoubtedly terrified, he would not be so overwhelmed by it that he wouldn't, at least, contemplate escape. Adults with life experience behave very differently to the young and immature. They know the risks. Teenagers have risk running through their veins. Bored of being cooped up in his surroundings with no clear end in sight, I reckoned it was a fair bet that Jake had fled the safe house of his own volition and, luckily for him, before it was blown. This would, in part, explain Blake's timely call to McCallen. He was trying to flag up that the boy had made a run for it. The more I considered the possibility, the more plausible it seemed, although it didn't resolve why anyone, other than Lygo for reasons best known to himself, would bother to attempt to kill him at this late stage. I could understand why I remained a target, but not the boy.

Right now, I needed to get the hell out of the area but I calculated that, if Jake had engineered his own escape, chances were he'd be lying low within an eight kilometre radius of the safe house, in which case I was already on the wrong course, on the wrong train, looking in the wrong place. I thought about contacting McCallen to tell her this. I swiftly decided not to. One: she wouldn't believe me. Two: it would compromise the pair of us. If I risked return I'd walk straight into trouble. Three: I didn't want to follow the curve of events. I wanted to ride them.

With hindsight, I should have asked more questions. I'd been too persistent with regard to Lygo and less persistent with the person who mattered most. I didn't know Jake Wilding's old haunts. I didn't know his friends or whether he had any. I didn't know his current state of mind. I could only guess based on personal experience.

My mind reeled back fifteen years.

Numb, raw, silenced, this was what I'd felt. Unhinged and disconnected, this was what I was. Any illusion I'd ever had that my life was in control vanished without trace. Overnight, I was plunged into an atmosphere of denial and blame, silence and recrimination. People can react quite oddly in the aftermath of violent death. Looking back to when my mother was alive I saw the world in colour; with her death my vision changed to black and white. I wondered how Jake Wilding now viewed the world.

The train arrived at West Croydon shortly after six-thirty in the morning. I took a tram to East Croydon station and, using a pay phone, called Jat. Despite the hour, he answered after two rings.

'Can you talk?'

'Uh-huh.'

'How's the little brother?'

Jat let out a groan.

'Not good then?'

'That's the problem. He's too good.'

Instinctively I bent one knee slightly, shifted my weight, and turned my face away from the glass and anyone walking by. 'When he isn't at the mosque or attending meetings he spends every waking moment lecturing us about the evils of the West. Apparently my weakness for the odd pint condemns me to an eternity in damnation,' Jat said with feeling. 'My parents are tearing out their hair.'

'Have you managed to turn anything up?'

'Not really.'

I blinked, wondering whether Jat was onto something without being aware of it. The Muslim/Jewish dimension was like a thorn in my side.

'Thing is, I need to keep tabs on Khaled so I'm playing along, acting like I've seen the light.'

'I like your thinking.'

'I can't promise anything. It's a real long shot.'

'Do what you can.'

I said I'd phone him again when I could. His was a fruitless endeavour, perhaps, but I appreciated the effort. Next I caught a mainline train back to Victoria. I had two destinations in mind.

First, I needed to refuel. Finding the nearest food shop, I bought sandwiches and

take-away coffee. Afterwards I went to a public lavatory and took advantage of the washroom facilities and freshened up. Wiped out with exhaustion, I'd neither slept much nor shaved in a couple of days. My new stubbly look suited me. It also helped conceal the damage Yuri had inflicted on my face.

I took a bus, changing twice to avoid detection, and arrived outside Jake Wilding's former home before mid-day.

Sheeted scaffolding covered the front of the house. Cordoned off as a crime scene, it immediately assumed a bleak and lonely appearance. Like a sentinel, a solitary policeman stood outside. Word would have leaked out that the boy had been taken, or escaped, dependent upon whichever view the powers that be subscribed. This didn't faze me. Wilding's home should have been where the cops were on high alert. Understanding how they operated, I gauged it the least likely place. The policeman looked bored and cold and complacent, the likelihood of him springing into action remote. With regard to the alarm, I'd memorised the original code. If it had been changed I could over-ride it. Where there's circuitry there's a connection that can be cut or reconfigured.

Pulling my cap down well over my face, I walked past the house, turned right at the second turning and made a big loop round until I was parallel to the rear of the property. That's when I spotted a Volvo parked some distance down the road, an unmarked police car, most likely. Inside, cartons and paper coffee cups littered the dash, and a man and woman ate a selection of fast food. From the way they were going at it, I reckoned it was the first time they'd had a break in hours. This was good. Hungry people are sharp. Food has a sedative effect on the brain. I needed the cops to be as sated and lethargic as possible. I wanted their senses blunted.

Still left me with a problem: the road was busy.

Out of ten ordinary people, perhaps eight would notice my

aberrant behaviour. Of those eight, six would be suspicious. Of those six, less than half would be determined enough to contact someone in authority. However you multiplied it, I was the equivalent of one person away from immediate arrest. A bad man, undoubtedly, but I was no fool. I took nothing for granted. One person was all I needed to completely screw me.

I took a deep breath and in full view of passing traffic and pedestrians, scaled the high wall as fast as I could, dropping down onto the other side. I waited, blood pounding through my head, expecting the alarm to be raised. Nothing happened. Keeping close to the larch-lap fencing that formed a natural boundary with next-door, I sprinted across the garden towards the patio and back entrance. Inside, a rear lobby contained the security system. I slid the disabling device from my jacket, held it up to the window, and a minute later walked inside, closing the door silently behind me.

It felt strange to be back, a form of sacrilege. Immensely cold, the place had a dead and musty museum-like quality, like it was frozen in time for future generations. The damp and fetid atmosphere smelt of chemicals, a result of the crime scene techs at play. I imagined them soft-shoeing around in their moon suits, taking photographs, measuring distances, lifting every available print, dusting surfaces, removing articles, removing doors, everything bagged and tagged and signed for. Moving like a wraith through the lower floor, I noticed for the first time the ornate cornicing, the dado rails, the solid wooden staircase, French windows, feature fireplace, stylish laminate flooring. I admired Mary Wilding's bold choice of colour: bright golden yellow softened by grey, and navy combined with peach. The woman had style. Home was important to her, perhaps not as much as her career, but it mattered. I didn't think I understood this before.

I paused outside a downstairs room, a dining room I imagined, for no other reason than it revealed a chaotic scene of overturned chairs, broken ornaments, pictures ripped from walls. Overkill, I thought. Something about the arrangement of smashed-up tables and chairs came across as theatrical and staged, giving an impression of a burglary rather than evidence of one taking place. I glanced across to the opposite room and discovered the same degree of vandalism. It startled me. Professionals didn't leave traces. Nothing in the act sat well with the cool, clean way in which Wilding had been killed, inclining me to think that someone other than a professional was responsible for the destruction. Had the place been left unguarded I'd have put money on Yuri. The rage behind the wanton vandalism bore his hallmarks. As it stood, I couldn't say.

Pondering this, I crept upstairs; retracing my steps and following the exact route I'd taken on the night of Mary Wilding's death. Her bedroom had been stripped. The door had also been removed, only the wooden base of the bed left in place. Briefly squatting beside it, I recalled my own sense of surprise and dull realisation that another had been there before me. I remembered her hair, the way her arm hung down, the softness of her middle-aged flesh. I thought about how I'd justified her demise and compared her to a long list of others who'd also sold their souls for money. People like me.

Straightening up, I decided to check out the other bedrooms, of which there were two. Neither reflected recent occupation by a teenager. No lads' mags, no litter, no clothes or clues about school or mates. Admittedly both had received the full forensic treatment. Even so, it struck me as profoundly odd, almost as peculiar as the absence of photographs in the house.

I moved on to the study. Soulless and barren, stripped of computers and filing cabinets, the desk cleared and a hole in the floor where the safe had been removed for examination. Hard to imagine the scientist ever working on her private scientific papers here. I scanned the books on the shelves, thick scientific tomes and journals, as you'd expect. No novels.

I turned on my heel, retreated to the space behind where the door would have been. With my eyes closed, I replayed the exact moment when Jake Wilding flicked on the light, met my eye, and our lives became irrevocably and inextricably linked. Floppy hair, lantern jaw, jeans, jacket, trainers and…

A torrent of questions exploded in my head. How come he was fully dressed at that time in the morning? What was he doing? Had he been out? Where had he been? *'Who sent you?'* he asked. As odd a question now as it was then. Did he expect someone? And if he did, did he tell McCallen this? Did he name names? And if so, had McCallen decided to keep me in the dark?

Shaky, I sat down at the top of the stairs. I wasn't given to crazy ideas but Jake Wilding was the last person to see his mother alive. He was also her next of kin. Blood connections carried weight. In other circumstances, he'd be viewed as a potential suspect. So what was I really thinking? That Jake was in some way connected to his mother's death? Lygo's voice wormed its way into my brain: *'A child?'*

I checked myself. Lygo was a crook. Evidence surrounding the boy was circumstantial, nothing more. Not only ridiculous and unthinkable, it was without motive. The expert way in which Wilding was killed, alone, the precision required, ruled Jake out.

So where was he now? Held in a dark, dingy basement, fleeing for his life, or on a mission to find the man who he believed killed his mother? I shook myself for making a classic mistake, Reuben's voice like a taunt in my ear. *Never second-guess someone else's actions by considering how you would behave in the same situation.*

Back to basics then, to the information, the prize, the reason half the security services in the world were tearing around the country. Only a fool would believe that McCallen was telling me the full version. Too often I'd noticed something else flit behind her eyes when she spoke. I wished I knew what that was and yet I dreaded it.

With a strong sense of coming full circle, I started over again.

From the moment I'd entered Wilding's room I'd assumed the involvement of another assassin. Lygo had given the impression that the data had fallen into other criminal hands. I thought back to our conversation. He'd been keen to quiz me, anxious to find out if I had a clue about who had it. Was it possible that the laboratory had been set up but never used?

I got to my feet, slipped back downstairs and instantly braced. I had company: voices; key in the lock; people. I swallowed at the prospect of arrest followed by a lifetime's incarceration, if I were lucky. Blood rushing through my temples, eyes fixed doggedly ahead, I took a big gulp of air, kept moving on leaden legs, willing my way to freedom. Not for my sake, but for those I didn't know.

One more step then another. Chill air behind me as one door opened and another closed. Silently I left the house the way I'd come in. By the time I got back to the road, my pulse had settled and the Volvo had gone. The team, if that's what they were, inside Wilding's home, chasing shadows.

CHAPTER TWENTY-FOUR

With Britain unusually gripped by Arctic conditions, it took me over an hour to reach Reuben's home in Chiswick. Snowing hard, roads in chaos, spin of tyres on untreated surfaces, London had ground to a standstill.

Reuben projected the affable and easy-going side of his personality when he opened the door. 'Joshua, come in, come in. Anyone told you your face looks like a smashed-in watermelon?' he chuckled. I smiled, snake-eyed, and followed him into the kitchen. 'I was making coffee. You want some?'

I nodded and watched as he poured boiling water into a cafetiere and retrieved another mug from the cupboard. He didn't ask where I'd been. He didn't ask what I'd been up to, what misfortune had befallen me, or who had rearranged my features.

'Are you alone?' I said.

He glanced at me, a quizzical expression in his dark brown eyes.

'Only last time I was here,' I began, 'You had company.'

He didn't respond straight away. He took cream from the fridge, poured it into a jug and set it on a tray together with a bowl of brown sugar. I watched his every move knowing that if he chose he could strike and strangle me with his bare hands. 'Really?' he said mildly. 'I don't remember.'

'Three wine glasses on the table, one clean, one yours, one used.'

'Your powers of observation remain impressive.'

'They should be. I learnt from the best.'

Reuben flashed an appreciative smile. He walked towards the steps that led down to a dining area and motioned that I follow, which I did. We pulled out chairs, sat down opposite each other, the table between us. I looked into his eyes. He held my gaze, steady.

'Why did you do it?' I said.

His eyes flickered in the dull winter light. 'Do what?'

'Betray me.'

'Joshua,' he spread his wide, mobile hands. 'You've lost me. I've done nothing but help you.' I nodded slowly, pretending to buy the lie. 'I made a promise, remember?' he said.

'Yes, I do.'

A faraway look entered Reuben's eyes. Immediately the years peeled back, making him appear much younger. I found it disturbing, as if he were dragging me back with him.

He spoke slowly, weighing each word, weaving a story. 'Your grandfather was a mabuah.' A non-Jewish informer and part of Israel's invisible army of helpers. 'He was Israel's friend and Israel does not forget its friends.' I knew this well, just as I knew that Israel did not forget its enemies or that Reuben had once been a katsa, a Mossad field agent. 'You remember him?'

I did. He'd been an investment banker. Populated by rich and powerful men, the world of high finance seemed strange and shadowy to me at the time, still did. It was never openly stated but I gathered that over many years grandfather pulled influential financial strings for a country that was not his own. To this day, I had no idea why. My grandfather was not the sort of man you'd call approachable. I think, even before my mother's sudden and violent death, he'd viewed me as a nuisance, an encumbrance in his life. It's why I'd been so beguiled by Reuben. By comparison, Reuben was charismatic and confident and amusing and I was flattered by his attention, as was my mother, I remembered.

'Yes, Reuben.'

Reuben nodded, satisfied. I thought he was going to tell me something important. Instead, he leant towards me, conspiratorial, his voice soft. 'Do you think of your mother, Joshua?'

Uncomfortable with the question, I leant away from him. Nevertheless, I replied truthfully. 'More often than ever these days.'

'A fine woman. Of course, she had problems, as do we all,' he said tactfully. The 'problems' as Reuben so quaintly put them was her strong addiction to alcohol and prescription pills. It led to a certain amount of domestic chaos. To protect me from it and long before her murder, I'd spent significant periods of my life with my grandparents. I think it contributed to my solitary nature. In spite of this, I'd loved her like no other, with passion. When she was well she was the best. She could light a room. Men fell in love with her. They consumed her. Although this did not please me, it did not surprise me. I understood. Her beauty was the big turn-on for most of her admirers. Others were drawn to her slightly feverish, vulnerable nature. I don't know what did it for Michael Berry, why he felt drawn to her. I'd never wanted to stop and consider it.

Reuben's voice continued to drip into my ear. 'Your grandfather, and indeed, your grandmother never really recovered from your mother's death.'

Their lives disintegrated as did mine. My grandmother took to her bed, my grandfather to mute isolation in his study. I was caught in my own personal maelstrom.

'It was not your fault, Joshua, but afterwards you became an immensely sad and disturbed young man. And so I promised to take you under my wing.' Reuben did not need to say this. I knew how the story went.

222

'It was not my only promise,' he continued. 'I swore on oath to your grandfather that I would find and bring to justice your mother's killer.'

I straightened up. This was something I had never heard before. I rubbed at an imaginary stain on my jeans. When I spoke I had difficulty in concealing the pain in my tone. 'You used me.'

He flicked a smile. 'I trained you and we used each other.'

I drank some coffee. My hand trembled. 'And your masters, were they aware?'

Reuben shook his head. 'Of course not, it would have been viewed as unorthodox.'

'So they knew nothing of me?'

'They didn't need to know. Besides, I believed you'd come to your senses.'

'You didn't think I'd stay the course,' I said with a dry laugh. 'You thought I'd buckle.'

'Yes.'

'But I didn't.'

'No.'

'So what was I, some kind of experiment?' I had a dry acrid taste in my mouth and my voice sounded bitter. I couldn't help myself.

'I thought training would help, that it would give you a sense of purpose. It was important someone believed in you.'

You stole my trust, I thought, at a time when I was vulnerable and trusted no-one.

'When I saw how good you were...' His voice briefly trailed away. 'Joshua,' he leant towards me, wonder in his eyes, 'you learnt more in twelve months than most agents in three years.'

'You never said.'

His eyes hardened. 'I wanted you to convert, is that not enough?'

Strange to say, I remembered the suggestion. For the life of me, I couldn't recall my response. Academically, I could be quite lazy. The hours devoted to learning Hebrew held little appeal. National service in a strange land also repelled. Physically strong, I already had a highly developed sense of my own power and strength. More importantly, and thanks to Reuben, I had found my confidence. Reuben had channelled all my teenage energy into a killing machine. In essence, he'd created a monster and the monster got out of hand.

Interpreting my silence as a slight, he rasped, 'You could have served the greatest nation in the world.'

But I didn't. 'I went and did what I had to do.'

Reuben's top lip curled in disdain. 'You killed for money.'

I wasn't going to debate the immorality of what I did. I was in no position to make judgements, let alone argue a defence. 'What did you hope for, that I'd wind up in a dark foreign alley with a bullet in my head?'

'It has been known,' he said coldly.

'Why shop me now?' I felt consumed with white pain and anger. I should have known that friends and those closest to you often prove to be the greatest traitors of all.

Reuben's voice dropped to a low animal growl. 'Because you came back.'

I let out a laugh, something I do when under pressure. 'But…'

'My crime was to train you,' he spat. 'Your crime was to return.'

My fate sealed from the moment I walked through the door, it came as a shock. 'You double-dealing bastard.'

Reuben's fist hit the table with such force the china shook. I pulled the gun. One of my early lessons in self-defence was to shoot with accuracy from a sitting position. Reuben knew it. I knew it. He stayed very still. It felt odd to threaten the only man I'd ever trusted.

'I am very old. It will serve no purpose if you kill me.' He jutted out his chin in a gesture of defiance.

'It will serve *my* purpose. Let's get this straight,' I said. 'This business with Wilding, you decided to use me again, didn't you?'

Reuben smiled. 'In the service of my country I will do anything.'

Must be nice to feel that passionately about a cause. I let my finger play on the trigger. As much as Reuben thought he understood me, I understood him. At heart he was a survivor. He wouldn't go easily into the night.

'What do you know about Frank Lygo?' I said.

'Nothing,' Reuben blinked.

My smile was chill. I rephrased the question. 'Who is Frank Assad?'

'Former CIA turned rogue agent and the man who we suspect recruited your services,' he said, a mocking note in his voice.

'You knew all along?'

'I did not know,' Reuben said flatly. 'After your first visit I made enquiries.'

'You talked to your old pals?'

Reuben smiled. 'Once a spy always a spy, isn't that why you came to me? I am not the only user, Joshua.'

Colour spread across my cheeks like spilt red wine. 'Go on,' I said, the gun steady in my hand. 'What did you discover?'

'Assad has been on a Mossad hit list since he killed one of our own.'

'Explain.' The fibre in my voice made plain that this was an order. Reuben issued a tired sigh, something in his exasperated expression reminding me of my grandfather.

'For decades we've had a policy of infiltrating our field agents into the highest levels of government in the Middle East.'

'Successfully?'

'Extremely,' Reuben said. 'For historical reasons, and ever since the Americans' Beirut station chief was kidnapped and assassinated, the Americans have not been so fortunate. They haven't hadn't had a station in Tehran for years and any attempt to pitch to agents has largely met with failure. They have a long and depressing roll-call of scientists and others who have been killed by Middle Eastern governments on suspicion of spying.'

'But Assad was different?'

'Very,' Reuben snapped a cold smile. 'Empathy is the most important asset for a successful spy and Assad had empathy in spades.'

'The power to manipulate.'

'Too crudely put,' Reuben grimaced. 'Even the most unsophisticated human beings know when they are being controlled. It takes real skill to persuade others to trust you. Something you have yet to learn, I suspect.'

Inside, I boiled. Outside, I didn't so much as move a muscle. I kept my face poker straight. 'Tell me more about Assad.'

'A talented operator, he could smell weakness in a man. He had the knack of picking out those who were greedy from those who were needy. He could differentiate between a true idealist and one who masqueraded as an idealist.' With his extra-sensory powers of perception, I wondered what Lygo had seen in me. Nothing, I hoped. 'But Assad had one major flaw: arrogance,' Reuben continued gravely. 'He thought he was cleverer than even his own masters. Assad was not in the game to help his country. He was in the game for himself, doing deals on the side, drugs mostly. Half of Iran is addicted,' he added with distaste.

'And his path crossed with a Mossad agent?'

'Yes.'

'And Assad killed him because he'd discovered his little scam?'

'Because Assad was discovered running arms deals and supplying to Muslim groups with links to al-Qaeda.'

Christ. A toxin that would destroy the white population would be of immense interest to Islamic fundamentalists and Assad/Lygo already had those contacts in place. Such a commodity would surely fetch eye-watering amounts of money. I wondered just how much Lygo expected to be paid.

So far, Reuben had made no mention of Frank Assad's scientific interests or indeed the Russian scientist, Petrov. No mention of Assad/Lygo residing here in the United Kingdom either. This didn't mean to say that he didn't know. We weren't exactly trading information and I wasn't about to enlighten him.

'Is that why you sent me to watch McCallen? To establish a link between Assad and the new Muslim splinter group?'

'It was hoped it would yield fruit.'

But it hadn't, or at least it hadn't yet, and I'd failed to report in as expected. 'And when it didn't you had me followed.' Israeli surveillance teams were the best in the business. They could easily have watched without my noticing. Then I thought about the unknown team in Barcelona. I guessed that even the best had off days. Unless it was a deliberate ploy to shake me up and force me into making another mistake.

Reuben looked through me. He didn't say yes. He didn't say no. Either he knew more than he was letting on, or simply played enigmatic for effect. Why Mossad wanted to remove me remained a mystery. Perhaps it was a simple case of guilt by association. I put it to Reuben.

'No,' he said gravely. 'During the course of your killing spree...'

A pulse ticked in my jaw. 'I'm not some psychopathic high-school drop-out.'

Reuben ignored my protest. 'You got in the way of an under-cover operation.'

Shit, I thought. Ignorance was no defence. I'd messed with those on the side of the angels. Forgiveness was not high on the Mossad agenda, largely with good reason. My days were numbered.

'When, where?'

'I have no details,' Reuben said, a shrewd gleam in his eye.

'Then give me the broader picture.'

'I have no picture,' he said, stubborn as an overpaid company chairman hanging onto his entitlements.

My mind raced with locations and times and targets, like the German banker who I'd 'persuaded' to vault a metal railing and glass barrier and make an exceptional leap from the top of a hotel in Shanghai into the Huangpu River below. According to the media report, he'd been under considerable strain after making a series of flaky decisions that had lost his bank a ton of money. What was not generally known: the man, a violent paedophile, had killed two young boys during a ten-year period. Or was it the bomb I'd placed underneath the car of a Serb wanted for war crimes on a Paris street that had also killed his hapless female companion? Although I tried to force connections, I failed to make a link that stood up to any form of scrutiny. I could only imagine that I'd unwittingly screwed one of their operations and possibly destroyed years of planning. 'If I'm on a Mossad hit list I have a right to know why,' I glowered.

'A right?' he sneered.

'Tell me, damn you.'

Reuben gave a dismissive shrug. Generous with information when it suited, he preferred to retain the whip hand in matters that one day might also threaten Israel's national interests. A chilling thought suddenly occurred to me.

'If Mossad found out that Wilding had something they wanted, would a team have gone in and lifted the information?'

'Of course,' Reuben said evenly. 'And before you ask, anyone who trades in death can expect to pay the ultimate sacrifice. We've had our fingers burnt before.'

'She didn't trade,' I said, my overwhelming desire to protect the dead woman's reputation strong.

'Whatever.'

I narrowed my eyes. 'But Mossad didn't kill Wilding?' I had to be certain.

'Absolutely not.'

I watched Reuben's face for signs of deception. I could see none. 'Then who do you believe did?'

'We don't know.'

My trigger-finger tightened. Time to speak plainly. 'Who do *you* believe stole Wilding's secrets?'

Reuben slowly shook his head. 'I don't know that either. Perhaps the information was never there.'

My stomach clenched. I'd said the same only McCallen had dismissed it. My hopes briefly lifted. All this for nothing? 'Then why was Wilding murdered?'

Reuben shrugged. 'A question asked many times over. We do not always have the answers.'

I put the gun away, dejected, and stood up.

'I have it on authority that, while you remain in Britain, your safety is guaranteed,' he said, glancing up at me.

'And if not?'

He gave another lazy shrug of his big powerful shoulders. From a man who'd taught me how to make murder appear as a suicide, who'd given me lessons on how to conceal explosives, who taught me how to survive, this came hard. He'd cut me loose. He no longer cared. I'm not sure he ever did.

'Did you find Assad?' Reuben growled.

Deep in thought, I almost missed his question. 'No.'

The man who taught me everything I knew had forgotten that he'd also taught me how to lie with expert conviction.

'When you do,' he said darkly, 'send a bullet through his brain with our warmest regards.'

CHAPTER TWENTY-FIVE

Everything was swept away. No certainty. Nothing as it seemed. I'd spent days looking at the big picture, staring through the wrong lens, my past corroding my vision. And yet it was in my past the truth lay hidden.

While the hunt was on for Lygo, I went in search of Tilelli. This time I went straight to the basement bar on the Cromwell Road. It wasn't officially open, but Tilelli would sometimes have a coffee with the manager when he wasn't working. I didn't find Tilelli. I found Gaal, Tilelli's Somalian friend. Hunched over a glass of brandy in a darkened corner, he didn't notice my approach at first.

'Gaal?' I said, pitching up beside him. He turned and looked at me slow-eyed and without recognition. 'I was looking for Ron. Have you seen him?'

Gaal nodded. It wasn't especially cold in the bar but he shivered. Something was very wrong. 'I need to talk to him,' I said.

'Can't, man.'

'Can't?' I said, edge to my voice. I like 'can' so much better.

He snatched at his drink, took a big swallow, winced as though he were downing paraquat. 'He's dead.'

'Dead? When?'

'Early this morning.'

'Where?'

'Know the old gin warehouse in Dalston?'

Derelict for years, a bleak and melancholy assembly of broken down buildings, it stood on an expanse of waste ground. I nodded.

'Someone took him there, tied him to the undercarriage of his own car and took off with him underneath. He was dragged to death.' I imagined Tilelli's portly frame connecting with every piece of debris, every rock, every rise in the uneven ground, a truly terrible way to die. Wes's words to me at the hotel flashed through my mind. *They have their own for torture.*

Gaal turned to me, a wild, urgent look in his big eyes. 'I know what you do, Ronnie told me, but you wouldn't do something like that.'

He was right. I wouldn't. 'I'm very sorry, Gaal.' And I was. I also had the feeling that Tilelli had been killed because of me. Tillelli had put me onto Lygo, not willingly but under duress. My duress. 'What happened exactly?'

'Ronnie called me last night around ten o' clock. We were supposed to meet, right? He said something had come up, that he had to drive an important guy to a meeting.'

'Did he say who?'

'No.'

'Did he sound worried?'

'For sure. Ronnie said he was okay, but I knew.'

'You didn't push it?'

Gaal smiled sadly. 'I never asked those kind of questions. Ronnie did a lot of work for a lot of people, some of it shady.' A lot of it shady. With so many connections Ron Tilelli could have been taken out by any number of individuals. This could simply be happenstance. But the timing of his death and the manner in which it had come calling suggested otherwise.

'I got a text from him around one this morning. No message, only an address.'

'At the warehouse?'

He nodded. 'Think he sent it?' I said.

Gaal slowly shook his head, mournful. 'I don't know.'

'So what did you do?' I didn't think a man like Gaal would call the police, but you never knew. People acted weird in those kind of pressurised situations.

'I sensed something bad so I drove straight there.' Gaal's big eyes welled with fat tears and he began to sob. For a hard guy he did the crying thing with feeling. 'The police,' I said insistently, 'Do they know?'

Gaal wiped his nose on the back of his hand, leaving a snail trail of slime. 'I called from a phone box, didn't give a name, told them where to find him.' He drained the last of his drink. I bought him another. He looked as though he needed it.

'Before last night did he seem bothered about anything or anyone in particular?' Apart from me, I thought.

'Something was definitely going down. He was drinking more.' A heavy drinker in normal circumstances, Tilelli must have been shifting alcohol intravenously. 'The murder of that woman, the scientist, really upset him.'

'Why?'

Gaal shook his head again, his every movement laboured, like he was in slow motion. 'Seemed to take it personal, as if he were to blame, or something. And he acted more suspicious than normal. He started checking his car.'

'For bugs?'

'Uh-uh, underneath with a mirror.'

'Explosives?' I had a tingling flashback to the day when Reuben had taught me not only how to spot a bomb but attach one.

'Sure thing,' Gaal answered. 'We stopped meeting at his apartment. He said he didn't feel safe there.'

'Did he ever mention an American by the name of Lygo?'

Gaal thought for a moment, told me he didn't believe so.

'What about Frank Assad?'

232

Gaal tilted his head, thought again, and repeated the name. 'Maybe, I don't really remember.'

'Try.' This word was used extensively and repeatedly from my repertoire. I employed it most when I needed one crook to disclose vital information about another crook. Over the years, I'd perfected the tone and it worked. Gaal flashed me the same response I got from a lot of people: surprised fear.

'Ronnie got wrecked one night,' he said, breathy, 'started talking about the old days, before he came here.' I'd been treated to some of Tilelli's tales. He'd worked variously for the FBI, the CIA, and the Drugs and Enforcement Agency depending on what mood he happened to be in at the time and how much he'd had to drink. I suspected that he'd either known folk who had, or he'd attended several interviews and failed the selection process.

'I got the idea that he'd met someone called Assad back in the day.'

I frowned. 'You mean they worked together?'

'Search me, man.' Gaal issued an indulgent smile. 'Probably met in a bar. Actually, there *was* a guy who arrived in London not long ago who ran into Ronnie.'

'Think they were one and the same?' I said hopefully. Gaal gave me a wary look. To be fair, he was probably worried about my possible reaction to his lack of hard information. I flashed an encouraging smile, made out it was no big deal.

'Maybe. I'm good with faces, not names.'

'You never met him?'

'No.'

'When was this exactly?'

'Around ten months ago.'

'Did Ron ever speak about him again?'

'Never.'

Too much debris, too little detail; I had the feeling I was running headlong into a blind alley. 'Did Ron mention any particular places he'd worked in the States?'

'Nowhere special. He worked all over.'

So he said. A sharp pain inserted itself behind my eye. Felt like someone was plunging into it with a corkscrew.

'Always said he'd take me to St Louis,' Gaal said wistful.

I thought I'd misheard. 'St Louis, in Missouri?' The same birthplace as Frank Lygo, I registered.

'Where Ronnie grew up,' Gaal said. 'Ronnie sometimes talked about it. Place got hit real bad by unemployment, manufacturing industry collapsed, or something.'

I looked him straight in the eye. 'Gaal, can you take me to Ron's place, his apartment?'

'No way, man. Cops will be all over it.'

Knowing Tilelli's connections it wouldn't only be the cops. 'Tell me the address anyway.'

Gaal did, a second floor apartment minutes away.

'Key?' I said, holding out my hand.

'Hey, man, not sure.' Gaal's eyes rolled inside his head. I took out my wallet, started counting out twenties. The eyes focused. The key appeared in a flash. 'Got a phone number I can reach you at?' I said.

With a show of reluctance, Gaal fumbled through his pockets and drew out a fistful of cards, finally handing one to me. Name and number one side, image of two guys getting it on the other. Different. I slipped it into my wallet.

'Anybody else comes asking questions, you say nothing,' I said, handing him three hundred in cash. 'Stay low, out of sight, understand?' Gaal nodded uncertainly, scooping the loot inside his jacket.

I stood up, put my hand on his shoulder, patted it clumsily twice and left.

It didn't take long to cut through to the Old Brompton Road and into Roland Gardens. Slow day or slow effort, no sign of police or anyone else outside the apartment block. Yet. After almost being caught at Wilding's place, I wasn't about to get cocky.

I glided past a concierge talking to a deliveryman, and took the lift to the second floor, the door to Tilelli's apartment at the end. Without setting so much as a toe inside, I valued it at around one and half million in sterling. Either Tilelli was better off than I'd given him credit for, or he was renting.

I took out the gun and let myself in. No point in taking unnecessary risks. Took me seconds to clear two bedrooms, one en-suite; palatial bathroom; big open-plan reception room with expensive furniture, high ceilings and double doors leading to a kitchen kitted out with top of the range stainless steel equipment. To quote my Spanish friend Isabell, 'very on trend.' Or it should have been. But Tilelli lived like a pig. Dirty and untidy, with dumped bags of unopened food, the place stank of rancid food waste and booze, as evidenced by the number of empty bottles of sour mash whisky and Tilelli's favourite, Jameson. I doubted the place had been cleaned or dusted in years. It spoke of a disordered life. It spoke of emptiness.

I had little time to nail down Tilelli's last movements. At any moment the law or unknown others might show up. I swivelled my gaze to the sofa. An indentation in a big satin cushion implied recent occupation. Easy to imagine Tilelli's large frame sprawled in front of the television, Tilelli eating a take-away, the remains littering the surface of a light wood coffee table. Fused with concentration, I tuned out and imagined the scenario:

Tilelli gets a call.

Takes his phone from his pocket.

It's his mystery caller and he wants to meet.

Tilelli is anxious, frightened even, but he has no choice so he takes down the address.

I glanced over the debris for signs of a pad or piece of paper then realised my mistake. Tilelli knew the capital well, no need to write the destination.

Maybe he's a doodler.

I looked, hoped to find a note. Zero.

I took Tilelli's place. Seat and cushions reeked of unwashed hair and body odour, Tilelli definitely a man caught in the grind. I leant back. Rays from a feeble sun shone through the window and illuminated the foil carton and Tilelli's last supper and ...

I squinted and craned forwards, saw something scrawled, imprinted in the dust. *Jake.*

Quick investigation of the rest of the apartment yielded plenty of receipts for booze and cigars but no smoking gun, no hard connection to Jake Wilding.

Time to move out.

I made my way through snow-encrusted streets and took a minicab to Barnet. There, I spent that evening and part of the night holed up in a cheap motel. I hadn't found Jake Wilding, hadn't come remotely close to locating the boy in the flesh. I had a set of messy connections, a couple of possibilities and one probability, hardly anything to boast about. And yet...

Abandoning sleep, I rubbed my face and thought long and hard about Tilelli and his strong reaction to Wilding's murder. His recoil of shock and fear inferred he'd been party to information that until that point had little resonance. When told about Wilding he'd instantly painted in parts of a landscape to create an ugly canvas. I didn't think it connected to nerve agents and toxins and unspeakable weapons that could biologically exterminate half the planet and hurtle us back to the dark ages. Tilelli's response was visceral and personal. If Frank Lygo was not Tilelli's mystery friend, then who was?

I rolled over, hit the pillows, leant back and attempted to think as loosely as I could. I estimated both men were around the same age. I didn't know the size of St Louis but I guessed that it was within the realm of possibility that they'd grown up in the same neighbourhood. Maybe they were good friends and, something I'd noticed, best friends knew stuff about each other that nobody else knew. They had their secrets. It got me thinking. Had Tilelli known things about Frank Lygo that nobody else knew? Was

Tilelli a secret-keeper? For a man famous for his loose mouth, it seemed a stretch, yet it was worth closer examination.

Gaal told me that Tilelli and his mystery friend ran into each other, as if by accident. Lygo didn't strike me as a man who had coincidence in his vocabulary. Things happened for a reason. While it didn't make sense for him to engineer a meeting with someone who could potentially undo him, it had value if it was supposed to act as a warning. Tilelli might have been entirely ignorant of Lygo's grand plan, but he probably knew his capabilities, and if Tilelli had dirt on Lygo I thought it something more intrinsic and personal. Frankly, I was surprised that Tilelli had lasted so long. If I were Lygo I'd have taken him out in an instant.

I yawned and stretched. Exhaustion muddied my thinking. Wasn't good to speculate. Perhaps I was on the wrong track. But I wasn't on the wrong track about Jake Wilding.

Like Lygo, I didn't believe in coincidences. Bad stuff happened because of the warped desires of men. As for the wider picture, to my mind, events took place due to the collision of one reality with another. Came down to laws of probability. The probability that Jake's disappearance was unconnected to Lygo's I rated as one in a million. I didn't believe Lygo had burst into the safe house and taken the boy. I believed that Jake had burst out for the strongest of reasons. I didn't understand the nature of events, the timing, the 'how' of it, the evidential chain, to coin a police phrase, but I reasoned that Lygo and Jake Wilding shared something in common so obvious I wondered why I hadn't sussed it before: Jake Wilding wasn't gunning for me. He was gunning for Lygo.

CHAPTER TWENTY-SIX

I got moving around five, washed and dressed, stole out into the morning. It was cold, around minus eight degrees, and dark. Snow from the previous night had frozen, pavements lethal to traverse. Traffic moved gingerly. I hailed a passing cab and took a ride to Finchley. We travelled at a sedate pace. At that time my driver wasn't big on conversation. Suited me. At the very least I'd expected chat about the weather. Failing this, gossip about the latest politician to hit the buffers, or the death of a celebrity.

As a wanted man for all of my adult life, I'd learnt to live with risk. Sometimes it increased to white-heat proportions. At others, it faded away to nothing. Came down to resources and how those resources were deployed. For those reasons, I estimated my chances of hooking up with McCallen later on without incident as 50/50. After examining the safe house and Blake's last stand and following McCallen's debrief, the intelligence agencies had a brand new focus: Frank Lygo. Find him and they find the missing data. Find him and they find the boy. Technically we were on the same page. In reality we were chapters apart.

I knew little about sharp-end detection. My knowledge, based on years of experience, stemmed from moving in criminal circles. Three words in the form of questions cropped up incessantly:

motive, means and opportunity. The cops followed the same strap lines. Get the answers to these and you discover who has pissed on whom, and what's going down. So far I'd come up with two out of three and had a shaky grasp on the third. I recognised that I was fallible. This was good. Proved I was flexible in my thinking. I needed McCallen, the star in my dark night, so that I could narrow and nail down my theory and put it to the to test.

I paid the driver and walked the rest of the way on foot. I'd chosen Hampstead Heath, the viaduct. It couldn't be overlooked. Anyone skulking around would be spotted immediately.

I arrived two minutes after the appointed hour. McCallen was already on the bridge, leaning against the balustrade. Below shimmered an expanse of grey-green icy water. She looked pale in spite of a bracing wind. Dark shadows circled her eyes. I asked if she'd been followed.

She issued an exhausted smile. 'No.'

I asked if she was all right.

'Not the best twenty-four hours of my life,' she admitted.

'Kicked off the operation?'

'Uh-huh.'

'At least you handed them Lygo, that has to count for something.'

She agreed without enthusiasm.

'So what's the crack?'

'The brewery is receiving the full forensic treatment. We have a combination of teams scouring the country, hunting for Lygo, and every police force in the land searching for Jake Wilding. I take it you didn't find him?'

'No.'

She shivered. 'Bloody cold, isn't it?'

'And you're tired. Here,' I said, opening my coat, wrapping it around her, my body pressed against hers. I thought she might resist, but she didn't. I suppose we both felt dislocated and in need of human contact. I couldn't remember the last time I'd been this close to a woman and feeling this way. Not sure I ever had, come to think of it.

'You make a habit of this?' McCallen looked up at me with a laugh.

I suppose I could have asked her if she routinely consorted with assassins. 'Not especially.'

'I'm honoured then.'

'Honoured? Not a word I'm accustomed to.'

'No,' she said, thoughtful and serious again. 'Come on,' she pressed the flat of her hand against my chest so hard I wondered whether she could feel my heart racing. 'Tell me what you've been up to.'

'I went back to Wilding's house. It's all right, I was careful,' I added in response to her astonished expression. 'I wanted to run through events again. There were some inconsistencies, things that should have struck me at the time.'

She elevated an eyebrow, a searching expression on her face.

'Why didn't the assassin kill Jake Wilding?' I said.

'Because the boy wasn't his target.'

I shook my head. 'You don't leave loose ends.'

'You did.'

That was different and I wasn't going there. I came at it from a different angle. 'Jake Wilding was fully clothed when I surprised him.'

'Maybe he'd been out.' She quoted my own words back to me. *You obviously know little about the activities of teenage boys.*

'This is different.'

'Thought it might be,' she said with a dry smile.

'Fully clothed at four in the morning on a school night?'

She shrugged, didn't miss a beat. 'Bunking off is a popular pastime. Doesn't indicate a criminal mind. Anything else I should know?' Her tone inferred disappointment. I got the idea that whatever I said would be considered useless information.

'And he was singing.'

'Singing?' she snorted, unimpressed, 'as in drunk, or as in he had an I-pod attached to his ear?'

'As in he didn't give a shit.'

'Your point?'

'Why would he risk waking his mother?'

'God knows. Doesn't prove or disprove anything.'

'Not on its own, I agree, but when he saw me he asked a question. He asked who'd sent me. I thought it odd at the time. With hindsight it's positively weird.'

McCallen pulled a face. 'He was in shock. He thought you were going to kill him. He said the first thing that came into his head.'

'No,' I said. 'Trust me, if anyone gets an inkling they're going to be offed they don't ask questions.' I thought about the people I'd removed, those with sell-by dates attached to them. They had form. They had history. That's what I'd always told myself. It was a given that if you messed with the big boys you wound up in the sights of someone like me, a merchant of death. And they knew it. On the rare occasions when I'd revealed my face, I'd be faced with: *For God's sake, please don't kill me.* I didn't tell McCallen this. I was too ashamed. 'He expected something to happen, but he didn't expect me,' I said.

'You're not making sense.' The impatient note was back in her voice. She thought I was wasting my energies and hers.

'Hear me out. Downstairs was ransacked.'

'So what?'

'You knew?'

'Of course, we saw the moment we got there.'

So it wasn't a recent event. 'But it wasn't me.'

She rolled her eyes. 'Wilding's killer probably did it during his search for the data.'

'Not his style.'

'How do you know?' She braced, drew away slightly as if worried by what I might say next.

'Professional assassins don't leave a mess. They are cool and clean and tidy. It's about finesse. Anyone can pump a target with bullets from the latest sub-machine gun…'

'All right,' she cut in, 'I don't need the big sell.'

I flicked an apologetic smile. 'Let me ask you something, who made the original call to the police?'

'Jake Wilding.'

'At what time?'

'Seventeen minutes past eight.'

'At two minutes past five I was already riding a tube on the district line. Why did he take so long?'

'Because he was traumatised.'

'For over three hours?"

'So what do you suggest, Mr Bourne?'

I ignored the sarcasm. 'Because he was smashing the house up.'

'Is that supposed to be facetious?'

'Not in the least.'

'All right,' she said, as if humouring me, 'he was upset, distraught. He went wild.'

'Did he say he trashed the house?'

'Well, no.'

'Because he wanted you to believe it was the killer. He *wanted* you to believe that it was me.'

'Why?'

I didn't answer.

'What the hell are you suggesting? Because, if it's what I think, you couldn't be more off message.'

'Off message? Now there's an interesting phrase.' I was thinking about the toxin, and dirty dealings, and the targeted individuals it was destined to obliterate.

'How about plain wrong?' she flashed.

'He was the last person to see his mother alive. That means something.'

'It *means* he was subject to rigorous scrutiny right up until the moment he disappeared. He's undergone extensive psychological examination. His computer has been routinely checked for passwords and buried sites, as has his mobile phone. Frankly, if you weren't making such a despicable allegation, I'd find it funny.' She tried to push me away. I stayed put. If I told her I found her even more appealing when she was angry, I daresay she would have kneed me in the groin. I smiled. 'Inger,' I said softly, my mouth close to the perfect curve of her ear. 'Don't get so exercised. I am simply thinking aloud and outside the box. Everyone brings their own gifts to the table.'

'Bullshit,' she said.

'May I continue?'

'If you must.' She was cool and furious. I mentioned Tilelli. From her neutral reaction, she'd obviously not heard about his death. 'Ron Tilelli is a fantasist,' she insisted.

'I thought you guys had him on your pay-roll.'

She let out a laugh. 'He wouldn't scrape through our vetting procedures.'

'I did.'

'You don't count,' she flashed again. 'You're not getting paid. You're not anywhere.'

'I'm here,' I murmured. 'With you.' I pressed in closer. Any harder and we'd both break through the railings and into the water. A flush of colour splattered the top of her cheekbones.

'Tell me more about Tilelli,' she said hurriedly. I think she found me unsettling. The feeling was mutual.

I started from the moment I first put the bite on him to my meeting with Gaal the day before. 'Tilelli was brought up in St Louis,' I pointed out.

'Second largest city in the state of Missouri, so what?'

'Same place as Lygo.'

'Hell of a coincidence, nothing more.'

'Then why did Lygo take the trouble to look up Tilelli?'

'You don't know it was Lygo. Gaal hadn't a clue, from what

243

you've told me. And, besides, you don't know whether Gaal told the truth.'

'No reason for him to lie.'

'He could have been mistaken.'

'He could, but maybe Tilelli knew something which, under pressure, Lygo feared he might disclose.'

'Then why not simply kill him?'

'I think he did. Ron Tilelli was found dead less than twenty-four hours ago.'

She glanced away. For a moment I thought she'd seen someone approaching.

'What?' I whispered.

She shook her head. 'Nothing.' Whenever a woman says nothing it means something. I had the good sense to leave it – for now. I told her about Jake's name inscribed in dust.

She frowned big time, opened her mouth as if to speak, and closed it again. 'Mary Wilding,' I said. 'Tell me about her. You must have run a background check.' Standard procedure. Digging for dirt was nine-tenths of what spies did. Financial status, education or lack of it, relationships and unsavoury habits all fell under the spotlight. For the hundredth time, I cursed my own miserable lack of attention to detail.

'We did,' she said, clipped. 'Nothing came shrieking out of the woodwork.'

'Forgive me, but that's peculiar in itself. Everyone has skeletons. Most people have a hidden side.'

'From a hired killer that's almost amusing.'

I wasn't amused.

'As I've already told you,' she said breezily. 'Dr Wilding kept herself to herself. Married to her career. Happy with her own company.'

'She had few friends, is that what you're saying?' I'd assumed this but I wanted it confirmed by an expert. Call it a desire for corroborative evidence.

'Her work was everything to her. She lived and breathed it and had no time for anyone or anything else. So what?'

'That's my point. Where does her son figure?'

She looked away. I was pleased. It meant that she couldn't see the flash of satisfaction on my face. 'Tell me about her job.' I said, trying to catch her off-balance.

She turned back, stared at me hard. 'No.'

'How about edited highlights, career path, that kind of thing?'

'Perfectly average for someone of her high calibre.'

'I don't do average. Like to enlighten me?'

McCallen issued an exasperated sigh. 'Oxford graduate. A stint at Porton Down. Took a Sabbatical in the States. Early nineties, worked out in Russia on behalf of the British government. Joined Imperial College in 2000. Authored a number of papers on biological defence initiatives. Formed part of an expert team of scientists who met in Geneva in August 2010 to keep up to date and abreast of developments in the biotech field. The rest is history.' She didn't flush. She didn't waver. Her voice was ice-cool and matter-of-fact. I didn't bother to ask why she'd neglected to tell me this before. I took it as a compliment that she'd decided to take me into her confidence now.

'Where exactly did she do her sabbatical?' Wilding's stint in the States was big news to me.

'Harvard.'

Same place as one very dead scientist, I recalled. 'When was this?'

'Eighteen years ago.'

'You think Tilelli met Wilding there?' If they'd struck up a friendship, maybe it explained his strong reaction to her death.

'Jesus Christ, Ron Tilelli was a drunk. How could someone like that orbit Mary Wilding's sphere?'

Now I'd articulated it and she'd come up with a counter-argument, I thought she was right and I was wrong. 'Then how about this? Wilding hooked up with Lygo there.'

'Hooked up?' Her nose creased. Kissable, I thought.

'Eighteen years ago. Think about it. Gives a Sabbatical a whole new meaning.' To her ears, I was speculating like crazy, not something I'm prone to do, but I could tell from McCallen's astounded expression the suggestion had resonance.

'She got pregnant in the States,' McCallen said, the idea clicking. 'You didn't tell me that before.'

'Doesn't exactly fall under the heading of career path,' she said, sharp as a broken bottle.

Fair enough. 'Odds-on the father was American.'

'There's a lot of them to choose from,' she said facetious.

'Easy enough to check whether Lygo was orbiting her sphere at the time,' I said smartly. 'And I bet Tilelli, Daddy's oldest pal, knew about the child.' The reason he'd written Jake's name in the dust because he associated the boy with the father. She said nothing for a moment, considering the implications. Relentless, I continued, 'Lygo was the consummate spook. On the basis of his real life, he produced a fake. He knew Wilding all right, but not in the way that he said.'

Her face paled to the colour of fine porcelain. 'If this is true he ordered you to kill his own son.'

'Yes,' I said simply. As hard men went, Lygo was a prize specimen. Took one to know one.

'That's how Lygo was able to prepare the ground for Wes to put the frighteners on her,' McCallen said, suddenly animated. This part of the plan still didn't gel with me, but for now I was prepared to go with McCallen's flow, which was virtually in full spate. 'He knew which of Wilding's buttons Wes had to push.' She rippled with excitement, her body flexing. Completely wired. I could feel it through several layers of clothing. I wondered idly which of McCallen's buttons I needed to press.

'Explains why Wilding was prepared to give up her soul,' she riffed. 'She found out about Lygo and, realising he'd stop at nothing, she complied to protect Jake.'

It still didn't tell us who killed Mary Wilding. I told McCallen about Lygo's alleged terrorist links.

'With al-Qaeda?' she said, grave. 'Who told you that?'

There was a time in my life when I would have done anything to protect Reuben. No more. 'An ex-Mossad employee.'

'You keep strange company,' she said, instantly suspicious.

'Something we share in common.'

She looked straight into my eyes in a way that made me deeply uncomfortable. I wondered what she saw and whether she glimpsed a man with a black space where his emotions should be, a man with no soul. I cleared my throat. She nodded absently and adroitly pushed me away. 'I have to go,' she said. I stood aside. 'Right, then,' she added like a woman on a mission.

'Right,' I said, clapping my gloved hands together.

'Stay in touch, yeah?' She turned to walk away.

'One other thing,' I said.

'What?' Her eyebrows formed two angry darts. Her lips thinned. Impatient.

I took one step towards her, kissed her full on the mouth and walked away.

With the taste of McCallen on my lips, I headed back into the cityscape, more specifically to Waterloo to catch a train. Tilleli had been removed from the picture because he knew too much. Stood to reason Billy Squeeze remained at serious risk. Judging by his last call, this was something he already knew. Should Lygo come knocking on his door, I'd be lying in wait with or without Billy's approval. As for Jake Wilding, I couldn't yet view him with enough objectivity. I hoped the lad regretted his bid for freedom, if that's what it was. I hoped he was keeping his head down. I seriously hoped he wasn't in trouble or about to cross a line and change his life for eternity. Had I been a praying man, I'd have prayed he wasn't about to follow in the footsteps of a man like me.

While waiting for a train I put a call through to Jat from a pay phone. The tone of his voice instantly told me that he'd discovered something.

'Good news and bad,' he started.

'Let's have it,' I said.

'I've seen your guy.'

My pulse quickened. 'Where?'

'Wolverhampton. There's a meeting room over a chip shop he regularly uses, and he and his mates don't buy too many fish dinners.'

I thought about this. Saj, McCallen's asset, was undercover. Should I be surprised? 'Okay, what's the bad news?'

'Khaled is mixed up with them, not heavy duty, but they use him for running messages.'

'Any idea what's in the messages?'

'Fuck, no, it's all word of mouth, and I'm not inclined to push it with my little brother to find out.'

I rubbed my chin. My mind reeled back to the meeting in the gardens. McCallen had instructed Saj to persuade Mustafa to put out the word, to say they were in the market for receipt of the stolen data. 'Have you come across Mustafa?'

'Not so much as a squeak. Best I can do is keep tabs on my little brother.'

I did a quick risk assessment in my head and came to a decision. 'What you do about Khaled is your business, but consider your job for me finished.'

'Really?' The relief in Jat's voice was palpable.

'Really. I reckon you've already flown too close to the sun. Take care.'

I arrived at Sunningdale train station late morning and, flashing enough cash to put food on the driver's table for the next week, took a no-frills mini-cab to Billy's place.

The gates were shut. Pressing the electronic entry pad, I waited, my mouth close to the voice-receiver. Nobody answered. I tried again. Nothing. A break-in would trigger the alarm. For obvious reasons it wasn't connected to the local police station. Silent to the would-be trespasser's ear, the security device set off a signal within the house and served as a first alert so that Billy could take appropriate action. So be it, I thought. At least, I'd find out the score.

Taking a run at the gate, I leapt up, gripped the railings with both hands and hauled myself up a three-metre expanse of wrought iron. Wobbling at the top, I dropped cleanly onto the other side, knees bent, crouched, listening. A city boy by nature, I was uneasy in the country. I'd always preferred my mother's town apartment to my grandparents' pile in rural Gloucestershire. I hated the drab winter light when the sky, unbroken by towers and spires, seemed encased in muslin. I disliked the mud. I was all right with sheep and cows and pigs but I couldn't spend significant time with them. I wasn't into community living and the requirement for conversation and mischievous gossip. Never had been. Never would be. Taking all this into account, I felt more unsettled than usual. Everything was silent. No breeze. No birdsong. No whisper of falling leaves. In that surreal moment in time, I reckoned that fear had a colour. This, I imagined, was what it would look like if a biological bomb dropped.

I prowled forward.

The black and white timbered house, stark, like a deserted Tudor fortress, bore down on me as I drew close. Pressing my face against the glass revealed big rooms with ancient beams, comfortable furnishings, heavy drapes at the windows. I wondered what had happened to Billy's wife, his laughing daughters, the housekeeper, *Billy*.

With a deep sense of foreboding, I headed towards the stables, my imagination clipped by Billy's voice and the sound of Milo clattering against the cobbled stone, the heavy smell of freshly turned dung strong in my nostrils. The sliding door was padlocked. I shot open the lock, the noise from the silenced gun loud in the stillness, and walked inside and switched on the light.

Up ahead, the door to Milo's stall lay ajar. Flicking my eyes to the right, I checked to see if he'd been moved. The other four stalls were empty. I glanced up, half-expecting someone to drop down from the rafters. I didn't want to be caught out for a second time. No-one there. Right at the end, past the empty stalls, another door, closed, not locked. I inched my way towards it, stepped to one side and, using the muzzle of the gun, flicked the door open. A tack room, empty, that was all. Retracing my steps, fresh spots of blood formed an irregular trail in the sawdust. Crouching down, I could tell from the size of the droplets that they weren't the result of a firearm injury. Didn't look like much of an injury at all, to be honest. I'd seen worse after a punch to the nose.

Straightening back up, I followed the trail back to Milo's stable and stopped dead. Inside looked like the worst kind of back-street abattoir. Walls and floor sprayed with viscera and gore. Straw soaked in blood. Smell indescribable. On his side, Milo, eyes open, with a single bullet wound to his head, the rest of his magnificent physique unmarked. I edged forwards, boots sliding in the general slime. Extreme violence hung in the air like sea fog. Looking down, I noticed the stains on Milo's hooves, the way the hair on his powerful legs was matted. I stretched out a hand tentatively, felt for wounds, my fingers connecting with flesh and tissue and, I realised, human DNA. Then I saw it.

Partially obscured by Milo's hulking form, a mess of clothes and blood: a body.

I recoiled in disbelief, and thought of Billy, the way he'd snapped at me, the fear in his voice, the realisation that he'd asked one too many questions in dangerous circles. I had a strong stomach. I'd seen terrible things in my life. In spite of this, I fought a deep dark elemental fear. I wanted to walk away and never come back.

But I didn't.

There are twenty-two bones in the head and face, fourteen shape our facial features and I reckoned that every one belonging to the corpse was broken. One eye clean punched out, the other blown, teeth and nose gone, blood clotted in orifices, both natural and inflicted. Hair could have been any colour at all. Every facial feature was reduced to human soup. Had it been in a fire, it would be as equally unidentifiable.

I switched my gaze. Broken right arm. Shattered right hand as a result of a frantic attempt to ward off Milo's flying hooves, and ultimately doomed. I turned to go, saw something gleaming amidst the carnage, and stretching forwards, hooked it out. In the palm of my hand, a signet ring. Heavy-duty. Expensive. Platinum not gold. I looked back at the body in the straw, narrowed my eyes.

I'd found Frank Lygo.

CHAPTER TWENTY-SEVEN

McCallen showed up two hours after my call. In the meantime I'd searched the stables and walked the estate and drawn my own conclusions.

I met her at the gates, which I'd disabled. She drove a brand new black Mini Cooper S. Her own I guessed, the Lexus a pool car. I climbed in beside her. It was warm and I was tired. It felt good to be sitting down. We drove up the long drive, past the house and back down to the stables. 'In there,' I said.

'You're not coming with me?'

'In a moment.'

She gave a 'suit yourself' shrug and climbed out, leaving the car keys in the ignition. This was either a bad habit, or a misplaced display of trust. I reached across, took them, counted to ten and followed.

She examined the wreckage and made a sort of hissing sound. 'Play by the sword, I guess you die by it.'

After what Lygo had done to Ron Tilelli, I agreed.

'Who owns this place?'

I told her: William Franke.

'What's his connection?'

Without giving away all Billy's trade secrets, I told her that, too. 'The removal of Yakovlevich, Petrov, and Tilelli is part of a clean-up operation. I think Lygo came here to get rid of William Franke.'

'Except he hadn't bargained on his equine date with death,' she said with black humour. 'Where is our elusive Mr Franke?'

Good question. I'd devoted the last couple of hours to fathoming this out. So far, I'd failed to come up with a credible answer. 'He takes his family to the West Indies this time of year. Bearing in mind Lygo put the frighteners on him, he could have booked an earlier flight.'

'Just as well in the circumstances.'

I thought so, although the idea of Billy making a run for it did not sit well with my knowledge of the man. Also I couldn't explain why he'd leave a brute like Milo to his own devices. Seemed like McCallen was working along the same shout lines.

'Who shot the nag, do you think?'

I shrugged.

'Lygo?'

'Where's the weapon?'

'You've checked?'

'Yes. Not here,' I said.

McCallen let out a slow whistle. I didn't know exactly what she was thinking, but I was starting to see too much of a coincidence with Blake's murder. I squatted down on my haunches. 'See this,' I looked up at her, pointing to the trail of blood. 'I think Lygo was forced in at knifepoint.'

'By Franke?'

'Could be.' Not the type of man to respond well to threats, I wouldn't put it past him, although I couldn't imagine Billy taking a gun to Milo. He loved the creature too much. I told McCallen this. 'There are alternatives.' For dramatic effect, I paused. For dramatic effect, McCallen expressed her impatience.

'For God's sake.'

'Go back to the beginning,' I said, easy with it. 'Could be the original outfit responsible for Wilding's murder, if they exist.'

'*If they exist?*' McCallen groaned. 'Simply because we haven't found the evidence doesn't mean there isn't any.'

'Isn't that what one British Prime Minister said about WMD?'

'Can we stick to the point?' she said, borderline glacial.

Aside from the absence of proof, I wasn't a fan of the alternative outfit scenario. If an unknown guilty party had got away with stealing the data and kept it this quiet, they'd be insane to bump off Frank Lygo and draw that kind of heat now. I bluntly told McCallen this.

'Jury's out,' she said. 'Next.'

I didn't say. Just looked. I watched the growing restlessness in her eyes, the blinding realisation and irritation. '*Not* Jake Wilding.'

'It's a stretch but not impossible.'

'So is flying to the moon.'

I smiled. To my amazement, she smiled back then I realised she was trying to humour me. 'All right, why would Jake come here?'

'Because he followed Lygo.'

McCallen pulled a face. 'But Jake doesn't know Lygo.'

'We *think* he doesn't know.'

She put the flat of her hand up. 'Idle speculation. If and it's a huge if, Jake Wilding was Lygo's son, Jake knew nothing about it.'

'These company shrinks you mentioned, the ones who do the talking trip,' I said, 'was Jake ever asked about his father?'

'Of course.'

'And?'

'He was quite obviously clueless.'

Looked like that bit of my theory was falling apart. 'Presumably Mary Wilding wasn't quite so dim.' I didn't have her down for a loose one-night stand kind of a girl. 'Did she ever mention the father of her child to the outside world?'

'She never disclosed it and the police have interviewed dozens of her acquaintances and associates. Like I said, she was, by all accounts, quite a cool individual, kept herself to herself.'

'I don't buy it. We all have our foibles.'

McCallen looked me dead in the eye. What I'd give to be one of hers. 'Her only real Achilles heel in life was her son,' she said.

I thought back to my last visit to the house. Wilding came across as quite the homemaker. She liked nice things. An eminently grown-up environment with none of the usual debris and clutter associated with a teenage son, almost as though he'd never lived there. Something flickered at the fringes of my mind, a forgotten memory of the day I called to see my mother and registered that her addiction to booze was stronger than her love for me. Mentally snuffing it out, I said, 'How did Jake get on with his mother?'

'Okay. A bit rocky, as you might expect with an only child and him being a teenager.'

'Within the normal spectrum of volatile?'

'I didn't say it was volatile. I said it was okay.'

I wanted to quiz her more about Jake's relationship with his mother, but McCallen had that combative light in her eyes. Pushing her would get me nowhere. 'Fair enough,' I said, 'I accept what you say.'

'Good.'

'But what if Jake *did* find Lygo? Indulge me,' I said in answer to her sharp expression.

'Why would he do that?'

'Vengeance for sending me to kill his mother.'

'You should watch your back,' she said, droll.

'I'm serious.' More than I could ever say. She looked at me, didn't speak for five or ten seconds. At least that's how long it felt.

'You know, don't you?' she said, at last.

'Know what?'

'What it's like.'

Afraid that something in my bearing would give away the darkness inside me, I stared her out.

McCallen continued, relentless. 'Every time you talk about Jake Wilding you carry a certain expression.'

Razor-sharp edges sliced through the soft lining of my stomach. Uneasy didn't do it justice. I cast her a stony look. 'How's that for an expression?'

'Fine,' she said crisply. 'For a nasty moment I thought you were going to confide in me about a tragic childhood.'

'I wasn't. In my book people make their own choices in life. You choose who you want to be.'

'You don't believe we're products of our upbringing, however that pans out?'

'No.' After what had happened to me, I should have avoided any connection to violence, let alone murder. Instead, I'd embraced it.

She looked surprised by my candour. Whether or not she was pleased I found it hard to tell.

'I apologise,' she said.

'No need.' I meant it. Talk heavy if you want to but don't include me. I had no desire to revisit my past with McCallen on board.

She sensibly changed tack. 'Supposing for one second Jake was after Lygo, you're forgetting a number of critical factors.'

'Like what?'

'His age and inexperience. To pull off something like this requires a sophisticated mind.'

'You should know. Holed up with him for hours, you have a better handle on the boy's psyche than most.'

'I wouldn't say that. Debriefs in safe-houses are nuanced affairs.'

'How the hell do you *nuance* a seventeen-year-old?'

She crossed her arms, didn't look happy. 'I thought you said he was traumatised,' I reminded her.

'He was.'

'Maybe he's plain old-fashioned cunning.'

'You seriously think he fooled us?' She looked affronted.

'You said he was clever.'

'I don't ever remember saying that.' The penetrating look in her expression told me to back off. I didn't.

'You also suggested he was a truant.'

'What if he was? Look, if it bothers you that much I'll give you a thumbnail sketch and tell you what he's really like. It's actually quite easy,' she said, speaking to me as though I was a child myself, and one who needed calming down. Patronising actually, but it rolled off me like rain on glass. 'Jake Wilding is pretty typical.'

'Typical of what?'

McCallen suppressed a sigh. 'His age.'

I thought back to the seventeen year-old I once was prior to my mother's death. 'Bolshie and idealistic?'

'Anti tuition fees, anti-war, anti big business, into the green agenda, climate change, blaming the old for constraints put on the young. He's also materialistic, likes gadgets, and can't live without I-pods and Facebook. You get the picture?'

'I get *a* picture. What about friends, places he liked to hang out, girls?'

'He's a witness not a suspect,' she said, instantly guarded. 'I'm sure the MET would be happy to talk and give you the low-down,' she added with a thin smile.

McCallen's edgy response meant two things: now wasn't the time and I was dinging her alarm bell even if she wouldn't admit it. I smiled without heat. 'Something tells me you don't buy my theory.'

'Correct.'

'How about the Russian connection? Right up their street. Revenge for removing Yakovlevich.'

This got her vote. She flashed a winning smile. 'Russians, I like.' She took out her mobile phone.

'What are you doing?'

'Calling in.'

'Thought you were suspended.'

'I am, but now I've found Lygo…'

'I?'

Her top lip curled. 'You want to take the credit?'

I didn't say yes. I didn't say no. I was too mad.

'Look,' she said. 'I have a duty to report this. Think of the resources wasted by chasing a dead man.'

Think of your job, I thought. 'Go ahead,' I said, leaning against a stable wall. 'Why don't I wait for the cavalry to arrive?'

She closed the phone, appreciated my dilemma. More to the point, she had a dilemma all of her own: consorting with the enemy. How was she going to explain me away? Wouldn't look good on the C.V. I took her car keys from my pocket and jingled them in my hands.

'How the hell?' she flashed.

'Can I borrow the Mini?' I said.

'Why?'

'To hunt Russians.'

She shook her head in disbelief, thought for a moment, and laughed. 'Have it your own way,' she said. 'I'll get a lift back.'

'Don't you want to know where I'm heading?'

'I can find you anywhere,' she said, punching in numbers on her phone.

'Of course, I was forgetting you're a spook,' I cracked a smile.

She didn't so much as look at me. 'The car has a tracking device. You didn't seriously think I'd hand over my beloved Mini to an unreconstructed thug, did you?'

CHAPTER TWENTY-EIGHT

Chelsea. Rush hour. Blast of horn. Blare of lights. Dog eat dog. I finally arrived outside Yakovlevich's four-storey residence around six. Drapes drawn, shutters on the downstairs rooms closed. Nice to know Yuri would not be available for the welcome party.

I rang the bell. The butler came to the door with his coat on and bag packed. Flustered and clearly a man in a hurry, I don't know who or what he expected but it wasn't me.

'Mr Hex,' he said, snatching past me and tumbling down the steps. I watched him scoot along the street and he didn't look back. I suppose if your boss and his second-in-command have suddenly disappeared it makes a man jittery. Either that, or the FSB was breathing down his neck.

I walked inside, closed the door behind me, and switched on the lights. Before me a sea of misshapen objects, every chair, table, sideboard, sofa, covered in thick off-white coloured sheets. To be honest, I thought it an improvement on the original and crossed the floor to the staircase, my footsteps echoing in the silence.

Upstairs was the same. Fortunately, the booze remained. Not planning on going anywhere yet, I poured myself a large glass of whisky, pulled a sheet off Yakovlevich's cream leather sofa and spread out, the heel of my boots resting on a coffee table. Taking a long deep swallow, I thought about McCallen. I thought about Jake and me. Put me in mind of everything I'd spent fifteen years running from.

When someone you love dies you think you lose that person in one piece. You don't. There are increments. Bit by bit, your senses are ransacked and robbed. Images fade. A remembered touch vanishes. A voice drifts to nothing. That look, that gesture, the actual words and the way they were once spoken disappear. You may cling onto all of these things by their coat tails but, eventually and finally, you are left alone with a pile of dusty memories. Death does that.

And Jake Wilding would experience all of these things. Not yet. Not now. Later.

Your story is my story, I thought, but I genuinely hoped that Jake's ending would be different to my own.

In my despair, I'd turned to my grandparents. Rejected, I'd appealed to my father. I often think that if he'd embraced me as a son my life would have been different. Rejected again, I'd turned to Reuben, but by then the damage was done and something elemental within me altered.

Cast aside by a mother too bound up in her work, and failed by those who should have protected him better, Jake had suffered a similar fate. It bothered me. Betrayal did strange things to people. To those of a certain inclination it put them on self-destruct. I knew.

Adrift physically and mentally, with the only attachment to my previous life severed, it hit me that I no longer had a sense of my own identity. I no longer had a reason to be. My skills, if that was what they were, lay in a redundant art. Even the intelligence on which I'd prided myself didn't play any more. I was out of my league, out of my depth. But I was no quitter. I wasn't about to give up. Not now. Not ever.

I got up, found a bathroom on the next floor, stripped off my clothes and took a shower, hot then cold. I took clothes from

Yakovlevich's room: designer label underwear, designer label jeans, designer label shirt and sweater. They were too big but they were clean. I went to the kitchen, made myself a sandwich from the contents of the fridge: ham and cheese on rye. Pouring a glass of milk, I drank and ate standing up.

Next I went in search of Yakovlevich's study. Black and crimson décor and not a pornographic image in sight, it was located on the top floor.

Sitting down at Yakovlevich's large desk with its phone and the big man's smoking paraphernalia, I fired up a twenty-seven inch I-Mac, expecting it to be password protected. To my surprise, it wasn't and I went straight to the Google search engine and typed in ethnic-specific biochemical weapons. A whole tranche of stuff came up. I scrolled down and found a quote by William S Cohen, U.S. Secretary of Defence, dated April 28th 1997.

'*There are some reports, for example, that some countries have been trying to construct something like an Ebola Virus, and that would be a very dangerous phenomenon, to say the least. Alvin Toeffler has written about this in terms of some scientists in their laboratories trying to devise certain types of pathogens that would be ethnic specific so that they could just eliminate certain ethnic groups and races.*'

A newspaper entry for November 15 1999 stated:

'*Carried out at Israel's Institute of Biological Research, Israel is working on ethnic bio-weapons, which would hit Arabs not Jews.*'

I hoped they were still struggling with it.

Next up, a whole screed of information about possible forms of delivery. Tricky to release, small-scale attacks were apparently more likely if no less vile. Invisible and colourless, simple to conceal and transport, toxins could be weaponised in aerosol form and used with ease. There were other claims that veered into the realms of science fiction.

Working my way through the blurb, mostly described in cold and clinical terms, there was little posturing or overt sabre-rattling.

In common with the nuclear deterrent and the mutually assured destruction argument, the big powers considered it rational to have bio-weapons in the arsenal in the event of such weapons being used. If nothing else it would frighten the crap out of the other side and in so doing maintain peace, it seemed to say. Reduced to its basic elements: bio-weapons made what I'd done for a living child's play. Without underselling it, I'd taken bad guys out one at a time.

Mind throbbing with exhaustion, I nodded off in the chair, woke an hour later, thick-headed, disorientated. Connections flickered like Coi carp shimmering beneath the surface of a deep pool. Every time I stuck my hand in to reach they darted away. Tilelli and Lygo. Lygo and McMahon. McMahon and Billy. Dead Russians. Dead scientists. I realised then that, in common with McCallen, I'd run too fast and assumed too much. Unlike McCallen, I had an excuse: I was new to detecting.

I now saw that Wilding was last in a long list of 'removals'. Motivated by clearing the field, Lygo had ordered the murders of scientists and those associated with the programme in the States in exactly the same ruthless way he'd plotted to get rid of the mother of his child here in the U.K. I'd previously believed McMahon had carried out the killings. Mistake number one. Aside from McMahon's limited intellect, the U.S. murders were way too much for one man to carry out in the timeframe. The whole trick with assassinations: you do the job and get out. You don't hang around, tripping from one gig to the next. In other words, you don't stick around for applause. Do that and you're dead.

Mistake number two: No more than McMahon could operate a one-man killing spree, I didn't believe Lygo could operate easily with Mossad and undoubtedly the CIA on his tail. Not with that degree of determination and bloodlust against him. Not with the current terrorist threat level.

Mistake number three: Nobody had figured out or even

thought to ask where Lygo had been and what he'd been up to in the past three years. It had all been assumed. The more I thought about Frank Lygo, the more I realised he'd had serious help. How else could he have operated and found a safe haven in Britain?

In other circumstances, I'd have elected Yakovlevich with his extensive connections as a front-runner, but I believed, as I'd always believed, that Mikhail was a latecomer to the table, nothing more than an opportunist who'd strike a deal with the devil if he could make enough money out of it.

I looked at my watch, looked at the phone. Whenever Ellen Greco wanted to contact me she left a coded message at an American diner in town. I needed to speak to her now, but didn't want to run the risk of getting picked up so, for the second time in as many weeks, I punched in her number, waited for the connection.

'Ellen,' I said.

'Hey,' she said. 'Thought you'd never fucking call.'

'You got something?' I braced myself.

'Going to tell you a story.' She sounded playful. I wasn't in the mood, but in no circumstances would I ever tell someone as powerful as Ellen Greco to cut to the chase.

'I'm all ears,' I said.

'Steve and me once took a vacation in Dubai. Business combined with pleasure, you know?'

'I get the picture,' I said. Dubai the nerve centre for shady activities, I thought.

'A place with a lot of opportunity.' I heard her break off to chug on a cigar. 'It was back in the day when the whole area was one monster building site and foreigners were buying up land like it was the Klondike. Investors were doubling their money on properties within months. Anyways, we wanted a slice of the action. That's when I ran into Frank Lygo.'

'I thought you'd never heard of him,' I spiked.

'Honey, I didn't associate him with the type of guy you were looking for,' she said, noisily clearing her throat. 'I mean, with a name like that, sounds like one of those Irish hoodlums.'

'So what was he doing?"

'Investing, pure and simple, Lygo was out to make a buck. He was some kind of property magnate.'

'Property?'

'Sure, he was there with another guy, an Englishman.'

I sharpened. 'Who?'

'I don't remember the name. He was kind of quiet, a little guy, smart. Not someone to underestimate. We spoke mainly to Lygo because he was a fellow American, and the guy with the mouth and charm. I liked him and so did Steve. Said he was like a guy dipped in gold. We even considered running a little business with him.' She broke off to take another puff. 'Dubai's not so big and I was just thinking it might be a good starting point for you to find him.'

'Yes,' I said, numb. 'Good thinking. Thanks, Ellen, I owe you.'

Ellen let out a raucous laugh. 'Call it quits. Take care of yourself, honey,' and then she hung up.

I got up and tugged at the drapes, peeked out of the window into cold darkness and a street empty of suspicion. A couple of hours had passed and still no sign of McCallen. Snatching up the phone, I called her number. It went straight to voicemail. I left a message then, grabbing my jacket, bolted downstairs. As soon as Ellen had mentioned the quiet Englishman, the game was up. Lygo had been in Dubai with William Franke or, as I knew him, Billy Squeeze.

Furious, I drove to Farringdon where Billy leased an executive office suite off Gray's Inn Road. I'd been there once. I'd no idea under what banner Billy currently traded. It didn't matter. Whatever it purported to be, in reality it was a front, just like the man. His offer of help, fake concern nothing more than a string of lies designed to obscure. Even a fiercely intelligent man like Lygo hadn't banked on the feral cunning of someone like Billy Squeeze.

The office block stood out like a lighthouse at sea. Every window blazed with illumination. Twenty-four seven. British work ethic in full swing. Spotting a stationary white van advertising cleaning services, I tucked McCallen's car in behind. A female driver lumbered out. Stocky, square-boned, she wore an apron over a fleece jacket. Her dark trousers were short, exposing white ankles that looked too thin for the rest of her. Going round the back of the van, she opened a rear door and hefted out a housekeeping trolley, trundling it across the road, her thickset shoulders rounded, like she had all the cares of the world compressed inside her.

I followed at a distance, not too close to spook her, not too far away so that she couldn't hear me. As we both converged on the entrance of the building I made a pantomime of trying to find my security card. Close-up, I could see she was foreign, Eastern European maybe.

'Damn,' I said, catching her eye. 'I've driven all the way and left my clearance card at home.'

She gave me a cold 'whatever' glare.

A woman once told me that my whole face lights up when I laugh or smile. I think it's probably down to the fact I do either so rarely. I discovered that I could literally get away with murder if I flashed a grin at the right moment. All came down to timing. 'Hey, do you want a hand with that?' I said, a big blowsy grin on my face as I looked meaningfully at the cleaning-cart and the flight of steps to the glass-fronted doors.

Her features softened. Seemed that she didn't often receive offers of help. 'Here, let me,' I said, manhandling the cart.

'Thank you,' she said shyly and followed me up the steps. When we reached the entrance, she said, 'You want to go in?' She took out a pass from her apron pocket.

'That would be terrific,' I said. 'Save me a whole load of trouble.'

Inside, the grateful cleaner went one way. I went the other. Taking the lift, I rode to the top floor, got out and followed the corridor as it snaked round to the back of the building and to a door with a plaque: W.F. Good, Rich and Franke Public Relations Consultants. Had I been in a more accommodating frame of mind, I might have appreciated Billy's dark sense of humour. More in hope than expectation, I depressed the handle and pushed. Didn't budge. Slipping the gun from inside my jacket, I pointed it at the lock. Even with silencers guns made a noise. I hoped the steady drone of a vacuum cleaner on the floor below would mask it. About to fire, I heard movement on the other side. I stepped to the right, my back against the wall, listened as the lock turned and the door swung open. As Billy swept out, I darted close behind him, thick carpet muffling the sound of my footfall, and pressed the barrel of the gun to the back of his head.

CHAPTER TWENTY-NINE

Forcing Billy back inside, I flicked the lights on, LED judging by the glow, and kicked the door shut behind us. We stood in a small Reception area. Spying a door, I frogmarched him into another room that was large and square, two doors off, both open. A long rectangular chrome and glass table, ten chairs running down each side and one at each end, occupied the central space. An alcove to my left contained a cabinet and refrigerator. I imagined Billy holding court, doing deals, trading with whoever would buy his 'products' as he termed them, cocaine and heroin to the rest of us, and now something unspeakable.

I frisked him, confiscated his Beretta then, dragging out a chair, told him to sit. He sat. Until this point, he'd not uttered a single word. 'Where is it?'

'Where's what?'

'The fucking data.'

'Don't know what you're talking about.'

I slapped him hard once, nearly knocked him clean off the chair. A trickle of blood issued from the side of his mouth. He swallowed, wiped the blood away with his sleeve. His eyes locked onto mine.

'I don't have it, son.'

I knew in an instant he was telling the truth. 'Who has it?' I stared at him hard. He returned the stare. 'Billy, I don't have all day.' I drew back my hand, primed for another blow.

'Don't you want to know the crack with me and Lygo?'

'I don't have time.' But I stayed my hand. My breath came hard and heavy through my nostrils.

'That's more like it,' he said with a bloodied smile. 'Always enjoyed a chat. So many of the creeps I deal with are brainless morons.'

'This isn't a social. Talk, you cunt.'

He inclined his head as he spoke, anger coiled in his expression. 'You really should have left things be. I tried to warn you, but you wouldn't take the bait.'

'And what bait have you taken, Billy?'

'No need to be chippy. Business is business. There's a recession out there, or didn't you know? Only the flexible survive,' he added ominously.

'Flexible?' I snickered.

'What would you call it?'

'Mass murder.'

Billy clicked his tongue, shook his head. 'Pot, kettle and black, Hex.'

I bit down hard on my jaw. 'You've got one more chance to talk then I'm going to blow your kneecap off.' I took aim.

Billy fixed me with a contemptuous look. For a man facing unspeakable pain, I thought he was incredibly calm. Too calm. Or was I losing my touch? 'What do you want to know?' he growled.

'For the last time, who has the hard drive?'

He flashed a malevolent smile. 'When I'm good and ready. Don't you want to know how I met Lygo, how he figured?'

'You were responsible for him being trampled to death and that's all I need to know.'

'Frank Lygo only had himself to blame,' Billy said, his voice as inflexible as granite. 'You screw with your business partners, you get your comeuppance.' I almost laughed at its banality, 'Too many cooks' syndrome all too common in gangland circles. 'Lygo's problem was that he thought he was smarter than me,' Billy continued, his voice a low drone. 'Thought he was running the show. Insisted on using men not up to the mark, in my opinion, people like McMahon and that Spanish cop, Tony Blanco. Too fucking clever for his own good, know what I mean?'

'What about Wes?'

'My choice, my man. I like blokes who are expendable, if you get my drift,' he grinned.

I did. Trading on my ruthless reputation, I pointed the gun again, this time my finger dancing on the trigger. The grin vanished. He cleared his throat.

'Frank and me had mutual interests in the Middle East. He was shifting gear all over the place. Got good contacts and all, what with him being a CIA man. Did you know that, Hex, him being a spook?'

I grunted a yes. The sooner Billy got his showboating over, the sooner I'd locate the hard drive.

'Had a fine little earner going for a good few years, him and me. 'Course, his angle was different to mine.'

'How?'

'You know me. I'm a businessman through and through. Always looking for the main chance. Now Lygo was one nasty greedy son-of-a-bitch, but when it came to the Middle East, he got all misty-eyed. An idealist, see, and that's what did for him.'

'Not sure I understand.'

'Didn't appreciate the way the States in particular, and the West in general, waded into the Middle East. Me, I'm not one for politics. Waste of everyone's time. Anyway, had his fingers burnt; strayed too close to the action and got his cover blown. I wasn't best pleased, I can tell you. But then he came up with this plan. Fucking clever. 'Course, at the time, I knew nothing about biological gear. Going too fast for you, am I?'

I said nothing. I was worried by his cocky manner. Billy, somehow, had the drop on me but I couldn't work out how. I gestured for him to continue, which he did seamlessly.

'Like I already said, Lygo had these contacts, people who knew people.'

'Including terrorists?'

His face assumed a blank expression. He fell briefly silent. I lunged forwards, cuffed him once viciously with the barrel of the gun, not hard enough to beat him unconscious, just enough to cause pain and concentrate his mind.

'Jesus Christ!' he let out, awed as much by the sudden violence as the blood trickling down the side of his face and into the collar of his shirt.

'What was the plan?' I prompted him.

Billy scowled, features flaring with malice, the swagger momentarily battered out of him.

'Using his CIA contacts, Lygo got wind that the Brits were engaged in a strategic defence programme specialising in targeted stuff, ethnic-specific.'

A nauseating image of the young Korean couple flashed into my mind.

'These scientists,' he continued, his voice dry and without emotion, 'they create a toxin to do the business and then an anti-sera, that's what they call it, to counter the effects, a bit like giving a druggie smack and then dosing him up with methadone.' I thought the analogy piss poor, but I didn't have either the time or inclination to argue with Billy's warped sense of logic.

'So your interest was in the toxin?'

'Yes.'

'And the data for it was what I was meant to steal?'

'Yes.'

'And you took out a contract on Wilding?'

'Wouldn't you?' Billy said bluntly. 'She could have blown the whistle at any time. We knew she had the information. Knew where she kept it. Doing it our way kept things nice and tidy.'

Except it didn't.

'So how did Petrov fit into the picture?' I had a rough idea but I wanted to hear it from the main man. Billy crossed his legs in a casual gesture, at ease with the question.

'Lygo had all sorts of contacts and while he was in the Middle East he got pally with this Russian scientist, defector, or some such thing.'

'If Lygo had this guy's ear why hound Wilding?'

He flashed a grin, seemed to appreciate the fact that I was on the ball. 'The Russian was our chemist. For all we knew, Wilding could have been supplying us with an encrypted nursery rhyme. You know how it works, Hex. Never know if the merchandise is any good until you test it. Stuff gets spiked or proves bloody useless. Remember, we wanted a real premium product, something that would appeal to the Muslim terrorist market, and they ain't the sort of boys to get on the wrong side of,' he winked, 'trust me.'

I recalled Reuben's remark. *Muslim groups are always relevant. What if such a weapon fell into their hands?* I'd believed my old mentor had displayed the type of paranoia that comes with old age. I was wrong.

'I'm guessing the product would only affect the white population.' I said this nonchalantly, as if describing the merits of a new brand of lager.

'Got it. So we set him up here.'

'The Russian scientist, Petrov?'

'Yeah, with Lygo.'

'At the brewery?'

Billy's eyes narrowed. 'You went there?'

'I did.'

'See, that's my point about Lygo. He didn't tell me half of what

271

he was up to.' I wondered about the Tilelli connection, but didn't want to spoil Billy's narrative flow. At least I now knew that the toxin wasn't designed to target Muslims and Jews, as Lygo had told me. Not that it made me feel any better. Creed or colour wasn't an issue for me.

'About Petrov,' I prompted him again.

'Right, so while the Russian's settling in, Wes puts the squeeze on the doctor.'

'By issuing threats against her son?'

Billy nodded, a strange, malicious light in his eyes. 'Had things gone according to plan, you'd have whacked Wilding and we'd be in possession of the goods. As it turned out, I wasn't in full knowledge of the facts. It's what I mean about Lygo having his own agenda.'

'You mean Lygo and Tilelli?'

'Oh, him? Bloody joke of a man. And squealer. He was no friend of Frank Lygo's.'

'Is that why you had him offed?'

'Too right, killed him myself. He made a right fucking noise about it, too.'

I remembered the white fear in Wes's eyes at our last meeting in London. He wasn't frightened of Lygo. He was afraid of Billy. 'Jake Wilding,' I said. 'How does he fit? Is that what you meant about Lygo having his own gig?'

A shutdown expression entered Billy's eyes. I lunged forward, punched him hard in the gut with the barrel of the gun. He doubled-up, face contorted, bile spewing out of his mouth. I drew my hand back for a second jab. Billy nodded quickly twice. 'Jake Wilding is Lygo's son,' he gasped.

'You had no idea before the hit?'

''Course I fucking didn't know. Neither did you by the sound of it.'

'How were things supposed to play then?'

'A lot easier than they did,' he snarled, coughing up crap and spitting it onto the carpet. I let him recover then motioned for him to continue.

'Lygo told me that Wilding had a son, which was good as far as I was concerned because then we had leverage.'

'But Lygo had other ideas?'

'He convinced me that he could use the boy.'

'Use him?'

'Exploit him.' Billy inclined towards me as though sharing a confidence, 'Lygo was what you'd call psychologically savvy. Came with the job description. The way he explained it to me: Wilding had washed her hands of her son and the lad was a loner and would respond to a father figure. So Lygo turns up, the big man, the real deal in the boy's eyes because at last someone is taking an interest in him. Had a right shitty relationship with his mother, by all accounts,' Billy said, almost as an aside. 'And because Lygo is one smart son-of-a-bitch, he finds out how the boy ticks, what presses his buttons and he *presses* them.'

'So he got close?' I mumbled, recognising the scenario only too well.

'Crawled right up his arse and stayed there. Organised lots of little treats and get-togethers. Quality time, or some such crap. Burrowed his way into the lad's soul and into his brain.'

Straining to look at the situation from a purely professional perspective, I saw the benefits of having an inside man. Then I realised the full implications.

'That's how you knew about the safe.' Because Jake told Lygo, I realised. 'Did Lygo know that his son was going to be at the house on the night of the hit?'

'Said he did,' Billy glowered. 'Son or not, the boy was a liability.'

'You tricked me.'

'Yeah, well, business is business.' His eyes went cold as night. 'Didn't expect you'd be so fucking squeamish.'

An ugly silence descended. Others would have erupted with fear. I was too enraged. 'How did they communicate?' I said coldly.

According to McCallen, Jake's phone and computer had already been rigorously checked, and any connection, including to Lygo, revealed.

Billy just looked, mouth clamped shut, showboating over. Taking a leaf out of McCallen's book, I fired, deliberately missing his ear by a whisker. I watched him squirm, then repeated the question. This time he was more accommodating.

'Frank gave the boy his own separate phone and laptop so that they could keep in touch.'

Then where was it now? 'And at that point you'd still no idea they were related?'

'I keep telling you,' Billy growled, voice dangerously low. 'What's my mantra? Never mix business with pleasure. Don't make it personal. Never shit on your own doorstep. Worse still, Lygo brought the boy to my house. That's when I rumbled it.'

I blinked. Billy was moving too quickly. I tried to rein him back. 'Did Mary Wilding know about Lygo's contact with his son?'

'Not until the night she died.'

'She found out?'

'Yep, and a bloody great row took place between mother and son. Wilding threatened to blow Lygo to the police, but by then it was too late,' Billy said with fervour. 'Next thing I know, you've screwed up, the boy is a witness, and the data has gone AWOL.'

'So then you decided to shut everything down, remove any evidence?' Code for eliminating those who had any connections to the operation.

'With everything tits up, damn right. But Jake, strange to say, came to the rescue.' A dark smile touched Billy's lips. 'Lygo, for all his smooth-talking swank, hadn't a clue about the boy. That lad's golden.'

'You mean pliable?'

'Psycho, more like.'

My mouth felt full of stones. 'Jake Wilding was a willing player?'

274

'Peachy, ain't it?' Billy flashed a Machiavellian smile. 'He outma-noeuvred his own dad.'

I blinked, trying to take it in. 'But what about the threats?'

'Jake's idea. Pack of lies designed to throw off the cops and spooks.'

I thought perhaps the blood supply to my brain was compromised. For the first time, I felt a real stab of fear. 'The boy has the data, is that what you're saying?'

'Are you deaf or plain stupid?' Billy jeered.

'You're doing business with a deranged seventeen-year-old?' I was aghast.

'Trade,' Billy spat with savagery. 'That's what I do.'

The room went quiet. In a tailspin, I was critically close to losing control. I wanted to smash Billy's head to a pulp. I must have grimaced. Billy's eyes hardened. 'Don't fucking look at me like that. It's a poison; no different to the drugs I push. Kills a select group of people, a one-off and in one hit. It's controllable. It's not a fucking virus. It's not going to start World War III.'

Nihilism on a grand scale and it didn't matter a damn about the dangerous religious climate, the culture of hostility, the growing intolerance in the world, or which group of people it annihilated because the outcome would be the same. Billy was proud to play with fire in the name of Mammon. Blindsided, I closed my eyes, best I could to shut out Billy's self-righteous justification and the nagging voice in my head that told me I was no different to him, no different at all. My lapse of concentration cost me dear. I felt as if I'd been hit by a freight train. About to fire, a bright flash of light shot across my line of vision coupled with acute pain as my legs crumbled and the ground accelerated up to meet me.

CHAPTER THIRTY

I came to with the metallic taste of my own blood in my mouth. I didn't know how long I'd been unconscious. Right side of my face burnt where I'd been dragged at speed across a carpet. Head felt as though it were held in a vice. Pain punched through every muscle. Nausea gripped me in waves. On my side, shoulders and arms pinned, with hands tied tight behind my back, I couldn't move. At first I thought I'd been paralysed. Then I realised that the cord cutting into my neck was with trigonometric precision attached to both wrists and ankles. Forced into the ultimate restraint position, I was in agony. Any sudden movement I'd choke to death.

I flicked my eyes, trying to persuade my brain to focus. Terrorists and data, Billy and Lygo, then I remembered Jake Wilding. Escape was my top priority. Possibilities looked decidedly limited.

Footsteps. Soft tread. Shadow. Billy. He pulled out a chair, sat down, feet square, everything neat. He had the Beretta pointed at my head. Overkill. I was in no position to move at all, certainly in no position to do him harm.

'All's well that end's well,' he murmured, dull-eyed, surveying me from top to toe. With every breath the cord cut more deeply into my neck. Sweat seeped from my brow. Panic would be the death of me.

'Does the boy realise what he's trading?' I said.

'Yes.'

'What did you do? Dupe or drug him?'

Billy tipped his head back and let out a laugh. 'I did nothing of the sort. Nobody told him to do it. He acted off his own bat.' He leant over me, a baleful look in his eye. 'You really don't have a fucking clue, do you?'

I met his monstrous gaze. I thought I might throw up because I knew then what he was about to tell me. Lygo had already spelt it out.

'Jake Wilding killed his own mother,' Billy hissed.

Like twisting the kaleidoscope by a degree, the picture changed. Until that moment, and in spite of my own reservations and Billy's revelations, I'd wanted to believe that the boy, clever and idealistic, was easy prey, that Lygo with his expert skill at cultivating and turning assets had corrupted his son's mind. No longer so. The boy wasn't only guilty of cold, premeditated murder. He was guilty of matricide. I remembered myself at seventeen years of age: vicious, unstable and highly impressionable. But that was after my mother's death, not before.

Still I clung to the notion that Billy was muddying the waters. I let out a dry laugh. 'Impossible. Wilding was killed by injection. Doesn't get any closer. To do something like that he must have hated her.'

Billy loomed over me like a blanket of thick fog. 'He did, son. He did.'

I swallowed and felt my neck swell, the cord bite into my skin. My muscles shrieked as I strained to keep my hands steady. Circulation had vanished from my fingers. My feet were numb due to a lack of blood supply. If I lost all feeling I wouldn't be able to control the degree of torsion. 'Why?'

Billy shrugged his wiry shoulders. 'Why does anyone hate anyone?'

'His own mother?' I was in hell. My own past had shaped and blinded me to the unthinkable.

'The fact she put him into care might explain it.'

I was too stunned to speak. Bunking off, McCallen had said.

'Always had a toxic relationship, according to the boy,' Billy continued. 'Had a mother too caught up with her own life. Maintained she couldn't cope, or some such nonsense.'

'What do you mean?' It was the best I could come up with. I needed Billy to keep talking. Every word counted as a stay of execution.

He shot me a look and said, 'Usual story. Fell in with a bad crowd, and got to be a handful. Had him shipped out to a boarding school for delinquent boys when he was eleven. Posh institution-alised care, I call it.'

Sweat swelled out of every pore. I think my hands trembled but I'd lost so much feeling I couldn't be sure. I seriously didn't know for how long I could hold out. 'Tell me what happened at the stables,' I rasped, setting aside this brand new piece of information and the anger roaring through my veins.

'Lygo turned up unannounced, all excited,' Billy said. 'Fortunately I'd already sent the wife and kids away. He told me that the boy had escaped from the safe house and was in posses-sion of the information. Without asking me, Lygo lured him to my home.'

'With the intention of retrieving the data and getting rid of Jake?'

'Plan A, yeah.'

'So Jake came to the stables?'

'That's when things took an interesting twist.'

'Yeah?'

'He wasn't what I expected. Full of himself, confident, the lad oozed menace. Reminded me of you, to tell the truth, and he wasn't best pleased that his old man, as he saw it, had tried to get rid of him.' I thought back to that night. Coming face to face with me, I saw now why the boy assumed his father had double-crossed him. 'Could appreciate his point of view,' Billy said, taking up the story again, unfazed by the fact that he'd wanted Jake Wilding removed for reasons of his own. 'Lygo told him that there'd been a misunderstanding, but the lad wasn't having any of it.'

'Then what?'

'He said he wanted a deal.'

'A deal?' Spots danced before my eyes.

'A slice of the action, to play the game. Smart little bastard came empty-handed. Told us he had what we wanted tucked away in a nice safe place. I decided to take a punt on the lad.'

'What about Lygo?'

'He'd served his purpose. Milo did the rest.' His face suddenly clouded. 'I'll miss Milo. Had to shoot the mad old sod. After what he did to Lygo he'd developed too much of a taste for killing.'

'And Jake?' I stuttered. My body was in uproar, sinews, tendons, and blood vessels rupturing with strain. Let my hands drop to relieve the pressure and I'd slowly strangle myself

'Wasn't fussed,' Billy said with a raw smile. 'The lad's smart. In this game you have to be ruthless.'

I shuddered, not with exertion but rage, my real anger reserved for myself. 'Where is he?'

Billy cracked a cold smile.

'You killed him?'

'Don't be soft. He's young. He's hungry and sharp. Knows what he wants.' Billy narrowed his deep-set eyes. 'Given the right schooling, he should come good.'

'He's cool dealing with terrorists?' In the criminal stakes, the boy had done the equivalent of going from nought to sixty with no gear changes in between.

'Icy.'

'How do you know he's not playing you?'

'Because he needs me and I've already met the buyers.'

With Lygo leading the delegation. I wondered how the buyers would react to Billy and his junior sidekick. Came down to trust. Lygo was the face of the deal. He'd long cultivated his Middle Eastern contacts. His CIA experience, the fact he'd been working undercover in Iran indicated a man who not only spoke Arabic fluently, but who understood the culture. Billy was mistaken if he thought that he could move in as if taking turf from a competitor. I thought he'd badly miscalculated the nature of the beast. By his own admission, his purchasers were slippery.

'And you've struck a deal?' I strained to keep my voice as steady as my hands. I was getting dizzier with each passing second.

His eyes sparkled. 'All good to go.'

The only light in the darkness was that the blueprint had yet to be traded. Once the exchange took place, we were doomed. 'Where's the meet?'

A wide smile sprawled across Billy's face. 'You're nosy for a dead man.'

'One of your hidden sites?'

'Not that it makes any difference to you, but yeah.'

Narrowed it down to three locations. Billy was right: it made no difference. I was powerless to prevent catastrophe. There was nothing more I could do. I'd broken every moral code and I was about to pay for it with my life. But I *had* made a decision. Billy thought he was in control. He was wrong. All I had to do was let my hands drop. I swallowed.

Billy pointed the gun. I watched his eyes for signs that we'd moved into the endgame. Glassy and cold, they had that telltale lifeless appearance with which I was familiar. I transferred my gaze to his gun hand. Looked tense. He was getting into the zone, readying himself to dispatch me. One last question remained.

'Something I don't get,' I said. 'The toxin.'

'What about it?'

'You said it kills whites only?'

Billy's eyes glittered with malicious glee. He wanted me to beg. I repeated the question softly.

'Correct,' he said.

'Why the hell trade in a commodity that will kill you and your family?'

A wide wolfish grin spread across his features. 'Lygo and me weren't exactly on the same page but we were in the same book.'

I got it. 'You're Jewish?'

'And immune.' And, with his Arab blood, so was Jake Wilding, I realised with a jolt.

I played my last move. 'Intelligence services are already over-running your empire. They're at your house. They're at the brewery. They've been on your case from the beginning. And they know about Jake.'

Billy didn't miss a beat. 'Is that so? Then they'll know he killed one of their intelligence officers,' he sneered, voice cudgelling my brain,

'A setup,' I bluffed, muting my natural reaction. 'Nobody died. They deliberately let Jake go. They used him as bait to snare you. All that stuff about killing his mother was a lie. The boy's smarter than even you believe. He ought to win an Oscar.'

Time stood still. Men like Billy had degrees in double-dealing, bluffing and counter-bluffing. They recognised complexity. The successful bosses were the philosophers, those who could out-think and out-manoeuvre their rivals. I watched Billy's triumphant expression darken and collapse in confusion. His features went slack; skin paled to the colour of old snow. Had to rate as one of the most memorable moments of my wretched life, the sight of Billy Squeeze rattled.

Everything slowed. Room smelt of polish and sweat. Light more diffuse. I could hear Billy breathing hard. Now or never, I thought. As Billy's finger began to tighten, I let my hands drop.

CHAPTER THIRTY-ONE

The door burst open. The instinct for self-preservation kicked in. I fought to ease off the pressure. No use. Air rattled through my windpipe and disappeared. The harder I struggled the tighter the knot, the deeper the cut the more my throat was crushed. Conversely, my head felt pumped with gas, compressing my eyes and tongue, every pore of my body enlarged, divine retribution and payback no doubt for years spent garrotting, smothering, shooting and strangling the life out of others. Starved of oxygen, I began to lose consciousness. Everything that followed took place as a collection of monochrome images: chair ricocheting; Billy off-balance; shots fired, window exploding, showering glass; gun spinning. Two figures: Billy and McCallen, chill in her eyes, locked in combat, then McCallen and me, her mouth on my mouth.

'Breathe, you fucker. Breathe. Has Franke got the data?'

I came to. It wasn't an unpleasant sensation, a little like being kissed by an angel while a Challenger battle tank ran over my body. 'No. Where is he?' I managed to croak as McCallen cut through the remaining cords with a lethal-looking letter opener. Her hair was a mess. She had a cut to her mouth. Her right cheek looked red and shiny and swollen.

'He got away.'

'You let him go?' I groaned.

'Either him or you.'

I sat up. Every bone and muscle screamed in complaint. My larynx felt as though it had come within a millimetre of being crushed to dust. My bones howled as if I were fifty years older. The steep decline in adrenalin made me nauseous. I couldn't quite compute that McCallen had saved my life.

'You chose me?' My voice sounded as though it had been sanded with emery paper. I ran a hand over the back of my neck.

'Strange, I know.' She knelt on the floor. For a magnificent moment I thought she might throw her arms around me. She didn't. When she spoke she sounded weary. 'You think I only care about my career.'

'I think you care. Good enough for me.' Her kiss fresh on my lips, sweet taste of her in my mouth, I held her gaze. First to look away, she took a phone from her jacket and trampled the moment.

'I'll call this in. They'll need to get a bio-tech team down here, check the place for anything remotely dodgy.'

I had a flashback to men in white suits, breathing apparatus, contorted faces. No doubt, in the event of any kind of discovery, WC1 and surrounding area would be evacuated. I wondered how they'd pass it off to the media. Gas leak, probably.

'Hello, McCallen,' she said to whoever was at the other end. 'We need an all out alert on ports and airports for William Franke.' She briefly turned to me. 'Does Franke use any pseudonyms?'

'William French and Joseph Franklyn,' I told her, which she relayed back to base. After that

I tuned out. I thought it way too early to hang out the bunting.

'There's to be a meeting,' I said bluntly as she closed the phone.

She sat back on her haunches. 'What kind of meeting?'

'The kind you've been trying to prevent.'

If I'd come at her with a knife, she couldn't have looked more startled. 'Go on.'

'I don't know where, Billy didn't say.' I wanted to keep that to myself.

'Billy? I'm not following. You said he didn't have the data.'

'He doesn't, but he knows who does.' I sounded as angry as I felt.

'Are you going to just sit there? Who the hell is it?'

'Jake Wilding.'

McCallen's lips parted. 'Jake?'

I confirmed his relationship with Lygo, told her how he'd killed his own mother and stolen the material.

'No, that can't be right. You said yourself it was a professional job. Think about it, the killer used a syringe.'

'To impress his son Lygo jawed about his CIA days. I'm guessing it included tried and tested methods of dispatch.' Same as Reuben once instructed me in the Dark Arts. Easy enough to get hold of a gun if you knew the right people, easier still for a teenage boy to get his hands on a syringe.

'You're talking cold, premeditated murder, for God's sake.'

'I know what I'm saying,' I said deliberately.

McCallen was adamant. 'No, Billy played you to shift the blame.'

I'd already considered this and discounted that possibility. As far as Billy was concerned, I was about to die. No need for lies. 'I don't think so.' I watched her face, which was without expression, unlike her eyes. They had a strange, luminous, knowing quality. 'Why didn't you disclose Jake Wilding's past? Why didn't you tell me that he was sent away to a school for delinquents?'

'Wasn't relevant.'

'Seems pretty relevant to me.' She failed to meet my eye, glanced away, shifty. 'Why exactly was he sent away?' I said. 'I assume it wasn't for shoplifting.'

'Extortion.'

'He had criminal tendencies, for God's sake. Did it never occur to you that...'

'Hardly grounds to murder his mother,' she sniped back.

'But if you're looking for motive it's a damn good place to start.' Also explained why Wilding had crumbled under pressure. Deep inside, I bet she felt guilty for sending her son away. Whenever I saw my mother she'd be over-the-top, buying me stuff I didn't want, taking me places I didn't wish to go in a half-baked effort to make amends for the fact she only saw me for a third of my life. 'When exactly was the prodigal welcomed back into the fold?'

She ignored my sarcasm. 'He wasn't. For the past several months he's lived a rather nomadic existence.' She glanced away again. I caught a bad vibe.

'So he wasn't bunking off, as you said.'

'No,' she said quietly. 'He got kicked out.'

'For what?'

This time she met my eye. 'Having a homosexual relationship with one of the younger boys.'

I hitched an eyebrow. McCallen stared straight at me, or rather through me. I saved my best line until last. 'You should also know that Jake Wilding killed Blake and acted as an accomplice in his father's murder. Quite the all-rounder, isn't he?'

If she was stung by what I said she didn't show it. I guess she was on overload. Without much hesitation she assumed a smooth mask of cool professionalism. No surprise with so much at stake. 'Are you certain that Jake Wilding has the data for the genetic blueprint?'

'I am.'

'Did Billy actually see it?'

'No, Jake kept it…'

'What did Billy say exactly?'

I repeated it again word for word. She swallowed. 'Who's the buyer?'

'He wasn't specific. Billy said the product would appeal to the Muslim terrorist market.'

'Think Billy will show empty-handed?'

'No, but Jake will.' And I have to find and stop him.

She collapsed back on the carpet like a deflated plastic swimming aid.

'Is there a problem here?' I said.

She swallowed, lifted her eyes to mine, nervous. I reeled back over conversations we'd shared, the slightly off-centre expression in her eyes, the way I had the feeling that she knew more than she was prepared to let on. Then I recalled her meeting with Saj, the shock on his face, the unspoken, the unwritten, the unthinkable. Secrets, I thought. Dirty secrets.

'Wilding worked on a variety of programmes, in a defensive capacity,' she added swiftly.

'You strike first, we'll strike back,' I said, remembering my recent sortie on the Internet. Defensive or offensive seemed like a thin line to me.

'Yes.'

'Which presumably means we developed all sorts of nasties to remove the opposition.' No point beating around the bush. Lygo had been right in one key respect. And Wilding, being the bright intelligent woman that she was, suspected her scientific endeavours would fall into the wrong hands. I put this to McCallen.

'Exactly.'

'How exactly?'

She let out a heavy sigh. 'Because of the highly controversial nature of Wilding's work, special safeguards were put in place in the event of this kind of threat.'

'You mean there's a protocol?'

She agreed with her eyes. 'What she left in the safe contained a sting in the tail.'

I frowned. 'But it's only computer data contained on a portable hard drive. That's what you said.'

'No, that's what you assumed. It's a little more than that,' she said gravely. 'The data for the blueprint is contained inside a small aluminium case, military grade, seven inches by five, built to withstand shock, vibrations and water.'

'Why?' I said dully. I had a rough idea but I wanted to hear it from McCallen. I wanted her to spell it out. Make people tell it the way it is, there's less room for obfuscation, or prettying it up. I also wanted to her to think that she was no better and no worse than someone like me.

'It contains the type of sting that on opening destroys the information and kills those who attempt to use it.'

'Sounds fair.' I hadn't factored in Jake. I hadn't factored in the ethnicity aspect. Black, green or white, bad was bad. When it came down to it we all bleed the same. Then I remembered that Wilding was scheduled to hand it over herself. 'Christ, she was planning to turn herself into a chemical suicide bomber.' The only way she could protect her son and not have to live with the consequences of her actions.

'That's right,' McCallen said. 'But there's one small problem,' she continued, averting her gaze, 'In the right conditions it will also eliminate anyone within a twenty kilometre radius.'

CHAPTER THIRTY-TWO

'What? Are you all fucking crazy?' Billy's words battered my ears: *It's a poison; no different to the drugs I push. Kills a select group of people, a one-off. It's controllable. It's not a fucking virus. It's not going to start World War III.*

McCallen stood very straight, unbending, her expression cool and stark. I looked around the room, disorientated and appalled. Billy, I could hunt down. Jake was an altogether different prospect. 'Saj, the guy you met in the park,' I said urgently.

'How did you…?'

'Doesn't matter, call him.'

'Why?'

'Because he has his ear closer to the ground than you think.' In truth, Jat hadn't been able to confirm much about him either way. The absence of the main man, Mustafa, triggered my suspicions but, in reality, I was going on pure gut instinct, a simple measure of the desperation I felt. Fact was I'd bust my balls to find the prospective buyers. If that meant acquainting Saj with my fist to help him re-evaluate his sense of priorities, fine by me. 'Get him on the phone now.'

'I don't take orders from you,' she snarled, switching back to full-on disdain mode.

Screw that. 'When are you next scheduled to meet him?'

She kept her voice low, edgy. 'Today.'

'Neat coincidence, isn't it?'

She shrugged.

'What time?' I said.

She didn't answer.

'What fucking time?' I didn't raise my voice, no need.

She let out a sigh, as if it were no big deal, and glanced at her watch. 'In three hours.'

'Same place?'

She narrowed her eyes. I narrowed mine. Letting status get in the way of timelines was her big weakness. She needed a major lesson in pragmatism. 'Who called for this meeting?'

'He did. Means he has something.'

'Means he's setting up a smokescreen.'

'His intelligence has always been first rate,' she protested.

I'll bet. I stretched my limbs, stood up, slid McCallen's car keys from my pocket, put them on the table, and headed unsteadily for the door.

'Where are you going?'

'Leaving you to do what you have to do.' And play your dirty games alone.

I limped out of the office, took the stairs down and exited the building. As I walked slowly along the street I heard a car brake at speed behind me. Two doors opened and slammed shut then I heard the noise of receding footsteps. Backup. I didn't turn round. I didn't flinch. I felt like a guy who thinks he's following a Rolls Royce when in truth he's been following a dustcart and it stinks. I needed to get cleaned up and grab something to eat. Ideally I wanted to sleep but that wasn't an option.

It felt warmer outside than it had for some time. The rawness had disappeared. Clouds flirted with the sun. It wasn't quite so universally grey. I registered these things by default. I had one main objective: retrieve the data by any means. Billy I'd hunt down and kill later. To achieve my goal, there were intermediate steps. I didn't think of consequences. It was too late for that. As for the myriad powers of law enforcement, I reckoned they had enough to handle without bothering me. Yet.

First step: go to the lock-up. There, I picked up a canvas shoulder bag containing a set of Tornado Night Vision goggles. Top of the range, second generation, and costing a shade under four grand, the lens gave a 6.3 magnification, the built-in infra-red viewing in zero light conditions. My other piece of emergency kit was one of Isabell's customised violin cases. Inside a German manufactured Heckler and Koch MP5 Kurtz. 'Kurtz' meant short. The H&K model was exceptionally compact with a short barrel and no shoulder stock. In other words, it had an appealing characteristic: mobility. Light, with a robust grip, it could be transported in a laptop case or concealed under clothing. Discharging nine hundred rounds per minute but firing single shots and three round bursts when required, it was my choice of a highly versatile weapon. I took it out, ran a standard check, loaded a magazine and fitted it snugly back inside. Should my German friend and me split up, I packed a Colt semi-automatic into my waistband, a blade into my pocket together with a box of matches.

Second step: Oxford Street. I went into the first big department store, headed for the men's section and, using different concessions, bought a new set of clothes, black jeans, black shirt, black sweater, black jacket, and a hat with a wide brim. Paying in cash at each, I made for the disabled toilets. Lots of space and the only place to have a top to toe wash in private. They even provided the soap. Freshened up, I changed into my recently acquired jeans, sweater and jacket, secured my weapons, glanced in the mirror and, in spite of a red-raw weal on my neck, flashed a wolfish grin at my reflection. I reckoned I had enough stubble on which to successfully strike a match and start a fire. Metaphorically speaking, that was exactly what I was about to do.

Third step, and possibly the most important: refuel. Keeping it simple, I stayed in the same department store, took the escalator to the third floor cafeteria. All the time my eyes were alert to trouble, to someone following me, Mossad or MI5, or someone who bore me a grudge from more than a decade ago. Kill a significant number of people and you gather enemies like women acquire shopping vouchers. I saw nothing suspicious, but I took nothing for granted. People stood out in public places when alone and I was never more alone than now.

I picked up a tray, loaded it with juice and fruit, some kind of meat pie and chips, and full strength tea with plenty of sugar. I added a couple of plastic bottles of water, sparkling and still, to keep for later. A little over an hour had passed, left me just under another two hours to eat and drink and get to Kensington Gardens. Provided there were no hitches.

I sat down at a corner table with a good view of the entrance, ate methodically, slowly, my entire being centred on Jake Wilding. I wondered how he'd managed to evade detection. I wondered how he'd survived. At night, temperatures had dipped to sub-zero. I doubted he'd slept rough. It's difficult to abandon family even if it's dysfunctional, tough to leave familiar places, personal significant landmarks for good. And he would have had to have money. However resourceful, he needed loot. Sharper, more feral, than I'd been at the same age, he was much cleverer than I believed. Sociopaths were like that. And Jake Wilding was one of them.

I finished my meal, dumped the empty tray back on a stack of others and descended three floors to street level. My intention had been to saunter down Oxford Street like a busker in search of a prime position, and catch a tube from Marble Arch to Kensington High Street, the Palace Gardens minutes away on foot. I changed my mind.

Eating is the best displacement activity there is apart from sex. The time spent forking food into my mouth had freed up my thinking. Nobody had watched me. The lack of surveillance struck me as strange. There could only be one good reason and it wasn't down to overstretched resources, but the simple fact that there was no need. The same surveillance officers who'd be watching Saj would also be on the lookout for me. The gardens were a trap. To visit them invited trouble. More importantly, they were a waste of precious time.

Unlike McCallen, I believed Saj held the key to the identity of the buyer. Saj wasn't the voice-piece, the equivalent of the press officer for the organisation he served. He was a decoy from the main event and McCallen and her ilk had fallen for it. If I got picked up now, game over.

I headed towards Piccadilly. Sun had broken through. I felt good, limber, any soreness from my muscles and tendons eased. It felt great to be alive. I put my positive mood down to what I sensed was showtime. The next twelve hours would be defining.

Putting myself in Jake's shoes, I imagined him holed up some-where waiting for a call. In the absence of communication, what would he do? He wouldn't lose his bottle. He'd come too far with little encouragement. As far as he was concerned he had nothing left to lose. I think he'd brazen it out in the way young men tooled up the world over, secure in their own immortality, believe that they're untouchable, that they'll never get caught or hurt. Not one of them ever thinks they'll die.

Still didn't answer my question as to why Jake's name was written in dust in Tilelli's flat. The more I considered the whole Tilelli, Jake, Lygo triangle the more I realised that I'd been looking at the wrong shape. I'd assumed Tilelli's connection to Lygo was predicated on a childhood relationship. Whether or not this was true was insignificant. Lygo was outside the box, not inside it, almost peripheral. The man I'd so easily dismissed was funda-mental.

Ron Tilelli had always been good company, a great raconteur on the right night with the right audience, the typical gay friend much beloved of women of all ages. But now I understood that it was a brilliant cover for a man who knew more than he ever got paid to tell.

Like McCallen, I'd always believed Tilelli to be a fantasist, his extravagant claims fuelled by a heavy-duty booze habit. I didn't know whether or not Tilelli had met Dr Mary Wilding during her sabbatical. If he had the two might have become special friends, with Tilelli uniquely in the know about Jake's parentage, and therefore his reaction to Wilding's death, in every sense, genuine. And yet, like a shot from a Val sniper rifle, I realised I'd missed something obvious, a strange idiosyncrasy that, when put together with other details, formed a wider picture. It explained how Jake had managed to stay under the radar for so long after he fled the safe house. It explained where he'd stowed the data after he'd killed his mother: somewhere familiar, somewhere he felt safe, and somewhere he called home. Tilelli's shocked response was due to a relationship to Jake Wilding, not Jake's mother. And he was afraid of him.

I found a pay phone, took out Gaal's card and called his number. He answered, sounded nervous then relieved when he realised that it was me.

'Gaal, did Ronnie have other places he stayed?'

Gaal hesitated. 'Well, sure. Depends who he was with.'

'I mean somewhere regular, somewhere private? You said you'd stopped meeting at his apartment.'

'Oh yeah, we used to hook up at his gay bar in Vauxhall sometimes, but not for a while.'

'I didn't know he owned a bar.'

'Has done for a number of years. Ronnie had a bolt-hole there, his secret place.'

'Does anyone else know about it, the police, for example?'

Gaal let out a derisory laugh. 'No way. It was registered in a different name.'

I asked for the address, thanked Gaal and took a Victoria line tube from Green Park. I thought fleetingly of McCallen, wondered how she would feel if she knew that I was safe and well and out of reach. Nothing probably. Too consumed in the moment, too caught up in the fallout.

From Vauxhall tube station, I walked the short distance to Kennington Lane and found the bar, as Gaal described it, set back from the road in between a dry-cleaners and a shop selling fancy dress. Except it wasn't really a bar in the accepted sense, more of a sauna and massage joint spread over what looked like several floors. An open door and lights indicated that it was up and running for business. I stepped inside a lobby. Modern. Bleached wood. Halogen lighting. Two cream leather chairs and a low table. Tasteful. There were two doors off, one on the left and marked private, the other marked 'entrance'. The back wall had a rail with coats and jackets and lockers like you find in a swimming pool changing room. I set the violin case down. A semi-naked foreign-looking guy emerged from the entrance and greeted me with a friendly 'Hola'. He had eyes the colour of ripe blackberries and wore a white towel louchely draped around his nether regions. Clearly a gym fanatic, he had impressive pecs, his torso rippling with musculature. Not my thing, but I recognise a good physique when I see one.

I said, 'Hi.'

'Six pounds for a locker,' he said. 'Rubbers are free.'

'I don't want a locker.' Or rubber.

He elevated a dark eyebrow, eyes raking my build, admiring. 'For your clothes,' he said.

'My clothes are fine where they are.'

He laughed lightly, no hostility in his voice. 'You have to remove your clothes. They are the rules.'

'I don't play by the rules.' Clearly, he wasn't picking up my vibe.

He laughed again. 'I like this joke. You have not been before. This is no problem. My name is Ramon. I will show you round.'

Before he got into an illustrated guided tour, I said, 'You have rooms here?'

'Many,' he said, eyes smiling.

I guessed he was thinking video rooms, dark rooms and orgy rooms. If I told him I was looking for a boy, things would only get worse. Time to make myself plain. 'Ron Tilelli sent me.'

Something flashed behind the man's eyes. His pleasant open features meant he was easy to read. First I saw fear then I saw him take the decision to lie. 'I know no-one by that name.'

I whipped the Colt from my waistband. He looked down at it and did what most people do: froze.

'I'm not here to hurt you, Ramon, but please don't bullshit me.'

From the way he was looking at me, he clearly thought I had a hand in Tilelli's demise. With no time to explain, I forced the pace and increased the pressure. 'Tilelli owned this joint. He had a suite here and I think he had a guest, am I right?'

He nodded, fixated on the weapon, everything around him apart from me blanked out. I didn't like scaring a decent man but I had no choice. I picked up the violin case in my free hand. 'Show me.'

He turned slowly, walked towards the door on dead legs. I followed, my body pressed closed to his, the muzzle of the gun pressed hard into the small of his back the only separation between us. The door opened out onto a dark corridor, dimly lit, the atmosphere intensely hot, steamy, sound of running water, and grind of techno-pop through overhead speakers.

Stairs ahead, plush carpet, iconic gay memorabilia adorning the walls. A number of naked men carrying towels walked past laughing. One looked back over his shoulder. Misreading the body language, he blew a kiss in my direction. We walked past a bar area, lights twinkling, screen on the wall showing guys getting it on, past closed doors, past doors ajar, heaving silhouettes inside. Sex hung heavy in the air, the smell of it and sound of it.

Another flight, narrower, cubicles on either side, then we turned down a corridor to more closed-off rooms, lights overhead like those you find on a runway. Up onto another floor where my Spanish guide stopped outside a room with a fish-lens spy-hole in the door. He crooked his index finger, tapped against the wood nervously. By my reckoning, the boy had two guns, Blake's and Lygo's. I didn't want the Spaniard in the line of fire.

'It's fine,' I said. 'I'll take it from here. You can go now. Tell no-one about this or I'll hunt you down, comprender?'

From the look on his face and the speed with which he left, he got the message. I knocked again, louder, gave it ten seconds then, back against the wall, shot the lock. I expected return fire. Giving it another few seconds, I slipped inside and checked and cleared the rooms. There was nothing because there was nothing. Empty. A blast of cold air buffeted from an open window, curtains blowing in the icy breeze.

Jake, if he was ever there, had disappeared.

CHAPTER THIRTY-THREE

I went straight to the window, stuck my head outside, and looked down on the surrounding streets with its mishmash of roofs and buildings, alleys and yards. No fleeing figure. Measuring the distance to the ground by sight, I reckoned it was around nine metres. Doable if you had the right gear, or you were a free-runner, or you had courage. I tried not to think what might happen if Jake had already delivered the goods.

I said the room was empty. Empty of people, but not empty of things. Aside from a double bed, there was a sink and basic wardrobe and a rail brimming with the kind of hoodies and T-shirts, jeans and canvas shoes found in 'Top Shop For Men'. Posters of bands I'd never heard of hung on the walls. Used cans of soft drinks and half-eaten trays of food, signs of recent occupation. And it smelt of sweat.

I started on the bed, tore off the sheets and mattress. Something went flying, clattering across the thinly carpeted floor. I picked it up, turned to the window and smiled. Not only had the occupant left in a hurry, he'd got careless. I opened up the phone, checked the list of contacts. The names made interesting reading: Frank, Ron and Billy, all three fitting snugly into the cast of players, no Jokers in the pack.

Next I checked texts, last entry received from Billy with today's date and timed at mid-day. It read: Move out. Meet as planned. Nine. Nine at night? Nine in the morning? An address with the number nine? I had no idea. A glance at my watch told me that it was coming up for four in the afternoon. More in hope than expectation, I called Billy. The number failed to register. Seemed to me that, without the goods, Billy had nothing to trade. Also seemed to me that he was letting the boy make the meet alone, exposing him to danger. Billy was, in effect, passing a death sentence on him. Had it not been for the rigged gear, I'd have been tempted to leave it at that.

Slipping the phone into my pocket, I moved onto the wardrobe, opened the doors. Inside revealed a scrumpled up hoodie, dirty socks and underwear. Picking them out, I felt something hard beneath the layer of clothing. For a heart-stopping moment, I thought I'd unearthed the case housing the data, but as my fingers connected with plastic, I realised it was a laptop. Sliding it out, I plugged the lead into the nearest socket and fired it up. The screen-saver featured the open jaws of a cobra. After that I was sunk. Password protected, probably encrypted, it could take days to decode. With time in short supply I picked up Jake's phone and, taking the obvious route, dialled an expert.

'McCallen,' she said.

'How was your meeting?'

'Where are you?' Snap in her voice.

'A gay sauna.'

Stunned silence. Recovering with commendable speed, she said, 'Have you found Jake?' Meant she hadn't.

'I've found a laptop and phone, which I believe belongs to Jake Wilding. I can't get into the computer because it's password protected. Thought you might be able to help.'

'Is this a wind-up?'

'No.'

'Give me the address, I'll be right over.'

Not so fast. 'Thought you'd be chasing down the Asian lead.'

'Not me. Been handed to another section.' She didn't sound thrilled.

'Whatever Saj told you,' I said, 'he's lying.'

'You can't know that.'

'I can guess.'

'Guess away.'

'He's going to tell you what you want to hear. I bet he said the handover was going to take place tonight, somewhere in Wolverhampton.'

'How the...'

'There you go. Who's receiving the delivery?'

'No further details,' she replied tight-lipped.

I waited a beat, actually several beats. I quoted her favourite line. 'When are you going to learn to trust me?'

She didn't respond. Clearly, I wasn't high on her list of confidantes and she wanted to keep it that way. 'Lygo and Billy are on Jake Wilding's list of contacts,' I told her, careful not to reveal the Tilelli connection. I didn't have time.

She didn't put me through the third degree. She went quiet, lowered her voice, grain in the tone. 'The address, Hex.'

I gave it. 'And as a token of good faith I'll leave you the computer.'

'You're not staying?'

I hesitated and in the silence realised that I had a choice. I could run away or I could risk my life. My death, should it come, could be terrifying and painful. In the bad old days this would have been a no-brainer, survival my only priority. Now it didn't matter. Everything I'd lived by, all the choices I'd made, my justification for being had fallen apart. I cut the call then registered I had a major problem: transport. Usually an employer took care of this, but the employer, in this case Lygo, was dead.

I left the room, navigated my way through a maze of dingy chambers and corridors and naked men and returned to planet

Earth where I found Ramon in the reception area. Evidently shaken up, he was talking in low tones to the man who'd blown the kiss. Ramon shrank away at my approach.

'Thanks for that. Appreciate your co-operation,' I said, aiming to strike a more measured and reassuring note. 'One of my colleagues will be arriving shortly. You'll need to escort her upstairs. Nobody must enter the room until then.'

'Are you police?' It was the kiss-blower. He stood in front of me, arms crossed, challenge in his voice.

'No.'

'So who are you?'

'Can't say.'

'Why not?'

Ramon broke in. 'It's okay, Steve, leave it.'

'No, I won't leave it,' Steve said, petulantly turning his attention back to me. 'Now are you going to tell me, or what?'

I wondered what the hell this guy did for a living. Seemed like one of the myriad rules and regulations types spawned in the last decade. Time to exploit his belief-system and turn it to my advantage. 'Sorry, it's classified.'

'Official then?'

'That's what classified generally means,' I said unsmiling. The persistent line was starting to needle.

'Are you with the security services?'

I let the silence do the talking. Technically I couldn't be accused of telling a lie, not that it bothered me. Ramon was quicker off the mark than his curious friend.

'Fuck,' he let out.

'It's fine,' I said. 'You're not in trouble. Consider it a discreet visit. Ever have much trouble with customers taking drugs here?'

Ramon paled. 'We have a strict no drugs policy.'

'Which you enforce?'

'Si, yes.'

'So no shooting up on the premises?'

Ramon spread his hands. Beads of sweat gathered above his upper lip. 'It is not allowed.'

'Let me put it another way, have you ever found needles?'

Ramon swallowed. The guy called Steve broke in, hawk-eyed. 'What are you going to do, prosecute us? Surely your time would be better employed catching terrorists.'

I restrained the urge to rough him up and, addressing Ramon, offered assurances. 'Like I said, nobody is in trouble here. I only want answers to questions.'

'Si,' Ramon said. 'But we do our best to find out who and get rid of them.'

'Thanks for being so frank.' Easy enough for Jake to get his hands on a syringe then, I registered. 'Now, either of you got wheels?'

'Motorbike, why?' Ramon said nervously. He'd lost all his bounce and shine. He looked terrible. I really was screwing with this guy's day.

'I want to borrow it.'

Steve's jaw dropped open. He looked at his friend in astonishment. 'You're not going to…'

'You'll get it back,' I assured Ramon.

'Sure,' he forced a smile, my threat to his person fresh in his mind. 'I'll get my keys and helmet.' He disappeared through the door marked *Private*.

Deeply dissatisfied, Steve threw me a mean look. The gap between his feet widened in a vain attempt to square up and intimidate me, difficult to pull off when you're five nine and with nothing more than a towel wrapped around your waist. 'Can't the security service afford its own transport?' he sneered in disbelief.

'Government cuts,' I said.

The door swung open and Ramon briefly re-emerged with a biker's helmet and a set of keys. 'Bike's in the yard out the back, I'll show you.'

I flashed a *good to have met you* smile at Steve and followed Ramon into an office area with computer and filing cabinets, and out through a small kitchen, down two steps, past a store and then down another two steps into a small brick-built yard, mostly overgrown, with a gate leading out onto the street behind.

I am not given to overt demonstrations of emotion but the sight of the Harley-Davidson propped against a wall blew me away. Different to the average machine, this was a 350cc ex-Nato model, a MT350. Exceptionally quiet – a pre-requisite for despatch riding on a battlefield – they are also one hundred per cent reliable. Unglamorous, no attitude, and therefore invisible, I couldn't have picked a better mode of transport for the job.

'Nice bike,' I said, appreciatively.

'Si,' Ramon said, evidently glad to gain my approval.

I secured the violin case in the rack on the back and jumped on board.

'Don't worry, I'll take good care of it.' I powered up the ignition, the vibration running through my legs like a jolt of electricity.

As Ramon performed one last act of kindness and opened the gate, I sped out and saluted him goodbye.

CHAPTER THIRTY-FOUR

I don't play roulette. I have never played Russian roulette. I'd only ever enjoyed games when the rules were mine, the odds stacked in my favour, when I could win.

This time there were no rules.

I was severely handicapped.

I could lose.

And if I lost…

There were three options, three possible locations. If the buyers had arranged to meet somewhere else, I was screwed. I could only go on what I knew, that Billy was a force to be reckoned with, that he wouldn't take unnecessary risks, and that he called the shots. To believe anything else was negative thinking.

Billy used three locations for transacting business. Choices were a disused warehouse on a stretch of riverside near Deptford, an abandoned car wash in Hackney, and a vast sprawling godforsaken site of underground tunnels and bridges and empty buildings between Harlow and Epping. These places were not my milieu, my normal sphere of operation. They were familiar only in the sense that I'd overheard Billy talk about them. Perhaps there were other locations. Perhaps he'd contacted Jake and aborted the entire plan. More likely, Billy was busy covering his rear, going to ground until the heat died down. Bad guys always took care of number one.

I ruled out the car wash on the grounds it was too exposed. Fine for meetings by day, a dead loss for those by night, any activity destined to draw attention. I ruled out the Deptford location because of the tightened security surrounding the Olympics and the East of London. It might not extend as far as Billy's waterside retreat, but it wouldn't be my first choice if I were al-Qaeda, or some associated splinter group – important to consider the potential client in this type of circumstance. That left the site between Harlow and Epping. Most of it underground, remote, a maze of exits and entrances on different levels, I thought it suited the occasion. For me, it was a nightmare. I only knew of its existence. I'd never actually been there. I was going in blind. Not the way I liked to work. Added to this, I was a one on one operator. I wasn't a soldier and had no combat experience to speak of. I'd no idea how many terrorists would show up. I presumed there'd be a main man, Mustafa, perhaps, and several henchmen. Then there was the problem of intercepting the boy and getting my hands on him before Mustafa and his mates worked out that half the welcome party was missing.

I wondered again how much money would be put on the table, how much for such a commodity. Money had been my life-blood, my measure of success and means to persuade those, often of a reluctant persuasion, to do what I wanted. No doubt about it, money was more than currency. It talked, concealed, dictated and lied. Days ago, and if I'd had enough, dirty though it was, I would have put in a counter-bid. It would have been the smart move. But I didn't have enough.

All this was running through my head as I drove through Elephant and Castle and over London Bridge towards the A10. Only as I negotiated the roundabout that would finally lead onto the M25 did I finally make up my mind, open up the throttle, take the third exit and accelerate towards the motorway and the unknown.

The night spat rain. Lights from oncoming traffic punctuated the darkness. Always better at action than inaction even though inaction dictated ninety per cent of my time, I still felt good. My muscles shrieked, but mentally I was in the right place. All that would change if I'd made the wrong call.

Fifty-five minutes from leaving Kennington Lane, I took junction twenty-six and followed the signs for Loughton then Epping and Harlow. Rain increased to a steady chill drizzle. Traffic light: only passing cars and tractors. I was deep in Essex hinterland, in a maze of quiet and forgotten places, ridges and valleys buried within remote tracks where railways lines had once run. Like a monument to the fallen, a water tower loomed ahead. I drove past and veered off onto the next dirt track, a car's width wide. Scraps of remembered conversation flickered in my head, of markers and signals and killing grounds.

I rode on. A squally wind picked up, blowing directly into my visor. After a few hundred metres, I came to a gate. Up ahead a hill speckled with starlight. I climbed off the bike, pushed it into the hedge, ditched the helmet and put on the night vision goggles and, taking the MP5 from the case, scanned the horizon.

No sign of animals. No sign of people. No bad guys. No noise.

My boots slipping on scree and tree stumps, I moved slowly, picking my way, the penalty for not being able to thoroughly scout the position beforehand. Cresting the hill, and partially obscured by foliage and brambles, the remains of a bridge. I halted, checked the night skyline once more, and keened the air for sound of movement.

Nobody in sight.

Wind the only sound.

I edged forwards again, taking it steady, making good progress. Within a couple of metres of reaching the bridge everything changed.

A figure appeared, a lookout.

Unmistakable outline of a Kalashnikov AK47 slung over a shoulder.

Red glow of a cigarette.

Lazy.

Stealth and brute force required.

I rested the MP5 on the ground, slid the blade from my jacket and snaked forwards. In one finely tuned movement, I rushed him, clamped one hand over his mouth and drew my knife hand across his throat. Takes strength and precision. Cutting through cartilage and tissue is like cutting through rubber, and if he wets himself or defecates you know about it.

I did what had to be done. A lot of blood but not much noise. I slid his body to the ground, removed the man's fancy leather sling housing the AK and put it on, picked up the MP5 and crossed the bridge elated, not out of triumph, not because I'd reduced the odds by a factor of one, but because I had certainty. I had the right location. I was in business.

On the other side of the bridge, two stone pillars, gateposts and a set of rusted metal steps. I shimmied down as quietly as I could, which sounded pretty loud to my ears, and found myself outside one of many entrances. I glanced inside the first three. Not much other than broken bricks and chunks of stone and hundreds of empty metal tubes. Graffiti decorated the brick-built walls.

I moved on, speeded up. As soon as the man upstairs was discovered, the shout would go out, the alarm raised.

Ground felt soft, strong smell of vegetation and floodwater against the breeze. The next aperture had an open metal door, racks projected from the wall inside, and remains of a rusted oilcan lay squashed like road-kill in a corner. Someone had attempted to start a fire. No glowing embers. No smouldering ash. Didn't look recent. A rat scurried over the front of my boot and shot out into the night.

I cleared two more entrances, both piled high with rubbish, metal shopping trolleys and old bicycles and general detritus. Another housed the remains of two wooden benches, black and rotten, degraded by water and foul smelling. The next two similarly empty then I came to a hatch with a white painted number nine above. Remembering the message on the boy's phone, I headed inside.

Another expanse of garbage. This had the addition of an old pump valve half hanging off a wall with a knackered-looking boiler standing next to it. On the facing door a sign read: Danger: No Admittance.

I admitted myself.

There was light.

There was sound. Human. Foreign.

Switching off the goggles, I stared at the honeycomb of derelict chambers and corridors lying in wait, any one of them a fast ticket to disaster. Billy's cocky voice flashed through my mind. This was his place, all right, his identity stamped all over it.

I eased forwards, sliding from one dead space to the next, the only guide the clamour of voices in a tongue that was not my own. Suddenly, a figure, the boy, and the reason I'd come.

I took a step forwards.

Ice-cool, he took a step back.

His eyes were hard and feral, soft downy beard concealing the lower half of his face incongruous. He wore a rucksack on his back. I guessed it contained the aluminium case with the data for the genetic blueprint and booby-trap device inside.

In the space of a few weeks he appeared to have grown up or maybe it was the gun in his hand that gave an impression of maturity and masculinity. Conversely, the tense, edgy way he held the pistol made me believe he might fire a shot by accident. I'd never faced a child soldier but I reckoned this was as close as I was going to get to the experience. Didn't particularly appreciate it. I pulled off the night vision sights. I hoped to frighten him.

He wasn't frightened. He had all the bearing of a killer. I made no allowances. Guilty of many despicable crimes, matricide didn't rate amongst my sins.

I fixed him with a level, dead-eyed stare. 'Billy isn't coming. He set you up, just like your dad.'

The tip of his tongue flicked out, catching the corner of his mouth. 'You're lying.'

I shook my head. 'You see him here?'

His eyes drifted to a point beyond me as though Billy might magically appear out of the dripping walls. 'What have you done with him?'

I shook my head grimly. 'I haven't done anything.' Haven't had the chance, but I will, I thought.

He chewed his lip. Hand shook a little, one finger snapping at the trigger. Eyes as restless as they were chill. Volatile and dangerous, this was too fluid a situation for my liking. Now was not the time to tell him that Tilelli was dead. Then again, maybe he already knew.

'Without Billy you can't trade,' I said.

A cold smile cracked his face, looked like a moon with no night. 'You're wrong. I don't need Billy. I don't give a shit. I've got plenty to sell.'

'It's not what you think it is.'

He cocked his head. 'Something you don't seem to understand, I don't give a flying fuck.'

'I understand all right. Everyone has to make a few quid when they can, but there's one big flaw in the plan. The goods are rigged.'

'Rigged?' His smile thinned.

'Booby-trapped.'

'Fucking liar.'

'Jake, why would I lie? I've never lied to you. I'm the guy who spared your life, remember?'

Confusion registered in his eyes. Then he got angry. 'Don't fuck with me, you cunt. You came to kill me. I know you did.'

We were back to the fluid situation again.

'You're wrong,' I said without accusation, my voice neutral. 'I came to get you off the hook. Attempt to trade that stuff and, not only does the data get destroyed, but you're going to kill a lot of innocent people, yourself included.'

He shook his head vigorously, eyes manic. 'She wouldn't do that.'

'She?'

'My…' he faltered. He had a wild look on his face. Lasted several seconds. 'My mother,' he said, uttering the words like they were a curse.

'Wouldn't she? Are you sure?' I took a slow step towards him. I didn't doubt he could shoot me. Once the taboo is broken, it gets easier. Billy was right about Milo. He'd developed an appetite for killing, for savouring the taste of blood in his mouth. Nothing much can be done about it. Jake Wilding was like Milo, but he was also like me in one small respect. He wanted to live. I recognised the hunger in his eyes. He knew that the moment he went to pull the trigger, I wouldn't hesitate to fire. I could only pray that, if he forced my hand, the subterranean location would provide protection to those within the twenty-kilometre radius. I took another step towards him, my eye catching something to the right. 'You know she would,' I said. 'She'd do anything to protect her work. That's why she sent you away. She rejected you, Jake; put you into a special school, didn't she? Didn't have time for a kid in her life. Too time-consuming. Too inconvenient.'

'Don't you fucking come any closer,' he snarled through blood-less lips, eyes lit with hatred.

Time to tear it up.

I switched the MP5 to single shot; twisted away, hit the man creeping out of the shadows dead centre. Not my normal modus operandi, but it did the job. Twisting back, I barrelled into the boy, striking him hard across his forearm with the barrel of the gun. He let out a scream and the gun spun out of his hand. I kicked the weapon away and, as he tried to make a run for it, grabbed hold of him by the scruff of his neck, would have beaten the crap out of him given a more leisurely schedule. By now I could hear loud shouts coming from the other end of the building. So far, two down and I had no idea how many more to go.

I leant in close to Jake, his rucksack a lethal buffer zone between us. He clutched his arm. Looked to me like it was broken in a couple of places. Least of his problems, I thought.

'Is it inside?' I demanded.

He spat in my face. I grabbed his damaged arm and gave it a twist. He didn't hesitate. He didn't lie. He let out a scream and gasped, 'Yes.' Amazing what a moderate amount of force can do. I ripped open the top of the canvas, plunged my hand into the opening and pulled out a miniature-sized metal case.

'It's all in there,' he said, his voice unsteady. He looked white as though he might throw up. I shoved the case back and dropped the night vision binoculars into the rucksack, bulking it out then grabbed hold of him.

'You will do exactly as I say. You will not speak unless I give permission. You deviate from the plan and I'll rip this damned chemical cocktail out of the bag, open it above your head and unleash hell. Trust me, you'll plead for me to kill you.'

I had a practical problem. Too many weapons, not enough hands. A burst of firepower concentrated my thinking. I pulled aside, let off an answering round from the AK, and heard the distinct rat-a-tat-tat as a round ripped into the near distance. Wrapping my left arm in a tight vice around the boy's neck, my right hand gripping the Kurtz, I pushed him forward into the next aperture. It felt clumsy, laboured, like pushing a fruit machine up a mountain. Another round of firepower sprayed the walls. Guns are like engines. Spend enough time with them you get to read their note. This was of a slightly higher pitch, staccato, like hundreds of coins shaken in a bag. Made in Israel. Uzi. Probably the mini. I wasn't a fan. Most guns recoiled upwards. These bastards recoiled down. Easy to shoot yourself in the foot.

I let it die down then shouted out. 'Don't fire. I have what you want.'

Brief silence then someone let off a round. Whoever it was got a bollocking – expletives sound much the same in any language.

More silence then a voice called back. 'Who are you?'

I'm not that familiar with the Midlands but, care of Jat, I recognised the Birmingham accent and this was as Brummie as they came. 'Billy sent me.'

'Where is Billy?'

'Couldn't make it.'

Another brief silence.

'Are you alone?' the voice said.

'I have Frank Lygo's son with me.'

'Frank is our friend. Where is he?'

I took a gamble. 'He's dead. Billy killed him.'

This time the silence was followed by a fierce exchange of foreign voices. It occurred to me that fundamentalists of any persuasion didn't listen, deafness the single trait that best defined them. At last, it went quiet. The Brummie voice spoke again. At least the guy was prepared to make some pretence of hearing me out.

'Put down your weapons, walk this way and we will talk.'

I ground my jaw so hard I thought a tooth cracked. 'Doesn't work like that. I have the goods inside my jacket,' I lied. 'You should know that the boy's rucksack is rigged with explosive. You try to shoot either of us and we both go up and you lose what you came for.'

Seconds thudded past.

'All right. Understood.'

'Put down *your* weapons,' I shouted.

Loud metallic clatter as several pieces hit the ground. I wasn't

311

fooled. All I'd done was reduce the amount of weaponry pointed in my direction.

'I'm coming towards you now,' I called. Forcing Jake forwards, my eyes flicking from right to left, we shuffled down a central passage, past another labyrinth of empty rooms without doors, each step as if we were walking towards a scaffold and execution. The boy moved like he had lead in his pants. Acute pain had a strange effect on him. I wouldn't say his spirit was crushed, but it was certainly dampened.

The corridor opened out into a large derelict garage with inspection pits and bits of rusting machinery. An old Vauxhall Cavalier lay rotting in a corner. At the end, near a wide entrance that led to cold night and open ground, the remains of a machine for dispensing air and water. The only modern addition, a portable trestle table on which sat a black leather attaché case, four inches deep with stylish gold double locks, presumably containing the money. I reckoned the case was a Bellino. Italians led the field for this type of hand luggage. Steeped in *Mafioso*, they'd had plenty of practice.

I worked out the maths.

Between freedom and me, three men.

One I recognised.

They spread out in a classic threat formation: Saj, McCallen's asset and all round snake in the grass in front, a man flanking each side, stalking towards us in an attempt to split me from the boy. It's what I'd have done. If a bodyguard made the classic mistake of sandwiching himself in between the client and assassin, it made the assassin's job ten times easier. Unfortunately for them I was familiar with the move and I wasn't shifting.

'Stand back,' I threatened, '*All* of you.'

The two on the flanks, both in their mid-twenties at a guess, glanced back at Saj, their leader. A muscle ticked in the main man's neck. His dark eyes flickered greedily, every bit of his mind focused on me, the one that had the goods, the one who called the shots. He nodded for his compatriots to back off.

'Hoodies, take them off,' I growled.

They went through the same performance for a second time. Hoodies came off, revealing holstered weapons. Saj also removed his jacket, the only bulge the left-hand pocket of his shirt in which an old-fashioned cell-phone the size of a small brick resided. A definite lapse in style, I reckoned.

'Weapons,' I stated. No need for a command. They were getting used to how this was swinging. Several pistols hit the deck. Once upon a time, I'd have been interested in the particular hardware. Pressure and changed status dictated otherwise.

'Jeans, off.'

A collective groan went up, but they did as they were told.

'Move away from the entrance,' I said. 'You, too,' I told Saj who reached for the case.

'Lift it up and drop it onto the floor. Slowly. Do not open it.'

'As you wish.' Accommodating and urbane, he hefted it onto the concrete. Consistent with the contents, it fell without report. Had it been a heavy thud I'd have suspected arms. He squatted down, looked up at me through a fringe of jet-black lashes. 'You wish to count?'

A shrewd man would have said yes. The money could be counterfeit, less than the agreed price. Probably dirty. If clean, I wondered who'd laundered it. The money trail was of infinite interest in normal circumstances. These weren't normal circumstances. 'No. Drag it with you.'

He shot me a quizzical look, shrugged and changed position. As they moved round, I moved anti-clockwise, dragging Jake with me, my back towards the open entrance.

'I see Frank's son is hurt,' Saj said, solicitous.

'He'll get over it.'

Saj's men exchanged worried glances. One gabbled something to Saj. Saj gabbled back.

Sounded angry. 'We would like to see the product now,' he said composed, all charm, sophisticated and infinitely scary.

'Not until I speak to Mustafa,' I said.

A thin, cunning smile touched the man's lips. '*I* am Mustafa.' Neat trick. Explained how Jat had been unable to locate him. I wondered how McCallen would react to being duped.

'Right, Mustafa. Here's the thing. We've changed our minds. There is no deal. You hang onto the cash. You walk away. We walk away.'

He let out a laugh, sounded like the grind of metal on metal, then his face darkened and his eyes locked onto mine.

'I'm serious,' I said, taking another step backwards.

'So am I. I had a deal.'

'Deal's off.'

'I want to speak to Billy.'

'Go ahead, call him.'

Surly, eyes still holding mine, Mustafa reached for his phone, held it in the palm of his hand, the expression on his face deadly. Something was wrong. I dropped my gaze, stared at the phone, or more specifically the antenna. Same size, same shape, same appearance as an older model, the antenna gave the game away.

Accurate at up to twelve metres, this was no style-lapse.

Pushing the boy to the ground, I jumped back and twisted away as Mustafa flicked his thumb over the keypad, hitting the seven key and discharging four rounds in quick succession, one grazing the side of my left hand and missing the boy's back and rucksack housing the container by millimetres.

Couldn't let him get away with that.

Flicking the selector switch on the Kurtz to automatic fire, I let off a burst for each man. All three collapsed like skittles at a bowling alley.

With five men down in total, the data with its deadly cargo in my possession, my troubles should have been over.

I was wrong. They'd only just begun.

CHAPTER THIRTY-FIVE

The loud roar of an engine and the sight of blazing headlights forced me to make a rapid reassessment. Like the unexpected discovery of a fish-bone in your throat, I knew I was in trouble. Grabbing the boy, I half-ran, half-dragged him in the opposite direction over uneven ground, the way ahead pitch black and directionless. A sudden shower of bullets sprayed overhead followed by the sound of a loud bang as a generator kicked into action and the entire site lit up like Wembley Stadium.

I glanced back over my shoulder. Four armed men clambered out of a jeep. With death in their eyes, they sprinted towards us. I turned, let off a burst, and dived with Jake behind a pile of pallets, the brief hiding place disintegrating as another fusillade ripped into and shredded the wood. Wrenching the rucksack from the boy, I swung it onto my back. To the left, I saw a slab-sided building; jaws open one side, around two hundred metres away. I pinched the boy's good arm at the elbow, looked into his eyes, told him to make a run for it. Others would have left him to take his chances. Perhaps I should have done. My decision to protect him was a messy combination of honour and altruism and wanting to clear my name. I wasn't going to get banged up for a murder I hadn't committed.

'I'll cover you,' I said.

He didn't question me. He didn't speak. He was panting hard with pain. Self-preservation kicking in, he took to his heels. Scenting an advantage, the men unleashed another volley, earth and dust rising around the lad as he zigzagged across the lumpy ground. I stood up, sprayed the pursuing figures with firepower from the AK. Three went down. Should have left one. It didn't. Several more had joined the party.

I ran, kicking up the dirt, the earth beside me punched with machine gun fire, and scooted into a large flimsy-looking wooden shed in which ancient-looking helicopters and bits of old machinery stood mute and accusing as if I'd disturbed their peace. I could see no means of escape. Jake had recognised it, too. He broke into a laugh. It sounded dry, without mirth, haunting. 'They're going to kill us.'

'Shut up.' I could see his point. We'd been funnelled into a kill-zone.

'Get as far back as you can,' I shouted. 'Use the machinery as cover.'

I hunkered down as bullets spat and zinged off the metalwork with the arrival of the extra gunmen. Whoever they were, and in spite of their weaponry, they didn't strike me as disciplined. Not that I was complacent. Killing a man was a numbers game. Any one of them could get lucky, including me.

I flicked my eyes to the front. The attackers were splitting up and creeping closer. I didn't know how many against two. More accurately: I didn't know how many against one, not terrific odds, not disastrous. This wasn't *Zulu*.

Glancing across at the boy, I edged backwards. Nothing at the rear other than a couple of metal drums containing God knew what, and a small tank on wheels, a bowser. I suspected it had once contained aviation fuel. Maybe it still did. I moved in front so that anyone who tried to kill me, with luck would hit the container.

Bagging their interest bought me another burst of fire. Not close enough to the bowser, but too near to me.

And they were advancing.

Flicking the H&K selector to three round bursts, I took aim. As the next dark face appeared, I removed the top of his head. Odds increased in my favour.

Made them mad as hell.

Another salvo of firepower sliced towards me, this time it winged wide and spray peppered the tank. From a hole near the bottom, blue-coloured liquid spurted out. Drawing fire, I zipped out of my hiding place and let rip another burst, a scream of pain confirming that it had found its mark.

I was cracking the odds against me.

Excitement flickered in the pit of my stomach. Time to change tactics. With a yell, I darted out and sprinted back towards the rear of the building, and drew level with Wilding's son. I wasn't interested in his expression, or what he was thinking. I only wanted to make sure he was playing the game. As expected the remaining men moved forwards and let off another deadly fusillade, ensuring the tank was further punctured. More fuel seeped out from a hole in the lower half. Meant it was mostly empty and filled with plenty of vapour. I could smell it.

I rested my weapons on the ground, lifted the rucksack off my back, took the matches from my jacket and turned to Jake. Dirt on his face, sneer in his eyes, fear and pain had failed to loosen the hard 'fuck you' edges.

'On a count of three, throw yourself forwards and jump into that inspection pit,' I said.

He shrugged a whatever.

'Your choice. You die if you want to.' Then, clutching the rucksack like a prop forward about to score a try, I lit the match and on the count of three, flicked it onto the leaked fuel and hurled myself inside next to Jake. There was a mighty explosion as the fuel ignited and burst into flames. Heat powered over me, scorching my back and singeing my hair. One attacker was engulfed in flames; the remaining men on fire and screaming in panic as the blaze rapidly caught the flimsy wooden walls and roof and spread at speed.

I twisted my head towards Jake. Hand clasped over his mouth, eyes red-ringed from smoke, and his jacket burnt from his back, he'd survived. He knew it, too. He grinned and for a fleeting moment I forgot who he was and what he'd done. I remembered that he was once innocent like me, that he'd had hopes and dreams, and that somehow, somewhere things had got snarled up and gone bad in his head, and then everything went wrong in a life when everything had already gone wrong.

The moment passed, vanished into thin air. Reaching across, I hauled him up by the remains of his clothing, clambered out and dragged him into the night. No sooner than we were clear, a loud explosion ripped the remaining roof off and all three walls collapsed.

Close call.

I walked away a little, swung the rucksack from my back, rested it on the ground, put down my weapons and gulped in a lungful of fresh air. A loud report followed by a burning pain in the top of my left arm made me spin around.

'Don't move.'

I stayed absolutely still and blinked in the uncertain light. Warm blood trickled down the inside of my jacket and onto my hand, and my face stiffened at the sight of Jake awkwardly holding one of the dead men's Kalashnikov's.

'Nobody screws with me,' he spat, his face a picture of malevolence. 'I've got plans.'

I made no sound. This was it. An ignominious end, any concern I felt reserved for those I'd failed.

'Aren't you going to beg?'

'Not my style.'

A sneer crawled across his lips. He lowered the gun, aimed it at my knees. 'We'll see, shall we?'

I braced, expecting the inevitable. A single shot rang out. Startled, I scooped up the Colt single-handed and twisted and fired it at the man powering towards me, younger than the rest, his clothes in tatters, face black with fire. As he jack-knifed into the dirt, I wondered about his identity, wondered if his name was Khaled, wondered if he'd had a brother called Jat. Although the man had inadvertently saved my life, I followed up with a double tap: *snap, snap*. Game over.

Noise overhead, I tilted my gaze towards the sky and a single helicopter's searchlights. Looked like it was official. Looked like it was heading our way. Wondering if McCallen were on board, I glanced across at Jake. Face down in the dirt, body at an awkward angle; part of his head was blown away from where the bullet had made its entry.

Exhaustion and pain sweeping over me, I sank to the ground. When McCallen arrived I was still on my knees.

CHAPTER THIRTY-SIX

She let me go.

Apart from the pilot, she'd come alone. Good from my point of view. The conversation went something like this: McCallen asked if I needed a doctor.

I said, 'I can take care of it.' I reckoned it was a through and through. Painful, messy, not life threatening.

She insisted on taking a look then patched me up from a medical kit stowed in the chopper.

'You'll live,' she said, looking in the direction of Jake's body. I shook my head, gave a shrug, got to my feet and walked away a little. I found it hard to describe my feelings. All I knew was that I felt something. Not for Jake – the boy was warped – but for me, for loss and how I'd allowed it to change me and commit me to a life of strange beds in strange rooms, sometimes, not often, in the company of strangers. 'Here, you'll be wanting this.' I handed her the rucksack and wondered whether Wilding's spirit would be pleased. I didn't ask McCallen what she was going to do with it, or whether the contents would be clinically destroyed, or what would happen next. I didn't want any part of it and I was tired and weary.

She opened it up, looked inside, a wide smile of satisfaction breaking over her face. 'Fantastic, thank you.'

She didn't thank me for saving her career, but I think that's what she meant. Not that it mattered. I didn't want her gratitude. By carrying out this small act, I only wanted her to recognise that behind the soubriquet there was a real person, a man with a background, a history, a man with desires and virtues, who was not all bad.

'How did you know where to find me?' I wasn't that curious. I was stalling for time.

'The computer: Jake received a message from Billy stating the location.'

'But you didn't know I'd be here.'

She flashed a smile. 'You always were a safe bet.'

'Was I?'

She didn't reply. The smile faded a little. I recognised that serious look. It meant business. 'We'll have to debrief you.'

I shook my head. 'All you need know is that Saj and Mustafa were one and the same, the rest you can work out.' She reacted exactly as I expected: tense and brittle and cool. I didn't care. I simply wanted to feast on her for one last time. Eyes like traffic lights on go, body all curves and valleys, she looked quite beautiful. I think she read the desire in my expression because she blushed.

'Not sure how I'm going to explain you away.' She gave an awkward glance back towards the pilot.

I turned to go. 'You'll think of something.'

'Wait.' She took two steps towards me. I hoped she might reach up and slip both her arms around my neck, press her lips against mine full-on, her tongue in my mouth, her teeth against my teeth. 'Hex, you understand that there can never be anything between us?'

'Yes,' I said with less emphasis than intended, 'of course.'

'But I really like you.'

'It's cool. Inger, you don't have to…'

'I do,' she said softly. 'I mean it. For a bad man…' she faltered.

I forced a smile. 'I'm not so bad. Is that what you mean?'

She shook her head. 'What you've done here tonight, don't you see, you've saved lots of lives?'

I supposed I had. 'Then it's a start.' I smiled as I walked away.

'I still have your number,' she called after me.

'Me, too.'

I returned the bike, got properly fixed up with a doctor I knew well, and went to ground. I'd done this dozens of time before. The location was always different but the routine, in the sense I had one, stayed the same. I ate. I slept. I read. I exercised. I unravelled. The order varied, but this was my basic rehabilitation programme. It usually lasted a couple of months. Any less, I wasn't fully rested. Any more, I got edgy, too unpredictable. In other words: dangerous. Not so this time.

During my sabbatical I studied the news. A gift to conspiracy theorists, Dr Mary Wilding's murder continued to dominate, and the death of her son explained as suicide, adding fuel to the flames. Given time it would drop out of the headlines bit by bit. As for the scare, the threat of national disaster, the smashing of the terrorist cell, the hunt for Billy Franke, there was nothing. In the context of McCallen's world, the greatest screw-ups were never discussed and successes rarely received the light of day. With the panic contained, I assumed the current government was doing the equivalent of kicking the can down the road until it got itself lodged underneath a cabinet minister's car. I didn't call Jat to find out whether or not Khaled was still running with the pack, or whether he'd gone out one night never to return. I had unfinished business.

Nobody can stay out of circulation forever. At some point, and even with an army of protectors, you have to show. Billy was particularly disadvantaged. He had family. He had colleagues. He had a corporation to run. To my certain knowledge, he was still in the country. I was at a disadvantage only in so far as Billy knew me and understood I'd be gunning for him. To further complicate matters, as soon as I came into play, I ran the risk of being picked up by MI5 or the police.

This time I did my homework thoroughly. Adopting a variety of covers, I went after anyone who knew Billy Franke, anyone with whom he had dealings, however loose. If word got back to him, I didn't care. I listened well; silences, carefully chosen words, the saying of one thing that meant another, of particular interest. And I bribed. There's a certain pattern with this part of the game, a set of internal rules. Reducing it to its most basic elements: somebody hears from someone who talks to somebody else. There were pitfalls. Like Chinese whispers, facts could get distorted or lost in translation.

Eventually I found out from a man who ran a garage who knew the owner of a certain car leasing business that Billy had been on the move in the same manner of a fleeing dictator, never staying more than two nights in the same place. Calling in favours from some of the hardest bastards in the business, Billy had promised deals on which he couldn't deliver.

There is no sadder sight than a man down on his luck. Men in the criminal world fear this more than anything else. To them, vulnerability is a disease. They think it contagious. When hard men discover the truth they always cut themselves loose. It's a given. Within two months of my return to the streets, and three weeks after that, faces were talking and I had a lead.

Paddington station has five exits, links to the underground and sixteen platforms. Plenty of scope for manoeuvre. Piecing together disparate bits of information, Billy planned a trip from the train station on a certain day at a specific time, destination unknown, but probably heading south. That's all I knew, better than anything that had come my way to date.

Around seven-thirty in the morning on a Wednesday in late January I strode into a main concourse alive with disgruntled commuters and harried station staff, the place erupting in chaos at cancelled services due to bad weather. It wasn't busy; it was insane and ugly, the atmosphere ripe with division and anger. Not ideal. You'd think the general atmosphere of mayhem provided a perfect habitat in which to insert myself. It didn't. It made it harder for me to pick out someone watching me. On the upside, it made things tough for Billy, the chances of him boarding a train to make an escape reduced to zero.

Aware Billy had made efforts to change his appearance, I did a tour of the station concourse with an open mind. Eyes are the most difficult to disguise. Cleaners, vendors, rail officials fell under my scrutiny to the same degree as the travelling public. Without success, I finished up near the departure board, the most popular gathering place at a station. Nagging at the back of my mind the worry that Mossad was still out to get me.

I like doughnuts, the hot off-the-plate variety. There's not a huge amount of skill attached to their creation. Hot oil, pre-prepared dough, deep-fry around three hundred and seventy degrees for between a hundred and a hundred fifty seconds, job done. The best I'd ever tasted were in Illinois. The smell of sweet sugar-dough that morning made me drool. Hungry, I approached a doughnut stand close-by. Manned by two guys, one sliced dough inexpertly with a cookie cutter, the other flipped donuts in the seething fat. Slow and subtle, neither had a clue, and I didn't think it was related to their shortage of culinary skills. Surveillance of sorts, but not the specialists Reuben had warned me of. Or maybe I was getting jumpy and seeing things that didn't exist. I looked at my watch, wondering where Billy had got to and whether I'd been sold a lie or my information was dud.

'Double espresso,' I said, making heavy-duty eye contact with the biggest, 'And two ring doughnuts.'

'With you in a tick, mate,' he said, faffing around with a coffee machine.

'When you're ready,' I said with an icy smile.

Eventually I was handed my order. I paid and, taking a bite, wandered off in a wide arc, then put my hand in my pocket and pulled out and dropped a piece of litter on the ground, hoping it wouldn't be seen by one of the permanent army of cleaners. Still chewing, I headed for a nearby phone booth and picked up the phone as if to make a call. From here I could observe on three sides, including the area where I'd dropped the fake receipt for one of my fake identities. Sure enough, a young blonde with a neat walk crossed over, bent down as if to adjust her shoe and scooped up the receipt. Gotcha. I was, by no means, out of the woods. Small, low-level teams could be the most formidable, an irritation I could do without.

Suddenly I noticed Billy, thin as a stick, wearing straight-legged jeans, brown leather flying jacket, trainers. He'd let his hair go grey, long at the sides, the thick sticking-up look now feeble thatch on top. His face looked gaunt and had a yellowy sheen, eyes still and unfathomable. When he walked he moved with his body pitched forwards, head down, no eye contact, desperate to avoid attention. My first hurdle was to shake off the surveillance team. If they were intent on getting me here in a public place, I was sunk. However, if these were preliminary steps to killing me outside, I stood a chance of being able to carry out what I came to do. I'd worry about them later.

I sauntered over to a flower stand with a nice loose gait. The blonde followed. I turned and smiled at her.

'Is that something on your collar?' I glanced at the inductor tab on the lapel of her coat. Five centimetres in length, plastic, it transmitted signals to the earpiece fitted on the same side. Instinctively, she looked down, looked back up, her cheeks crimson. 'Here, let me help.' I reached over, twisted it off, dropped it on the floor, ground it underneath my heel and walked away.

She didn't follow. Nobody did. I'd performed one sudden manoeuvre, enough to shake off those inside, but not enough to deter watchers posted at the exits, or Billy.

He twisted away, barged through a crowd of Chinese students and jumped on board a nearby escalator heading to the

Underground. I veered left, didn't look back, kept right moving. The blonde might have fallen into step behind me, or maybe someone else. I didn't know. I didn't care.

Four lines out of Paddington; four separate groups of people; plus those whose train journeys had been cancelled, the place was a scrum. Faces intent, purposeful, it was like travelling amongst a trail of fleeing refugees. A woman stumbled, sprawled across the dirty floor, gathered up her handbag and half-crawled out of the way. Nobody stopped. Nobody asked if she was hurt. Nobody paid her attention. Me included.

Billy cut down towards the circle line. Needing him to believe that he'd lost me, that he was safe, I stayed at a respectful distance and fixed my gaze on the back of the person immediately in front. My brain, meanwhile, tracked the nape of Billy's neck, his head, the most vulnerable part of a human's body.

We arrived at the platform seconds apart, Billy up by the tracks, me behind, seven or eight people deep. I stood back, rounded my shoulders, and bent one knee to reduce my height. Noise of the approaching train was muted, muffled. As I expected, Billy turned, took one long last look back. Simultaneously, I lowered my gaze, displayed an unusual interest in my footwear. When I looked up he was facing the track again. The tension had gone from his stance. He stood feet slightly apart, grounded and relaxed.

The Underground was alive with British Transport Police. CCTV worked on a consistent basis here, and any incident involving injury or fatality studied at length. With no room for mistake, I pushed away bleak and distant memories of hot air and blinding lights, of heat running through my veins and giddy hammering in my chest, and moved forward in sinuous motion; the closer to Billy, the more dangerous for me.

Rumbling now. Roaring sound. In those penultimate moments, I remembered the smell and tang of vengeance. In my mind, I saw Michael Berry tumble onto the train tracks.

Billy turned towards the oncoming train, looked towards what he believed was salvation. I turned with him, mirroring his every movement. Great rush of air then lights then...

He glanced back, saw my face, his own frozen in shock. No time to cry out, he stumbled and toppled onto the track. Some commuters surged forward, some retreated in horror. A woman screamed and the speeding carriages finally stopped. Hoping to beat the inevitable lockdown, I slipped away, retraced my route, and headed for the nearest exit. Daylight ahead, almost clear, the blonde with the crimson cheeks stepped out of nowhere and blocked my path.

'You, again,' I said. I'd made a classic mistake of worrying too much about danger behind me instead of concerning myself with trouble ahead. I let my hands drop to my sides. No point in causing alarm. She met my eye unsmiling. I believed it was my turn for a bullet in the brain and realised that there was only one thing in life that could be taken and not returned and that was time, and I so badly wanted my time over again.

'We are grateful to you,' she said. She didn't explain who 'we' were. 'But I must warn you, Mr Thane, next time you may not be so lucky.'

I stood mute. I wanted to thank her. I wanted to say that I'd bear it in mind. Most of all, I wanted to tell her, *assure* her, that I'd use my reprieve to be a force for good. I remained speechless. The messenger turned on her heel, crossed the road and disappeared into a neighbouring street. I let out a liquid breath and stood quite still.

There is an Israeli saying. I don't know the literal translation but it states that the person who saves one life saves the world. I reckoned my life had been saved that day. Not entirely certain it was deserved, I stepped out into the cool morning light and wondered where to go.

KILLER READS

DISCOVER THE BEST
IN CRIME AND THRILLER

Follow us on social media to get to know the team behind the books, enter exclusive giveaways, learn about the latest competitions, hear from our authors, and lots more:

/KillerReads 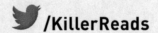 /KillerReads

Printed by RR Donnelley at Glasgow, UK